T0355935

Praise for Jam

In this powerful novel of unquenchable faith in the midst of persecution, Jamie Ogle excavates the stories of the legendary Nikolas of Myra. The turbulent Roman Empire comes alive through expert research and vibrant settings, but the journey of the characters transcends the centuries. Breathtaking and deeply inspiring, this is a story readers will hold in their hearts long beyond the last page.

> **AMANDA BARRATT,** Christy Award–winning author of *The Warsaw Sisters,* on *As Sure as the Sea*

With rich detail and beautiful writing, Jamie Ogle has written my new favorite book of the year—*As Sure as the Sea.* The diving aspects and incredible depths to the story are a testament to this author's brilliant research. I found myself craving to be a part of the early church (which was not an easy life!) and relating to Demi in profound ways. I devoured the book and yet, I didn't want the story to end.

> **KIMBERLEY WOODHOUSE,** bestselling and award-winning author of *A Hope Unburied*

A terrific read, rich in historical detail. With vividly drawn settings and complex characters, Jamie Ogle brings ancient Rome to life in this immersive and heart-wrenching story about early Christians who sacrificed everything for their faith. Fascinating from the first page to the last.

> **FRANCINE RIVERS,** *New York Times* bestselling author, on *Of Love and Treason*

Jamie Ogle has breathed pulsing, throbbing life into third-century Rome in this profoundly moving episode in the saga of the early church. Fans of Amanda Barratt's novels and Francine Rivers's Mark of the Lion series will rejoice over this astounding debut. It's one of the best novels I've read all year.

> **JOCELYN GREEN,** Christy Award–winning author of *The Hudson Collection,* on *Of Love and Treason*

What a triumph! *Of Love and Treason* is for anyone who's ever wondered why bad things happen to good people. It offers no cliches or easy answers. . . . A tender love story and boost to faith!

MESU ANDREWS, author of *Brave*

Of Love and Treason overflows with heart and hope, courage and conviction. . . . [A] well-researched, timeless novel set in third-century Rome.

LAURA FRANTZ, Christy Award–winning author of *The Seamstress of Acadie*

A beautifully wrought tale. . . . Jamie Ogle is a brilliant storyteller with original, heartfelt stories to tell!

JOANNA DAVIDSON POLITANO, author of *The Elusive Truth of Lily Temple*, on *Of Love and Treason*

Ogle provides an illuminating peek at the lives of ordinary Romans. . . . A well-plotted story of politics and love set against the drama of the early Church.

HISTORICAL NOVEL SOCIETY on *Of Love and Treason*

AS

SURE

AS THE

SEA

JAMIE OGLE

Tyndale House Publishers
Carol Stream, Illinois

Visit Tyndale online at tyndale.com.

Visit Jamie Ogle's website at jamieogle.com.

Tyndale and Tyndale's quill logo are registered trademarks of Tyndale House Ministries.

As Sure as the Sea

Copyright © 2025 by Jamie Ogle. All rights reserved.

Unless otherwise noted, all cover and interior images are the property of their respective copyright holders from Adobe Stock, and all rights are reserved. Woman in boat © Kateryna Kukota/iStockphoto; belt © maryviolet; white gown © faestock; cloudy sky by Amanda Mocci/Unsplash.com; fruit © b.illustrations; sack cloth © sutichak; fabric texture by Engin Akyurt/Unsplash.com.

Author photo by Jodi Sheller, copyright © 2022. All rights reserved.

Cover designed by Eva M. Winters

Edited by Sarah Mason Rische

Published in association with the literary agency of Gardner Literary LLC. www.gardner-literary.com.

Unless otherwise indicated, all Scripture quotations are from The ESV® Bible (The Holy Bible, English Standard Version®), copyright © 2001 by Crossway, a publishing ministry of Good News Publishers. Used by permission. All rights reserved.

James 2:16 and 1 Thessalonians 4:13-14 are taken from the Holy Bible, *New International Version,®* *NIV.®* Copyright © 1973, 1978, 1984, 2011 by Biblica, Inc.® Used by permission. All rights reserved worldwide.

Luke 17:33 is taken from the (NASB®) New American Standard Bible,® copyright © 1960, 1971, 1977, 1995, 2020 by The Lockman Foundation. Used by permission. All rights reserved. www.lockman.org.

Matthew 10:33 is taken from the New King James Version,® copyright © 1982 by Thomas Nelson. Used by permission. All rights reserved.

As Sure as the Sea is a work of fiction. Where real people, events, establishments, organizations, or locales appear, they are used fictitiously. All other elements of the novel are drawn from the author's imagination.

For information about special discounts for bulk purchases, please contact Tyndale House Publishers at csresponse@tyndale.com, or call 1-855-277-9400.

Library of Congress Cataloging-in-Publication Data

A catalog record for this book is available from the Library of Congress.

ISBN 978-1-4964-7971-6 (HC)
ISBN 978-1-4964-7972-3 (SC)

Printed in the United States of America

31	30	29	28	27	26	25
7	6	5	4	3	2	1

For Phil.
We're having a good time.

PART ONE

*"One gives freely, yet grows all the richer;
another withholds what he should give,
and only suffers want. Whoever brings
blessing will be enriched, and one who
waters will himself be watered."*

PROVERBS 11:24-25

ONE

Seawater closed over her head with a roar of bubbles in her ears. Twenty-year-old Demitria closed her eyes, body relaxing, heart slowing as the stone tied around her ankle pulled her to the depths of the Mediterranean.

The rush in her ears quieted to a dull hum, punctuated by the familiar clicks and burbles of the underwater world. She opened her eyes. Sunlight poured in brilliant shifting shafts through the cerulean water, illuminating the rainbow of coral and plants studding the rocky seafloor, fast coming into clear view. She scanned the bottom, eye snagging on a flash of red in the shadow of an outcropping. The coral stretched from the seabed like an arm, fingers splayed, reaching toward the light above.

There you are.

As the stone hit the bottom in a cloud of pale sand, Demi slipped her foot from the loop in the twine and kicked toward the coral, scanning the bottom as she swam. Air bubbled out between her lips.

She wiggled the little iron hammer from the mesh bag tied around her waist, fighting to stay near the seafloor as she made her way toward the coral. Prized for its mythical powers of protection and healing, and for the way the blood-red color didn't fade to white when harvested and cut into beads, a piece of coral this size might have fed her family for months. Too bad Mersad, self-proclaimed *jeweler of the seas* and their controlling employer, would get the lion's share of the profits.

Remorse flickered through her as she smashed the hammer against the coral, red fingers snapping free. Fish scattered from the destruction in flashes of silver and yellow. Demi tucked the coral into the bag and paused to run her fingers over the jagged space scarring the reef. What a waste. To destroy something so beautiful for the vanity of red jewelry. At least Mersad used divers to harvest only the red coral, instead of dredging the seafloor with weighted beams and destroying entire coral beds like other harvesters. Even so, she much preferred oyster hunting to coral collecting. Though not always reliable for pearls, at least oysters served the dual purpose of filling their bellies.

Curious fish darted around her legs, fins whispering against her skin.

A large shadow flickered over her. She looked up to see her brother, Theseus, swimming for the place where the reef swelled upward in a near vertical wall. Only a year younger, his strokes were sure, strong, and so much like their father's.

How had three years passed since Pater, Mitera, and Hediste had been so violently taken from them? Three years since she and Theseus had filled Pater's place as Mersad's best divers—for quarter pay. Not that either of them would dare complain. They were among the lucky few Christians to have jobs.

Lucky. A strange word to use in these times.

Six and a half years ago, after a seer had accused Christians of interfering in her attempts to read the future for Emperor Diocletian, the emperor had passed a series of edicts and demanded the other three rulers of the Roman tetrarchy enforce them in their own regions. The first edict had removed Christians from the military and public office; the second called for the imprisonment of church leaders and the burning of Christian literature and Scripture. The latest edicts had mandated all citizens of the empire to burn incense to the emperor and the chief god of the empire, the Sol Invictus. In return for declaring the emperor as lord, they'd receive a *libelli* token which enabled them to work, buy, and sell. Living without a libelli was difficult, and in some regions violently prohibited. Thousands upon thousands had lost their lives refusing to utter the words "*Kyrios Caesar.*" Caesar is lord.

Demi's lungs began to burn, and not from the lack of oxygen. Without libelli, she and Theseus shouldn't be able to hold jobs, but Mersad was no fool. He'd employed their father and knew they were the best divers in Myra and Andriake. He'd never asked to see their libelli, and if he suspected their beliefs, he kept it to himself. But he paid them less and less each season, as if he knew they wouldn't dare complain.

Theseus slipped toward a tangle of red growing in the shade of a rocky outcropping. A good find. She twisted and started to follow, her gaze catching on a fist-sized shell. Her heart beat a double rhythm. Coral be drowned if that oyster held a pearl. She released more air and curled downward, kicking toward the rough, dark prize.

She tried to wiggle the shell free. No good. Her hand slipped and a thin stream of pink swirled from one of her fingertips followed by a stinging burn. She took up the hammer once more and attacked the shell, jarring it free. The protest in her lungs turned insistent.

Tucking the oyster and hammer in the mesh bag alongside the coral, Demi arced upward. She glanced toward Theseus.

Bubbles from her own startled exhale clouded her vision but not the image of her brother, locked in a struggle with a thrashing moray eel. Longer than Theseus was tall, the moray's mottled brown-gray skin flashed in the light as it writhed, jerking her brother with it.

Let it go, Theseus.

And then she saw he couldn't.

The moray's ugly jaws were locked on her brother's wrist.

Blood swirled in the water around them. Her chest burned as she started for Theseus, black spots dotting the edges of her vision. She'd been down too long.

Demi straightened and made for the surface, panic and prayers jumbling in her mind. Theseus was sure to follow. *Surface at the first sign of trouble.* That was Pater's rule, pounded into their ears since childhood. She tilted her head back, spitting saltwater and sucking in a lungful of air as she emerged. Calm sea breezes ruffled the turquoise water, the sun shining white in a cloudless sky. Perfection masking the terror below.

She turned in a circle, scanning for her brother's dark head above the waves. They'd hunted eels before while they dove. Dragged them out of the depths and wrestled them into the boat. Why did Theseus not surface now? Perhaps he couldn't.

Demi drew another breath and ducked under, working the tiny stone knife from her bag as she kicked downward. The roar of thrashing bodies deafened her ears.

Morays were not normally aggressive, but they wouldn't back down from a fight if they wanted one. She'd heard of another diver who'd been bitten on the ankle and the moray wouldn't—or couldn't—release him until after he'd killed it. A fight with a moray was often a fight to the death. But whose? A burst of fear and anger drove her forward. She'd lost too much already. Her parents, her sister, her future husband. A pang shot through her chest.

She would not lose her only brother too. Scrambling for her knife, she swung hard, striking toward the eel's slithering spine. The animal recoiled but didn't relinquish its grip on Theseus's arm. She slashed at it, but the jerking and thrashing made accuracy impossible. The flick of a dark tail struck her shoulder. She reached for it. Missed.

Pater's voice echoed in her ears again. *Surface at the first sign of trouble. Your life is worth more than all the coral or pearls.* Maybe to Pater. Not to Mersad.

Theseus beat at the bulging head as the eel writhed. Frustration mounted. Why wasn't he—her gaze lowered, and then she saw it. Her brother's foot caught in the coral.

Demi curled downward, fingers shaking and fumbling as she exchanged the stone knife for her coral hammer. Theseus jerked his foot, but it stuck fast, blood swirling in the water. She cracked the hammer against the coral, scattering a slow spray of shards. Free. She pivoted toward him, pointing upward.

Her hand drooped.

Theseus's arms and legs splayed, limp. Eyes open, face slack. He drifted away from her, the eel clamped to his wrist and curling beside him like a thick oily ribbon in the water.

Fear struck like a knife to her heart.

Not Theseus too, God. Grant me strength.

Ignoring the moray, she tucked an arm around Theseus's chest and kicked, propelling them upward, dragging the struggling eel behind. Her prayers and strokes grew stronger with the streaming light, blocked only slightly by the dark shadow of the boat. The rope ladder dangled over the side, frayed ends waving in the water. God be praised they'd remembered to leave it out this time.

Demi sputtered as her head emerged then ducked under once more, her free arm flailing for a grip on the boat. She kicked, bracing Theseus's back against her chest as she swam for the ladder, fighting the downward pull of the moray. Her muscles ached and shook.

Steady. Steady. Be strong. Theseus will not die. Not if I can help it.

She gripped the wet ropes, wrestling Theseus's head and one arm through the ladder before scrambling up herself. *In the event of an accident, secure, leverage, and pull.* Pater's voice ran through her mind, as clear as if he were standing beside her barking the emergency orders himself. She spread her feet, gripped the top of the ladder, and heaved with everything she had.

The eel roiled and fought.

The opposite side of the boat rose up behind her, threatening to capsize. With a final burst of strength, she rolled Theseus inside. Demi fell back, landing on baskets of coral fragments and oyster shells. The boat rocked from side to side as she scrabbled through the mess, searching until her fingers gripped the extra knife. The eel curled and twisted. She threw herself on the slimy body, fighting it still as she hacked at the head. The eel never once loosed its grip on Theseus. It thrashed, even headless, as she flipped the tail to the end of the boat and dropped to her brother's side, the moray's jaws still clamped to his bleeding arm.

Lungs heaving, Demi flopped Theseus onto his back, dropping her whole weight against her fists on his wide chest.

"Wake up, Theseus." Her voice sounded strange to her ears. Strangled and choked. "Come on. Wake up!" She screamed the words into his still face, willing him to blink, willing his mouth to twist into that lazy grin of his that had won the heart of her best friend.

Theseus lay in a pool of brine and blood, droplets on his tanned chest gleaming like shards of red coral.

"Please, Theseus." Her voice dropped to a whimper. She stared at him, as if by sheer will and determination she could make him draw a breath. "Don't leave me here alone. Not you too."

Demi pumped at his chest again, tears rolling down her cheeks, movements jerky and weakening as the seconds scraped by. Nothing.

Do not take Theseus too, God.

She couldn't go through it again. The loss, the fear, the terrible . . . loneliness.

Take me too. Why won't You take me too?

"Where are You?" The question came on quivering lips. "Do You hear us? Do You see Your people anymore?"

Theseus lay still.

God was silent. And she shouldn't be surprised. Not after what she'd done.

Tears burned. She sank back against the side of the boat, chest aching, pressing the back of her hand against her teeth as sobs rolled up her throat.

Nydia would be devastated. Demi's best friend had set her heart on marrying Theseus since she was twelve years old.

I'm sorry, Nydia. I'm so, so sorry.

Theseus lurched upright, spewing water. He twisted to his side, shoulders heaving as he vomited into the bottom of the boat.

Sobs strangled by a cry of relief, Demi scrambled to support him, unable to speak. Shells and coral fragments cut into her knees.

Theseus flopped back, staring at the sky. Coughing. Breathing. Alive.

Thank You.

Demi cradled his head, stroking the hair from his face like she'd done when he was hardly more than a baby and she, barely old enough to remember. His dark eyes connected with hers, then went distant as his body began to shake.

TWO

THE MAN WHO'D SOLD HIM the boat was a liar. Early that morning, it hadn't mattered to Nikolas. He'd seen with his own eyes that the boat wasn't as seaworthy and sturdy as the man claimed, but he'd thought he could manage it. He'd spent two years at sea on his father's merchant ship, after all. Not that that had ended in great success either.

"Fool," Nikolas muttered, cupping his hands and scooping water over the side of the boat. The memories were easier to keep at bay if he was busy.

The wood wept. Saltwater snaking in through a maze of worm holes. After two hours it swirled over his ankles, soaking the crates and bundles stacked around him.

Did gold rust?

He eyed the distance to the shore. Perhaps he could land the boat, hide the goods, and continue to Andriake on foot. He could always come back later by land or boat. Perhaps that was an even better plan than the original. If the others knew the cargo he carried, they'd only ask questions—or worse, they'd know who he really was. Or at least who he *had* been.

Water lapped a little higher. Nikolas bailed faster.

Lord, see me safely to land.

He drew a dripping hand to his brow, squinting against the sun and the turquoise sea glittering with a crust of diamonds. Beyond, the Taurus Mountains tumbled toward the Mediterranean in a mottle of pale almond and gray limestone broken by bursts of palms and oleanders mingled with bright sprays of blooming fuchsias. He wasn't far. The coast was familiar from the last time he'd traveled this route—only then he'd been carrying a message for the pastor in Myra from the pastor in Patara. He'd never anticipated arriving in Myra for Pastor Tomoso's funeral. And even less, to step into the house and find himself awarded the dangerous position of replacement leader, no matter that he was years too young. Times were desperate, and men . . . they were not as old as they used to be.

As terrifying as the prospect had been, Nikolas knew he wouldn't refuse. An odd peace had come over him when he'd accepted, and he clung to the memory of it. Perhaps, after he'd failed everywhere else, this was where he actually belonged. Leaving his hometown hadn't been difficult. His memories there were not good, and the rumors still swirling about him were even worse. There was nothing left for him there—aside from a boatload of gold, which he'd gone back for. Possibly one of the biggest mistakes he'd ever made.

Nikolas glanced around him. Nothing but dazzling sea and sun, a welcome sight for a man who'd spent the last few hours slipping behind rocks and small islands to avoid being seen by early morning fishermen, but for a man about to go down with his boat?

Blood and panic raced through his veins.

Calm yourself, Niko. You can swim.

Mostly.

An orange had freed itself from the sack in the prow and bobbed against his calf, its skin glistening. They were small. Leftovers. Probably no good anymore, but that morning, as he filled the questionable boat with every *aureus* he could carry, the little sack of oranges had remained close. Silly, he knew. But every time he bit into the tangy flesh, he felt again the grief over his mitera's passing and saw the toothless grin of the little girl who'd found him sobbing on the beach in Myra so many years ago. A bit ragged and in need of the food herself, she'd offered her orange to him instead. And while it hadn't erased his grief as she had claimed it might, knowing someone saw his pain, cared enough to help . . . He'd never forgotten it.

Nikolas had planted the seeds in a tiny pot on his windowsill, carefully tending the fragile seedlings through the neglect of his brother and pater. Through the pain of their deaths. Hiring men to relocate the potted trees to his uncle's monastery had been the largest expense of moving there and had come with the additional cost of being labeled a wastrel in need of reform. Not a new epithet. He'd ignored it as he had the others and planted the trees at the edge of the monastery grounds. They'd finally borne fruit two years ago, despite being stunted and scorched after the monastery had been burned and abandoned.

Nikolas swallowed back the burning in his throat and lifted his chin. Surely God would not lead him this far only to let him drown now. When the four emperors had passed the series of anti-Christian edicts, escalating from simple expulsion of Christians in government to the massacre of thousands, he and a few others had escaped the attack at the monastery. In the following years, he'd done his best to help the battered church in Patara as church leaders were arrested, homes and Scriptures burned, and whole families executed for refusing to declare their allegiance to the gods of the empire. And when the church in the next city had welcomed him—and begged him to lead them—he couldn't refuse. The remembrance of his calling brought reassurance, quenching the panic. For now.

A bit of white flashed near an outcropping of land. The sun on the water? The sail of a small vessel? The signal?

He had to be close. Titus had given clear instructions not to sail into the port of Andriake but to stop just shy in a hidden cove. He would be there waiting to unload and hide the cargo, though he had no idea what it was.

Wind struck Nikolas's face. Finally. He adjusted the tattered sail, limping the boat closer to the rocky beach. The wind played a twofold game of filling his sail and kicking up waves. He bent to scoop again, water playing at his calves now. The faster he sailed, the quicker the boat seemed to fill. His mind raced. What to do?

Is this how I lose everything, Lord? Have You spared me and everything I own, just to take it all now? Perhaps it was no less than what he deserved after what had happened.

The boat hit a wave. Nikolas flailed for a grip on the side and leaned too far. The leaky vessel tilted, water inside rushing toward the low side. "No, no, no." He flung himself toward the high side—too late. The edge dipped beneath the surface. Water rushed to his knees, then his waist, and then Nikolas found himself floundering against the pull of the water as his boat disappeared beneath him, sail and all.

He sputtered in the brine and blinked water from his eyes, kicking and propelling his arms forward and back, unwillingly embracing the water that had welcomed him. The crystal blue around him bubbled like a boiling pot, then went smooth and innocent. As if it hadn't just devoured his inheritance in one burbling gulp. It wouldn't be so bad if he hadn't lost all the oranges too.

His stomach felt as though it were tied to the boat. Sinking to the depths.

Never put all your money into one vessel, Niko.

His father's shipping mantra echoed in his mind. Solid advice. Though it had always seemed metaphorical. Until now. He looked down, the bottom dark blue and obscure. Why had he even bothered going back for the money? Hadn't Uncle always said wealth was the cause of greed, and sin, and destruction? Wasn't that why they'd hidden it away in the first place? To keep him from himself? Nikolas shut his eyes. Was it greed and sin that had driven him to fetch the gold? It wasn't like he was going to buy an oceanside villa with a red door and a pretty courtyard with three orange trees or anything.

A wave slapped him in the face like a reprimand. Nikolas coughed and spat. "Fine. I was tempted. But I didn't do it."

He sighed. Why had God bothered to give him wealth at all if he couldn't use it? Uncle had often spoken of ways God had unmistakably stepped in and supplied needs. Was this going to be one of those times? He hoped so, because instead of sweeping in like a hero to rescue the floundering church in Myra, he'd arrive empty-handed and in need of aid himself.

He eyed the distance to the shore. *If* he arrived at all.

Nikolas blew out a watery breath of surrender. "Lord, I am Your servant. I'll do what You ask, and I'll do it how You want me to."

As if in answer, a small orange orb burst from the water and fell back with a splash, bobbing in front of him. Heat seared behind his eyes. No matter how dire it looked, he was seen. Cared for.

"Thank You."

Nikolas tucked the orange down the neck of his tunic before setting his gaze ahead and angling for shore.

THREE

TEARING A STRIP from the hem of her already short swimming tunic, Demi made quick work of securing it around Theseus's arm above the eel's head. Ramming a piece of coral beneath the strip, she gave it a twist, slowing the flow of blood. She tore another strip to bind the cuts on his foot.

"Stay with me, Thes." Her words emerged far steadier than her hands.

Demi cast a glance at the sky, sun high overhead. Where to go? Mersad's private dock for his divers would be dead at this time of day. No help to be found there. And while the port of Andriake would be bustling with docking merchant ships, sailors looking for drink and women, and carters hauling goods to warehouses, it was too great a risk for a woman with an incapacitated guardian to seek help there. It was far likelier for Theseus to be dumped overboard and she dragged onto a slave ship. She couldn't risk the port now.

She looked at Theseus. They couldn't risk waiting for dusk either. They'd have to beach in the cove. The path was rougher but a far shorter walk home than docking at Mersad's pier and trying to navigate the crush of people moving to and from the larger city of Myra barely a mile inland. From the cove she could drag Theseus home herself or leave him alone and run for help. Though neither option sounded ideal, they offered the only way to save her brother.

She set her chin, and the sail. Ahead, faded almond limestone tumbled into the sea-foam and obscured the entrance to the sandy cove.

"We're almost home, Theseus. Not long now."

Even draped with both of their outer tunics, Theseus shivered. Eyes closed. Too pale.

The swish and crackle of waves grew louder as they approached the shore.

Demi glanced at her brother and back toward the cove, expertly maneuvering the boat around rocks hidden just below the surface.

"Nearly there, Theseus. Stay with me."

With a hiss of sand on the hull, the boat beached, and Demi leaped out to drag it farther in. She swept aside shells and coral with her foot as she climbed back inside, kneeling to shake Theseus's shoulder.

"Wake up, come on."

Her brother's eyelids fluttered, and he moaned, rolling toward her as he struggled to sit up.

"That's it, come on." She shoved her shoulder into his armpit, wrapping her arm around his waist, using every ounce of strength she had to hoist him up. At nineteen, her younger brother had grown bulky with muscle in the last few years.

"So dizzy." His words slurred, and he swayed, body shuddering. "Cold."

"Come on. Step over the side. Don't pretend you're too tired to walk. I'm not carrying you home anymore. I stopped falling for that years ago."

His lips twitched, then wobbled as he concentrated on lifting one leg over the side of the boat, then the other. They stumbled forward into hot sand.

"My arm."

"I know."

"Get it off."

She glanced at the eel's head, slimy brown and shining in the sun. Jaws bloody and clamped to his wrist. "I can't. We must find Cato, all right?"

Theseus grunted, feet dragging with every step, breaths ragged. "Can't breathe . . . stop."

"Not yet. Keep going—" She went down hard on her knees as

Theseus pitched forward and she tried to break his fall. Demi rolled him to his back, sand clinging to his skin. She slapped his cheek, dark and prickly with stubble.

"Theseus." His name caught on the lump rising in her throat.

Lord, help us.

"Is he well? Can I help?"

Demi whirled, sucking in a breath.

A young man sloshed through the shallows near their boat, water-logged tunic clinging to his heaving chest as he bent and gripped a boulder for support. He slicked waves of dripping brown hair from his eyes as he looked toward her, gulping air as if he'd been under too long. Help? He looked ready to keel over himself.

She turned back to Theseus lying motionless in the sand. Experience told her not to trust strangers. Even those who looked friendly and safe. Safety was a dangerous illusion that got people killed. It was the reason her parents and sister were dead. The reason her betrothed, Alexander, had been murdered. And yet? At her prayer, this stranger had come right out of the sea. Odd. Miraculous.

She shut her eyes. Could he possibly be an answer to her prayer?

Not likely. Not anymore.

She turned back to him. "What are you doing here?" She winced at the harshness in her tone. *Tread carefully. Theseus depends on you.*

The man straightened and staggered forward, tugging the front of his tunic away from his body. "I had boat trouble."

She scanned the cove. Empty. "You don't have a boat."

"Yes." A wince. "That is the trouble. And you?"

Tears rushed her eyes and her lungs shuddered at her next inhale. "A moray."

The man knelt across from her, Theseus between them. "Could he walk if we supported him? Or shall we try to carry him? I believe the port is not far, but . . ." He cast a doubtful look toward Demi's arms, which she returned. *He* didn't look like he spent his days in the gymnasium either.

She hesitated. She wasn't going to the port. Couldn't bring Theseus to the normal village physician without showing libelli—which she didn't have. Couldn't risk bringing this stranger to their home. Her pulse kicked up, a bead of sweat tracing her spine.

Theseus moaned.

Her gaze darted from the stranger to her brother, and back. If she didn't allow his help, she'd never get Theseus to safety on her own. And he needed a physician. Now. She could figure out where to take him on the way.

"Let's carry him as far as we can." She scrambled back to the boat and snatched up their outer tunics wadded into the prow. She spread Theseus's larger one on the ground and they rolled him onto it before covering his shivering form with her long *chiton*.

"Can you lift his shoulders? I'll take his feet."

The stranger gave a nod.

Scrambling to stoop at Theseus's feet, Demi gripped the edges of the tunic-turned-stretcher as the stranger leaned down, his brown hair catching the sun as he gently crossed Theseus's arms over his chest so they wouldn't drag.

Considerate.

He wrapped the top edges of the tunic around his wide hands and met her gaze, sun glinting in warm hazel eyes. "Ready?"

She nodded.

They stood slowly, Theseus half-suspended and half-dragging between them.

The stranger gave a nod. "I'll follow you."

Her bare feet slid in the sun-warmed sand, unseasonable Aprilis heat radiating against her legs as she maneuvered Theseus toward the faint path leading to Andriake. She shuffled backward, water spraying from her wild curls as she whipped her head back and forth from the path to her brother swaying between her and the stranger.

The beach narrowed to a footpath twisting over a rocky arm separating the cove from the harbor on the other side. Sweat trickled down her hairline. The tunic slipped in her grip. She tensed her fingers.

"It's slipping, set him down."

They lowered Theseus to the path, the stranger straightening and pressing fists into his lower back, face tilted away from her in an expression of discomfort. Demi gasped for breath and flexed her aching fingers, a mounting dread building in her stomach. She would have to bring this stranger into their home. Or, at least to the place she considered home since she and Theseus had been forced to flee the house they'd grown up in after their parents' arrest. It wasn't the most secure place, nor the most sheltered, but she couldn't bring the stranger to one of the secure safe rooms. And the man would think it suspicious if she insisted they leave her brother in the citrus grove outside the village. Home it was.

She bent, gripping the stretcher once more. "Ready?"

The stranger nodded in response, his eyes skittering away from her as he squatted and lifted. Threads snapped in the fabric, but it continued to hold.

Before them, the path smoothed and cooled as they descended the rock berm into the citrus grove, air cloying with a sweet, tangy scent of early spring blossoms. New grasses tickled her legs as she ducked branches and wove between trees. Her stomach churned the closer they drew to the edge of the port village, dilapidated fishermen's huts solidifying between the branches.

Neck and shoulders aching, Demi shuffled her heels backward and kept her head twisted over her shoulder. She had to ask. Even though he was gone, Pater's rules stuck close. *Trust no one until you ask the question.* Her pulse kicked faster. Mouth dried.

"Do—" She licked her lips. Blew out a steadying breath. "Do you know the way?" She squeezed her eyes shut, waiting for the confused answers to follow. *What way? Of course not, I'm following you.*

Silence. For one step. Two. Three. Four.

He didn't answer.

Maybe he hadn't heard. She turned, and this time his gaze didn't skitter away as it had before but locked on hers, steady.

His Adam's apple bobbed in his throat. "The way is narrow." His words were soft but steady in the way his gaze was. Fixed and solid.

The breath left her lungs in a rush that brought another flood of tears to her eyes. She faced forward, only to find the path was indeed narrowing before them, slowly filling in with refuse and the crumbling huts of the abandoned quarter of the fishermen's village. Had he really known the answer? Or was he simply observing?

Demi sucked in a breath. "There is another path, broad and easy." Her words were tight, strained. Her shoulders ached.

Please, let him know the answer.

"Broad is the way that leads to destruction."

Her chest shuddered with a relieved sob that threatened to undo her grip on her brother's feet. The answer to her desperate plea for help felt like extravagant grace.

Thank You. Thank You.

They didn't speak again, but Demi felt the tension between them ease. She led them down a rocky gully and across the shallow stream trickling through the bottom and wending its way to the harbor.

"Nearly . . . there," she panted, smearing sweat from her cheek with her slimy bare shoulder. The village refuse dump spread before them, crumbling huts of the often-flooded and now abandoned fishermen's village surrounded by heaps of broken pottery, discarded furniture, and bones. Chickens bathed in the dust while several goats wandered, golden eyes on the alert for anything green. A mangy dog panted in the shade of a single standing wall.

Farther off, higher on the hill, the inhabited portion of the port village appeared mostly abandoned at this time of day while the men and boys cleaned their fishing nets in the harbor and the women and girls sold the night's catch in the morning market. Demi let out a breath of relief. They could make it without being seen.

She flicked a glance over her shoulder at the stranger, shod in a single shoe. "Watch where you step. The dye-makers dump their old murex shells here."

He gave a nod.

Theseus moaned and thrashed his legs. Demi lost her grip on the tunic, and he thumped to the ground.

"Thes—what are you—"

His uninjured hand batted at the sky, legs kicking in sluggish motions.

"Theseus, you're all right." She cradled his face.

He fought to sit up, gasping and coughing. "Can't . . . breathe."

Her heart skittered and jumped. "Yes, you can. You're breathing now."

"My arm . . ."

"I know. I'm going to get Cato, all right? Let's get you home first."

Theseus pitched forward, moving his feet beneath him. Demi and the stranger moved to either side of him. She dug her shoulder into Theseus's armpit and pressed into her legs, hoisting him up. The stranger did the same. They half dragged Theseus between them as they staggered forward. Thorns grew in scraggly patches throughout the dump but in cultivated thickness around the crumbling hut ahead. She directed the stranger to the entrance facing away from the village—less an entrance and more of a tunnel. They dragged Theseus through it.

The house was roofless like the other ruins in the dump, abandoned after one too many spring floods. Demi pointed to a stick shelter in the corner where two grass mats lay neatly rolled. She kicked at one and it unrolled with a flap.

"Lay him here."

They dragged Theseus to the mat and flopped him onto his back.

Demi's breath came in short, burning bursts and her arms shook. "Theseus?" She pushed his shoulder. He didn't move.

"Thes? If you die after I dragged you all the way here, I'll never forgive you." Tears edged her voice. It wasn't true. She held her fingers over his nose and mouth. Soft, warm breath met her touch.

"I'm going to get Cato, all right? I love you." Demi pressed a kiss to his forehead and pushed to her feet. She turned toward the stranger sitting with his arms over his knees. Panting. "Thank you. I can care for him from here."

He looked up. "Are you hurt?"

Her brows knit and she looked down at her swimming tunic, clinging to her frame with sweat and blood. She crossed her arms over her chest. "No. Just—" She snatched her chiton from where it puddled near Theseus and wrestled it over her head.

"If you need to fetch the physician, I can stay with your"—the stranger twisted toward Theseus—"husband?" His eyes flickered toward her.

She ran a hand through her tangled curls, fingers shaking. "Theseus. He's not my husband."

"Theseus," he repeated, and offered a cautious smile.

She wanted to protest. Surely this man had other things to attend. Yet the thought of leaving Theseus alone, defenseless, chafed. "I don't know you."

"Nikolas . . . from Patara."

Nikolas. Patara. Something about those names rang in her ears as familiar but she couldn't place why.

"Nikolas." She gave a nod. "I am Demitria, daughter of Anatolios. Thank you."

"It is as it should be for followers of Jesus, yes?"

Relief crashed through her chest. "Yes."

"Theseus is safe with me. Find your physician."

Demi stooped to press another kiss to her brother's damp forehead, then fled, leaving him with a stranger, and wondering if she'd made a terrible mistake.

FOUR

OF ALL THE WAYS Nikolas had envisioned arriving in Andriake, doing so while carrying an unconscious man with the jaws of a beheaded eel clamped to his arm was not one of them.

The young woman had left, her wild curls casting a large shadow on him as she darted through the low door, leaving Nikolas and Theseus in . . . What was this place exactly?

Sunlight poured in overhead, beams and roof tiles rotted and crumbled long ago, leaving nothing but walls and overgrown weeds. Nikolas shut his eyes and rested his head on his knees, strength depleted from all the day had brought. Running, hauling, rowing, swimming, dragging—was this how Olympians felt after competing?

He tried to scrub away the mental picture of the woman as easily as the thorns obscured the house. That scrap of faded gray linen, tied in two knots at her sun-bronzed shoulders, only made it halfway to her knees and left shapely arms and legs burned into his brain. She hadn't offered much beyond the Scripture, their names, and the fact that the half naked man she'd just kissed was not her husband. Brother, maybe. Hopefully. Although he'd never minded a difficult task before, the prospect of leading a church with Corinthian morals wasn't a challenge he was eager to take on.

Restless, he pushed to his feet and paced the dirt floor. A breeze ruffled through the undergrowth, choking the interior of the house, carrying with it a damp scent of fish and decay. He rolled his shoulders, the wet fabric of his tunic clinging and constricting.

Theseus moaned.

Nikolas scanned the area around him. A three-legged stool squatted near a cracked terra-cotta firepot that was little more than a clay cylinder standing on end with a hole for the fire on the bottom and a broken bowl over the top hole. A chipped clay cup and unbroken amphora sat next to it. He sniffed the contents of the amphora as he poured it into the cup. Water. Not wine. Though he never drank it himself, the lack of it now was too bad for Theseus's sake. He shuffled back across the room. Pain burned the sole of his bare foot and he paused to pull a shard of pottery from his heel. He tossed it aside with a *clink* and knelt beside Theseus.

"Can you drink?" Nikolas touched his shoulder.

Eyelids fluttered. "Demitria?" The name came slurred and thick.

"She's gone for help. I am Nikolas. I'll stay with you until she returns." He tipped the cup toward Theseus's lips.

Theseus struggled to sit up. "My arm." He squeezed his eyes shut.

Nikolas gently pressed his shoulder. "It's best if you lay still for now, until the physician arrives. The eel's head is still attached."

"Get it off." Theseus spoke through gritted teeth. "Please." He tilted his head away, blowing a long, painful breath through his lips.

"Soon." Nikolas rose and searched through the refuse, finding a bit of cloth that looked somewhat clean. He wet it and swiped at the blood covering Theseus's arm and hand, careful to stay well back from the wound. He wouldn't risk removing the eel's head without a physician present in case the rows of needle teeth had severed veins. Blood formed a sticky pool beneath the injured arm. He moved down to clean the man's foot, unwrapping the hasty bandage and waving flies away from the shredded skin, oozing and dark with drying blood.

Nikolas froze, struck with the eerie remembrance of being here before. His breath caught, jaw clenched. No. Not here, exactly, but kneeling beside his own brother, hearing his father beg Amadeo to live when it was clear by the blood, he was already dead. Would he always be haunted by the memory? He wished he could recall other things. Mitera's voice or Pater's laugh. The way they'd prayed with him and

Amadeo as children. Those memories rested in his mind as colorless fact, and the last ones—the feel of Pater's waxy skin as he bathed it, the rasp of labored breath, the smell of death—those memories lingered, ever vivid and tinged with pain and the breathtaking cut of his father's final accusation.

It should not have been Amadeo who died.

Nikolas shoved to his feet, eyes roving the overgrown room for something to do, some way to help. Best to stay busy. The memories couldn't rise if he moved.

Stones scrabbled outside. Nikolas spun toward the sound, in two steps placing himself between the helpless man on the floor and whatever was trying to find its way into the house. A wild dog? He kept his eyes forward and bent, picking up a fat stick discarded beside a line of dirt-filled, broken pottery. Who saved broken pottery? Or collected dirt, for that matter? The thorns around the low door rustled. He straightened, gripping the makeshift club as a dark furry patch emerged and then Demitria burst inside, flipping curls out of her face.

Her gaze went first to him, then dropped to Theseus. "How is he?"

"Eager to get the eel off." Nikolas tossed the stick behind him as she crossed the room and knelt by Theseus. "Did you find the physician?"

She nodded. "Phineas will be here soon."

Theseus groaned, half opening his eyes. "Not Cato? Let me die."

Demitria gave a wobbly smile. "You're lucky I found Phineas. You know how fond Cato is of removing limbs." She lifted the cup Nikolas had left beside him and tipped it to his lips. "Here, take a drink."

Theseus gave a weak shake of his head and let his eyes drift closed.

"Theseus, you need to drink something." Her voice wobbled, a note of panic lacing through it.

"I gave him a drink while you were away." Nikolas reached out, nearly touching her shoulder, before jerking his hand back, curling his fingers at his side.

She stood and turned toward him.

"Thank you." Her voice caught and her eyes raised to his. They were a deep, rich brown that he might have called black had the sun not illuminated a glimmer of mahogany—or maybe it was the tears rising in them that did it.

"Theseus is all I have left in this world. If I lose him too . . ." Her lips trembled, and just for a moment he glimpsed a haunted pain in her expression. She shuttered it nearly as quickly, tilting her face away and smearing the back of her hand across her cheek. Dried sand crumbled down the front of her blood-smeared chiton that had once been a pale yellow.

He didn't need to ask why she was alone. The code she'd spoken on the way here had revealed enough. Hadn't all Christians lost someone close to them? And yet, he wanted to ask, wanted to hear *her* story, to see if the haunted look in her eyes matched the one he felt in his own soul. But those questions wouldn't come. Now was not the time.

He tipped his chin toward the blood streaking her clothes. "Are you certain you're not hurt?"

Demitria looked down at her chiton, haphazardly tied at one shoulder and hanging loose and shapeless to the tops of her brown feet. She shook her head, shaking fingers running over the patch of dark blood marring one hip. "No," she whispered.

Perhaps he should go. It seemed his work here was done. Theseus was—Nikolas glanced at the sparse shack—*home*. The physician was coming. And he had a meeting of his own he'd surely missed. And yet, that seemed less important than ensuring there was nothing more to be done here first. "Can I do anything?"

Stones clattered outside.

"Demi? It's me, Phineas," a man's voice called.

The thorns snapped and crackled. Nikolas stepped around Demitria and grasped a leather bag that was shoved through the tunnel entrance. A man who looked about forty crawled through the opening behind it.

"Sorry it took me so long. Sophia gave me the message and I got here as soon as I could." He pushed to his feet and looked up for the first time, gaze narrowing on Nikolas. "Who are you?"

Nikolas took a breath to answer, but Demitria pushed forward, grabbing the physician's arm.

"He helped me carry Theseus home. Come." She dragged him toward Theseus.

"Can we trust him?" The whispered words, not meant for Nikolas's ears, reached them anyway.

A shrug. "We'll have to."

Phineas knelt, dragging the bulging leather bag against his side as he did so. "Thes, what have you gotten yourself into this time?"

Theseus groaned. "Where's your pater?"

Phineas chuckled. "You're in good hands with me. I'll have you know, three out of my last dozen patients made a full recovery. Demi, I need heated water."

Demitria darted for the firepot and set to building a fire faster than anyone else Nikolas had seen. Finally. Something to do. He scrounged through the weeds for more fuel. Climbing vines revealed tiny cucumbers, and squatty plants hid infant eggplants beneath toothy leaves. The place wasn't overgrown with weeds at all. It was a garden. He handed Demitria a handful of sticks. "Can I do anything else, or—"

"I need another set of hands," Phineas called over his shoulder.

With Demitria busied with the fire and water, Nikolas moved to help.

Phineas gestured toward the eel's head. "Push the head forward and keep tension here, as I sever the lower jaw from the rest of the skull. The teeth point backward toward their throat so a bite this deep is impossible to release without removing the head in pieces. Good. That's it."

Nikolas gripped the sticky head, turning his eyes away from the crackling slice of Phineas's knife.

"Sorry, Thes. Not long now," Phineas reassured.

Theseus gritted his teeth, releasing a guttural groan as the jaws clamped tighter on his arm for a moment.

"You can let go now."

Nikolas relinquished his grip on the eel's head and sat back on his heels, wiping his hands on his thighs. Phineas wiggled the top half of the skull forward and off the arm.

Theseus bit back a noise strangled between a whimper and a roar. Demitria stooped beside Nikolas, the hem of her chiton brushing against his bare foot. She pressed the back of her hand to her mouth.

Nikolas's stomach lurched. The man's wrist looked like something a novice butcher might sell for half price at the meat market. On the poor side of town. At the end of the day.

Phineas bent closer, examining the wound with his fingers. "No teeth left behind that I can tell. Let's get the lower jaw remov—"

"Shh!" Demitria held up a hand, her body going rigid as she listened. "Someone's outside."

Nikolas twisted toward the tunnel and stood. How could she hear anything else over Theseus's moans and the—

Demitria shot to her feet and wrapped her fingers around Nikolas's arm.

"Don't move," she hissed.

Stones clattered. Thorns rustled, then stopped.

His heart lodged in his throat.

Demitria spread her feet, fists clenching and shoulders rolling back into a ready position, as if she were about to single-handedly fight off whatever came through the tunnel. Who was this woman?

"Demi? It's me."

Demitria released her breath as another form crawled through the opening.

"You've got to do something about that tunnel. I'm too old for this." The man stood, joints cracking, and Nikolas recognized him at once. Titus Didius Liberare. Tall and broad shouldered, his bearing was distinctly military, though he had to be over sixty. Scars covered his arms, and a silvering beard attempted to cover the ones on his face and neck.

Demitria stepped toward him. "Titus, what are you doing here?"

"I was at the cove and saw your boat and the blood." Titus's words bore a slight Latin accent, as if Greek was not his native tongue. His gaze shifted to Nikolas and sank with relief. "Pastor Nikolas. I'm relieved to see you here. I went to meet you at the cove as we agreed, and I didn't see your boat."

Nikolas shifted. "Yes, well. There was a bit of trouble with that—"

"A moray bit Theseus," Demitria broke in. "Phineas is here."

Titus's attention snapped to her and then to the men behind. "How is he? What can I do?" Concern sharpened his tone.

"He's agreed to raise my patient recovery average to four out of twelve," Phineas called over his shoulder. "And I will not accept anything less."

"There you have it." Demitria's smile was weak.

Titus leaned to the side, peering at Phineas around Demitria and Nikolas. "Tell me what you need, and I'll do my best to get it here."

As the physician listed items, Demitria turned to Nikolas, those nearly black eyes meeting his with a shine of tears.

"Thank you." Her smile was grateful, if trembling and troubled. "Though I'm sorry this was your welcome into Myra."

"I'm glad to help." He crossed his arms, feeling the lump of the orange still tucked into his tunic.

"Are you hungry?" She spun to the vine-covered wall before he could answer and began shifting through the vines.

He pulled the orange from his tunic and rolled it between his fingers. *Don't do it.*

Demitria turned around, thrusting a handful of tiny cucumbers toward him. "They're small and not nearly enough to—" Her gaze dropped to the orange he extended toward her with a wince.

"It's silly, but . . ." Nikolas couldn't bring himself to explain further. To repeat the words the toothless little girl had once spoken to him.

Demitria's brows drew together and her other hand reached for the orange in jerky motions as if she felt as awkward as he did at the exchange.

Stupid, Niko.

She took the orange and transferred the cucumbers into his hand, eyes sweeping up to meet his again. "Thank you."

"I'll pray for a quick recovery." His fingers closed over the tiny, prickly fruit.

Titus stepped away from Phineas and looked toward Nikolas,

expression torn. "I hate to leave like this, but we need to go, Pastor. There's trouble at the school."

Anxiety and relief clashed in Nikolas's stomach.

He'd nearly forgotten. The *school.*

FIVE

WITH HER BACK AGAINST THE WALL, Demi wrapped her arms around her knees and shut her eyes. Theseus slept on his mat, helped into the easy slumber by Phineas's poppy tincture. Her every sense hovered over the sound of his breathing. Even, and yet . . . did it catch? Hesitate? Was that a gurgle in his lungs, or only in her mind?

Stop.

He was going to be fine. Provided he actually rested, and infection didn't set in, and the fever didn't linger, and—*stop*. Theseus hadn't died. He was alive. That's what she had to think on. Not the what-ifs. Even so, her mind ran. She'd left Theseus with Phineas long enough to return the boat and explain to Mersad about Theseus's injury—though she'd left off just how serious it was. They'd be back in a day or two, she'd promised. They couldn't risk Mersad assigning their lateen to other divers. Too many lives depended on that boat for far more than coral and pearls.

Searing heat rose behind her eyes. How had a routine day turned to such a nightmare? Demi swallowed the lump rising in her throat. Fear added an extra rhythm to her heart. Both she and Theseus had been swimming before they could walk. Though Pater had hounded them with his rules, it hadn't occurred to her that the sea could betray her. Turn treacherous. People, yes. But the sea? *Her* sea? The betrayal stung, and a familiar shame crept up her spine. She should have known. Should have prepared. Should have thought of the possibilities. She'd let her guard down and failed the ones closest to her . . . again.

Demi reached up to push the hair from her eyes and caught sight of blood smearing her fingers. She froze. Stared. Turned her shaking hand over in front of her eyes as her gut twisted and threatened to spill what little it contained.

It wasn't the first time she'd had blood on her hands.

Guilt in her soul.

She shoved to her feet and crossed to the bowl of water next to Theseus. Splashing water over her hands, she scrubbed at the stains. If only the past could be erased as easily.

Stones clattered outside the walls. Two sets of footsteps. Demi straightened, drying her hands on her chiton. She held her breath. Overhead, the deepening sky was streaked with pink and orange.

"Demi? It's us. Will you help with the basket?"

Nydia's voice cut the tension stiffening Demi's spine.

"It's nearly dark. I didn't think you were coming." Demi stooped near the low opening.

"Pater said Phineas gave him a list. And Mater packed food. She said we could stay with you." Wicker crackled against the thorn bushes. "We need a better way into this place. I hate this thorn tunnel."

"Better safe than fighting stray dogs."

Nydia grunted in a way that said she didn't quite agree.

Demi pulled the basket through as Titus's daughter followed on her hands and knees. Nydia twisted to free her chiton from a thorn, then emerged from the tunnel, braid snagged and mussed. Her adopted eight-year-old brother, Rex, followed.

Nydia flung her arms around Demi. "How is he? How are *you*?"

Tears threatened and Demi swallowed them down. "I'm fine." The lie slipped easily through her teeth as she drew back. "Theseus is resting."

Nydia peered past her, and Demi nudged her forward.

"Go see him. Phineas gave him some poppy tincture to ease the pain and help him sleep."

Nydia crossed Demi's garden to where Theseus's mat lay beneath the awning. She let out a long breath and gazed at him tenderly, as if trying to memorize his every feature.

Rex leaned to one side, peering around Demi to Theseus but not going any closer. Dim light from the firepot glinted on his golden hair and pale eyes the color of sea glass.

"Thanks for coming with Nydia, Rex." Demi tried to catch his eye.

Rex stared at Theseus, unblinking. "Is he dead?"

"No." Her answer came quick.

"He's so pale." Nydia's dark braid, streaked with honey-gold strands, slid across her back as she looked from Theseus to Demi.

"He's strong. It's just his wrist." Demi paused. "And his foot. But you know how Theseus can be. If his nose runs, he's certain he's going to die."

Nydia bit back a wobbly smile.

"He will be well. Phineas said so." She did not mention his patient averages as she settled beside her friend. The physician's numbers were less assuring than his words.

Rex sat too but kept his distance from Theseus. "Where's the eel?"

She'd carried it back from the docks after she'd returned the boat, but sent it with Phineas. It was a shame to waste so much food, but she'd never be able to stomach it. "Phineas took it with him."

"Tell me what happened," Nydia urged gently. "Pater tried but—"

As Demi recounted the ordeal, her heart began to race again and her palms started to sweat. When she'd finished, Rex gave a satisfied nod at the tale and stood, crossing the garden to poke at the vines and hunt for frogs.

Nydia lowered her voice. "I saw Pastor Nikolas when he and Pater came home. Pater said he helped you bring Theseus home?"

"Yes." Demi wove the fabric of her chiton through her fingers. "What a welcome, hmm? He was very kind."

"Yia-yia had some of the church widows over today, helping in the *kuzina*. They were not so kind about him. You know how some of them can be."

Demi nodded. She'd been at the receiving end of more than a few sharp comments. Women should pursue a quiet life in the home, not spend their days doing a man's job—and such a job—in the sun all day, diving for coral and pearls, naked, or nearly so. She could understand their cutting remarks, deserved them, and worse—but Pastor Nikolas?

"What could they possibly say about him? A man they've never met."

Nydia glanced at Rex and leaned closer. "He's from Patara. *Nikolas of Patara?*" She raised her eyebrows, as if that was supposed to mean something. "Second son of the wealthiest shipping tycoon on the Mediterranean? He might as well be a prince."

So that was why his name had sounded familiar.

"Some say he murdered his father to take over."

Demi scoffed, gaze drawn to the little orange gleaming on the wall niche. Murderers did not have soft eyes like Pastor Nikolas. And they did not give oranges as gifts. "No one who has committed murder becomes the leader of a church."

"The apostle Paul did." Nydia shrugged. "With God's help, people can change."

Could they? Could *she?*

"Then it doesn't matter what they say, does it?" Why she felt the need to defend him, Demi didn't know. Perhaps because if the church widows knew what she'd done, they'd not just spread malicious gossip. She'd be cast out for good. A man like Nikolas didn't deserve to be spoken of like that.

Nydia reached for the basket she'd brought. "Forgive me. I shouldn't have repeated any of that. Yia-yia rebuked the widows for gossiping and perhaps I ought to scrub my tongue too." She lifted a cloth-wrapped jar from the basket. "Stew?"

Rex bolted toward them at the word. "I'm starving."

Nydia ruffled his hair as he plopped beside her. "Mater would never let that happen and you know it."

"You can have my portion, Rex." Demi smiled. "I'm not hungry."

"Lies. You're always hungry." One of Nydia's eyes scrunched as she studied Demi. Nydia had inherited her mother's beauty and curves, and her father's dark-blue eyes and ability to find things others wanted to leave hidden.

Demi averted her gaze. Too late. Nydia had seen something and was immediately on the hunt.

"What's going on, Demi? What aren't you telling me? Is Theseus worse than Phineas said?" The jar of soup lowered to Nydia's lap, her knuckles whitening. "Tell me. I can take ill news, but I can't stand false hope."

"What? No. Nothing like that."

"Then what?"

Rex took the jar of soup from his sister and tipped it to his lips.

Demi's stomach churned. Nydia might be her dearest friend in the world, but even she didn't know how far Demi had fallen. Her mind ran. What else could she admit instead? Something mortifying but not exactly condemning. She shut her eyes and blurted, "I've been in my swimming tunic all day."

"So?" Nydia's brow furrowed in confusion before her eyes expanded to the size of an ocean sunfish. "You mean, you met Pastor Nikolas in your tiny swimming tunic?"

Demi nodded. It sounded worse when Nydia said it like that. She lifted her shoulders. "I was so consumed with helping Theseus, I didn't even notice until he said something."

"Well, at least . . ." Nydia paused, as if searching for something to say to ease Demi's discomfort. It was a long pause. "At least you don't dive naked like everyone else."

Demi snorted. "Comfort Pastor Nikolas with that thought, will you?" She winced. "Never mind. Don't."

Rex slurped. Nydia pulled the soup jar away from his lips and poked his shoulder. "Save some for the rest of us, you." She passed the jar to Demi. "Chin up. Act like nothing happened and maybe he will forget."

Wasn't that what she'd been doing all these years? Acting like nothing had happened? She knew firsthand that she could pretend it away all she wanted, but the guilt would never go anywhere.

"Tell me some good news, Nydia."

"We're here. And Rex saved a few swallows of soup for you."

Demi smiled. "I'm glad. You're good friends."

"The best. Now, eat this." Nydia pulled out several fist-sized loaves of *pelanos* bread and passed one to Rex and another to Demi.

Demi's mouth watered. No one baked like Nydia's mother.

"Yia-yia only let me take the misshapen pieces, but they'll still taste fine."

"Misshapen?" Demi lifted her nose and waved her away. "Take them back."

"No! I'll eat them." Rex dove for the bread.

Nydia laughed and lowered her voice. "I have to tell you, Yia-yia is quite taken with Pastor Nikolas. She keeps talking about how handsome he is."

Demi swiped a piece of bread and bit into it, her eyes closing of their own accord. "She didn't douse herself in her matchmaking perfume, did she?"

Nydia shook her head. "Only because Mater hid it. But she's got that concerning gleam in her eye again."

Demi chuckled, imagining Pastor Nikolas's discomfort as Yia-yia Beatrix waved a glass vial beneath his nose and spouted the attributes of her famous "mysterious and exotic" scent for men.

"Yia-yia claims it's her scriptural duty to remove singles from Myra. Do you remember the arguments she had with Pastor Tomoso?"

Demi nodded. After Emperor Diocletian had passed the edicts banning Christians from public office and the military, Pastor Tomoso had refused to allow marriages. He'd claimed that the Lord was returning at any moment, and believers were better off devoting themselves to Scripture and good works rather than the distraction of building families. Some agreed. Nydia and Theseus had simply never spoken of their growing affection, while others, like Alexander, had been angry. He'd refused to break their betrothal, insisting that Tomoso would soon see reason, but it hadn't mattered. Alexander had died at the hands of a festival mob, and in the years that followed, everyone—herself included—had been too busy trying to survive the edicts to argue for marriages. The violence ebbed and flowed now, increasing around pagan festivals and dying out in between.

Demi sipped the fragrant broth left in the jar.

Nydia looked over at Theseus again. "I just want him to live. Now that we have a new leader, I'd hoped . . ." She bit her cheek, stopping herself from voicing the old longings.

Demi scooped a bite of fish with her fingers and handed the crock back to Nydia, refusing to let her own disappointed dreams sour those of her friend. "He'll pull through. And perhaps Pastor Nikolas will allow you two to marry, and Yia-yia will calm down."

Nydia laughed. "Have you met Yia-yia? No singles are safe."

Demi offered a tight smile and shoved the last bit of bread in her mouth, failing to smother the burn rising in her throat, the bloody images flashing through her mind.

Nydia was wrong. No one was safe.

SIX

IF NIKOLAS HAD TO GUESS, the problem at the school seemed to be the fact that there were no students to be found. The place appeared wholly abandoned—and in great haste. Apple cores, waxed tablets, papyri, and styli littered the floor of the main room. Titus skirted toppled benches and kicked aside a discarded shoe, at ease with a mess that made Nikolas's skin prickle.

He looked around the empty room. "Where is everyone?"

"They're in here." Titus crossed to a row of tall wooden cupboards with pointed tops.

They both couldn't be talking about the students.

He swung open the doors of the cabinet on the far-left end. Instead of scrolls, Titus pulled out a rack of wooden swords.

Swords?

Interest flared. "What sort of school is this, exactly?"

"The normal kind." Titus rapped on the back of the now-empty cabinet.

The *normal* kind? Nikolas had been led off to school by a servant pedagogue for his entire adolescence. Not once had he seen swords in the cupboards. He might have actually excelled in his studies had they included swords. Perhaps his had not been a normal school.

The back of the cabinet gave way and Titus motioned Nikolas inside.

Definitely not the cabinets he remembered from his own childhood. He certainly would have enjoyed school more if there had been hidden passages.

Nikolas stepped inside and blinked against the sudden dimness. A lamp on a shelf cast the room in guttering orange light and shadow. Stacks of crates and rows of barrels came into view as his eyes adjusted. Bare shelves lined the top half of the room, clustered with empty jars and amphorae. Bundles of carded wool tumbled like snow-covered peaks from one corner of the room to the center, where nearly a dozen people waited.

Nikolas froze, mind racing backward to the attack at the monastery. Monks trapped behind stone walls, screams and swords cutting through the darkness. The cramped, lightless cellar where he and several others had hidden.

Titus nudged him forward. "This is the *koinonia* I was telling you about. And these are the elders and a few of the deacons and deaconesses of Myra and Andriake."

A ragged breath scraped back into his lungs.

Of course. A meeting. Not a trap.

Nikolas swallowed the dryness in his throat and pressed his shaking fingers against his thighs. Titus had tried to explain the situation in Myra and the way the church gathered food and stored it in caches around the city to be distributed by the deacons to those in need. This must be one of those communal storage places.

"Glad to see you all again." He recognized a few faces from when he'd stumbled into Pastor Tomoso's funeral and had been unanimously chosen to be the new leader of Myra's churches. Never mind that he'd only been there to deliver a message, and that he was five years shy of the traditional pastoral age of thirty, and that there were others more qualified, if less willing. Church leaders were the first to be hunted down and arrested, and few were eager to step into such positions anymore.

Titus pulled the door shut behind them. "We all wanted to gather in one place to greet you and—"

"Air our grievances," someone in the back interrupted.

Titus turned and shot a look of warning toward the speaker. "Inform you of how everything works."

One by one, the elders gave their names and introduced the deacons and deaconesses who helped them care for the small groups of believers they led in various sections of the city. Nikolas's head spun, trying to absorb it all. To match names with jobs and regions although he hadn't a clue where any of the streets were.

"We decided it was safer to divide into smaller gatherings, rather than to meet as one large body," Titus explained when the last elder had introduced himself, "though all of us try to meet together at the river each month. But don't worry about remembering everything right now." Titus waved a man forward. "Xeno has agreed to guide you on your visits to each of the small gatherings."

That was a relief.

The man who came forward was perhaps slightly older than Nikolas and bore an eager expression contrasted by an almost reverent hug. "I couldn't believe it when they said you'd agreed. Welcome, Nikolas of Patara."

Nikolas's smile faltered at the knowing way Xeno spoke his name. And yet, was it too much to expect that no one had heard of him? Of stories that came with his name? He cleared his throat. "Thank you for volunteering as guide."

Xeno grinned. "Glad to."

Titus broke in again, all business. "Each of these elders have several deacons and deaconesses in their charge who supply food and ensure needs are met. Various food caches and safe rooms are spread throughout the city to ensure that if one is discovered, all is not lost. The koinonia, here, is one of them. We also trade for goods and supplies from our brothers and sisters upriver in the farming villages."

"I see." Nikolas nodded. Before they'd been betrayed, the monks near Patara had conducted similar trades with the Christians in that city.

"But all the caches in the city are as empty as this one." A man unfolded from the bales of wool and crossed the room with one stubby hand extended and the other pressed against his barrel-shaped chest. "Crescens," he introduced again.

Nikolas nodded and gripped his hand.

Able to see Nikolas better now, Crescens took him in with a glance. "You look young." By his tone, it was not a compliment.

Nikolas ignored the slight. Hadn't they known that already? "Why can't they be filled?"

Crescens crossed his arms. "Our contact at Hadrian's Granary said the grain is gone." The room was silent at the news, suggesting the others already knew of this development.

Titus squinted. "Gone, or he won't sell it to us?"

"Dioscorides doubled the bribe, and he still said the same. It's empty. There's no grain in the city—or at least nothing left in the public granary."

Crescens's words settled in Nikolas's gut like his boat had settled to the seafloor. Without grain, everyone in Myra and Andriake would be in want, not just them. "What's being done for the poor outside of the church?"

The elders and deacons stared at him, as if his question was too ludicrous to answer.

Xeno shifted beside him. "We can't keep ourselves fed, much less anyone else."

Crescens nodded. "The festival of Artemisia begins soon, and all business in the city will shut down for the entire month of Maius. Between the caches, there's a handful of this and a jar of that—we've got nothing to live on." He turned to Titus. "Send word to the runners that we need to go upriver for supplies. Now."

Titus let out a long breath. "One of the runners was injured today. Badly. He'll not be going upriver for months. Maybe not ever."

Now the room rumbled with murmurs. Crescens muttered under his breath and kicked at an empty crate.

Nikolas scrambled for a plan. If they wanted him to lead them, then first things first. "Let's pause and pray. The Lord will—"

"You've spent the last, what, six, seven years sequestered in a monastery?" Crescens barked a laugh, then gripped the back of his neck, as if to collect himself. "Praying is not wrong, it's just . . . you don't know what it's like here. You have no idea the danger, the secrecy, the . . . the *toll* it takes on a body just to survive from one day to the next. We can't trust anyone, we're starving, and you expect us to just sit around and pray—and what? God will pour down manna from heaven? It doesn't work like that."

Nikolas clenched his teeth against a defensive response. He'd spent barely two years in the monastery and the rest dodging capture in Patara while doing his best to help the church there. He wasn't naive to the danger. Nor had the monastery protected him from it. The opposite, really. The price of disobedience to the emperor had been paid in much blood. But an argument now was not needed.

Give me wisdom to navigate this, Lord.

"I never suggested it was a simple thing." Nikolas worked to keep his tone even. "Only that the Lord is glad to give direction to those who seek Him." He turned to Titus. "Is there food upriver?"

"It might as well be in Nicomedia if we can't get it," Crescens muttered.

Titus ignored Crescens and focused on Nikolas. "Yes."

"You need a man to go upriver? Send me. I'll go." The words left his mouth of their own accord—not that he would have stopped them. He'd refused to help once before and vowed never again. And yet, why was no one else volunteering? He shrugged away the doubt niggling at the back of his mind and forced his chin up. "The sooner I know how the trade network runs, the better."

The room was silent.

"It's . . . not a bad plan," Titus said, nodding slowly and looking about the room as if waiting for someone to raise an argument. No one did. "Then it's settled."

The others began to shuffle toward the door as if the pronouncement brought the meeting to an end. Titus rubbed his temples and opened the door as the men and women filed past, offering Nikolas the right hand of fellowship and belated murmurs of welcome.

Crescens huffed as he moved toward the door, pausing near Titus. "Send word when they're on their way, and I'll have everyone ready to transport."

They? Nikolas glanced at Xeno. "Do you go upriver too?"

Xeno shook his head. "There isn't room for more than two in the boat, and none of us have experience on the water."

"I see." He wasn't certain his own experience would be much help. "So, who else is going?"

"Titus can fill you in on the details." Xeno lifted a hand toward one of the other men who was headed for the door, gesturing for him to wait. He glanced back at Nikolas. "I'll be here tomorrow afternoon to bring you to Theodore's group. You'll like them."

Nikolas nodded. "Thank you."

Xeno gripped Nikolas's hand and leaned closer with a conspiratorial squint. "Good luck with her."

Her?

Xeno released his hand and slipped through the doorway. When Nikolas emerged into the schoolroom, it was empty once more, but this time, the benches were righted and the floor clean of debris.

Titus replaced the rack of wooden swords and closed the cupboard doors. "You did well. In times like these, when brothers are here one day and gone the next, it is difficult to build close bonds. But they will welcome you better in time."

Perhaps after Nikolas had proven himself by going upriver, they'd be less standoffish.

His father's harsh voice echoed through his mind, reminding him that whatever he did would never erase the one thing he hadn't done. Perhaps he'd never belong. Perhaps . . . being the outsider was what he deserved.

Titus swung an arm toward a dim hallway in the opposite direction where faint clatters and loud aromas emerged. His wrist twisted at an odd angle, as if he'd broken it and it hadn't healed properly.

"The kuzina's this way. It smells like the evening meal is ready."

Nikolas followed. "What did he mean, *Good luck with her?*"

A slight smile tugged at Titus's mouth. "Demitria. Theseus's sister. She'll be the one going upriver with you, though I'm sure she'll need some convincing."

Sun-browned skin. Black eyes. Wild curls. The images flashed through his mind with startling clarity at the mention of her name. Titus kept talking. Coral divers. Impeccable character. Highly trusted.

Theseus's sister.

Somehow, those were the only words he heard.

SEVEN

As Nikolas followed Titus into the kuzina, the aroma hit him straight in the gut. Fish, herbs, and bread. His mouth watered and his stomach cramped. When had he eaten last?

A fire smoldered in the mouth of a large clay stove that branched into three upright tubes where sputtering pots nestled over the openings. Two women bustled about the room, sweeping the pots off the stove and onto the table when the men entered.

Titus caught the younger of the two women by the waist and pressed a kiss to her cheek. She murmured a greeting and smiled up at him, the scar marring her temple puckering as it disappeared into gray-streaked hair.

"Pastor Nikolas, I believe you met my wife, Iris, on your last visit?"

Iris turned her smile on Nikolas, brighter and less soft than it had been for Titus.

Nikolas nodded. "Yes. I—"

"Thank the Lord you've arrived safely!" A tiny woman, white curls springing from her head with the same energy reflected in her eyes, rounded on Nikolas and threw her bony arms around his waist. "We welcome you, gladly." She drew back to cup his face in her silky hands and turn it from side to side as she nodded. "The Lord has blessed you indeed. This makes my work so much easier. It won't be long before you're snapped up."

Unease edged his gut. How did such a tiny, pink-clad woman manage to sound so threatening?

"And this is Beatrix." Titus's belated introduction didn't slow the woman for a moment.

Beatrix tugged at Nikolas's chin so his gaze met hers. "If you need a new scent, I have just the—"

"Mater." Iris pulled away from Titus and gently removed the old woman's hands from Nikolas's face. She turned a sheepish smile toward him. "We're glad you've arrived safely, Pastor. We've been looking forward to your arrival."

Beatrix nodded, rheumy eyes sparkling with a concerning eagerness.

"I'm glad to be here too." At the admission, a bit of the tension in his stomach eased.

"I hope you don't mind a quiet meal. So many wanted to meet you, but we thought it safer to introduce you in smaller gatherings." Iris gestured to the corner where a low table sat, ringed with flat cushions. "You both go and sit."

Nikolas sank onto a patched green cushion across from Titus. The stone monastery he'd lived in was neither furnished nor heated. Uncle had abhorred furnishings. Especially cushions. He'd insisted that discomfort kept one close to God. If that was true, Nikolas should feel closer to God in Myra than anywhere else.

He cleared his throat, shoving the thoughts aside. "The school is impressive. I've never seen the like."

Titus nodded and looked around the room. "Lady Isidora and her husband, Evander, have been quite generous, allowing us to live here. There's a room for you too. I'll show you later."

He went on to explain that while Lady Isidora was a believer, her husband was not. As one of Myra's ten elected decurions who aided the two city governors, Master Evander had been "invited" to pay for a public work to benefit the city. Lady Isidora had convinced him to build a school for laborers' children.

"He provides the funds and Lady Isidora sees to the administration, and ensures we have all we need," Titus finished. "All of us who work here are believers, although there have been many . . . new hires in the last few years." Titus didn't need to elaborate. The solemn silence said enough.

"And it's . . . we are . . . *allowed* to work here?"

Titus waved his hand in a so-so gesture. "Master Evander posted the notice of government compliance outside the door. And it's just assumed that we are all compliant as well."

Compliant. Devoted to the gods, carriers of libelli. Nikolas's stomach twisted.

Titus continued. "You must know we're only using a building, not . . . we haven't personally burned incense and we don't plan to. But if we can make a difference in this city, then we will work. As long as God allows."

"And I am to pretend to be an instructor at this school?"

Titus rubbed the back of his neck and didn't quite meet his gaze. "Not *pretend* exactly. One of our instructors bolted in the night, and . . . We have other tutors, but I hoped you could take over—only for Latin in the mornings. I helped where I could, but I'm better equipped to train the boys with a gladius than a stylus." He raised both hands with a sheepish grin. "You may find your students a bit boisterous. My apologies."

That explained the swords.

Nikolas let out a breath and found himself nodding in agreement to the plan, though his mind wandered back to his own education in Patara. Sweat dampened the tunic beneath his arms. Much to his pater's shame, he'd barely completed the levels and spent far more time with the disciplinarian than he'd spent conjugating Latin, which few spoke in the Greek-influenced Eastern Empire. He'd hoped in coming here that he could *do* something, not be reminded at every turn of all the things he hadn't done. The prickle of guilt had become a constant companion.

Iris lowered a tray of fish stew and bread onto the table.

Nikolas's stomach rumbled. "Thank you for your hospitality."

Iris waved him off with a smile. "Of course. This is as it should be."

Beatrix stepped between them. "Here you are, Pastor Nikolas."

His nose burned as the elderly woman stooped and held out a steaming bowl. Her floral scent set his eyes watering and clouded the aroma of the stew. He accepted the bowl quickly. "Thank you, Beatrix."

The old woman beamed. "Try it," she urged, snapping straight and looking for all the world like she was about to bounce out of her skin in excitement.

He took a tentative sip. His mouth filled with perfectly salted broth, swimming with flaky white chunks of fish and colorful vegetables.

"Delightful."

Uncle hadn't bothered overlong on cooking. He believed food was meant for sustenance only, not enjoyment. Enjoyment led to gluttony. Nikolas didn't agree. Especially now.

The others took their bowls and sat, Iris settling next to Titus, who tucked his arm around her. He whispered something in her ear, and she swatted at him, chuckling.

Something flickered in Nikolas's mind. A remembrance of his parents. The soft look in his pater's eyes when his mitera entered the room. The light that had gone out in him when she'd died. The anger and accusation that had replaced it when Amadeo followed her. Though he sat surrounded by kind people, loneliness crashed over Nikolas like water over his boat and left him floundering. He bowed his head, thankful when Titus prayed over the meal and he could press the memories back where they belonged. His fingers twitched against the cushion. *Lord, I need something to do.*

Iris turned a welcoming smile in Nikolas's direction. "And how were your travels, Pastor Nikolas?"

He jerked his head up in tardy response to the amen.

Utter failure.

"Eventful." He tried not to let the disappointment edge his words. Not even Titus knew what his boat had carried. "But I arrived in one piece, so I cannot truly complain."

"Titus said you were shipwrecked like the apostle Paul?" This from Beatrix, who looked at Nikolas in wide-eyed wonder. "You know he started the church in Myra on one of his missionary journeys?"

Nikolas smiled. "Patara's too."

"And you swam to shore?" Beatrix's fingers fluttered in front of her lips.

Nikolas nodded and took another sip. Apparently in the few minutes Titus had taken to dash back before the meeting with the elders, he'd been able to pass on more information than just Phineas's list of medicines for Theseus.

"In time to help Demitria drag Theseus home," Titus added.

Nikolas shifted, heat crawling up his neck at Demitria's name. He cleared his throat. "The Lord provides help in the strangest of ways. I pray he will recover well."

"Indeed." Beatrix plied him with the tray of bread. "He's going to marry my granddaughter, Nydia."

"I see. Congratulations." Nikolas accepted a round of bread and took another sip of broth. When his bowl tipped back down, Beatrix's unsettling smile was fixed on him from across the table.

"Delicious," he offered, awkwardly raising the bowl in toast.

"Pastor Nikolas"—her smile never wavered—"what are your thoughts on marriage?"

EIGHT

DEMI'S SKIN PRICKLED AS SHE ARRANGED the thorns across the tunnel entrance. The cool dampness of an early summer breeze washed over her. She inhaled the freshness, tinged faintly with the stench of herbs and salves Nydia had delivered for Theseus's arm. He'd been coughing and fevered for the last few days, and Phineas had been in and out of the crumbling safe house at all hours until the fever had finally broken. Theseus was not safe yet, but without a fever, his outlook was not so dire. Phineas spoke of moving him to a room in Myra where he would be closer and easier to observe. Though she hated the thought of moving him, it was not a bad plan.

Demi wove silently through the fishermen's huts, knowing the men had already left to find the best spots before dawn broke. She'd attempted to return to work, not because she'd wanted to, but because she couldn't risk Mersad giving their place and boat to another set of divers. Mersad had simply pressed a few coins into her palm and insisted she return home to care for Theseus. Better to lose a few days' work from them both than lose his best diver. At least their jobs were safe . . . for now. But how long would Mersad feel so generous? And in their absence, would Ennio and Pelos make another appeal for their sons to take over Demi and Theseus's boat? If Theseus did not recover soon, she'd have to convince Mersad to let her dive alone. Maybe she'd ask if Rex could act as her spotter. He was only eight and the help he could offer was minimal, but she'd try anything before she lost access to the boat.

A breath of relief left her lungs as she passed the last straggling huts of the port village and entered the citrus groves clustered between the port of Andriake and the city of Myra. She'd made the trek hundreds of times with Theseus, weaving along the worn trail others might mistake for a goat path. The smooth dirt beneath her bare feet was as familiar as her boat and yet it felt strange, and somehow wrong, to be traveling it alone. She forced one foot in front of the other, denying the thoughts that told her it would be far easier, far safer to turn back and go home.

Do not neglect meeting together.

Despite the slight wobble in her knees, Demi lifted her chin and pressed on, clinging to a deeper truth. That if she did not go on, did not make it to the meeting, she would miss out on the only thing that truly mattered. If only she'd clung to that truth sooner.

The river chortled against the rocky banks and the path grew soggy beneath her feet. She passed the city to her left and wove through the crumbling shantytown that spread outward toward the riverbank, the foot of the mountain crowding it all. Against the starlit sky, the necropolis of ancient tombs carved into the face of the mountain spread a backdrop across the cliffs behind the city, curving around the outcropping and following the Myros River inland. The tombs towered over the river, facades of homes and temples stacked one upon the other. Some doors remained sealed, while others gaped with jagged holes like mouthfuls of broken teeth. Death leered over her head. She shuddered and dropped her eyes to the path instead.

As Demi rounded the final bend, the brush gave way to a rocky clearing. She slowed, the only sounds the ruffle of wind in the leaves and the chuckling of the river. Then a single voice rose high, reedy.

"Let it be silent.
Let the luminous stars not shine,
Let the winds and all the noisy rivers die down;
And as we praise the Father, the Son, and the Holy Spirit,
Let all the powers add, 'Amen, amen.'"

Demi had always loved this part. This beginning in the silent dark. No way to discern their numbers. There might have been five or five hundred. But when the singing started, voices rose from all around. In front, behind, close to the river's edge, and up near the tombs. The darkness crafted an illusion of isolation, but the worship left the deception shattered. They were here. Together. Believers of Andriake and Myra shoulder to shoulder. Their songs uniting with believers spanning time, centuries, and the empire in a way that the darkness could not overcome. She drew the knowledge around her like a mantle—protective, warm, comforting.

A single lamp drew her eyes to one of the lower tombs, broken open and standing empty as long as the oldest among them could remember. Pastor Nikolas perched stiffly on the edge of a rock near the opening, singing, though she couldn't hear his voice over the others. His brown beard clung to the angles of his jaw and appeared newly grown—perhaps an attempt to make him look older, though he couldn't be much older than she was. Had he had the beard before? She couldn't recall. As the singing ended, he stood, hands shifting from his sides to clasped in front of him and back to his sides as if he wasn't sure what to do with them.

The singing fell away, heads lowered, hands lifted.

"The Lord's blessing—" Nikolas stopped, cleared his throat, and tried again, louder. "The Lord's blessing on you all." His voice shook slightly. "I am Nikolas of—erm—newly elected bishop and leader of Myra and Andriake."

He dropped into prayer as suddenly as a diving stone plunged to the depths of the sea.

Demi lowered her chin in tardy response as Nikolas prayed for those present, then cracked open a waxed tablet inscribed with the names of other church leaders within and without the empire and prayed for each of them as well. Demi wondered how many on the list still remained on this side of heaven. Letters from other churches had been scarce of late.

Her throat burned. There had been too many taken too soon. She longed to pray, to ask God if He saw their suffering, if He saw how the emperors picked them off in twos and hundreds. To ask when He would step in and save His people, set all things to rights. And yet, she dared not ask, had no right to do so. She had no right to even stand where she did, though she couldn't bear to be anywhere else. Longing and unworthiness beat a constant battle in her chest.

She swiped at tears. Nikolas called the readers forward and she strained to see who they were. Each of the readers had been entrusted to hide and care for a certain portion of Scripture, so in the event of arrests, not all of their Scripture would be confiscated. Diogenes and Justin came forward.

Demi hung on the words as Diogenes read from his portion of the Psalms, the psalmist's longing for justice resonating with her own questions. Justin followed with a lengthier portion from the account of the apostle John. *In the world you will have tribulation. But take heart; I have overcome the world.*

It was not a promise of ease, but a promise of suffering, of trial—more than that, it was a promise that in the end, the suffering would not have the final word. The promise tugged at the questions in her heart, inviting her to set them free, to take comfort, but how could she? When Pastor Tomoso had insisted that she could never be forgiven? Never be set to rights?

Nikolas stood again, this time leading them in a prayer of thanksgiving. The joy in his voice carried through the clearing, pushing back at the ache in her chest. Could joy exist in such times? When was the last time she'd felt anything remotely like joy?

A nudge on her arm. Her eyes opened and she saw the others moving forward toward the cleft in the rock where Nikolas passed out loaves of bread for breaking.

She joined the line and shuffled forward to take a piece of bread and drink from the shared cup in celebration of what God had done. A king became a servant, brought life from death, made beggars into sons. The world would never be the same no matter how the emperor schemed to return to the old ways and the old gods. But celebration in an unworthy manner was forbidden. And of all of them, she was most unworthy.

She kept her eyes downcast as she tore a bit of bread and placed it between her lips.

"His body broken for you," Nikolas murmured as he offered the cup.

She took it, the clay warm from his hands. She tilted it to her lips, but didn't dare drink it. Not with the stain on her soul.

"His blood poured out for the remission of sins."

But not hers.

A flash of memory. Another's blood pooling on the paving stones, her hands slick with it. Tears burned her eyes, and she made the mistake of looking up and meeting his.

"Demitria, will you stay a moment?"

Nikolas's low request sent a warning jolt to her pulse. Could he sense the guilt she carried? Did he know the bread still rested on her tongue, that she'd only pretended to drink? Everything within her wanted to act as if she hadn't heard. To simply turn and run. She forced a breath into her lungs.

"Yes." Her assent was little more than a choked whisper.

He gave a nod and offered the cup to the elderly woman next in line.

Demi stepped to the side, swiping the crumb of bread from her mouth and flicking it to the ground, lest she heap another sin upon herself. Her pulse thundered louder than the surf beyond the rocky necropolis. Nikolas didn't know her secret. Couldn't know it. So then what could he possibly need to talk to her about? He'd probably inquire about Theseus, and she'd be on her way. Yes. That was it, surely.

The crowd thinned, laborers leaving for their work as the sky began to lighten. At last—and all too soon—Nikolas approached, Titus with him.

"How is Theseus?" Titus asked.

The tension in her shoulders eased slightly. "His fever broke. Phineas is ecstatic, of course."

Titus's mouth twitched. "So I heard. What do you think of moving him to"—he glanced around and lowered his voice—"the safe room behind the sponge and pumice stone shop? The owner is a friend of mine. We can trust him, and Theseus will be closer to Phineas."

She hesitated. They'd never stayed in Myra, only Andriake, in the sea caves, or the crumbling hut, or beneath the stars in the cove. Her family had lived in Andriake for generation on generation, waking with the screech of gulls and lulled to sleep by the booming surf. The thought of leaving it, even going a mile, seemed both a betrayal and a loss. But it was for Theseus, and Titus would not have suggested it if it were not for the best.

She bit her lip and gave a nod. "If you think it's safe."

He nodded. "Much better than that roofless place in the dumping grounds. Especially if it floods again. And . . ." He glanced at Pastor Nikolas still standing quietly to the side, listening. "If we can help look after Theseus, it will free you to go back to work. We—another trading trip upriver is needed. Necessary. Before Artemisia."

Her head had started to shake before he finished. "Theseus isn't strong enough to go, and I can't do it alone. It'll be hard enough to convince Mersad to let me take the boat by myself. I meant to ask you if I might borrow Rex in the mornings, to be my spotter."

"Excuse me, Pastor Nikolas?" A withered hand pawed at Nikolas's sleeve. "Could I speak with you a moment?"

Nikolas nudged Titus. "I'll just be a moment. Good morning, Amata." He stepped aside with the old woman, and Titus turned back to Demi.

"We thought it best if you take Nikolas with you. So he can see firsthand how the supply run works."

"No."

"Why not?"

Because he unnerved her. "It's dangerous. And he's only just arrived. If we lose him now—"

"Who said anything about losing him? You're taking him upriver and coming back down. Same as always."

"You know there's more to it than that." She crossed her arms. "We've finally got a leader again and you want to risk his life fetching grain? You know the rule. We don't make important members take unnecessary risks."

"Isn't everyone important?" Nikolas edged between Demi and Titus, forming a tight circle.

"Different members, different skills, different jobs," Demitria recited, inching back and turning to Nikolas. "We don't move people from one job to another without reason. You are our leader, not a supply runner. I'll find someone else."

"Who?" both men asked in unison.

Demi faltered, running through the list of men who would qualify and coming up short. They were either dead, elderly, infirm, or had no experience on the water. Even Titus had an arm that never quite worked properly after an injury in the military.

"How can I be a leader if I sit back when there's work to be done?" Nikolas asked. "I can handle a boat."

"I thought yours sank." The words slipped out before she could stop them.

"Demi." Titus's tone chided as much as pleaded. "The elders agreed that the sooner Nikolas knows how everything works, the better."

She glanced at Nikolas, who was watching her with an expression she couldn't decipher. Judgment? Amusement? She didn't relish the thought of spending hours with him upriver, but ultimately, her feelings on the matter weren't as important as ensuring the survival of the church. If the elders trusted Nikolas enough to show him the supply chain, and trusted her to be the one to reveal it, then how could she argue?

"I'll pick him up on the riverbank just upriver from Mersad's dock." Her outward resistance gave as her gaze flickered from Titus to Nikolas. "Try not to sink my boat."

NINE

XENO MET HIM AT THE CORNER of the school where a street vendor roasted sticks of spiced meat over a pot of coals during the day but had gone now that dusk was falling. Nikolas's stomach rumbled despite the small bowl of stewed vegetables Beatrix had served for the evening meal. The food had grown more meager as the meals went on, and he realized Titus and his family must have saved rations for weeks to serve what felt like a feast his first night.

"Ready?" Xeno pushed away from the wall and swung into step beside him, his long arms swinging.

"As ready as I'll be."

They left the corner and the tantalizing smell that lingered in the air and pressed forward into streets heavy with the scent of flowers. They wove around garland sellers, slaves, and housewives in harried last-minute preparations for the monthlong festival of Artemisia which celebrated the richness and favor bestowed by the goddess Artemis. Doorways and windows sagged beneath swags of bright flowers and greenery, creating the illusion of vibrant life and abundance bursting from the very city itself. Caught up in the excitement, children wrapped themselves in the extra greenery and paraded about until the adults demanded they stop touching it. The streets were buoyant with anticipation, but Nikolas felt the weight of the undertow that always followed the pagan festivals.

Statues of Artemis—lauded as a perpetual virgin, mother of the earth and of harvest and plenty—perched in windowsills and in wall niches with her arms open to all. The benevolent virgin mother was the one the people loved, but few set out images of Artemis the cruel and vengeful huntress. The one with blood on her hands and death in her wake. Some claimed that there was no harm done in hanging a few flowers and celebrating the bounty of summer gardens and fishing, but like the bright flowers over the doorways that crumbled to dust in the summer heat, Artemisia had always turned quickly from celebration to hunting, terror, and death.

Nikolas quickened his steps. "How many gather with Elder Timothy?"

They turned down a quieter street that stretched upward with uneven stone steps. Palm branches swayed overhead, outgrowing the confines of their courtyards and shading the street against a sun-drained sky.

Xeno shrugged. "Eighteen perhaps? A few family remnants and older individuals."

Nikolas nodded. The other small gatherings had been about the same.

"Don't worry. They won't be as bad as a room full of eight-year-old boys, I'd guess."

Nikolas laughed. "That depends on how likely they are to have handfuls of crickets and a grass snake."

Xeno chuckled and shook his head. "I wish I could say for certain."

By the time they neared the top of the street, Nikolas's tunic stuck to his chest. The moisture in the evening air made it hard to breathe, and the buildings, radiating the day's heat, also restricted any cooling breeze the sea might have offered. He turned back to admire the pink-and-orange-streaked sky and the wave-ruffled sea, marred with a few late merchant ships making for the safety of the harbor before dark.

Nikolas turned to face Xeno. "Have you always lived in Myra?"

"Yes." Xeno lifted a hand and pointed over the city, where painted rooftops cascaded below them toward the sea. "That house there, the white one with the blue roof, belonged to my family."

Nikolas felt his eyebrows flicker. A large house. "What did your family do?"

"We dealt in fish. Buying from local fishermen, preserving it, and shipping it off to other cities. It was a good business." Xeno raised a small smile. "Not that our business or paltry city villa could hold a lamp to yours. We didn't have a country estate."

An itchy sensation crawled up Nikolas's neck as he shrugged. "None of it matters now, does it?"

"Does it bother you to speak of it?"

Again, Nikolas shrugged. "My pater spent his entire life building the business, investing, amassing everything he could. I didn't . . . enjoy it like he did." Nikolas turned and climbed the street once more, the memories making him restless. It wasn't that he hadn't enjoyed it— he'd loathed it. But not for the reasons one might have imagined. Not because he didn't have a natural affinity for business like Amadeo had, but because, no matter how hard he'd tried, he hadn't been good enough.

"Was everything confiscated during the edicts?"

Before answering, Nikolas glanced at Xeno, noting the way his gaze strayed to the blue rooftop in longing. He wasn't going to admit that he'd found a way around the edicts. But truthfully . . . "I lost everything important long before then."

Xeno stared at the rooftop. "It is the same for me. The house, the business, the wealth . . . my family—of course." He sighed. "Sometimes I dream of having it all back—especially the food. Think of what we could do with it."

Nikolas nodded in agreement. Not a day had gone by that he didn't think about the gold at the bottom of the sea. The good it might have brought. He didn't mention it to Xeno. His friend had enough weighing on his mind.

He followed Xeno down a side street where they ducked into the recessed doorway of a rug shop.

The oily scent of wool filled Nikolas's nose and he blinked against the dimness. Rugs hung from wooden racks on the walls and layered a large table in the center of the room. Xeno paused and flipped through the edges of the rugs on the table before making his way toward the man at the back.

"I'm looking for something with an unfading beauty. Something unique and lasting."

The man studied first Xeno, then Nikolas. "If you will wait, I may have something for you."

Xeno nodded and the man disappeared behind a curtained doorway. Xeno stepped away and casually ran his hand over a rug hanging from the wall. "Exquisite," he murmured. "I had one like this."

They didn't wait long before the man returned, gesturing them behind the curtain after a quick glance around the otherwise empty shop. The room behind the curtain was dim and filled with rolled rugs crowding every wall. Nikolas followed the two men through the maze, nearly treading on Xeno's heels when he suddenly stopped. The darkness fled, retreating away from a triangle of light that appeared when the man flipped back another heavy tapestry, revealing yet another room lit from within. He stepped aside and waved them ahead of him.

Rugs covered the walls of the room and hung suspended from the ceiling on ropes, the purpose not for beauty but to silence the hum and whisper of the crowd of people huddled within. A bearded man moved toward him—Timothy, as Nikolas recalled. He held out a hand which Timothy gripped, yanking him into a hug.

"Pastor Nikolas. We are so glad you've come." He released Nikolas with a hearty shoulder slap. "You must forgive us, but caution is of the utmost importance as I'm sure you know."

He nodded, a bit of the tension seeping from his muscles at the rather boisterous welcome. "I do."

Timothy stepped back and introduced the people sitting in the shadows of two oil lamps. The names whirled in Nikolas's mind, lost against the flurry of faces and murmured greetings. He'd never had Amadeo's gift for remembering names. Perhaps he ought to keep a list, check it before he went out.

They scooted aside to allow him a space on the floor in their circle and filled him in on the Scriptures they'd been studying. He answered their questions the best he could, grateful for the time of careful study at the monastery—however torturous the sitting still had been.

"Artemisia will be upon us soon." As soon as Elder Timothy spoke the words, fear seemed to descend upon the room, silencing the rest of the questions. "Evil surrounds us, steals our lives and our peace. Do you have wisdom to share on how we might better survive the coming terror?"

All eyes turned to Nikolas, filled with apprehension and longing. As if, by some miracle, he could provide a way out. He shook his head and noticed the expressions fall.

"You're better able to survive than most churches I've seen. But I think it would benefit us all, instead of looking at all the evil and quaking at its power and terror, to lift our eyes to the hope we have. The anchor for our souls that evil cannot touch no matter how hard it tries to shake us. I'm reminded of Peter, when he tried to walk on the water. The waves were high and rough, but Peter only fell when he took his eyes from Jesus. This earthly life is short and full of strife, but there is a better, truer one coming. Let us set our gaze there."

The room was silent, eyes slowly shifting toward Timothy, as if to verify that this was advice they ought to follow. The familiar sink of rejection pitted in Nikolas's stomach, even as he told himself this was as it ought to be. He could not expect to sail in—or swim in—and be blindly obeyed. It would take time to earn trust. No one here knew him. *Thankfully.*

He shifted and found Xeno's gaze on him. So, *almost* no one knew him. It wasn't as comforting as he'd thought.

TEN

"DEMITRIA."

Demi froze, her fingers just grazing the ropes mooring her white and yellow lateen to Mersad's dock. She straightened and turned.

"Mersad."

The dock shook as Mersad walked toward her. Large boned, and heavily mustached, her employer appeared every inch a man who was not to be trifled with. But beneath the exterior, Demi knew he had a soft spot—right where his money belt rested.

"How is Theseus? Don't tell me he's dead and that's why you're here alone."

She shook her head. They'd moved Theseus after the river meeting and he'd seemed to improve enough over the last few days under Phineas's close care that Demi had felt easier leaving him to go back to work. "No. He's recovering very well, though not well enough to dive just yet. But soon," she rushed to add. "And I'm not alone. I've brought help." She pointed to Rex, waiting in the boat. "He'll be my spotter until Theseus is better."

Mersad waved a hand as if uninterested. "Is Theseus well enough to be left alone? You're my best diving team but I'm not so selfish that I'd put Theseus at risk to have you here."

Did he care so much? Was that why he paid them barely enough to live on? She dug her toes into the rough wood of the dock, trying to keep the bitterness turning her belly from creeping into her voice. "Friends are caring for him. He's not being neglected, I assure you." Besides, she needed access to the boat again.

Mersad's lips twitched. "It's not your pretty friend, is it? Under such care I'd be surprised if Theseus recovers at all. I know I wouldn't want to, with such a nurse as that."

Rex spoke up from behind. "It's my sister."

"Rex." Demi's voice emerged tight. "Make sure we have the diving stones settled in the center." She'd told him several times already not to speak until they left the docks.

"Come, come!" Mersad slapped Demi's shoulder with a meaty hand as if she were one of the men. He laughed as she took a step forward to keep her balance. "It's a joke, yes? Be careful out there." A touch of concern lit his tone. "I don't like my divers to be without a proper handler."

Demi tried to smile as she turned back to Mersad, as if his comment hadn't filled her with disgust and unease. Her lips felt tight. How did he know about Nydia? Was he watching them? She'd have to tell Titus the roofless house in the dumping grounds was no longer safe.

"I'll be fine. I've been handling this boat since I was a child—and diving long before that."

"Don't take any unnecessary risks."

She raised an eyebrow. "Unless it comes with great reward."

Mersad laughed, and she sidestepped to avoid another slap to her shoulder. He smacked his thigh instead.

"This is why I like you, girl. A great diver and spirited too." His gaze lingered on her long enough to prickle the hairs at her nape.

She edged for the boat. "I need to go, or I won't make it to my best spot at good light."

Mersad waved her off like a pesky child. "Go. Go. May Poseidon reveal his treasures to you."

Demi turned back to the boat and loosed the mooring lines before pushing it away from the dock and leaping aboard. That had gone better than expected—and somehow worse, when she considered the comment about Nydia. She scooped up the paddle and dug it into the water, maneuvering around other dive boats bobbing on their moorings before setting the triangular sail.

A red lateen with blue markings darted out from the docks, careening in front of hers. Demi slammed her paddle into the water, missing a collision by inches. The other boat was crowded with men. Ennio and Pelos, sons of Lynos, bane of all the other divers, watched her with smug expressions as their sons worked the paddles and sped out in front. She met Ennio's hard eyes with a glare of her own as she worked to face her boat forward again. Much more difficult without Theseus's help. Ennio glanced at Rex with a smirk before shifting his gaze to Demi and letting it drop over her in a look at once threatening and condescending. Curses and coarse laughter trailed the red boat like a net.

"Go faster, Demi, the red boat is winning," Rex urged, standing in the prow and pointing.

On the contrary. The red lateen couldn't leave fast enough.

"Sit down, Rex. It's not a race. And you should never tell people about your family."

Rex dropped into her old seat in the prow but couldn't contain his excitement. He exclaimed over and pointed at every boat he saw, chattering all the while about the merits of different types of frogs and where they could be found. His presence filled the boat with energy, and she was glad Titus had agreed to let him skip lessons and accompany her.

Demi left the mouth of the Myros River where Mersad's docks were located and headed for the western coastline, hoisting the sail before crossing in front of the harbor of Andriake. The port village sat on a peninsula, caught between the large inlet of the harbor and the wide mouth of the Myros River.

Her sail caught the wind with a jolt and Rex tumbled backward into the middle of the boat with a shriek of delight. Demi couldn't help the laugh bubbling up inside as the boat picked up speed. Wind roared in her ears, tugging tears out the corners of her eyes. Rex scrambled back into his seat and leaned forward, shouting into the wind.

Keeping one eye on Rex and the other on the coastline, she headed for a reef she and Theseus had discovered a while back and hadn't fully explored due to the coldness of the water. The reef was riddled with underwater caves where the red coral liked to congregate in the shadows.

Fortunately, the water had warmed enough now that she should be able to explore.

Standing in the rear of the boat, feet spread, she relished the crispness of the wind snapping at her chiton, yanking her curls over her shoulders. She shut her eyes and breathed deep, filling her lungs with the familiar scent of brine and coastal cedars. Nothing was so exhilarating as the wide-open sea. It could be treacherous, sneaky—but catch it in a sweet temper, and it was glorious.

Demi turned toward the east just as the blinding orange orb of the sun burst from the dark line of the sea.

O Lord, our Lord, how majestic is your name in all the earth!

She missed the way Pater couldn't help but break into a song or Psalm each time the sun rose over the rim of the water. No matter the place or who was within earshot. He'd made it seem so natural, so easy, to be so bold. She'd wished then, as she did now, that she could have been the same. If she had, things would have been much, much different.

When she noticed the small Greek islands in the distance whose cities seemed to spring up out of the sea itself, Demi knew she was nearing the place. There. Just on the mainland, the narrow white face of a limestone cliff. Demi dropped the sail and the boat coasted forward. She drew out the paddle.

"Watch at the prow, Rex. The reefs can rise nearly to the surface here, and we don't want to get stuck."

The water grew lighter in color, the bottom mottled with dark spots. She set the paddle aside.

"Help me throw the anchor over."

Eager to prove himself, the boy scrambled to help. They rolled the stone anchor overboard, laughing as the splash doused them with spray.

"Will you teach me to dive too?"

"Not today. I need you to stay in the boat and draw up the coral basket when I fill it." She pointed out the basket and rope, explaining how she'd fill it, tug the rope, and he'd draw it up with her following it to the surface to ensure nothing tumbled out.

"Understand?"

Rex nodded and fidgeted. "I just have to sit here?" The allure of the dive boat was fast fading from his eyes.

"Your job here is very important. You must guard the coral and oysters I bring up and keep the seabirds from carrying them off. They especially love the oysters."

"Me too." Rex rubbed his belly. "How long do you stay underwater? What if you get swallowed by a fish like Jonah?"

Demi chuckled. "I don't think I'll get swallowed by a fish, but so you don't worry, let's practice. I'll hold my breath as long as I can, and I'll count how many times you recite the Lord's Prayer. Then you can do that while you wait and know when you can expect me to surface."

Rex brightened. "All right. Go."

Demi took a breath and settled into her seat.

Rex began reciting. *Our Father in heaven, hallowed be your name . . ."* He squinted at her face as he spoke as if trying to catch her breathing. Demi lifted one finger as he finished, the recitation taking about thirty seconds. She nodded for him to continue. Rex started over. When Demi held five fingers up, he let out an exasperated sigh.

"Are you still holding your breath?"

She nodded.

He continued.

Ten fingers. She started over. Thirteen. Seventeen. Twenty.

She took a breath. "Done."

Rex flopped backward dramatically. "Good. I can't do it anymore."

She laughed. "You don't have to. This was just a practice, so you know how long I'll be down there. But this first time I won't be down for long." Demi unpinned one shoulder of her chiton and shimmied out of it, kicking it onto the plank bench as it slid down her legs. Then she hopped, feet first, over the side of the boat. The first leap of the day was her favorite. The crash and roar of the sea in her ears. The shock of cool water on her skin. She spat brine and took a breath as her face broke the surface. The boat bobbed nearby, Rex leaning over the side.

"And forgive us our debts—That wasn't very long."

She swiped a hand over her eyes. "Not yet, I was just getting in . . ."

A red and blue lateen edged over the horizon, sending shivers racing over her arms. What were Ennio and Pelos doing here? They always went east. Dread built in her chest.

Lord, protect us.

They'd not done anything worse than toss insults toward her and Theseus in the past, but even so, the prospect of enduring them without her brother's presence unnerved her. Six men crowded the boat, making it appear much too small, even though it was larger than her own. Where could they even fit coral with so many bodies? She scanned the rest of the reef. In the distance, two fishing boats bobbed, mere flecks on the horizon.

Show no fear. Her father's voice echoed in her mind.

Ennio's sons dropped the sail as the boat approached the reef and took up paddles to navigate the sudden shallows.

"Out here all alone?"

Ennio's voice sent another wave of chills over her. Demi treaded water, turning to keep them in her sight.

"Someone has to keep Mersad in coral."

"And you think that's you?" Ennio cursed and the other men laughed. The boat coasted so near she was forced to move out of the way.

"What are you doing here? You're far from your own waters."

Pelos sneered. "We are free to go wherever we wish."

Her arms moved back and forth.

"We heard Theseus was injured and wanted to offer . . ." Ennio paused to search for the words that emerged like a foreign phrase. "Well wishes."

Her eyebrows flickered in surprise. Truly?

"You won't be able to meet your quota for long. I've already asked Mersad for your lateen. It's time we grew to two boats."

One of the sons, near her age or older, leaped from their boat to hers. Rex, to his dear credit, stayed silent and took a step backward, his blue eyes rounding.

"Hey!" Demi swam for the boat, inwardly kicking herself for forgetting to flip the rope ladder over before she jumped.

"What do you think of it, Tychon?" Ennio called.

Tychon ran his hand over the cheery yellow paint and fingered the sail. "She'll do."

Demi heaved herself up on the edge of the boat and scrambled inside, streaming water. "Get out."

Tychon towered over her, though, upon closer inspection, he appeared to be less than eighteen. He raised a self-assured brow and took a step closer. "Or what?"

Anger flushed her cheeks.

"What are you going to do? Hmm?"

Do not cower.

She clenched her jaw and stared back until a lazy grin spread over his face. Without breaking her gaze, he raised a hand and caressed the mast.

"She'll do," he repeated.

Her lip curled. "Get out of my boat."

Tychon chuckled and swung away, taking two running steps and a leap before landing back in the red lateen.

Unfortunate. It would have been far more satisfying had he miscalculated the distance.

Demi stayed where she was, arms crossed and glaring as Ennio directed their boat out of the reef and back along the coast to the east. They'd be far better divers if they dove more than they tormented others. She let out a breath, relief washing over her, followed quickly by waves of dread. She had to meet their quota until Theseus recovered. Mersad was loyal only to his money belt, and if Ennio and Pelos convinced him their sons could bring in more than her, it'd be over. She'd lose the means of providing food for the church, and the last connection to her family.

ELEVEN

"HAND OVER YOUR VALUABLES and no one gets hurt."

Nikolas stiffened as a blade pressed against his ribs. "I don't have anything to give you." A trickle of sweat edged his hairline.

A pause. "Let us go an hour early and no one gets hurt."

Nikolas spun and swatted the wooden sword away. The cluster of eight-year-old boys sitting at his feet leaped to theirs, erupting in cheers and shouts. The freckled vagrant grinned and leveled the sword at Nikolas's chest.

Nikolas shook his head. "You are risking too much for the sake of one hour, Paros. I see we're going to need to work on our negotiating skills." He turned to the rest of the boys. "Now, what is the proper way to handle poor negotiations?"

There was much shouting, but "Punch him in the nose!" seemed to be the ruling consensus. Nikolas raised his hands and his voice. "No one is punching anyone in the nose. Paros, I'll take the sword please—*not in the ribs*—thank you. Sit down, sit down."

The boys immediately dropped to the floor, hands in their laps, mouths shut, blinking at him dutifully. Well. He must be getting better at the classroom control issue Titus had warned him about. He cleared his throat.

"Yes, well. As I was saying—"

The pairs of eyes all shifted to his left. Knowing it was probably a trap, Nikolas turned anyway, and froze.

A woman stood behind him, red silk fluttering around her ankles and ropes of scarlet beads looping her neck and wrists. Honey-colored curls cascaded over one shoulder, and amusement played at her lips. She was beautiful and—recognition dawned. Nikolas's chin dropped in time with his stomach, mind racing. She was *here*? How had that happened? He'd taken such pains, such care to never be—

"I'm so glad to finally meet you. I am Lady Isidora."

Lady. She had done well, then. He'd heard she and her two sisters had married, but hadn't known the particulars. He shut his eyes, chin still plastered to his chest. Perhaps she wouldn't recognize him. Perhaps she didn't even know the part he'd played in her life. Best to pretend ignorance.

A small hand appeared in front of him, presumably for him to take, to bow over. He did. Woodenly. Hoping she couldn't feel the dampness of his fingers.

"Nikolas . . . my lady." He straightened. Made the mistake of meeting her searching gaze.

She offered a tiny smile. "I wanted to be certain it was really you. Wanted to"—her voice dropped—"thank you for what you did in Patara, for my sisters and me."

He felt the blood draining from his face. Would she tell? Spread the news far and wide, making life as unbearable here as it had been in Patara?

She reached toward him, stopping shy of touching his arm. "I saw my pater chasing you that night—he didn't know then what you'd done. Not until he came home, and saw the gifts—"

"I should have been more careful."

"You should know—you changed our lives with your kindness. Pater's too. I don't know why you didn't want anyone to know what you'd done. It is not . . . how men of wealth usually do things." Her gaze lifted to the school hall where her husband's name had been carved into the plaque by the door—inside and out—to ensure no one forgot who the school's benefactor was. She shook her head. "It wasn't fair, what people said about you. Especially after you came home without your pater."

Not fair maybe. But that didn't make the gossip unwarranted.

"You would not have done what you did for us if you were truly . . . what they said you were."

The way she refused to even speak the word was a kindness he felt to his bones.

"I've wanted to thank you for years."

His eyes jerked to hers. "Are you happy?"

She gave a troubled nod. "I have everything I could ever want. I only wish . . ." She bit her lip and repeated with some determination, "I have everything I could ever want."

He understood. From what Beatrix had told him, he knew Master Evander had forbidden Lady Isidora to worship with them, but that she also came regularly to "check on the school" and study Scripture in a private room with Iris and Beatrix.

He took a breath. "Thank you . . . for the school. And all that it does."

"I've had a good example." Lady Isidora's gaze shifted past him to his students, mouth twitching. "It is the least I can do. Good day, Master Nikolas."

He bowed and she cast a smile on the boys before sweeping into the back rooms where Iris and Nydia taught girls to weave. Nikolas let out a breath. Though it hadn't lessened the weight on his chest, time had been good to Isidora. It set his heart at ease, knowing that something good had come from his actions. He rubbed a hand over the back of his neck as he turned to his students.

"Now. Where were we?"

Elders and deacons had come and gone throughout the day, meeting with Titus in a small backroom office that was crammed with broken benches and crates of nearly destroyed school supplies. Nikolas had eyed the meetings, feeling more and more like an outsider, or a child relegated to simple tasks, not trusted enough for larger, more important things. Perhaps after he'd proven himself by going upriver with Demi they'd accept him.

When the last student left for home in the high heat of the afternoon, Nikolas sought out Titus and found him alone in the back room, balancing the school accounts at a rickety desk. He looked up when Nikolas knocked on the doorframe.

"Well? How did it go today?"

"Only one attempted mutiny."

"Only one?" Titus laughed. "Things are improving."

"Maybe. Although I think they're planning something bigger. There was a lot of whispering in the back."

"If they try to convince you that the previous instructor took them to the library, don't believe them. It's a trick. As soon as your back is turned to fetch a codex off the shelves, they'll be next door swimming in the baths."

"You speak from experience?"

Titus shrugged. "Swimming was a better idea anyway."

Nikolas chuckled and kicked the toe of his sandal against the doorframe. "You had a lot of visitors today."

"Yes." Titus did not elaborate. Nor did he look up.

A familiar sting struck the center of Nikolas's chest. His pater had often been bent in the same posture as Titus, bowing over his ledger books and accounts, Nikolas relegated to the side. The monks had treated him much the same. He'd lived with them, worked with them, but they'd always kept him at arm's length since he'd never joined the order. Was he so difficult to accept? It hadn't been a problem in most circles when he'd had money. People had clamored after him then, and while he didn't want to repeat the manipulative chaos that followed, it reminded him . . .

"I noticed there seem to be a lot of beggars in this city."

Titus nodded and ran a finger down a column of numbers. "Times have been difficult with the poor harvests the last few years."

"Is there anything we can do to help?"

"We can barely keep our own people fed, much less anyone else."

"But are we not called to do something? These people . . . have no hope."

Titus shifted and looked up at him, resting his elbow on the desk. "In case you haven't noticed, we're suffering and dying as well, Pastor. And you've seen the koinonia. We've nothing to share."

There was no way around it, then. He needed the gold. If the church wouldn't, or couldn't, help, he'd do it himself. All he needed was—

"You're meeting Demi tonight, yes?"

Nikolas nodded. His pulse jolted and a strange twisting in his gut accompanied her name. He shifted, the palms of his hands going damp. Were the elders at all concerned about sending an unmarried man and woman upriver alone at night? The monks would have had a fit.

"Is there . . ." He paused, unsure how to ask the question. "Will Demitria be . . . uncomfortable with—I mean, she doesn't know me."

At this, Titus looked up. "Are you going to make her uncomfortable?"

"Yes, exactly. I mean—*no*. Are you asking me?" His face was getting hotter by the word. "I'm only . . . I don't want anyone else to . . . misunderstand." Why was this so hard? Perhaps he shouldn't have broached the subject at all. No one else had raised any objections.

Titus gave a nod of apparent understanding and set aside the stylus. "Demi and Theseus . . . what they do for the church isn't known by many. It's safer for everyone that way. And in times like these, what a situation looks like becomes far less important than what it truly is. Demitria's character is impeccable. I trust her completely, and in trusting her with you, I'm trusting you as well. None of us can operate without trust."

The words were a comfort as much as an unnecessary warning.

"Of course." He shifted. "Can I help you with anything?"

"How good are you with math?"

"Better than an eight-year-old boy, thankfully, but I'm even worse at math than Latin."

Titus chuckled and waved for Nikolas to sit. "I never thought I'd have so much in common with a tutor. I was always the one in trouble."

"Same." Nikolas offered a half-hearted grin.

A knock sounded at the door and Iris stepped in without waiting for a response. She set a plate between them, not quite filled with a meager ration of green and purple olives, crumbly cheese, and two small, boiled eggs.

"I thought you might be hungry, Nikolas." She smiled. "There was a lot of shouting today."

"A bird flew in." Or someone had let it in.

Iris nodded as if that sort of thing happened every day. She patted his arm as she turned to leave. "I listened a bit today. You're doing a wonderful job."

The burn in his throat was unexpected. He coughed.

Titus protested. "No compliments for me?"

She laughed. "Good gracious, Titus. You're like an eager puppy. I can't have your ego swelling. You'll be impossible to live with." Her smile said otherwise.

Titus's mouth twitched. He reached across the desk for an olive as Iris shut the door behind her. "She loves puppies," he muttered, and shook his head. Instead of swelling with ego, Titus seemed to sink as he leaned back in his chair and popped the olive into his mouth. "I don't deserve that woman."

Nikolas balanced a bit of cheese on a purple olive. "Which of us deserves anything good? Yet that is grace, isn't it?"

"And a lot of forgiveness." Titus swiped the olive pit from his mouth and rubbed a hand over his scarred neck. "But that's a story for another time." He nudged the plate closer to Nikolas as if he'd suddenly lost his appetite. "Best eat quickly. It'll be a long night. You may want to nap."

TWELVE

THE MOON HUNG IN THE SKY, too close to full for Demi's liking, but Titus had been watching the rotations of the harbor guards and he'd assured them that tonight was the night to leave. They were a day away from Artemisia and already the guards were lax. Whatever her misgivings, Titus had never led them wrong before.

The water shimmered. Pearls scattered across a cascade of black Eastern silk.

The wind would be with them tonight. And good thing. Because the eager way Nikolas was rowing in the prow wasn't helping much. They hugged the shoreline, navigating away from Mersad's pier and into the wide mouth of the Myros River.

Pater had always said the river was getting smaller, shallower each year, filling in with more and more silt from the mountains, and that one day it would be little more than a trickle in a dry river bottom. Demi wasn't sure it looked any different than it had when she was a child. And for that, she was thankful. She navigated up the deep shoreline, silently slipping alongside the press of trees clustered near the riverbanks, which gradually gave way to fields of wheat and emmer and rows of vegetables, studded with the brick houses of farmers.

Nearly a mile from Andriake, the city of Myra spread over the foothills of the Taurus Mountains, reaching up the slope to where another temple to Artemis Eleutheria, the guardian of liberty, sat like a glimmering crown at the top of the ridge nestled between the city watchtowers. Firepots flickered at the front of the terrace, bathing the temple in a glow of golden light. It was pretty in the darkness. Even beautiful. But the sight of it sent a coldness to Demi's belly. The outward allure held a hidden evil that permeated everything and yet seemed innocent. Full of light, flowers. The breeze carried a faint scent of temple incense, and her stomach jerked in revulsion as images flashed before her eyes.

Blades. Blood. Her sister's hand jerked from hers.

Demi gripped her knees, trying to force her heart to cease thrashing. *Not here.* She swallowed, blowing a slow breath between her lips. She would not lose control now. Especially not in front of Nikolas. Pastor Tomoso had already declared Demi's judgment, and no doubt Nikolas would agree with him. He might have been kind and compassionate toward her on Theseus's account, but that would change for certain if he knew what she was. What she'd done.

Though the night was cool, a trickle of sweat edged her hairline.

Calm yourself, Demitria.

She sucked a deep breath, holding in briny air mingled with citrus blossoms and rosemary and fish. She tried to cling to the memories it always evoked. Of family meals on the rocks, Pater's boat beached nearby. Juice of citrus fruit running down her chin, clinging to her fingers. Laughter, love, belonging. Those memories were fleeting. Harder and harder to grasp though she held on with everything she had.

Beneath the guardianship of the crowning temple of Artemis, the face of the Taurus Mountains rising above the city was riddled with ancient tombs carved into facades of homes and temples painted in vivid blues, reds, and yellows. Those families of Lycia past had worked long and hard to preserve their names and legacy in stone, and yet had disappeared from myth and memory all the same. An ache swelled at the thought. Would she be like them? She worked hard and risked much to create a good name and reputation among her friends, but would it only last as long as the lives of those who knew her? Did any of it even matter?

The river curved around the steep, protruding arm of the mountain, hiding the city and necropolis from view. Tension eased from Demi's shoulders. She let out a breath. The most dangerous bit was over, at least until the return trip.

Safely out of view from any city dwellers, Demi raised the sail and adjusted it to catch the wind. The boat jerked, nearly dislodging Nikolas from his seat.

She leaned forward, speaking in low tones. "This next section is rocky. I can't see well from the back, so your job is to watch for darker patches in the water that the moon doesn't illuminate. When you see one, you'll have to tell me if it's left, right, or straight ahead."

"All right."

Silence.

Demi shifted. Was he feeling as awkward as she? Nydia would chatter up a storm to set him at ease. What to talk about? Probably not how other divers dove naked.

"You are from Patara, yes?" Safe enough.

"Yes." He turned slightly, his voice carrying over his shoulder. "Have you ever been?"

"I saw it from our boat once. But I was little."

"It's lovely. Miles of powdery white beaches. Sea turtles come ashore by the hundreds to nest every Iunius. Though there are probably a few eager ones starting to come in now."

"That would be a sight to see. How are you finding Myra?"

"Less turtled. Rock ahead."

"Where?"

"Right—er—left. Go right!"

Demi jerked the rudder as Nikolas leaned hard into his paddle—not quickly enough. The boat scraped against the boulder, the hollow grinding of impact loud and echoing off the high mountain walls rising up on either side of the river.

There goes the paint.

"I—I am . . . Forgive me." Mortification thickened his whisper.

Demi blew out a breath. It was a simple mistake. "It's all right," she whispered back. "That happens from time to time. A risk of going upriver in the dark." Maybe the scrape had been below the waterline and Mersad wouldn't notice. And perhaps now would be a good time to broach the question lingering in her mind since their first encounter. "So, how did you manage to sink your boat?"

Nikolas made a noise in his throat she couldn't quite decipher. Laughter? Irritation? "Worm holes." He didn't elaborate.

"Have you spent much time on the water?"

He hesitated. "It's been a few years, but I . . . spent some time at sea with my pater." He mumbled the last bit, as if he hadn't wanted to reveal it fully.

Nydia's words rang in her mind. Nikolas of Patara. Second son of the wealthiest shipping tycoon on the Mediterranean.

She was glad he couldn't see the heat rising in her face. Of course he'd spent time at sea. Perhaps she ought to have paid better attention to the gossip in the women's baths.

"So . . . you're used to big boats, then—ships." Stupid. She needed to stop talking.

"I wouldn't say *used to*, exactly. I didn't really have much to do with it all." He cleared his throat. "I admit, these are not great qualifications for helping with this."

"You're doing just fine."

"Right."

"Thank you for—"

"*Right.*"

The warning registering at the last moment, Demi veered left, narrowly missing another boulder. *Focus, Demitria.* Perhaps she ought to concentrate more on navigating and less on trying to set Nikolas at ease. They settled into silence, though the frogs singing along the riverbanks in varying tone and rhythm had other ideas. Weaving through the last section of rocks without incident, Demi relaxed in her seat, steering by moonlight while Nikolas paddled in the prow.

"You don't have to paddle anymore," she whispered. "Not with the sail."

Wood knocked against the side of the boat as he drew the pole inside. "I've never been good at sitting idle."

"There'll be work enough soon."

One silent hour slipped into two. Demi tried to keep time by the moon's migration across the sky, wishing Theseus were here. He knew better than she how to calculate time by the ever-changing moon. She'd never paid much attention. Unless the moon could calculate how long she needed to hold her breath to reach the best coral, keeping time seemed a silly thing to worry about.

"We're getting close." Her whisper seemed to echo. "Not far now."

"This must be beautiful in the daylight." Moonlight illuminated his profile as he tilted his head back to take in the mountains tumbling into both sides of the river.

"I wouldn't know. I've never been."

"You've only been upriver in the night?" Surprise lifted his tone.

"It's the only time Mersad won't miss this boat, and we've less chance of being caught by the harbor guards."

"The boat is . . . not yours?"

She caught the edge of unease in his voice. "It's not stealing. It—the boat belonged to my pater before . . ." Her pulse skittered as her mouth stumbled into dangerous territory. "When Pater was arrested, everything we owned was confiscated. Mersad was . . . I suppose you might call him a friend of my pater's. He took the boat in a show of support for the emperor. But when things calmed down, he searched us out and offered us Pater's job. Mersad asks no questions so long as the arrangement benefits him, but I do not think he would keep quiet if he were questioned. We do our utmost to keep that from happening."

"I see." The tone of his voice seemed to imply that he now understood her hesitation to bring him along. "And yet you do this every month?"

"Sometimes twice. Especially during harvest."

"Why *you*? Are there no—"

"Shh!" She held up a hand. Something dark moved on the bank. "What—"

"*Shhh!*" She pointed to the rocky shoreline. Nikolas's profile followed her gesture. Demi held her breath and watched, heart rising to her throat.

The dark shapes were still, thin, but not quite tall enough to be human. Was someone sitting and watching them? The boat glided nearer. Demi's breath sounded loud and ragged to her ears. The shapes on shore lowered and elongated, following the boat in the silent and graceful movements of large cats.

"Leopards," she whispered, her heart suddenly thrashing wild energy into her limbs. "Two of them." A rare sighting. The usually invisible cats were often trapped for use in gladiator fights.

"Will they be a problem?"

"I don't know. I've never seen any this close to Myra before. Though that doesn't mean they haven't been here all along."

At the sound of her voice, the leopards stopped, heads turning toward the boat, features as indistinguishable as Nikolas's. Bushes soon obscured them from view, but not from mind. Would they follow the boat? Stalk them to the cache cave?

Neither spoke, both keeping their gazes fixed on the shore, searching for movement, for a hint they were being hunted. The current slapped at the hull of the boat and Nikolas's paddle trickled water as he resumed paddling.

All too quickly the curve of the river announced the end of the route.

"We're here." Demi steered the boat toward shore, dropping the sail and clambering forward as Nikolas guided them closer to the rocky shore with the oar. Not quite successful in pushing the leopards from her mind, Demi grabbed the mooring line and hopped over the side before she could reconsider. Cold water splashed to her waist, and she gasped. Theseus usually did this part, but he'd never jumped so soon.

She swam the boat toward shore, mentally adding a new rule to her list. *Don't jump so soon.*

Mud oozed between her toes as she neared the bank, reeds rustling against her shoulders. She tied the line to a boulder and Nikolas stepped off onto dry land much like she used to. Together they unloaded the goods for trading onto a pile. Neither was attacked by leopards. So far so good.

"Take as much as you can carry." She slung a basket of dried fish over her shoulder and tucked two rolls of cloth under her arms. "This way."

The rocky shore glowed white, interspersed with boulders and gangly black bushes. The cave was not far from shore but well hidden. Demi reached the tall cedar tree marking the entrance and dropped the cloth and basket to drag away the branches obscuring the entrance. She reached inside but didn't need more than her nose to tell her what the cave held.

"More wool."

She'd hoped there might be cheeses and grain inside. Food was always more welcome than work, but Demi knew the wool would turn a tidy profit once the elderly widows had cleaned, carded, and spun it. They could always use a bit of money for bribes and rent, and silence was growing expensive. Demi emptied the cave while Nikolas took the first load of wool back to the boat and returned with the rest of the trade supplies.

The exchange of goods took twice as long as it normally did with Theseus, when they both worked in wordless tandem, each seeming to know what the other was thinking. But once directed, Nikolas didn't hesitate. Nor did he once complain.

After the cave had been emptied and refilled, Demi fought back a yawn as she dragged the branches over the cave entrance. She picked her way back to the bank, glancing over both shoulders. Had there always been so many leopard-shaped rocks and tree trunks? She hurried as fast as she dared in the dark, meeting Nikolas at the boat, which he'd loaded . . . shockingly well. Their cargo was balanced to perfection, each item nestled precisely against another. He was better at this than Theseus. A glance at the sky told her it was a good thing, too, because they had no time to rebalance. Even with the currents on their side.

"Want me to push us off?" Nikolas asked as she drew closer.

Demi shook her head. "I've already gone in. No sense in both of us having to sit in wet clothes."

Nikolas looped the mooring line and climbed in while Demi shoved against the prow, pushing them into the current. The mucky riverbed dropped away from her feet, and with a gasp, Demi found herself clinging to the prow, nothing but water beneath her. She kicked, trying to propel herself high enough to flop over the edge. Water weighted her chiton, and the current tugged at it, tangling it around her legs.

"Here." Nikolas's palm appeared next to her own. "Take my hand."

She gripped his hand, and he hauled her up, straining against the pull of the current. Demi clambered over the side, streaming water into the boat and all over him. "Thank you. I wasn't ready for that drop-off. Theseus usually does that part."

"Why didn't you let me do it?"

"I didn't want you to get wet too."

"Too late for that now."

"Sorry." Demi gathered her skirt and wrung it over the side of the boat.

"No . . . I—*I'm* sorry. I've made a mess of everything tonight. Nearly crashed us . . ."

A huff of laughter escaped her chest. How long since she'd laughed? "That was nothing. If you bottom us out on a reef, then we'll have problems."

He let out a breath, teeth flashing white in the moonlight as he offered a small smile. "Does this mean I'm not banned from your boat forever?"

"That depends." Her lips pricked into a sweet smile that he probably couldn't see. "You never finished telling me how you sunk your boat."

THIRTEEN

THE CITY WAS STILL QUIET as Nikolas trudged back to the school, limbs weighted with exhaustion. Of the two instances he'd spent considerable time in a small boat, he couldn't be certain which time he'd been gladder to climb ashore. True, the first time he'd nearly drowned, and tonight, he'd at least never gotten completely drenched. So that was something. He wasn't sure how Demi could do this month after month. They'd stopped multiple times as they neared the city, sorting and stashing goods in various caves along the riverbank. Demi had explained that the deacons would come later and bring everything into the city for safekeeping and distribution.

His arms and shoulders ached. The two years he spent at sea trading with his father hadn't been this labor-intensive—nor as enjoyable. Both his father and Amadeo had been passionate about goods and prices and finding the best of both. They'd worked tirelessly with a single-minded drive that Nikolas had both admired and despised. He had not shared their passion and in return they had not shared their time. There was room for one passion in their family and Nikolas had failed to find it. But Demi? She risked her life to care for the church, to help those in need. For once, that was work he could pour himself into with no regrets, no hesitation. Though it would be easier if his gold weren't resting on the bottom of the Mediterranean.

He'd nearly told her about it half a dozen times that night. Nearly asked if perhaps she'd help him find it. But he couldn't make the words come. For once, he'd been just Nikolas. Not a murderer, a usurper, or a degenerate failure of a son. He knew those things were lies. Rumors spread by envious gossips looking for an easy target. But they needled him all the same. Agitating those tender places where the lies felt more like angled versions of the truth. Because he hadn't been a good son, a good brother, a good man.

Would he have to reveal who he was—who he'd been—to gain her trust, her help?

Dawn broke over the city, ruffled and gray, drawing the darkness from the shadows like a fisherman drew his net. Flower garlands adorned windows and doorways, especially heavy on the streets where the goddess would be paraded on her way to the sacred pool for her yearly bath. Soon the streets would bustle with flower carts and women laden with overfilled market baskets making last-minute preparations. But now the streets slept as the sun edged toward the horizon. He could think of nothing but his own bed, sleep, the better perspective gained at the end of a good rest.

Nikolas rubbed his grainy eyes, wishing his bed would be the first thing awaiting him. Breakfast would come first. Then he'd attempt to teach Latin to a room full of eight-year-old boys who could talk of nothing but catching frogs along the riverbanks.

"Have you a spare coin?" A rasping voice broke through his thoughts.

Nikolas stopped, eyes searching for the owner of the voice as his hands went to his chest, his side. Nothing.

A hopeful face raised toward him from a ragged bundle slumped inside the narrow mouth of an alley.

Nikolas's heart dropped with his hands. "I . . . no. I've got nothing. I'm sorry."

The dirty face gave a resigned nod and rested once more against the side of the alley, as if that was the only answer ever received, and the expected one. It was all too familiar. A request for help. Nikolas's refusal. Perhaps it wasn't right to call it a refusal this time, when he truly didn't have a coin, but would the end result be the same?

It should not have been Amadeo who died.

His hands went again to his side, his neck, as if a second search might produce what the first had not. Still no money pouch. A burning rose in the back of Nikolas's eyes. "Truly. If I could help, I would."

Lines flickered in the forehead. "Sure. Sure."

Nikolas turned away, struggling to swallow back the lump rising in his throat. He needed his money. *They* needed the money. The help it could provide. *Give me wisdom to plan this properly.* Regret added extra weight to his feet. If he'd only been more careful. Less reckless, less impulsive, impatient . . . he should have waited and found a better boat. Taken more trips and risked less . . . Why were his best efforts always met with failure?

Never put all your money into one vessel, Niko.

He sighed. Regrets were of little use now. What was done, was done, and his energy was better used solving the problem at hand.

More easily determined than done.

He paused at the door of the school, bolted against him at this hour, and knocked in the pattern Titus had instructed. He waited. Shifted. Knocked again. It opened, and Iris greeted him with a smile before stepping back and letting him in.

"Is all well?" She shut and bolted the door behind him.

He nodded. "Everything seemed to go smoothly."

"Good." She led the way to the kuzina. "Breakfast is ready, and you'd best sit and eat quickly. Your students will arrive soon and with the festival starting tomorrow, you can be sure they'll be boisterous today."

He hesitated in the doorway, glancing over his shoulder as if the beggar slumped just behind. "Actually, I think I'll take my breakfast on a short walk, if that's all right."

As the last student dashed out the door as if he had a viper on his heels, Nikolas sank to a bench and rubbed his eyes. *Lord, have mercy.* Why had he chosen today of all days to have his students begin their Latin recitation of *The Aeneid*? He propped his chin in his hands, gaze falling on the codex propped open on his desk. Nearly ten thousand lines, spanning dozens of volumes. Even though they were only reciting the first few stanzas, at the stumbling rate they were going, it was going to take years to finish the first codex.

Why had he even tried to teach today at all? Especially after Paros

had released a dozen fat crickets. Where had he kept them? And then
someone—or several someones, he wasn't quite certain—had released
a troop of frogs. Trying to wrangle a classroom of young boys after that
was like . . . trying to wrangle a classroom of boys after the release of
crickets and frogs.

He pushed to his feet. Frogs might have left his Latin lesson in
shambles, but at least he could set the room to rights. Tantalizing smells
drifted down the hall from the kuzina, quickening his pace. His stomach
cramped after his skipped breakfast.

Before he could investigate the source of the aromas, Beatrix hobbled
down the hall, a bundle in hand.

"Ah. Done for the month." She studied his face and gave a nod. "And
not a moment too soon, I see."

· He smiled and pressed a fist to his lips, trying and failing to stifle a
yawn.

"Before you retire to your much-deserved bed, could you deliver this
to Theseus?" She held out the bundle. "I thought to send it with Nydia,
but I'm not sure where she's gone off to."

The bundle released fragrances of fried chickpea cakes and stewed
vegetables. His stomach growled as he took it with a nod.

Beatrix patted his arm and nodded toward the bundle. "There's more
where that came from when you return."

He grinned. "That's the best news I've heard all day."

The walk to the storage room behind the sponge and pumice stone
shop was not far, but the streets, clogged with the bustle of last-minute
shoppers and decorators, slowed him. He finally twisted into the narrow
alley, dark with shadow and lit by a thin sliver of light from the far end.
His whole body ached as he moved to the door, inset in the wall. Voices
raised inside made him pause.

"I never took you for a coward, Theseus." Nydia's voice was high,
snappish.

"You deserve a whole man."

Nydia growled. "You think I only loved you because you had two
working arms? What kind of woman do you think I am if my love rests

on the number of limbs you possess? God will provide for us, Theseus. He always has."

"Then He'll provide some other two-armed man to care for you properly."

Nikolas knocked as something crashed inside, drowning out both his knock and the words jumbling together as the two inside argued over each other. He hoped no one in the sponge and pumice stone shop could overhear, or this might no longer be a safe room. He knocked louder.

The door flung open. Nydia's eyes went wide when she saw Nikolas. She twisted past him, yanking the door shut behind her.

"Everything all right?" Stupid question.

Nydia dashed a hand beneath one eye, swiping away tears. She lifted her chin. "No." Her voice dropped. "But he won't listen to me, so . . . God go with you." She stormed down the alley wearing an expression that dared anyone to try to stop her.

Nikolas hesitated, then took a breath and stepped inside.

Theseus slouched against the wall, his good hand braced against his forehead and his shoulders in the shape of defeat. He looked up as Nikolas entered and his expression followed his shoulders.

"Pastor Nikolas."

Not exactly a welcoming greeting.

"I brought food." Nikolas tugged the door shut behind him and dropped the bolt into place. He crossed the room, skirting racks of drying sponges, heavy with smells of the sea, and sat across from Theseus. Dim orange light from a single clay lamp served to deepen the hollows beneath Theseus's eyes.

"I couldn't help but overhear . . . you seemed to have a disagreement with Nydia?"

Theseus sighed, the muscles in his jaw tightening. "Will you talk to her? She won't listen to me."

"She said the same about you."

He shook his head. "But if she heard it from you, she'd listen."

"And what is it you think she should hear from me?"

"That we can't marry."

"Why not?"

Theseus stared at him. "You can't be serious. Look at me." He gestured to his arm, wrapped in linen bandages and resting against his stomach. "Even if you let us marry, I can't provide for a wife, a family."

"*If I let you?* It's hardly up to me."

"Pastor Tomoso didn't allow anyone to marry for the last seven years. He said Christ was coming soon and we were better off preparing for His arrival than satisfying the lusts of our flesh."

"Pastor Tomoso refused to marry you?"

Theseus nodded. "And we honored him—albeit grudgingly sometimes—but now Nydia has it in her head that you might believe differently."

"I do."

Theseus heaved a wry laugh. "Of course you would. Now that I'm incapable of providing for a family."

"You're not incapable, Theseus. You're still healing. And even if it doesn't heal properly, Titus has a bad arm too. It's why he was discharged from the army, if I recall."

"Yes, but Titus isn't a diver. He doesn't need both of his arms to make a living."

"I'm sure there's something else you could do."

"Something else?" Theseus repeated the words as if Nikolas had suddenly started speaking Latin. "My father and grandfather and great-grandfather have all been divers. What else is there for me?"

Words came back to him, the same words his uncle had spoken to him after his father died and left him a shipping enterprise he didn't want. "Where there is breath and life, there is purpose. You'll find it if you look."

Theseus huffed and looked away, then chewed his lip as he turned back to Nikolas. "You think so?"

Nikolas nodded. "I do."

Theseus's gaze caught on the bundle in Nikolas's hands, and his eyebrows flickered. "What did Yia-yia send?"

FOURTEEN

DEMI POURED A TRICKLE OF WASH WATER over the tiny seedlings stretching for the faint light filtering in through the cracks in the shuttered window. Silly things to plant. Orange seeds and peach pits. Fruits she'd likely never reap. It would have been far more practical to plant fast-growing things like greens, but there was something hopeful about these tiny seedlings, stretching for light. Growing even in the darkness and straining for a future day when they would flourish. Bear fruit. She ran her fingers over them, their flimsy stalks bending and strengthening as she hardened and trained them to stand strong one day when they faced real wind, real storms.

A rock clunked behind her. "I can't do this."

She turned and eyed Theseus and the diving stone he'd been attempting to wrap with twine. "It's been half an afternoon. You can't expect to train yourself to tie perfect knots with one hand in a day."

He sighed. "How much more of this?"

"It's only been a week."

Seven days confined to the safe room as the monthlong festival of Artemisia began and all trade, work, and school in the region came to a halt. The drums and music at the temples could be heard night and day, throbbing throughout the city. The statues of Artemis had been taken down from their daises and paraded through the streets to the sacred stream flowing from the fountain near the oracle of Apollo. There, the statues were bathed, dressed in new linen, and wreathed in flowers before being carried back into the city amongst raucous dancing and singing. These first weeks were ones of celebration. The next two would prove deadly.

Once the priestesses of Artemis and priests of Apollo had properly revived the ardor of the people with celebration, wine, and feasting, they would question their thankfulness. They must prove their gratefulness for the bounty given by their mother goddess. To show proper thanks, they must show proper devotion. To show proper devotion, they must stamp out all things Artemis hated. And Artemis hated Christians. Or so said the priestesses.

"I still can't move my fingers." Theseus's whisper echoed off the walls.

"It's early." She squinted at him. Was it the close air and dim lamplight sending that sheen across his forehead? Or was the fever back?

He raised his injured arm and stared at it, lips tightening in concentration as his fingers merely twitched. He let his hand fall back into his lap. "I'm useless."

"You're not useless. So you can't use your hand yet; give it time."

"I can't sit here day after day. I need a job."

"We'll find one for you. But no one's working for the next few weeks anyway." Demi sat opposite him, drumming her fingers on her knees. She'd give anything to be diving today, but even Mersad wouldn't risk angering the deities to line his purse.

Theseus let his head drop back against the wall and shut his eyes. "Artemisia is the worst."

She studied him. "Are you feeling feverish again? You look pale."

"Of course I'm pale. I haven't seen the sun in weeks." His lips seemed a little too tight. Probably just restless.

"Have you talked to Nydia lately?"

He hesitated. "I saw her a few days ago. Why?"

"You seem . . . different."

His Adam's apple bobbed. "Pastor Nikolas was here. He . . . he's not opposed to marriage like Pastor Tomoso was . . . He gave me hope."

Demi's eyebrows flickered. "This is you being hopeful?"

"I'm just . . . trying to figure out a way to support her first. I can't exactly ask Titus if I can marry his daughter without a way to put food in our mouths." He gave a shake of his head. "So far I've failed at everything."

"You've been tying twine for half an afternoon. That's hardly failing at everything."

"Everything I've *tried*."

"You're as dramatic as the hypocrites in the theatre. Perhaps you ought to try for work there." She sat on a crate opposite him. "If you've found hope, perhaps Nydia would like to know of it. Last she told me, you'd told her to marry someone else."

"You talk about me?"

"Of course. I'm the only one who can truly understand her frustration at how stubborn and pigheaded you are." She threw up her hands in a show of mock irritation. "And still, somehow we love you."

"Could you love me with less nagging?"

"Impossible."

Finally, that lazy grin of his, twitching through the misery on his face. "You're a pest, you know."

"I know." She smiled and took up the seagrass twine she'd been braiding, fingers falling into the rote rhythm she'd learned in childhood.

Theseus sighed and pushed to his feet. "Fine. I'll go talk to her."

Demi's head jerked up. "Not *now*."

"Why not? The streets are quiet. I can stagger through them as well as any of the drunkards out there."

"It's too great a risk."

He ducked under a line of sponges, angling for the door. "The deacons go out during Artemisia. Nikolas still makes his rounds."

What had she done? Demi dropped the twine and scrambled after him, slapping an arm over the bolt on the door as he reached it. "Not because of *love*," she argued, as if that were the most foolish of reasons.

His eyebrows wrinkled. "Of course it's because of love. Why would anyone do anything, if not for love?"

He tried to push her aside, but Demi stood fast, pulse thrashing in a panicked rhythm. "I just wanted to cheer you up, not make you do something stupid. Just *wait*. It's not time—"

"If not now, then when?" His good arm dropped, and his voice followed, thick with a sudden emotion. "We're not guaranteed another hour, another day." He shook his head, voice plummeting further into a choked whisper. "I don't think I kissed Mitera goodbye that morning, and Hediste was still asleep when I went swimming with the other boys."

Demi froze. He carried regrets from that day too? And yet, they were nothing compared to hers. "Theseus . . ."

He pushed her hands away from the bolt and this time Demi withdrew, her strength fleeing as it had that long-ago day. She spent every waking moment trying to make up for that one terrible mistake. Who was she to keep Theseus from doing the same? Her throat burned.

Theseus eased the door open and slipped halfway out.

Demi grabbed his shoulder and parroted one of Pater's oft-spoken rules. "Don't take any unnecessary risks."

Theseus turned back and raised a mischievous eyebrow, looking more like himself than he had in weeks. "Unless it comes with great reward."

Theseus's knock didn't sound until after darkness had fallen and Demi could no longer see to braid more seagrass twine. She'd lain on her mat, waiting for him to return, keeping herself awake by replaying her conversations with Nikolas. If his views on marriage differed from Pastor Tomoso's, might there be other differences too? Might . . . might there be forgiveness for one such as her? Though they'd ended the river trip as tenuous friends, she wasn't sure she was ready to bare the darkness of her soul.

When the coded knock came at the door, Demi leaped to her feet and let Theseus in. She clutched the thin linen blanket around her shoulders as he twisted inside and lowered the bolt across the door once more.

"Well?"

"Have you been awake the whole time?" He shuffled through the darkness toward his sleeping mat.

Demi followed, dread gnawing at the edges of her stomach. He should sound happier. Why wasn't he happy? "Did she refuse? Why do you sound like your boat sank?"

Theseus dropped to his mat and let out a long breath. "While I was there, we received word that Dioskorides, Crescens, and Hermaios have been arrested. They'll be executed tomorrow, most likely."

The breath left Demi's lungs. The three men, two of them husbands and fathers, and the other elderly, were all elders and deacons, pillars of Myra's church for as long as she could recall. She dropped back to her own mat, knees watery and shaking.

"What happened?" Her fingers tented over her mouth.

"I don't know. Only that they were coming back after distributing the supplies you and Nikolas brought, and drunken revelers found them." His voice dropped, cracking. "They've . . . endured much already."

Demi's eyes slammed shut against the heat of tears. Shame swelled in her chest at the same moment, images flashing in her mind. The blur of her mitera's face as she was ripped from Demi's grip. The wild look in her eyes before Demi and Hediste were surrounded and cut off from view.

Theseus was saying something, praying aloud maybe. But Demi couldn't hear him over the shouting in her head. Hot tears ran down her face, but in her mind it was the spittle of the man with murder in his eyes as he rained curses on her head. Didn't she care that there was no rain? Didn't she care that the gods were angry with the unbelieving Christians and withholding a bountiful harvest? If she truly loved everyone as Christians claimed to do, she'd do anything in her power to help. But would she burn a pinch of incense to appease the gods and stop the starvation? No. Because Christians were selfish and hateful.

She winced even now at how she'd shrunk beneath his insults and the twisted lies. She hadn't been able to defend her beliefs. She'd shrunk even as her little sister had straightened, staring down their accusers with fire in her eyes and declaring, "True love does not allow another to do whatever they wish, especially if they're heading for destruction."

They'd struck Hediste down, kicked her face with a sickening crack. Demi had screamed. Fought toward her sister, but rough hands had clawed her away. Shoving, tearing at her hair, screaming nightmarish threats into her ears. They'd smear her breasts in pitch and light them on fire, slice her open from naval to neck, stuff her body with grain and throw her, mercilessly alive, to the governor's pigs to fatten them for his feasts. She'd tried to stop her ears, knowing they were not idle threats, that they'd done those same things—and worse—to so many others before her. But their words took hold, fear turning her limbs to water.

And when they'd shoved her before the altar smoldering in front of the brass-plated images of the emperor and the Sol Invictus, she'd fallen. Hands and knees sliding on paving stones slick with her family's warm blood. They'd thrust a bowl of incense beneath her nose, crushed leaves and fragrant seeds and flowers, making her stomach jerk. Someone shoved her hand into the bowl and ordered her to throw it on the altar.

Just a pinch. Just dead leaves and flowers. Just a few meaningless words. *"Kyrios Caesar."* Caesar is lord.

Fire from the altar glimmered on knife blades, as the men drew them slowly. With purpose. Her whole being trembled, inside and out.

Just grass. Just leaves.

"Demitria," Theseus's voice called to her—but, that wasn't right, he'd not been with them that day in the market. "Demitria. It's all right."

An arm came around her shaking shoulders, drawing her back into the darkness of their little hovel. Her breaths came ragged, sobs tearing through her chest instead of blades. Oh, that it had been blades. Blades and glory instead of cowardice and shame.

"Shhh, Demi," Theseus murmured. "They are true to the Name. We must pray that they will have courage and hold fast. We mustn't mourn like those who have no hope."

She gripped his hand in both of hers. He didn't know. Couldn't know. That she hadn't been true. That she had no hope.

Whoever denies Me before men, him I will also deny before My Father.

Pastor Tomoso had preached those words at every riverside service, and in her moment of testing, she had not come forth as gold. She'd burned the incense. Denied the Name.

I'm sorry. I'm so sorry.

It didn't matter that she'd also burned the libelli they'd given her. That no one else had known she'd been taken with her parents that day. That shame and remorse had become her constant companions as she sobbed herself to sleep nearly every night since. She'd volunteered for the dangerous task of trading for supplies upriver, hoping to train herself in courage, absolve her lack of it. But in the end it wouldn't matter. In her moment to prove herself, she'd fallen short, and barred herself from heaven.

FIFTEEN

GRAVEL AND SHARDS OF POTTERY crunched beneath Nikolas's feet, and Xeno muttered under his breath as the crumbling insula they'd just left was swallowed in the shadows behind them. Holes gaped between the few roof tiles that remained, and the walls were lined with water stains from the spring floods. It ought to be wholly abandoned, but where would the tenants go? If one could call them tenants. Amata had said that a man came monthly and demanded rent. But for what? The place offered little shelter. If Nikolas ever recovered the gold, the first thing he'd do was provide a door for Amata and the two other elderly church widows who lived in that tiny room with her. Maybe he'd buy the whole thing.

He sighed. It all depended upon a rather large *if* sitting beneath the Mediterranean.

"I always want a good bath after visiting that place," Xeno said with a shudder. "I can't believe you ate the stew."

Nikolas shrugged. He'd hated to eat it too, but not for the reasons Xeno imagined. "Amata rationed her own food for days to be able to offer us something."

"Exactly. She needed it more than us. I did her a favor by refusing it. And by the look on your face, I think you wished you had too."

Nikolas's lips tightened. "Being able to receive a gift is just as important as giving one. Had I refused the meal, I would have dishonored her sacrifice, made her feel that her offering was not good enough." He'd felt that more often than he cared to think on. "I ate not to fill my belly, but to bless her."

Xeno was silent.

And if he were honest, Nikolas was glad. The last weeks with him had grown incrementally more difficult. The fawning and deferential treatment had increased to an uncomfortable level, and now this way he had of talking about others in a derogatory manner and acting as though Nikolas agreed with him because he too had been wealthy . . . Nikolas wanted no part in it.

Thunder rumbled in the distance and mist spat from the sky.

Amata and the other widows needed more food than the church could provide. That much was clear from the meal. And they needed wood too—or the women would only sacrifice their door for cooking fuel again. He ran his hands over his face, beard prickling beneath his palms. So many needs. So little money. So little help. His stomach sank again as he recalled the recent deaths of Crescens and the two deacons. He hadn't known them well yet, but the loss hit close all the same.

His first weeks in Myra had not gone as he'd anticipated. Instead of being able to provide for his church, he spent his days trying to remember Latin declensions and failing to teach them well. At night he and Xeno visited the small church gatherings, and in the afternoons he joined the deacons, poring over lists of names and numbers, trying to discern how little food each member could reasonably live on. Titus's contact in the agora had been successful in selling the wool he and Demitria had brought back, but not at a good enough price to buy lentils and chickpeas for everyone. They needed more.

They needed his gold.

A flash of lightning lit up the street, and a bell clanged repeatedly in the harbor.

"Look." Xeno elbowed him. "They've lit the tower beacon fire in Andriake."

Nikolas looked toward the port village and saw, indeed, a ball of orange flame rolling in the sky, guiding ships to the safety of the harbor.

"Sure sign of a bad storm." Xeno shook his head. "I used to be able to see the beacon from my villa, and I'd be an anxious mess worrying over my ships during every storm. I'm sure you know how that feels, especially since your ships carried much more valuable goods than dried fish. At least I can look at it now without a bit of worry."

But what of all the sailors at sea this very night? Sailors with lives and homes and families? Nikolas bit his tongue. He'd criticized Xeno enough for one night, and it never seemed to do any good anyway. He silently prayed for wisdom, patience, and safety for those at sea this night.

As they pressed deeper into the city toward the school, smells of spiced meat roasting in the temple altars perfumed the air. Nikolas's stomach rumbled.

Xeno inhaled. "Don't you miss a good slab of meat? Roasted with all the juices." He gave a moan. "My cooks had the best lamb roast you can dream of. Melted in your mouth. What I wouldn't give for a bite of that right about now, hmm? What do you miss?"

A good, silent walk. Again, Nikolas bit his tongue and instead mumbled something about winter venison. The mist fused into larger raindrops. Nikolas pulled the hood of his cloak over his head, shielding his eyes.

Passing the agora and the statue of Germanicus that towered outside the entrance, Xeno bade him good night and the two split up. Nikolas continued toward the city center, clustered at the base of the low mountain. The large temple complex of Artemis blazed inside a ring of firepots that thickened the air with smoke and incense. Rising above it, torches illuminated the hairpin path leading up the face of the mountain to the fortified acropolis and smaller temple crowning the ridge above the city. Torches danced on the farthest outcropping, and flutes kept time with small bodies in gauzy saffron linen, moving in the stomping steps of the Artemisia bear dance.

After two full weeks of nighttime revelries, the streets lay mostly quiet under the cover of darkness, though the festivities at the temples went on day and night. This year more than most. Perhaps they were extra eager to please the goddess after the previous summer's drought.

Nikolas dropped his gaze and pressed on. Myra's church had been established by the apostle Paul during his fourth missionary journey nearly 250 years before. In all that time, worship of Artemis had not diminished, though the church had remained strong. Tradition was a hard rod to break. The whole Lycian region of Antalya was steeped in the worship of their patron deity Artemis and her brother Apollo. When Gothic invaders destroyed the massive temple of Artemis in Ephesus, Christians had rejoiced, thinking the pagan worship and rituals would come to an end. Instead, the action only served to renew fervent worship, in hopes of incurring the goddess's favor again.

The heaviness of responsibility settled over him. *Lord, help me to be a good caretaker of Your church. Even the difficult members. Especially them.*

"Don't hurt me. I have nothing." A feeble voice spoke frantically as Nikolas turned a corner. Stones clattered as twisted feet slid over the ground in a vain effort to scramble away. Nikolas squinted, spotting a lump tucked against the wall. Lightning flickered, catching in whites of eyes wide with terror.

"I'm not going to hurt you." Nikolas crouched beside the old man and opened the bundle under his arm. "Have you eaten today?" He held out the last of the tiny chickpea cakes Amata had sent home with him. They were cold and slightly soggy now.

"Why would you care?"

The cakes disappeared from his fingers before he could respond. "I care because God cares."

"Tonight, I do not doubt it." The old man spoke around a mouthful. "I have never once doubted it."

Intriguing. "Of which god do you speak?"

"Our lady, the perpetual virgin, Artemis. She always cares."

"Do you think so?"

"Indeed. You offer me food from her hand."

"How can you tell her hand from the hand of any other god?"

"It is her festival that so warms your generosity, is it not?"

Nikolas straightened. "It's the sight of any in need that so warms my compassion."

The man tucked the remaining food behind his back. "Have you a coin, for an old man?"

Nikolas hesitated. Even after delivering exorbitant rent money for several safe rooms, he did have a few spare coins. But something about the man's greedy eagerness made him draw back.

The man gripped the hem of his cloak. "A coin. Just one. A small one—how am I to eat tomorrow?"

If one of you says to them, "Go in peace; keep warm and well fed," but does nothing about their physical needs, what good is it?

"I . . . just a moment." Nikolas took another step back, fishing in the neck of his tunic for the small bag that held a meager pinch of the smallest coins. He pulled one out, enough to buy several loaves of festival bread—or whatever the grainless equivalent was—and held it out. "Here."

The man leaned forward, reaching out feebly until Nikolas bent closer. Then he lunged, gripping Nikolas's wrists and shoving him backward.

"He's got a purse, boys!"

Stumbling, Nikolas fought the grip of the old man who no longer appeared so old or twisted. Miraculous what a bit of money could do for a man. Nikolas slammed against the stone wall behind him, more stars lighting the night for the briefest of moments.

A hand clawed at his neck, searching for the pouch strings. Nikolas shoved, sending the man reeling into the wall opposite. More footsteps snapped up the street. Not coming to his rescue. Nikolas turned and ran. He didn't dare lead them back to the school. But where to go? The long cloak weighed him down. So much for his attempt at blending into the shadows. Pounding footsteps behind him grew louder. Nikolas darted down a side street, then doubled back when he saw it was blocked.

A fist swung out, crashing into his eye. He stumbled. Two men gripped his arms, dragging him back into the alley and slamming him against the wall. Pain exploded through his abdomen, and Nikolas doubled over. With the flick of a knife, the strings of his purse disappeared from around his neck.

The man who'd taken the purse cursed. "Nearly empty."

The other sent a final blow to Nikolas's jaw, white light blasting his vision. "Give us your cloak and shoes."

Nikolas didn't resist as the cloak was ripped from his shoulders. He sank down, pain searing through his side as he untied his sandals and handed them over.

"Do you have a belt? That too then."

They snatched it from his hands and turned away.

Nikolas let out a breath of relief. Too soon.

The last man spun, a dark whirl in the alley. Nikolas didn't see the kick coming until pain exploded through his jaw.

SIXTEEN

DEMI LAY AWAKE IN THE DARK, listening to Theseus's even breathing. The morning after he'd returned with the crushing news of the three church leaders' arrest, Theseus had grown fevered again. In a panic, Demi rushed to find Phineas. It hadn't taken the physician long to find the trouble. Though the wound on his wrist had scabbed and outwardly appeared to be healing, the flesh beneath was putrefying. The only way to bring healing was to first tear away the scab and then clean the wound again. Even a sponge could not muffle Theseus's screams of agony. They echoed in Demi's mind even still.

"Please, don't take him from me, Lord." Her choked prayer reached the ceiling and bounced back at her the way they always seemed to. Tears burned the backs of her eyes and trickled into the hair at her temples. She didn't deserve to be heard. But did that mean Theseus would suffer? Had she doomed more than herself by her actions?

Something rustled near the front door. A rat? She stiffened, holding her breath.

Not a rat—not with Paul purring in the corner. The cat took his job seriously, attacking anything that dared get close to the sponges he guarded. Paul lifted his head, ears pricking toward the front door where the scraping grew louder. A stray cat or dog in the alley more likely, searching for scraps. Well, they'd not find any here.

A low moan. She glanced at Theseus. Stretched to rest a hand on his brow. Still hot. Still fast asleep. The moan was not his. Demi rocked to her feet, feeling in the darkness for a weapon. Her fingers closed around the handle of the water pitcher, and she hefted it. Half full. Heavy enough to do some damage. Her heart thumped as she crept forward, inching around crates of unshaped pumice stones and ducking lines of sponges drying overhead. Paul hopped up and joined her, rubbing against her ankles.

The rustling stopped outside the door. The owner of the shop rarely came to the storage room and even then, it was never at night. Her pulse hammered in her neck, the water pitcher shaking in her hands. Could she hit someone? Hurt them? The thought made her stomach twist. Then she glanced back at Theseus, fevered, defenseless. Yes. If anyone came through the door to hurt her brother, she'd knock them senseless.

The handle wobbled.

She tightened her grip, raising the pitcher.

The door thumped against the bar.

She drew a steadying breath.

Then a series of knocks and pauses released the tension in her shoulders. The pitcher drooped, sloshing water over her feet and Paul, who scrambled away with an irritated growl.

"Who's there?"

A grunt. "Nikolas."

She set the pitcher on the floor and yanked the door open. "What's happened?" she whispered. "Titus and Iris, are they—"

"All fine." Nikolas slumped against the doorframe, silhouetted against the starlit sky. "I made . . . a mistake."

"Come in."

He stumbled inside, hunched and limping, clutching one arm to his stomach. Demi shoved the door closed and bolted it behind them. Nikolas swayed on his feet. She gripped his upper arm and led him through the maze of stones and crates to her own mat.

"Sit here."

She stirred up the dying embers in the firepot, sending orange flickers dancing across the walls, broken by odd shadows from the hanging sponges. She turned back to Nikolas, sucking in a breath at the blood trickling from his lip into his beard and the bulbous swelling of his left eye.

"What happened to you?"

"I was out alone."

"You did this to yourself?"

"It didn't go exactly as planned." He touched his fingers to his jaw, wincing.

Demi poured water into a bowl and snagged a cloth from the table. She set the bowl beside Nikolas and wrung out the cloth, leaning forward to wipe his face. "What happened?"

He tugged the cloth from her fingers. "Xeno and I met with the small group in the insula by the river."

Demi watched as he swiped at his eye, his lip, and dropped the rag back into the bowl.

"Thank you."

She rolled her eyes. "You hardly did a thing." She dragged a low stool next to him and sat before scooping up the rag and dabbing at the blood drying into his whiskered chin. He flinched at her touch.

"Is Xeno hurt?"

"We split up as we normally do, but . . ." He shut his eye and sank back against the wall. "I was stupid. Tricked by a fake beggar and waylaid."

"Your compassion will be the death of you one of these days." Her tone implied how foolish he'd been. As if his face did not already prove it. Demi slid her fingers beneath his swollen chin, gently tilting his face toward the light. His beard was surprisingly soft against her fingertips. The sharp nob in his throat bobbed, but he kept his good eye shut.

"Does the rest of you fare as badly as your face?"

His eye opened, warm brown and flecked with dark spots. "I'm not sure it would be appropriate for you to check."

Heat flared up her neck. "That isn't what I—"

He pulled away from her touch. "I—I'm fine. Thank you. I didn't mean to bother you. I just . . . this was the closest place I knew."

"Is your arm injured?"

He looked down as if deciding, then shook his head. "My stomach hurts a little. But I'll be fine."

She rinsed the cloth and folded it, resting it gently over his swollen eye. "The more you say, 'I'm fine,' the less I'm beginning to believe you. Hold this here." His fingers brushed hers as she relinquished the cloth. Demi stood and set a bowl of water over the firepot to heat. "Perhaps some calendula *ptisana* will help."

Nikolas looked doubtful.

Demi opened a jar of dried yellow flowers and dropped a pinch into the bottom of a clay cup. For herself, she stripped a few leaves from the basil and mint plants drooping near the shuttered window and added them to the other cup.

He sagged against the wall and stared at his lap. "How is Theseus? I heard his fever returned."

She nodded, glancing at her brother still asleep on his mat. "The infection grew beneath the scab. It looked like he was healing and then . . ." She shook her head. "It wasn't real."

"Life feels like that sometimes." He sighed, voice dropping into a tone of thoughtful longing. "You run forward only to be shoved backward again."

She shut her eyes. *Yes.*

Nikolas took a breath that sounded as if it hurt. "My father was a shipping merchant in Patara. When he died, I inherited everything. A fleet of ships, warehouses of goods, a seaside villa, an estate in the hills cloaked in vineyards."

She knew that already, everyone did, though he'd never spoken of it before this. Remnants of refinement clung to his speech and movements, though no one could accuse him of snobbery. But why tell her now? She ran a finger around the chipped rim of the cup she'd prepared for him. He wouldn't complain, but it was tawdry compared to what he'd been used to. She checked the water and turned to face him, bracing her hands behind her back on the table edge.

"Did you lose it all after the edicts?"

Nikolas hung his head, gold tones in his hair illuminated by the firelight. "I wasn't supposed to inherit it at all. Didn't deserve to. But when it fell to me, and the first edicts passed, I sold everything I could and went to live with my uncle in a monastery nearby. So many needed help in those early days, and they would come to the monks pleading for aid. I started sneaking out at night. Doing whatever I could after the droughts, and when shipping started to fall apart . . . So many people were desperate—selling their own daughters as prostitutes." His voice cracked. "There were too many I couldn't reach in time."

"You did what you could."

He shook his head. "It's never enough."

Demi turned away, pressing her tongue to the roof of her mouth to stem the tide of tears rising in her eyes. After all he'd done, how could he possibly experience the same feelings she did? She'd never been more grateful for boiling water than at that moment. Demi kept her back turned as she poured it into the cups. Drawing a steadying breath, she turned and held one out to Nikolas.

He dropped the rag back into the basin and took the cup. Resting it on his knee, he watched the steam curl from its rim. "Everyone here expects me to close my eyes, to help only those within our gatherings, but it's killing me to walk by so many in need of hope."

"What could you possibly do?" Demi sank down on the stool across from him, her own cup cradled in her hands.

"I had plans." He leaned his head against the wall and closed the eye that wasn't already swollen shut. "Why do you do what you do, Demitria?"

The room had grown too hot. It was the wrong time of year for ptisana—why had she built the fire so high? She shifted, set her cup on the floor.

"My family." She looked over her shoulder toward Theseus, hoping his form would drown out the memories of the others.

"Ah, yes. The boat. Your family occupation."

Demi forced a nod. "Pater was a deacon. He went upriver before we did." She looked down, tucking her dirty feet beneath her stool. "It's so hard to fit into someone else's footprints."

Nikolas's sharp inhale drew her gaze. Pain contorted his face. His wounds must be deeper than he let on.

She turned toward him. "Are you all right? Shall I fetch Phineas?"

"No." He shook his head. "It isn't that. I . . ." Firelight played across the bruises darkening his skin as he let out a long breath. "When I sailed to Myra, I filled my boat with all the money I had left. And it all sank."

Her stomach dropped. She bit her lip, remorse swelling with each recalled comment she'd made about his boat. "I'm sorry. I shouldn't have teased you about it."

He didn't answer, only took a sip of the ptisana, and rested the cup on his knee once more. After a moment, his good eye shifted toward her, and his throat bobbed again. "What if we could find my boat? Recover . . . what was lost—even a little of it?" He winced and touched his lip that had started bleeding again.

Golden firelight leaped in the basin of water as she squeezed out the rag and handed it to him. With the price of food rising, rents going up, the price of silence increasing, that money would be . . . miraculous. But why was he telling her this? He barely knew her.

"Titus says your character is impeccable, that he trusts you. And after going upriver with you, I can see why." Nikolas pressed the rag to his lip as his eye crinkled in what might have been a wry smile. "I'm not one to ask for help, to ask someone else to take a risk in my stead—and if I meant to keep the gold to myself, I wouldn't ask at all, but . . . it isn't for me. And of everyone I know, you're the only one who can help."

Her chest tightened, squeezing as if she'd dived too deep. How could she refuse him? "Where did your boat sink? Could you remember the spot?"

"Near the cove where I met you and Theseus."

"How far from shore?"

He lifted his shoulders, winced at the pain the action brought. "Near enough to swim, but I don't know how deep."

The drop-off was gradual near the cove. Neither fishermen nor divers frequented the area due to the warm, shallow waters. "Mersad is very careful about keeping strangers out of our boats. He's worried we'll sell the coral to someone else. But . . . if you met me at the cove, perhaps . . ."

His eye shifted between hers, as if weighing how serious she was.

"I don't want to endanger you or Theseus. You already carry great responsibilities for the church with your boat."

An ache welled in her chest. "Sometimes it feels like nothing I do will ever be enough." Her words escaped in a whisper. She slammed her eyes shut, wishing she could call them back. Wishing that the courage she practiced in the dark on the river could somehow transfer to the daylight. And the past.

"I understand." Nikolas's answering whisper loosed the tightness in her chest. He looked down at his lap. "You know what money does to people. Everything I spoke to you was in confidence of your trust and silence. If we do this, no one can know."

She nodded.

"But perhaps you ought to discuss it with Theseus first. If Titus trusts him, so do I. If he agrees, then perhaps the three of us could . . ."

Demi nodded again, relief crashing through her at one less secret to carry on her own. "Theseus will be glad to have something to do. And you have my word that I will not speak of this to anyone else."

"We'll try to find it then," Nikolas agreed, tone still hesitant. His good eye flicked to her face. "But if it's too dangerous to retrieve, I need your word you will not pursue it."

"Everything is dangerous. It doesn't mean we give up."

His expression twisted. "I'm serious, Demitria. I won't put you at risk for a shipload of gold, much less a handful of coins."

Her eyes filled and she turned abruptly, stirring the fire. He wouldn't say that if he knew who she was. What she'd done. She forced the rising lump back down her throat and turned to him.

"I promise."

PART TWO

"What does love look like? It has the hands to help others. It has the feet to hasten to the poor and needy. It has eyes to see misery and want. It has the ears to hear the sighs and sorrows of men. That is what love looks like."

SAINT AUGUSTINE

SEVENTEEN

The warm wind in her face felt heavenly after a month shut up in the back room of the sponge and pumice stone shop. Judging by the way Theseus sprawled in the stern, face tipped to the sun, he felt the same. Demi sat on the edge of the boat and dropped her feet into the water. It eagerly licked up her calves and dropped back to her ankles as the boat rocked in the waves. The whole of the sea seemed to rise and fall as if the ocean breathed beneath them.

The ease Theseus seemed to have now betrayed the hesitancy he'd shown earlier in his diving attempts. He'd been reserved in the boat at first, stiff and keeping to the middle as if he feared getting wet. Demi could hardly fathom her brother fearing the water—the very place that felt the safest, most unchanged despite the chaos on shore. She could tell it ate at him, the way his legs had shaken as he stood on the edge of the boat, the way his lungs seemed incapable of retaining his breath, the way he'd lost control over his heart and it thundered wildly in his chest against his will. She'd seen the pulse hammering in his neck and didn't blame him for his fear. The last time he'd been in the sea, he'd nearly stayed there. Still, he'd tried to dive, again and again, each attempt worse than the last. Demi had assured him that it would take time, that his lungs had been injured and he only needed practice. She couldn't help but feel that every encouraging word she'd spoken was a lie.

"Well?" She slid a glance over her shoulder.

Nikolas stood in the prow, feet splayed for balance, facing the cove

111

where they'd just picked him up after his morning of lessons. Wind ruffled the waves of his brown hair, making it catch the light in streaks of gold.

"I think . . ." He paused, cocked his head to one side. "I think this is where I was."

One way to find out for certain.

Demi shrugged the chiton off her shoulders and arched her back, sliding off the edge of the boat and into the welcome embrace of the water. She let it pull her under, run its cool fingers over her scalp and through her curls. The welcoming hum and chuckle of the ocean calmed her thundering heart. The water was cloudy today, visibility low. It hadn't been a good morning for coral, and the afternoon wasn't looking promising either. She pressed lower and lower, searching first for the bottom, then for a sunken boat. A boat filled with gold. It was hardly believable. A story that might have been myth coming from anyone besides Nikolas.

Finally needing air, Demi allowed the water to propel her upward toward the dark oval of the boat. *Surface slowly. Divers have died emerging from the deeps too fast.* They might not have understood the reasons for them, but Pater's rules were never arbitrary. He'd never been wrong.

Until the day he'd said all was safe in the market. That the merchant was his friend.

When her head broke the surface, she blew out a watery breath, sluicing water from her eyes.

Nikolas met her gaze and slumped to sit in the boat. The skin around his eye had healed to a mottled green and yellow. "I turned around and you were just . . . gone." He ran a hand through his hair, looking adorably unsettled.

"I told him not to worry," Theseus volunteered, pushing to his feet. "How is it down there?"

"How long do you stay down for anyway?" Nikolas interrupted.

She pressed her arms forward and back, caressing the water as she stayed in place. One side of her mouth tugged up. "Rex could say the Lord's Prayer twenty times before I came up. Perhaps doing that will set your mind at ease."

He stared at her. "*Twenty* times? Impossible."

She shrugged. "Perhaps he recited it quickly."

His lips moved silently, gaze growing glassy with concentration as he recited, calculated, shook his head. "That's got to be nearly a sixth of an hour."

"Maybe. I don't know." She swam for the boat and pulled her shoulders up, locking her arms over the edge and tilting her face up to Theseus. "Visibility's not good today. It's deep here, but not a drop-off. I need a stone." She shifted her grip on the boat, holding on with one hand so she could swing the opposite leg up, hooking her heel over the edge of the boat.

Theseus bent to the pile of rocks in the center of the boat, each tangled in a web of twine netting they'd made during the month of festival. He fumbled over one, the fingers of his injured hand still unable to grip anything. Nikolas moved to help and hefted the jagged chunk of lichen-covered limestone onto the edge of the boat. Theseus looped the twine over Demi's ankle.

Nikolas's eyes went wide in horror. In the sunlight, they were a muddy mix of warm brown and dark green. His hand flung out to stop Theseus. "What are you doing?"

Theseus grinned. "If I was trying to drown my sister, I wouldn't have waited for a witness."

"Is that supposed to be comforting?"

"It's all right," Demi broke in. "We do it every day. Saves us energy and breath if we don't have to swim to the bottom every time. We can dive more times before we have to rest."

"All right . . ." Not sounding entirely convinced, Nikolas held the rock steady in a white-knuckled grip while Theseus finished looping the twine around her foot. "And then what? We just sit here and wait?"

Demi cocked her head. "Can you dive?"

"I don't know."

She gave a quick nod. "Then sit here and wait. Please."

"What if you can't get your foot out?" His gaze went to the loop around her ankle.

AS SURE AS THE SEA

"I have a knife in my bag." Demi patted the mesh bag at her waist, feeling the familiar shapes of her diving knife and coral hammer. "I'll be fine."

Theseus nodded, "On the count of three?"

"Feels wrong," Nikolas muttered, while Theseus began to count.

Demi sucked in a breath and released her hold on the boat as Nikolas released the stone.

And then the roar of bubbles in her ears. The tug of the stone at her ankle. She relaxed into the familiar rhythms and opened her eyes, the cloudy turquoise blue of the water shot through with shafts of white light. Water raked her hair from her face as the bottom came into view, pale sand broken by dark rocks and clumps of swaying seaweed. Fish scattered in sparkling shards. At the bottom, she slipped her ankle free from the twine, arms waving as she slowly spun, taking in her surroundings. No boat. No coral either.

She moved her legs, circling into an ever-widening loop as she scanned the bottom. It grew rockier farther out, stands of kelp and coral spreading in blooms of color. She headed that direction, mesh bag rubbing against her thigh as she swam. No gold winked from the sandy bottom, tinted a pale green and ribbed with waving current lines. What had she expected? To find a treasure on her first attempt?

Flashes of red snagged her attention. Kicking over a rocky rise, she saw crimson starfish studding the coral bed like flowers. Such beauty tucked far below the surface where few—maybe no one—would ever see it. Further exploration revealed nothing useful. Lungs burning and hands empty, Demi arced upward, angling for the oblong shadow of the boat above. A breeze stroked her skin as her head broke the surface. She blew out a whistling breath before filling her lungs.

"Well?" Nikolas knelt in the boat, gripping the edge and leaning toward her eagerly. "Did you see anything?"

She shook her head, rubbing the sting from her eyes and glancing toward Theseus. "Nothing of use to us or Mersad."

Nikolas sank back with a sigh. "I suppose it was silly to hope we'd find it on the first try."

Water lapped against Demi's chin. "Good things don't always come easily."

"It's too bad they can be so easily lost though." He shook his head. "I guess I was more hoping for my own sake. I hate to inconvenience you both when there's nothing I can do to help."

She gripped the edge of the boat and hauled herself up far enough to hook her elbows over the side. "You could get another rock for me."

Theseus handed her the waterskin and a date. "You'll need a rest after this."

She tipped the waterskin to her lips and nodded.

Nikolas chose another stone from the pile and heaved it to the edge of the boat as Demi crammed the date into her mouth and tossed the waterskin back to Theseus. She slipped her foot through the loop.

"On three?"

She nodded, breathing deep and relaxing as the stone crashed into the sea and pulled her down with it.

She found nothing resembling a boat or gold. When the light waned, signaling the time to return to the docks, Demi and Theseus returned Nikolas to the cove.

"Try again tomorrow?" Theseus asked.

Nikolas hopped over the side, splashing into the shallows. "Only if you have time." He glanced at Demi, huddled in her chiton against the cooling breeze.

She nodded.

Nikolas waded to the front of the boat and gave it a shove, freeing it from the sandy bottom. "Then I'll meet you at the docks and walk back with you."

Theseus nodded. "All right."

As her brother steered the boat around the rocky arm hiding the cove, Demi looked back just once to see Nikolas still standing on the beach watching. He lifted a hand. She returned the gesture and tried to stomp the jellyfish swirling in her stomach. They felt like hope. And that terrified her.

EIGHTEEN

TENSION BOUND THE STREETS OF ANDRIAKE like the ropes of a catapult. No children darted about, the way they usually did in the afternoons once chores and school were finished. Unease tightened around Nikolas's spine as he crossed the port village. Harbor guards lined the docks, guarding several moored ships. Odd, since no one else seemed to be about. The piers were empty of slaves loading and unloading goods.

The hair on the back of his neck prickled. What was going on?

His pace quickened as he crossed abandoned street after abandoned street. Where was everyone? It was as if the whole town held its breath, waiting for . . . what?

Pounding footsteps answered the question, announcing a runner before he swung around the corner in front of Nikolas, terror and anger in his eyes. The man was sunbrowned and dressed in the bleached garb of a sailor. Nikolas twisted to the side, barely avoiding a collision.

The sailor raced past, heading for the pier. "Captain! Ambush!"

More footsteps thundered behind him.

Nikolas flung himself against the side of a tavern as a herd of men surged around the edge of the building wielding clubs and wine amphorae. "Get him!"

In a moment, the streets were flooded with angry men. A tide rushing in with violence. A knot of sailors fought their way out of the tavern, surrounded on all sides by fists and shouts.

"Is this what you call Lycian hospitality?" one bellowed. A swinging club answered, and the sailor disappeared beneath the mob.

Pulse pounding, Nikolas fought to keep to the edge of the crowd. He had to find Demitria and Theseus. And they had to get out of here.

An elbow rammed his side. A foot crushed his. He stumbled into the back of the man in front of him, who raised a fist.

"Take them to the *Kranion!*"

"We didn't do anything!"

The crowd erupted, repeating the chant. "To the Kranion!"

The Kranion. The place outside the city walls where criminals were beheaded. The mob surged and Nikolas surged with it, caught in the undertow of violent humanity sweeping up the road toward Myra. His ears rang with shouts for blood and justice as he fought against the tide. Where were Demitria and Theseus? He prayed they hadn't gotten swept up in the mob as well.

Nikolas broke through the crowd, twisting down an alley and pressing against the sun-warmed brick of an oil and vinegar shop to catch his breath. Another group followed the angry crowd, these armed with swords and dressed in the sun-faded tunics of sailors.

"Liars! They did nothing wrong!"

Blood would follow this crowd. And he needed to find his friends before it did.

Nikolas spun into the emptying streets, racing for the docks along the river side of the port city. He scanned the shore, studded with fishermen cleaning nets, and the hum of anxious voices. Demitria's wild curls and Theseus's stocky form were nowhere to be seen. His pace quickened with his pulse. *Please, Lord, let them be here.*

"Nikolas."

He spun toward the voice, a shaky breath of relief crashing through his chest as Demitria waved from where she stood in a line of divers near the docks. Baskets of coral sat at their feet and every so often they shuffled a step closer to the men seated at a stained table, weighing coral and opening oysters. Unlike the others, no coral tangled above the rim of Demitria's basket, and a pang of guilt struck. How much might they have harvested had they not been helping him?

Beyond the line of divers, he spotted Theseus bent over in the lateen, readying it for the morning. He moved to help but Demitria flashed a palm toward him, a signal to wait where he was. Her coral was weighed and marked in a ledger and the few oysters inspected and dumped back into her mesh bag.

The shouts of the mob faded as she returned her empty basket to the boat and she and Theseus trotted down the dock toward him.

"What's going on?" Demitria cast an anxious look up the street.

He shook his head. "I don't know. Men attacked some sailors. I saw one running for the docks yelling about an ambush. I think the others are being taken to the Kranion."

Theseus frowned. "The Kranion? Without a trial? What did they do?"

"I don't know. But we should get off the streets. Best to be out of sight when the crowds go wild."

Demitria plunged ahead of the men as they veered away from the docks and the mob's stragglers, opting for the footpath nearest the river. Her hair flung back and forth as she looked from side to side and behind, worry pinching lines between her dark brows.

None of them spoke until the village behind them had been swallowed up by the citrus grove.

Theseus's breathing was ragged, he coughed and slowed.

Nikolas slackened his pace and fell back with him. Demitria plowed ahead, movements stiff and jerky.

"We can slow down." Nikolas called to her. "The mob is far away by now."

Demitria glanced over her shoulder and shook her head. "It's foolishness to let your guard down even a little. We're never safe. Never." Tears edged her words. "The moment you think—" She bit her lip and angled her face forward again, shoulders hunched and cowering.

How could this be the same woman who navigated a rocky river in the dark, who rescued her brother from an eel, who sailed and dove alone? What about the mob had left her so shaken?

Theseus sighed. "Let her go."

"Will she be all right?"

"In time, I hope."

Was now the time to act on pastoral concern and press for details? Or let it go, as Theseus suggested?

"Demi was betrothed once." Theseus spoke quietly, though Demitria was too far ahead to overhear. "Alexander was swept up in a mob like that . . . He died in courage for the Name."

Something snapped in Nikolas's chest. He knew what it was to lose someone in violence—perhaps not his betrothed, but grief and loss were painful no matter the circumstances.

"I'm sorry to hear of her loss." He swallowed. "Titus told me of your family as well. I . . . am sorry. There are too many stories like that. I don't know of anyone who is unaffected by the edicts."

Theseus only nodded.

"I lost my uncle after the first edict. The . . . monastery where we lived was razed. Nearly everyone killed." Even though it had been nearly three years ago, the shouts and cries, the odor of smoke and blood lingered in his mind, as surely as it did hers. Vivid. Heartrending.

"And your parents?" Theseus winced as the question emerged, as if regretting the asking of it. He'd no doubt heard the rumors.

Nikolas kicked a stone. "My mitera passed from the plague when I was twelve. Six years later my father and brother were both gone too, and I . . . the change was difficult. The emptiness . . . unbearable."

"The grief comes in waves." Theseus nodded. "Some days you can't breathe, and others . . . You don't realize you've forgotten they're gone until you go home and find it empty." He ran his tongue over his teeth and looked toward the river. "Those days are the worst."

"It's like you're hearing the news for the first time all over again." How many times had that happened to Nikolas? How many times had guilt flooded immediately after because he'd forgotten—and how could he have forgotten? Let himself enjoy an afternoon?

They pressed up the path in Demitria's wake, keeping her in sight and drawing silence around them in place of painful conversation.

Demi slowed allowing the men to catch up, flank her on either side. A small bag of mussels and oysters clattered against her thigh.

"Shall we try again tomorrow after your students dismiss?"

Nikolas recalled her empty coral basket. "I don't want to keep you from your work. The boat is important."

She lifted a shoulder. "The water wasn't good today for coral. Perhaps it'll be clearer in the morning, and I'll find more."

Theseus reached over and took the bag of mussels from her. He hefted it in one hand and frowned. "If you're going to dive for the gold in the afternoon, perhaps you ought to leave me at the cove. I can hunt the shallows for shellfish. There isn't a need for two of us to sit in the boat doing nothing."

Demi nodded.

Nikolas took a breath. "I could . . . try to help you look. I can't hold my breath for twenty Lord's Prayers, but I can swim."

Her bottom lip rolled between her teeth as she considered. "Maybe. If it's clearer, you wouldn't have to dive all the way down to see the bottom."

Ahead, the citrus grove gave way to a wan barley field, the city of Myra stacked against the steep face of the mountain behind.

Demi took a breath, as if to say more, but her chin came up sharp, gaze snapping toward the agora where the roar of the mob carried on the breeze. "We need to get off the street."

No one argued. Theseus took Demi's arm and Nikolas kept pace with them as they navigated streets clotted with people, most drawn in the direction of the commotion. When they reached the school, Nikolas shoved the door open and gestured Demi and Theseus in ahead of him.

"Titus?" He closed the door behind him.

Beatrix emerged from the kuzina. "He left earlier to meet with the tablet seller, and Iris and Nydia went to bring food to the widows in the river insula." She cocked her head. "I'm worried for them. What is the commotion about?"

Nikolas shook his head. "A mob from Andriake is headed for the Kranion. I don't know the particulars."

"Nydia and Iris are out there in this?" Theseus's voice had gone breathless and flat. He dropped the bag of shellfish on the floor with a clatter and turned to the door. "I'm going to look for them."

"I'll go with you." Nikolas moved to follow, catching the terror turning Demitria's face into worried lines. Her mouth worked, but no sounds emerged.

"You dear boys." Beatrix's smile was tight. "Go with God. And be careful."

There was a dull roar in the streets when Theseus opened the door. A woman herded her children into a doorway across the road as several young men ran past, heading toward the noise. They hadn't even taken a step through the door when a familiar voice screeched his name, laced with unfamiliar panic.

"Master Nikolas!"

A small body barreled down the street aiming for the open doorway. "Master Nikolas, please help him!"

Paros bolted through the door and rammed Nikolas, wrapping his arms around his waist. Nikolas stumbled backward, nearly tripping over a bench.

"What's wrong, Paros? Are you all right?"

"They took him." The boy stepped back and scrubbed at his tear-streaked face, gulping air.

"Who?"

"My pater. They're taking him to the Kranion and he didn't do anything wrong." Paros ran a hand beneath his streaming nose. "You have to talk to them and make them stop."

Nikolas glanced at Theseus, who met his gaze with an almost imperceptible shake of his head. He stepped outside.

"We've got to go."

"You have to come with me." Paros begged.

Theseus edged into the street, clearly wanting to wait for Nikolas, but not for long. "Nikolas."

Paros tugged on his hand. "Please, sir. He's been gone so long on his ship, and he just got home. He didn't do anything wrong. You gotta 'gotiate with them like you taught us. I can't do it right." A tear escaped his eye, and he rubbed it away.

Nikolas shut his eyes. It was a fool's errand, and he knew it. And yet . . . He looked down at the boy whose eyes overflowed yet somehow remained hopeful. Then he sighed and looked at Theseus. "Go on without me."

Theseus took off at a run.

"Don't be stupid, Nikolas." Demitria spoke through gritted teeth. "It isn't safe. You know mobs aren't safe. They'll turn on you in a moment and—" Her chin trembled, and she snapped her lips shut. Violent memories played out in the fear in her eyes. "If you go, you won't come back. You'll endanger everyone. What do you think you'll do against a mob like this? How do you know he doesn't deserve the Kranion?"

Paros took a step, straining at Nikolas's hand. *Keep quiet. Stay safe.* The elders had drilled those two rules into his brain at every meeting; it was the benediction given each time the church gatherings dismissed. And he couldn't live like that anymore. Afraid to help someone else because it might cause trouble for him.

He shook his head. "I don't know. But the least I can do is find out. And if he's one of the sailors they dragged in from Andriake, I know there hasn't been time for a trial."

"You're not a decurion. Let them handle this."

"What if they don't know?"

"Do you hear the commotion?" She threw a hand in the air. "How could they not know!"

Paros yanked on his hand. "Please. Please, hurry."

Nikolas glanced down at him. There was nothing he could do to stop an angry mob, but— "Where does Master Evander live?"

Demitria's lips tightened, her gaze locked on his. Her hands balled and flexed at her sides before she sighed. "If you go up—" She stopped, conflicting desires warring in her expression before deflating in surrender when her gaze dropped to Paros. "There's a back way. I'll take you there."

NINETEEN

Of all the foolish, reckless things.

They shouldn't be out, not with crowds like this. It broke every rule that had ever been drilled into her. Safety. Security. That was all that mattered anymore, and it was as fleeting as the color of dead coral. And yet—she glanced at Paros, the boy's grim face pale and determined—this mattered more, didn't it? Justice? Life?

The shops of the laborers' district fell away to broad streets paved in wide white stones as they climbed toward the affluent quarter. Here, not a bit of refuse or sprouting weeds marred the perfection of wealth announced in the rainbow of mosaiced walls surrounding the sprawling villas. Here, the walls kept out even the noise of the mob.

"Here." Demi paused before an iron gate, wrought in vines and leaves and painted in soft colors, so real she had to resist the urge to run her fingers over them. A guard stood on the inside.

Nikolas stepped forward. "We must speak with Master Evander."

"He is not receiving the riffraff today. Or ever."

Nikolas's voice went steely in a tone Demi had never heard him use before. "I am the Latin tutor at the school he funds. There's a mob, and I must speak with him immediately. For the sake of his reputation."

The guard let them in. "Wait here."

Paros tugged at his hand, whispering, "The mob isn't at the school."

Nikolas looked down at him and offered a small smile. "I never said it was."

Paros's eyes went round and he gave a conspiratorial nod. "Ahhh, you're 'gotiating."

Whatever that meant.

Demi crossed her arms and tapped her foot. Evander was as slow as a starfish in arriving. When he did, his blue robe billowed out behind him, resplendent as a rolling wave. He was flanked by four men in equally elaborate robes, all wearing matching expressions of irritation.

Demi's stomach dropped. *What have we done?* Five of the second most powerful men in Myra strode toward them, the same who'd presided over the sham trial of her parents and sister, deeming them worthy of a tortured death. A ragged breath scraped into her lungs, and she fought the urge to run. *Do not cower.* She drew back her shoulders. Raised her chin. Beside her, Nikolas did the same.

"Yes. What is it?" Evander's voice was tight and clipped. No time to be wasted now that he was here. The other decurions crossed their arms.

"There's a mob dragging men to the Kranion without a trial," Nikolas said.

"My pater didn't do anything wrong."

Evander's gaze flicked from Nikolas to Paros and back. "I thought this was about the school?"

"This is my student. I am his teacher, and you, sir, are a leader in this city. Will you allow justice to be thwarted in such a manner?"

"Last I checked, Latin tutors were not magistrates and judges."

"Evil prevails when good men are silent. It is my duty to the next generation to show them true justice and to speak on behalf of the innocent who cannot speak for themselves. I know you are honorable men and will execute justice."

"How do you know these men are innocent?"

"Are not all men innocent until the charges against them are proven? Justice will be perverted forever if you allow a mob to execute these men without a trial. How can you expect your citizens to respect and trust you in a higher position if you allow such a perversion of truth today?"

Was he threatening Master Evander? Something cold wrapped around Demi's heart. He was going to get them all killed. *Stop it, Nikolas. Be quiet.*

Evander's mouth set in a hard line as he stared at Nikolas. Then he blinked. "You said they were heading to the Kranion?"

Nikolas nodded.

"Then let us go quickly."

Evander led the way, and Nikolas and Paros followed, refusing to turn back and wait for justice to be done without them. Demi hesitated. Was she safer with Evander and the decurions in the mob? Or was it better to risk the crowds and return home alone? Nikolas took her hand and gripped it tight, tugging her alongside him.

"It's going to be all right," he murmured.

Lies. He wasn't a prophet. He had no idea what lay ahead. Everything within urged her to break free, to run. But her knees felt like jellyfish and she knew running wasn't an option. Not this time. Her pulse thrashed, drumming in her ears. She wasn't ready. The last time she'd been anywhere near the Kranion, she'd failed. How much worse to do it again in front of Nikolas? Each step that brought them closer to the mob boiling around the Kranion heightened her dread.

She heard the mob long before she saw it.

Just outside the city, men crowded the open *plateia*, where a square platform held an elevated dais on which criminals—or those accused of crimes—could be executed in full view. The shouting of the crowd grew less violent now that their bloodlust was about to be satiated. Would they truly go straight to execution without even the pretense of a trial?

Shoulders jostled against her own, the smell of sweat and anger clouding her nose. She tore her gaze from the platform and focused on Nikolas's wide shoulders. Why were they going closer? Wouldn't it be safer to watch Master Evander quell the crowd from the edge where they could escape quickly if needed?

Nikolas stopped her and Paros shy of the platform, as if finally sensing her hesitation. The crowd pressed her close against his side, and she didn't mind. Perhaps some of his courage would seep into her, and if not, then at least she'd remain upright if her knees gave.

At the center of the platform, several men forced one of the accused to his knees before a stained block of stone, pushing him forward so his chest and head lay flat over the top. The executioner brandished a sword.

"Tata!" Paros shouted.

Bearded cheek pressed against the stone, the captive's eyes darted for the crowd, fear etched into the lines of his tanned face.

Demi's mouth went dry, her heart sending quivering energy to her limbs. Why had she come? She didn't want to witness this punishment, this perversion of—

"What is the meaning of this?" Evander charged up the steps and wrenched the sword from the startled executioner's grasp. He threw it to the ground behind him. "When was the trial for these men? Where are the magistrates? Who sanctioned this execution?"

Demi held her breath. The other decurions swept up the stairs, forming a wall behind Evander. The executioner shrank back, stuttering. Evander raised a hand in a slashing motion. Three city guards stepped forward. The guards drew short knives and spread out, one to each prisoner.

"Paros!" Nikolas lurched forward, his hand wrenching from Demi's as he flailed for the boy who had darted into the crowd.

But the guards simply cut the bonds of the men and hauled them to their feet.

A small body burst from the mob, scrambling up the steps and barreling into the man who'd been bent over the stone block.

"Tata!"

The crowd shrank back like a receding wave. Bloodlust instantly replaced with shame, with unease, with—Demi found the same feelings flooding her. Shame. Unease. Embarrassment.

She'd begged Nikolas not to help. Been willing to let three innocent men die to keep the mob away from her and her friends. She'd been willing to allow justice to be obstructed so she could live in a sham of safety. So she could hide her lack of courage.

She'd failed again.

As Evander barked orders for the guards to transport the accused to the magistrates for a proper trial, the crowd melted away around them until it was only the decurions, a handful of tanned sailors, and Evander.

The sailor dressed like a captain clasped Evander's arm and bowed. "You've saved my only son among these men. What can I do to repay your goodness, my lord?"

Evander shook his head, as if to decline the offer of repayment. Nikolas released Demi's hand and moved forward.

"What are you doing?" she whispered.

He didn't hear her or ignored her if he did. "You're the captain of the grain ship in the harbor?" Nikolas asked.

The captain rose and turned to Nikolas.

Evander swept an arm in Nikolas's direction. "Here is the man you should thank. Without him, I would not have known of this."

The captain bowed toward Nikolas then. "I thank you, good sir."

"It was your man's son that alerted me." Nikolas pointed to Paros, hanging on his father's leg. "But if you long to show gratitude, show it to Paros, to the children of this city. Have pity on them and leave some of your grain behind. The city granaries are empty, and our children go hungry."

Evander's eyebrows flickered in surprise at the request.

The captain hesitated. "The grain is not mine to give. I merely transport it for another."

Nikolas nodded, disappointment evident in the movement. "Of course. I understand."

"But my master is a good man, and he will not let this thing go unrewarded. I will deliver a report of this to him, and I'm sure he will reward you in kind. What is your name, and where can he find you?"

Nikolas hesitated.

"His name is Nikolas," Evander broke in. "And you can reach him at the school for laborers' children in Myra."

TWENTY

The burble and whoosh of the sea filled Demi's head, slowed her heart, leached the tension from her muscles. Over the course of two weeks, they'd attempted to find Nikolas's gold three times, and this appeared to be yet another failure. At least Theseus was having better luck at the cove, gathering mussels for their meals. She slipped over a rocky ridge, startling a deep-red octopus that shot out in front of her. Green-and-purple snakelocks anemone and ruffled coral fanned between stands of waving kelp dotted with fish in a rainbow of color.

How creative and gracious God was to place such beauty here, where only her undeserving eyes would see it.

Undeserving indeed. Just that morning at the river meeting, the reader had shared a passage from Paul's letter to Philippi.

It is my earnest expectation and hope that I will not be at all ashamed, but that with full courage now as always Christ will be honored in my body, whether by life or by death. For to me to live is Christ, and to die is gain.

The words had struck. Shame and conviction flooding her heart again as they had daily since that day at the Kranion. She'd been ready to let her fear override godly justice and compassion for those innocent men. Had so easily convinced herself that it was better to let strangers die than risk her friends' lives. Why was it far easier to sin, than to sacrifice? How could others have so much courage and she had none when it counted? Perhaps there were no second chances for one like her.

A turtle rose from the bottom and drifted lazily beside her, shell the size of a large shield. She ran her fingers over the slippery smoothness of its back before it angled away from her, gliding over a large hole filled with lumpy rocks not yet covered in coral. Her gaze slid over it then jerked back.

The cloudiness of the water didn't allow a clear view, so she kicked closer. A wall of rock rose up on the back side of the hole, further shading the spot. Her heart stuttered as the point of a prow emerged from the shadows. Nestled inside, covered with a film of pale sand, sat at least a half dozen dark bags, mouths tied shut with leather straps. The mast was broken and missing, along with the sail. Both carried off by currents, most likely. Her lungs began to warn her that her time was fleeting. She pressed closer, fingers closing over the top of one of the bags before she gave a tug. Not a chance of getting them to the surface that way. They'd need a weighted rope and—

Movement out of the corner of her eye sent a shock to her pulse. She turned.

A moray poked its head out of the rocky outcropping, dark mouth gaping and snapping shut.

Demi reared back, horrifying images battering her mind. Theseus with an eel locked onto his wrist. Theseus, face still and slack, drifting away from her in the water.

She shot for the surface, arms and legs thrashing against the water. Out, she needed out.

A glance below told her the moray wasn't following, and only then did she recall her father's rules about slow ascent and the dangers of surfacing too quickly. She'd used too much energy racing upward and needed the air sooner than she was going to get it. A new sort of panic took over, stiffening her limbs and turning her movements jerky.

Finally bursting into the air above, Demi choked and spluttered, thrashing against waves that had kicked up while she'd been under. Her head slipped under. A hand gripped her arm and pulled.

Eyes blurred and burning from the salt water, she twisted and scrabbled for a handhold, clinging to Nikolas as her heart galloped a panicked rhythm. Her whole body shook. It was foolish. She knew it was foolish, but that didn't keep the terror from racing through her veins. His gold, guarded by a moray. She shuddered and coughed.

"We were just wondering where you were."

A voice that did not belong to Nikolas rumbled in her ear, sending a new burst of panic through her limbs. Demi swiped the water from her eyes and jerked backward as Ennio's laughter rang in her ears. He held her fast, even as her gaze raked the waves and landed on Nikolas standing in her boat, lines of his body tight, as if he was about to leap overboard and tear through the brine to get to her.

The red and blue lateen had come around the rocky arm of land at full speed, looking as if it meant to pass, but upon seeing Nikolas, they careened in close, casual questions floating over the waves. Good haul? What had they found? Where was Demi? Who was he? Did Mersad know he was there? Then Demitria had burst from the water and sent his pulse racing at her obvious panic. They'd hauled her in before he could move the boat closer.

"Let me go." Demitria jerked free of the man who did as she demanded and raised both hands as he took a step back.

"Easy." The man's voice dropped too low for Nikolas to hear.

The other men edged closer to Demitria, relaxed postures betraying a clear threat. Not taking his eyes from the other boat, Nikolas bent and hauled up the anchor, hand over hand, hardly noticing the weight of it. Words flew. Demitria's voice snapped, holding her own. He rolled the stone anchor over the side and yanked on the ropes to raise the sail. It caught the breeze, jerking the boat into motion and pulling it away from the red boat before he wrangled the wind and propelled it back toward it. Half the men watched him; the other half remained fixed on Demitria, as if Nikolas posed as much threat as a fly.

Pointing the lateen in the correct direction, Nikolas dropped the sail once more and steered up alongside the red boat. Two of the men caught the prow as he coasted close.

"Demitria, get in." His fists clenched of their own accord. Church leader or not, he'd not hesitate to "negotiate" with them if they laid a hand on her.

She didn't move, a hard gaze fixed on the tall man who'd pulled her from the water. Built of sinewy muscle, he was sun-darkened as a roasted chicken and looked to be nearing fifty.

"Well?" The man's smirk was self-assured.

"I'm not double-crossing Mersad. He's been nothing but generous."

"Too generous, some might say." His gaze flicked over her. "One might question why."

She shot him a withering look. "I'm a good diver."

A young man built of stocky muscle, wearing only a sun-bleached loincloth, straddled the space between both boats and peered into Demitria's coral basket. He barked a laugh. "You take on a partner and this is all you've got?" He looked at the other man and shook his head. "We'll get the boat, Pater. Never fear. If not this season, surely by next."

"Over my cold bones," Demitria spat.

Ennio raised his brows in a show of interest. "Then perhaps I'll leave you floundering in the water next time."

Nikolas's jaw went tight. "If she's truly no threat to you, as you claim, then perhaps you should keep to your own boat, and your own waters, and leave her alone."

Demitria turned and hopped the short distance between the boats, landing with a wobble and flare of her arms. The loinclothed youth returned to the red boat and two of the other young men raised the sail.

"Soon, little nymph." Ennio smiled.

Demitria lifted her chin and watched them leave, not turning away until they'd disappeared around the rocky arm. When they had, she slumped to her seat.

"Are you well? What happened down there? Who are they?"

"Too many questions, Nikolas." She hugged her knees and dropped her forehead onto her arms. "My head hurts."

He grabbed the waterskin from beneath the seat and nudged it against her arm. "Rest. Have a drink."

Hands shaking, Demi uncorked the waterskin and tipped it to her lips. Her eyes were bloodshot, expression weighted with exhaustion. She lowered the waterskin to her lap, corking the mouth once more. "A moray startled me," she admitted quietly. "I know it's silly, but I panicked. All I could see was Theseus when—I had to get out." She rubbed her hands over arms covered in gooseflesh, unwilling to look up at him.

He shook out her chiton and draped it over her shoulders. "But you're otherwise unharmed?"

She nodded.

Nikolas lowered himself to sit across from her. "And . . . Ennio, is it? Does he bother you often?"

She frowned and wiggled a finger into one ear. "He bothers everyone. Ennio and Pelos are brothers, not good divers, but they want their sons to be great. As you can see, they don't have enough room in their boat for everyone and want to expand. But Mersad cannot justify giving them another boat with their hauls so poor already. They think if they can run us out, Mersad will give them our boat and they will be more successful." She sighed and gripped the fabric tight beneath her chin as her teeth began to chatter.

"Will he do that?"

"I am . . . a little behind on my quota, but I can make it up." She shivered.

"Why didn't you tell me? You shouldn't have to sacrifice your boat for my—"

Her eyes met his. "I found it."

He froze, pulse jolting. "You . . . what?"

A tiny nod. A wobbly grin. "I found your boat."

"Truly? Where?"

She twisted, lifting a quivering arm and pointing at a specific spot in the glittering blue behind them. "It's deep." She turned back to him. "You just had to sink your boat into a hole guarded by an eel . . . But if we have a rope, we can fetch the gold, one bag at a time."

He stared at her, then back at the place where the sun lit the turquoise sea and made it shimmer like the silks his father had imported from the far east. Was it possible? So close and yet . . . His gaze dropped back to Demi, mind rolling back to the way she'd burst from the water, thrashing and choking. His heart had nearly jerked from his chest. He'd have dived after her if Ennio hadn't hauled her in.

"I—I'm sorry. I should never have asked such a thing of you. It was foolish. Selfish."

"Now that we've found it, how can you change your mind?" She lifted her head, confusion netting her brows. "Diving is what I do. What I've spent my whole life doing. And for the first time, I'm diving for a worthy purpose. Where do you think you'll find a diver who won't tell you he can't find the spot and then come back later and fetch it in secret?"

"You wouldn't do that."

"No." She shook her head. "And I'm the only one who wouldn't."

"But the moray . . ."

Demi chewed her lip, drew in a deep breath. "It startled me is all . . . I won't be caught off guard next time."

TWENTY-ONE

NIKOLAS WAITED IN THE HALF-PRICE AGORA where damaged goods and days-old bread were sold—when there had been grain for bread. He kept one eye across the street, watching as Theseus waited in line for Mersad's men to weigh Demitria's meager haul of coral and extract any pearls from the oysters she'd gathered. At the docks, Demitria tidied the boat.

After watching a street vendor for some time and not once seeing him ask for libelli, Nikolas risked a purchase. The three skewers were not quite filled with slices of eggplant and artichokes toasted over a firepot and sprinkled with herbs and fermented cheese. The scent had his mouth watering. He handed two to Demitria when she joined him to wait for Theseus.

"How's your head?"

She pinched her earlobe and tugged it back and forth. "My ear hurts more." She kicked at a stone in the street. "I panicked and surfaced too quickly."

"I'll send Phineas to you when we get back."

Demitria shook her head. "There's nothing he can do. If the pain persists, though, I may not be able to dive for a week or so. I'm sorry." She stooped and handed one of the vegetable skewers to a ragged boy, huddled next to a crate of molting chickens.

"Don't be. Has it happened before?" Inwardly chastising himself for already eating half, Nikolas handed the rest of his skewer to Demi.

"It happens to every diver from time to time." She caught a slice of eggplant with her teeth and slid it from the stick, offering it back to him.

He declined with a shake of his head, a familiar silhouette behind her snagging his attention.

"Basil?" He craned his neck. The man disappeared behind a cluster of women.

Demi frowned at the skewer. "It's thyme, I think."

Nikolas shook his head. Impossible. He was seeing things. He had to be. Another scan of the crowd turned up nothing familiar. The man who could not be his father's steward was nowhere to be seen.

Coincidence.

Footsteps trotted toward them and as Theseus approached, Nikolas tore his gaze away from the place where the man had disappeared. "We'd better get back. I have to meet Xeno soon."

Demi tossed the empty skewer aside and held out the last one to Theseus as they navigated the river footpath between Andriake and Myra. "How are your . . . meetings going?" she asked.

He shrugged. "As well as they can I suppose."

She looked up at him. "Is there trouble?"

"Not . . . trouble exactly." He rubbed the back of his neck. "It's . . . I'm new. And I know it'll take time for everyone to accept me. To trust me." He told himself that often and yet it wasn't quite enough to assuage the pangs of rejection and loneliness that struck him even now. He ought to be content to have a place and a purpose, if he couldn't have friends.

"We've lost many brothers and sisters." Her eyelashes flickered as she flashed her gaze toward him and then back to the path. Her voice dropped to an apologetic whisper. "Yours isn't a safe position."

His tone matched hers in volume, and that familiar swirl of disappointment and loneliness circled his gut again. "I know."

The reason he'd been chosen to lead hadn't been his education, or qualifications, or even that they'd respected him. Rather, it was primarily because he was a stranger, an outsider. He wasn't part of their beloved circle. When he was inevitably hunted down and killed, they wouldn't be heartbroken. They'd carry on as they had before he'd come. It shouldn't be a wonder to him that they were hesitant to offer friendship. They were only guarding their hearts. Perhaps he ought to do the same.

As Myra came into view, his pace lagged until he fell several steps behind Demitria and Theseus. If he was going to be the city officials' next target, perhaps he should keep his distance and not put them at risk of being associated with him.

Demitria twisted around to look at him, her hair leaving damp patches on her shoulders and the back of her chiton. "If I can dive tomorrow, we'll send word. If not . . ." One shoulder lifted. "Perhaps next week?" Her eyes glinted with excitement at the prospect and her smile—her smile made his heart do a strange lurch in his chest.

She was only excited about the money, he told himself. It was only anticipation of the good they could do with it.

He gave a nod. Neither she nor Theseus looked back again as they navigated the back streets and alleyways of the city. They drifted apart from each other, walking on opposing sides of the street, varying their strides so as not to walk in unison. Siblings and friends turned to strangers.

They were good at this.

Xeno waited at the school when Nikolas arrived, a wine amphora in one hand and a small bundle in the other.

"Are you ready? Where have you been? Titus said you've been gone all afternoon."

Nikolas hesitated. "I . . ." What could he say? He wasn't going to lie, but to tell the whole truth couldn't be wise either.

"I walked to Andriake and back." True enough. The omitted hours spent in the boat with Demitria niggled at his conscience. What would Xeno and the elders have to say about that? He swallowed. Possibly nothing at all. They were the ones who'd sent the two of them alone upriver at night, after all. Even so, he didn't elaborate.

Xeno eyed him a moment longer, taking a breath as if to press him further. But instead, he simply gestured up the street. "Shall we?"

Nikolas nodded and they set off. This evening they'd meet in the rug shop with Timothy's group again.

"Is that the amphora from Beatrix?"

Xeno nodded and held it out for Nikolas to carry. "It's in there."

The amphora was lighter than expected for its size. Beneath the lid, a cup of wine rested on a ridge inside the mouth of the jug, and when the cup was lifted out, the space beneath allowed for a scroll to be hidden inside. Thanksgiving wine and Scripture nestled together inside one vessel.

The streets steepened as they crossed the city toward Timothy's district. Laborers had returned to their homes for the evening meal, emptying the streets of eyes but refilling them with aromas of herbed fish, savory stews, and roasted vegetables. Nikolas's stomach growled.

Xeno inhaled and closed his eyes. "What I wouldn't give to have a loaf of steaming bread and a platter of baked sea bass swimming in lemon sauce."

"Me too." Nikolas's mouth watered. The few bites of eggplant had hardly satisfied the hunger pains gnawing at his belly. How long since he'd tasted such fare as sea bass and lemon sauce? Most meals at the monastery consisted of hard bread and watery fish stew.

"I cannot complain about Beatrix and Iris's cooking, though," he added, not to seem ungrateful. "It's by far the best I've tasted in years." Even if it was watered down and stretched as far as it could go.

"You are blessed then."

They fell into silence, Xeno's words hanging between them in a tone that didn't sound quite sincere.

Perhaps he shouldn't have said anything.

Timothy's group greeted them with less reserve than before. A small blessing. Nikolas emptied the wine into the goblet Timothy held and removed the small metal cup from the amphora. Tipping the jar, the scroll slid into his hand.

"What is it?"

"Isaiah. The first part." Nikolas held it out. "The whole thing was too large to fit, but I can bring the second part in a few weeks."

Timothy shook his head and raised his hands. "I don't want that one."

Nikolas blinked. "Why not? Didn't you want a new portion of Scripture to study?"

"I wanted one of the letters. I told you that."

"This is what I had. I think you'll find—"

Timothy put his arm around Nikolas's shoulders and turned him away from the group. They shuffled to the edge of the room. "The God of the Septuagint is an angry, vengeful God. We prefer to learn about Jesus instead. His love and acceptance."

Nikolas's brow furrowed. "What do you mean, the God of the Septuagint? There is only one God."

Timothy waved a hand, inclining his head. "Yes, yes, one God, three persons, of course. We simply prefer to worship Jesus. He is loving and kind, a welcome peace in the midst of the chaos around us."

Nikolas's mouth went dry. He couldn't let this slip past and yet, if he spoke up, it would cause one more wedge between him and this church. *Lord, give me wisdom to reveal who You really are in truth.*

"You say the God of the Septuagint is vengeful and angry, but we must consider what He is angry about. His wrath is not separate from His love. Rather, His wrath shows the depth of His love. It is the wrath of a husband and father who rises up to defend and save his beloved family against those things that would seek to destroy it. One is not separate from the other. Jesus' death on the cross displays the love of God and the wrath of God working together. His wrath on sin and His love for us—"

Timothy held up a hand. "Pastor Tomoso just gave me whatever Scripture I wanted to teach from."

Nikolas raised his chin. "The proper interpretation of Scripture is important, Timothy. You can't simply pick and choose which parts make you feel the best and then disregard the rest. It's all true or it isn't."

"How do you know Paul is right and Marcion isn't?"

Nikolas mentally ran over what he knew of the latter name. Marcion, whose teachings from a hundred and fifty years before still infiltrated the church and posited that God the Father was different than Yahweh, the God of the Hebrew Scriptures. Yahweh was an angry, inferior God, while the Father was full of love and compassion. This idea caused Marcion and those who followed his teachings to reject the books of the Septuagint and only cling to a few of the letters—so long as they did not mention the Hebrew Scriptures.

There was more to it, Nikolas knew, but . . . He felt his fingers slowly curling into fists. He'd never been good at fighting with words.

"Jesus upheld the Septuagint. He didn't destroy it, nullify it. He fulfilled it. The whole of it foretells of His coming."

"Yes." Timothy nodded. "It is fulfilled. So we can move on now to newer things. From wrath to love. A new creation, yes?"

"All of Scripture works in tandem. Jesus is the *logos*. The Word. He was in the beginning and has always been. How can you say—"

Timothy once again held up a hand to stop him. "Perhaps we'd best save this discussion for another time. Tonight is for unity and sharing the bread and cup of Thanksgiving." He held up his other hand still clutching the cup of wine.

"How can you partake of the Lord's Supper and believe Jesus separate from the Father—not even believe in—"

Timothy tipped his head toward Xeno, motioning him over. "Oh, we believe in Him; we just . . . don't like Him as much."

He might as well have punched Nikolas in the gut. Nikolas could say nothing as Timothy invited Xeno to walk him back to the school and all but shoved them from the secret room and through the darkened rug shop. Before he shut the door in their faces, Timothy pressed the scroll back into Nikolas's hand.

"God go with you."

In Timothy's mouth it was less of a prayer and more of a command. Nikolas looked down at the scroll, then slipped it up his sleeve, unable to utter the response. He simply nodded.

The humidity of the day hung heavy in the darkened sky. Not even the evening air brought relief. As Xeno and Nikolas descended the labyrinth of streets and stairs, their footsteps scraped over the flagstones.

"Did . . . did you know?" Nikolas turned to Xeno, who simply shrugged.

"Timothy has always had different ideas. He reads everything."

"Not everything," Nikolas corrected. "Not Isaiah. Not the Septuagint."

"But he's right about salvation. That's the most important part."

"There is no salvation in any other," Nikolas murmured. What Timothy believed was true. God was loving. God was kind. But if he disregarded the justice of God—among other things—then he was creating a god to suit his own desires . . . and leading others astray with him. As much as Nikolas wanted to find his place, to be known and belong . . . he couldn't in good conscience ignore this. His stomach twisted at the fight that was coming.

Paros and his other students thought him a master of negotiation, and yet, he'd never quite admitted that as a younger man he'd failed his rhetoric debate and stood silently against his opponent, soaking his tunic with sweat. He'd met judgment with the schoolmaster on more than one occasion, for turning to his fists when his words had not been convincing enough. The memory sent a wave of heated embarrassment over him again, followed just as quickly by a steadying conviction. He was no longer debating the merits of Greek versus Roman merchant ships. This was a matter of truth. Of life and death.

So, were fists truly out of the question, then?

TWENTY-TWO

"Are you getting up?" Theseus nudged Demi's shoulder.

She moaned, drew her blanket over her shoulders. "I'm so tired."

"You know what Pater always said. *Nothing cures the ailments like a trip to the sea.*" He coughed and tugged at the blanket, bracing one hand against the wall. She tried to hang on and failed. Cool air rushed over her.

"You are the worst," she grumbled, pushing herself up. As she'd suspected, the pain in her ear had kept her from diving for a full week. They'd not tried to rescue Nikolas's money during that time, though Theseus had attempted to dive for coral, with her as spotter. They'd brought in nothing and she'd spent most of the week trying to hoist his spirits. Still, the empty coral basket loomed, and pain or no pain, she *had* to dive today. She pulled at her earlobe, pain absent. A good sign, but the first dive would tell for certain.

With his good hand, Theseus poured two cups of water and set two pieces of dried fish on the table. He shooed away Paul who curled between his ankles and eyed the table, nosing the air with interest.

Demi gathered her dive bag and checked the tools inside. All in order. She lifted her cup and took a drink, the water soothing her dry throat.

Theseus rubbed his shoulder with one hand, wincing and swinging his arm in a circle. "I'm meeting with the elders tonight." He raised his gaze to hers. "Titus and Nikolas have put my name forward to become a deacon. They've been praying about it, and they will announce their decision."

She lowered her cup to the table with a clatter, heart seizing between conflicting emotions. "Why didn't you tell me?"

Theseus, a deacon? Pater and Mitera would have been overjoyed. And yet, fear nipped at the heels of joy. If he was chosen, he'd be hunted like a fish in a tidepool.

He must have seen the change in her expression. "Nothing's certain until they give their decision." He shrugged and lowered his voice. "I met with the elders and Pastor Nikolas a few days ago, and he spoke adamantly against the teachings of Marcion. He . . . was looking at Elder Timothy a lot."

"Is Elder Timothy a Marcionite?"

Theseus shrugged. "I don't know. He didn't argue back. Pastor Nikolas pulled me aside later to question my beliefs about the persons and oneness of God. I know it's important that I know what is true before I lead others, but all I'm going to be doing is distributing food." His lips tipped in a crooked smile. "At least I won't be sitting around anymore, doing nothing."

Demi slung the strap of her diving bag over her shoulder. "I'm sure you've spent more time hanging around the school's kuzina with Nydia than sitting around here." She slanted him a mischievous look. "Perhaps Titus is trying to get rid of you."

He tossed a sponge at her. "Perhaps you should mind your own business. Come on, we're losing daylight."

Hardly. The sun had yet to rise.

They stepped into the alley and headed toward Andriake, the air weighted with heat and water even this early in the day. They stuck to the river path, avoiding the main road, lined with centuries-old sarcophagi, resembling tiny stone houses with domed roofs. That reminded her . . .

"Do you think we can return home soon?"

Theseus shrugged and fidgeted. "It's been nice being so close to the others, hasn't it?"

"Being close to Nydia, you mean," she elbowed him, and he arched away. "When are you going to marry her?"

He gave a frustrated sigh. "I'd marry her now if I could. But where would we live? The safe room of the sponge shop isn't a home. There isn't room for all of us at the school—not with Nikolas living there. And I can't exactly ask Titus to let me wed his daughter and whisk her off to live in a dump. Literally." He muttered and ran a hand through his curls, every bit as unruly as hers. "She has no dowry either—not that I care, because I don't—it's just . . . I can't provide a home and she can't provide the furnishings. How are we to live?"

"Do you want me to scrounge about the dumping grounds for furnishings and move this wedding along?"

He laughed. "If you think that'll work."

"I'll do my best."

As the noon sun arched overhead, Demi drew in a calming breath tinged with warmth, flowers, and salt as Theseus angled the lateen for the cove where Nikolas waited on shore.

He raised a hand, and she returned the wave, wind tugging at her damp curls as the boat coasted to beach near him.

His teeth flashed white against the darkness of his short beard. "How was your morning?"

Theseus slung an empty mesh bag over his shoulder and hopped over the side before splashing to the shore. "Demi found some good pieces earlier, and I think we found a good spot to harvest for a few days." He looked at Demi for confirmation and she nodded, gesturing to the coral basket, nearly filled with scarlet branches.

"That's good."

Demi moved to the back of the lateen as Nikolas gripped the prow and pushed off the boat. He scrambled inside, soaked to the waist.

"How many frogs did you have in your class today?"

Nikolas chuckled and settled into the front seat, tipping his face toward the sun. "Twelve, that I confiscated. At this rate, I'm certain the next time we go upriver, we'll hear the frogs croaking in Latin."

She laughed. "I'm not sure I would be able to tell the difference."

"Oh, you'll be able to tell. Latin is so much sharper, more . . . punctuated than our flowing Greek."

She beckoned with a sweep of her fingers. "I'll need an example."

He rubbed his neck. "*Ut incepit fidelis sic permanet.*"

"What does it mean?"

"Loyal she began, loyal she remains."

Something cold and accusing crept up the center of Demi's chest, stealing her breath. Nikolas was right, Latin was sharper, slicing her heart into bloody ribbons as easily as a gladius. Her hand shook as she adjusted their course, squinting against the sun's glare on the water and checking several points on the shore against her memory of the location of Nikolas's boat. "I think this is right. Toss out the anchor."

She lowered the sail as Nikolas heaved the stone anchor over the side with a splash.

"You said you swam before you could walk. Is that true?" He turned toward her.

Demi shrugged, grateful for a change of subject. "I don't ever recall learning how to swim. Only swimming." She tucked a stray curl behind her ear and looked away. "I grew up in this boat. We were with Pater nearly every day, learning to dive too. Foraging mussels and urchins and playing about the rocks in the sunshine—just over there." She pointed to a familiar rocky outcropping, heart aching at the memories. The knowledge that memories were all they would ever be. "The sea and boat are more my home than anywhere else."

Nikolas pulled up the slack in the anchor rope and tied it off. "That must be nice, after all that has happened, to still have a place that feels like home." Pain and longing clung to his voice like barnacles to a boat. "I've never quite fit anywhere. Not even with my own family." He drew a quick breath as if he hadn't meant to reveal so much and glanced at Demi. "What I mean is, you're blessed to have a place where you know you belong."

She kept her eyes on the sea, quiet for a moment. "Sometimes, yes. But now the boat is empty of everyone that made it a home." The last words emerged in a rough whisper.

"You still have Theseus."

"About Theseus." She glanced at him quickly, trying to erase all traces of emotion from her voice. "I think I have you to thank for his change of heart."

His eyebrows flickered. "Oh?"

"You're allowing him and Nydia to marry. It's very kind and . . . he's more determined than ever to press on and find something he can do. You've given him hope."

"I'm glad to hear it. But it's hardly my doing. I'm not allowing anything God hasn't already allowed and encouraged. It's His plan for men and women to marry, bear children. Unless a person feels God has called them to a life alone, I don't believe it's right to refuse that."

Demi shook her head. "It's so odd to hear that after so many years of Pastor Tomoso urging purity and piety."

"Piety and purity are not incongruous with marriage."

She blinked at him. How different her life might have been if Pastor Tomoso had believed that. Might she and Alexander have wed? Had children? Would he have been more careful? Somehow, she couldn't imagine it.

He must have noticed her troubled expression. "Have I said something to pain you?"

Demi shook her head. "Do you ever wonder how things end up the way they do? What decision it was that brought a future tragedy—or how close a moment of joy had come to utter disaster?"

"Every day." Nikolas's jaw worked and he turned to face the shore where Demi's family had spent many peaceful afternoons. "I'm glad the memories you have of your family are happy ones. I know I had happy times with my family, but the things I recall most vividly are their deaths. And I wonder . . ."

Oh, but she remembered those too. She wished she could slam her mind shut as easily as her eyes, locking out the images, the screams and shouts that echoed. She swiped her cheek on her shoulder before Nikolas saw the tear. Too late.

"Demi—"

"I know it's not right to cry about it." She swallowed back the rising lump in her throat and checked her dive bag. Iron hammer. Two knives. Should she grab another? A shiver started up the base of her spine as the moray's dark head came to mind. Too bad she didn't have a spear.

"Cry about what?"

"That my family is gone."

"Who says it's wrong?"

"Pastor Tomoso said we must not mourn. Only rejoice because they are not dead, but alive with God—and I *am* glad. But sometimes . . . I miss them so much I can't breathe." She gripped her elbows, twisting away so he wouldn't see the tears burning her eyes. Pride and grief braided themselves around the memories of her family, making it impossible to tell where one ended and the other began. She scrubbed her eyes with her fingers.

Nikolas moved closer but stopped shy of touching her. His voice lowered with compassion and understanding. "Even Jesus wept when Lazarus died. He knows what it's like to lose someone you love. He wept even though He knew in a few moments Lazarus would live again. It isn't sinful to mourn, Demitria, or Jesus would have never done it. He shows us it's all right to mourn. It is human."

Her voice dropped to a ragged whisper, but still she refused to look at him. "Do you ever feel like you cheated death? Like you shouldn't be here?"

Nikolas didn't answer for the space of a breath. Two. "Yes," he whispered. "I do."

She dared to turn around, surprised to see her own guilt and vulnerability mirrored in his eyes.

He drew in a breath that seemed to steady him. "But we have to remember that it was not a mistake or accident that we remain. The Lord has prepared work for each of us and while we have breath, we have purpose."

TWENTY-THREE

BREATH. PURPOSE. Nikolas sank to the bench, waiting for Demi to surface again. His own words might be easier to believe if he hadn't failed at everything he tried. School, his pater's business, living with the monks . . . even his students hadn't learned the simple Latin poem he'd been struggling to teach them for weeks. But that wasn't the real reason he struggled to believe it. His own pater had struggled to believe it.

It should not have been Amadeo who died. Though he'd not spoken the exact words, the accusation in his tone and eyes said enough. *It should have been you.* The memory cut the breath from his lungs as effectively as if he'd plunged into the sea after Demitria.

"It wasn't my fault." He whispered the words now as he'd whispered them then. Only ever whispered. As if he couldn't quite believe it either. It didn't matter if he wished a thousand times over that it had been his own body crushed that day. It hadn't been. And he had to live with the fact that his brother had needed him, had asked him to help, and Nikolas had been so tired of being overlooked and ignored, that he'd refused. See how Amadeo liked being cast aside for once, second best. He might not have been Cain, deliberately crushing his brother's skull with a club, but he'd turned his back in anger, envy, and Amadeo had been crushed anyway.

Nikolas forced himself to breathe. The air, heavy with moisture and salt, pulled him back to the boat. He paced from one end to the other, rolling his shoulders to loosen the tension binding them. He didn't mind the boat. The extra time spent with Demitria. The sun on his skin, and glittering on the water. It was the cursed idleness that made his mind run with thoughts and memories that were going to drive him mad. It didn't help that Demitria seemed to be as plagued by the past as he was.

Swiping away a bead of sweat trickling along his hairline, he squinted, searching the water for her dark head popping up between the waves. What if something happened down there? What if the loop in the twine tightened and she couldn't slip her foot free of the diving stone? What if the moray attacked and the two knives she'd taken with her weren't enough? What if she was in trouble right now and he couldn't do anything?

"Our Father in heaven, hallowed be Your name . . ." How many times had he recited it? He turned and paced the boat from prow to stern.

"Your kingdom come . . ."

What if she never came up?

"Your will be done on earth as it is in heaven."

What if she died trying to find his stupid—

"Nikolas."

He spun at the sound of her voice, flinging his hand out for support against the bare mast as the boat rocked beneath him.

"Careful." A grin played at her full mouth. "Don't sink my boat."

"I can't do this."

Demitria swam closer, dark curls slicked back off her forehead and swirling about her shoulders. Diamond drops clung to her lashes, making her look every bit a sea nymph.

"Can't do what?" She pulled herself up on the edge of the boat and flailed an arm toward the waterskin.

"This." He flung a hand in a vague gesture around the boat, then bent to hand her the waterskin. "Wait around. Do nothing. What if something happens to you down there?"

"I've got two knives still." She tilted the waterskin to her mouth.

"Even so. I hate standing about while—"

"—other people work. I remember." Demitria swiped the back of her hand across her lips and dropped the waterskin. She splashed back into the brine, water closing over her head just for a moment. She popped

148

back up, working a branch of coral out of her bag and flinging it into the boat.

"I've got a few oysters too, but only Mersad can open them for pearls." She tossed those in next. "You can put them in that mesh bag and hang it over the side to keep them fresh. Just make sure the bag is tied to the lateen." One more oyster clattered at his feet. "Haven't found your boat again yet."

"Can I help? I can't dive as deep, nor hold my breath as long as you, but surely two sets of eyes are better than one."

Water lapped at her chin. "I can't force you to stay in the boat. But I will need you in here to draw up the bags once we find them again."

"Agreed."

She ducked under and didn't reappear.

He hesitated, then simply shucked off his leather belt and sandals and hovered on the edge of the boat in his tunic. *Lord, bless our efforts.*

Water crashed in his ears as he dropped over the side of the boat, bubbles rushing past his body like they had the day the sea had swallowed his boat. As the roar faded to a burbling hum, he cracked his eyes open. The saltwater stung. How did Demitria do it? He squinted and curled downward, stroking toward the bottom where green-tinged sand rippled in the currents, studded with dark rocky patches. Fish darted in front of him, disappearing between stands of pink coral and into cracks in the rocks. Pressure built in his lungs before he made it halfway down to a coral-covered ridge where Demitria hovered as she wiggled an oyster free and tucked it into the bag floating by her side. She shook her head at him, her curls spreading and waving around her head like the branches of an oak.

The pressure in his lungs grew urgent and he arched upward, his body pushed toward the surface as if the sea was rejecting him. At the surface, he rolled to float on his back, gulping deep breaths. His nose burned. This was harder than it looked. Another deep breath. He lowered beneath the water, pushing downward into the cloudy turquoise. A dark shape darted past in a spurt of bubbles that tickled against his neck. He caught sight of a sharp fin. But from the rear he couldn't tell—shark or dolphin? It ignored him, a good indication he didn't need to make for the boat. Yet.

He couldn't get low enough to see anything distinctive on the bottom before he ran out of breath again. Nikolas arced back to the surface and rolled to his back once more, chest heaving.

"Having a nice rest?"

Nikolas jerked upright, arms and legs flailing.

Demitria laughed, spitting brine between her lips as she appeared beside him, treading water.

"I'm exhausted." He tilted his chin up, mirroring her motions. "I don't know how you do this all day."

"Practice."

"I couldn't get low enough to see anything."

"You have to release your breath as you descend." She turned toward the boat. "But it's all right. I found it."

His movements faltered, water rushing to his ears, in his mouth. Nikolas choked, spat, and kicked after her. "You found it?"

She scrambled up the ladder and he followed, streaming water.

"What now?" He tugged his tunic away from his body, angling to keep her out of his line of sight. She might not realize the way her tunic clung to the contours of her body but he—he needed something to do. Occupy the hands and the mind.

Demi leaned over the side, squeezing water from her hair. "We move the boat over there." She gestured with a vague jerk of her chin. "I dive with the anchor rope, tie it to the bags, and you pull it up."

She made it sound so easy.

Nikolas set to work hauling in the anchor while Demi raised the sail and set the boat in motion. He enjoyed working with her more than he'd anticipated. As he rolled the anchor into the boat, Demi was already untying the other end from the mast and fastening one of the diving stones to it. She reached over and tugged another line, dropping the sail.

"Leave the anchor in here. I'll dive with this stone and the rope and when you feel two sharp tugs, start pulling up the rope. I'll follow the bag up."

"Could we just put the bags into the coral basket and haul more up at once?"

She shook her head. "I can't lift the bags into the basket, and the basket isn't strong enough for that kind of weight."

She checked her mesh bag and left her hammer behind but kept the two knives. Her eyes made a quick scan of the boat. "Everything's in order then." She picked up the dive stone, her confident movements betrayed by the tightness in her smile that did not quite mask the uncertainty in her eyes. "Be up soon."

"Be careful."

She nodded.

"I'm serious. I want the good we could do with that gold, but if it comes with a risk to you, it's not worth it."

"Everything we do is a risk, Pastor." She hugged the diving stone to her chest, anchor rope trailing from it.

"Demi—"

She took a step backward and disappeared into a ring of white foam.

TWENTY-FOUR

BUBBLES SLIPPED FROM HER LIPS as Demi tied the rough rope around the mouth of the dark leather bag. She glanced over her shoulder. No sign of the moray, but the water was cloudy today, obscuring a clear view of the reef around her. Fins whispered against her legs, sending a shudder through her. They'd never bothered her before.

Please keep Your eels in their tunnels.

She finished the knot and gave two sharp tugs on the line snaking upward and fading into the nothingness of blue. The line went taut, then the bag slowly started to lift, upsetting a puff of pale sand as it rose. A handful of bronze coins on payday had seemed like a fortune to her. What would it be like to own bags full of gold and silver? Demi tilted upright and slowly followed the bag to the surface. Would the knot hold? If it didn't, would the bag break open when it hit the seafloor?

She spat water when her head emerged into the bright sunshine and blinked Nikolas into focus. He stood in the boat, one foot braced on the side as he pulled hand over hand on the rope. He smiled when he saw her.

"It worked?"

"See for yourself."

With a final heave, the bag emerged from the sea and landed in the boat with a *thump*. Nikolas stared at it, hands braced on his knees. "I still can't believe we found it, that you could retrieve it." His eyes lit with a wild excitement as they met hers. "Can you imagine what we can do with this? Rent, grain, medicine . . ."

We? Demi angled for the boat. "You're a wonder-worker, Nikolas."

He shook his head. "That title belongs to you. I sank the boat, if you recall."

Demi hooked her arms over the edge of the boat and turned a smile on him. "Oh, I do."

His lips twitched. "Of course you do."

"But I meant that we've never had boatloads of money before you arrived."

"If there's anything wondrous about any of this, it's that God cares for His people. In spite of our faults."

Nikolas handed her a waterskin and two dates before untying the sack of coins and retying another diving stone to the end of the rope.

She pressed at her ears, hollow sounds remaining, but no pain. Exhaustion rolled over her. Diving to that depth took a toll. "I can get one more today, but perhaps if we had more ropes next time, I could secure two or three at once and we could be finished."

He studied her. "Only go again if you truly think you can. I'm in no hurry. The money isn't going anywhere."

Demi nodded. If anything, she needed to get this job done so she could focus solely on coral once more. Her hauls had fallen sharply. "I can do one more."

As the second bag neared the boat, Demi swam past it and surfaced first. "Nearly there," she gasped, swiping water from her eyes.

Bare feet braced on the edge of the boat, Nikolas leaned down and hauled in the rope, straightening and leaning back for the most leverage. Demi stroked toward the ladder, fingers just brushing the rung as Nikolas tumbled backward. His bare feet flew into the air along with the rope, which flailed against the sky like a writhing snake before flopping into the boat.

Demi hauled herself up on the edge of the rocking boat and peered down at Nikolas sprawled across the bottom. "Are you all right?"

Nikolas rolled to his side and rubbed his elbow. "The rope must have broken," he muttered. "But I don't recall seeing any worn spots." He shoved his feet beneath him, simultaneously coiling the rope between his hands. The end emerged, a limp sack still tied to it, dripping water.

"The bag broke." He pinched the bridge of his nose and heaved a sigh of realization. "I should have warned you there was one weak one."

"I—I can try to gather up what I can find tomorrow."

He shook his head, his bottom lip rolling into his mouth. "You're already doing so much. I won't ask that of you."

"You didn't ask. I volunteered. I'm going back down there anyway." She scrabbled against the side of the boat, foot failing to find the ladder. Her limbs shook, grip weak.

Nikolas stooped and tucked his hands beneath her arms and lifted her into the boat. Her legs wobbled and she collapsed to the bench, panting.

"Are you all right?" He knelt in front of her, concern and guilt etched in his expression. "I knew I shouldn't have let you go down a second time."

Demi shoved the hair out of her eyes with a shaking hand. "Don't get your tunic in a bunch. I'm not weak-kneed and breathless because of you." She reached for her chiton.

He grabbed it first and handed it to her. "Well, that's not what a man wants to hear."

She snatched the garment, then froze. She couldn't have heard him correctly. "What?"

Nikolas shoved to his feet and turned away, one hand wrapping around the back of his neck that looked awfully sunburned at the moment. "Nothing."

She wrestled her head into the garment and let it puddle around her.

He hoisted the sail. "I'm sorry, this whole thing is wrong. No amount of money is worth—"

"Nikolas." His name emerged sharper than she'd intended it to, but it had the desired effect of shutting his mouth. "I'm not a vase of glass. Diving is . . . the only thing I can do. I love it. I'm good at it." She waved a hand toward him. "So, whatever you're feeling guilty about, stop. I know my limits, and when I reach them, I'll let you know."

He met her gaze, a solemn and chastised look in his eyes. "Forgive me. I didn't mean to . . . belittle your skills." He looked at his hands, hesitating. "You're like no woman I've ever met."

Was that a compliment, or . . . She allowed a tiny nod and climbed to the bench near the rudder. "We'll pick you up in the cove tomorrow afternoon as usual then?"

TWENTY-FIVE

NIKOLAS GASPED AS HIS HEAD BROKE the surface and knocked against the side of the boat. He flailed an arm, gripped the edge, and hauled himself up to hook his elbows over the side as he'd watched Demitria do a dozen times. She mirrored the pose opposite him. Sans the struggling and choking.

She grinned. "I wasn't certain you'd make it."

He flicked his hair out of his eyes, panting. "And you find that humorous?"

"You're getting better. You just need to stay calm underwater, stop working so hard."

Easier advised than done.

After stashing the majority of the coins in the rocky cove the evening before, Nikolas had purchased several lengths of rope, and they'd drawn up the remaining four bags that following morning. The bag that had broken open left scattered coins along the top of the rocky ridge and down into the hole. Demitria gathered coins in the hole while Nikolas tried to pick them off the shallower ridge above it.

She looked down, fumbling with the bag at her waist. "What did you get?"

At her question, he inspected the mesh bag slung crosswise across his chest. "Three urchins. I didn't find the coin spot before I ran out of breath."

She flung two handfuls of coins into the bottom of the boat.

He raised an eyebrow. "Impressive."

She copied his expression, then flung down a third handful. The coins glittered in the sunlight.

Leaving his elbows hooked over the edge of the boat, he raised his hands in an awkward show of surrender. "My observation remains."

He tossed the sea urchins into the bottom of the boat and readjusted the strap of his bag, ensuring it hung securely. His eyes no longer stung and burned from being open underwater and he shot a grin at Demitria. "What say you? First one to bring up a coin wins?"

"Wins what?"

"Are bragging rights not enough?"

She balanced her stomach over the edge of the boat, leaning toward the middle to grab a stone and loop it around her wrist. "I thought we weren't to brag, Pastor Nikolas. The Scriptures say to let others praise you."

He mimicked her movements and chose his own diving stone, flashing a grin toward her. "Very well. The winner shall be praised."

The sharp corner of her mouth dug into her cheek as she smiled. Sweet—and yet, something mischievous danced in her eyes.

"Go." She disappeared.

Nikolas sucked in a breath and ducked under. Demitria's movements were more fish than human as she flicked her long legs through the water, each kick propelling her to the darker water below. Ahead of him by three boats' lengths. She must have taken the biggest stone. But as she'd said, he was getting better. He angled his body the way Demitria had shown him, although, she appeared to be withholding a few tips. He'd ask Theseus later—or maybe not. Theseus might have questions Nikolas wasn't sure he was ready to answer.

Murky blueness shifted into focus with rocks and rippling coral and the deep, shadowy hole that had swallowed his boat.

Demitria had already shed the diving stone and kicked over the rocky outcropping, her movements graceful and fluid as if she was part of this underwater world. She raked her fingers through the sand, searching for the stragglers that remained. He wrestled his wrist free of the stone before it hit the bottom and stroked toward her. A glimmer in the sand caught his eye. Demitria's too. His movements quickened.

They collided above the coin, shoulders ramming, hands digging into the sand. Grit clouded the water, tickling his arms, burning his eyes. She pushed him. He elbowed her back.

Demitria grinned, bubbles escaping her mouth with a garbled laugh. Shafts of shifting sunlight danced over her face and skin, her hair waving in the water like an anemone. Her eyes crinkled at the edges as she shoved at his shoulder.

He twisted, gripping both of her hands in his. The playfulness drained from him, leaving an awareness in its wake. He didn't want to let her go.

Demitria stilled and stared back at him, the coin long buried beneath the churned sand and, in that moment, forgotten. Their gazes held, as if seeing each other for the first time—and maybe he was. This woman was wildly brave and self-sacrificing. Beautiful and kind, compassionate. And he—he needed air.

The black slashes of her eyebrows crashed together. She yanked her hands, still captured in his, and lifted her chin toward the surface with an anxious nod.

Of course. He let her go and kicked upward, expecting her to do the same. When he broke through at the top, he scanned the turquoise sea around him. No Demitria.

"Demitria?" He swam around the boat. "Demi!"

No answer. His heart thrummed. Why hadn't she surfaced? Why hadn't he waited for her? Guilt flooded in a tidal wave. If anything happened to her . . .

He filled his lungs and curled downward, anxiety taking hold. *Lord, let her be all right.* All he could see in his mind were her wide eyes as she motioned upward. Why hadn't he let go of her sooner? *Stupid Niko.* Please let that not be his last memory of her.

The pressure of the water grew greater on his chest as he swam deeper.

Please.

A dark shape moved through the murky blue, slowly clarifying as it rose to meet him.

Thank God.

Demitria's sharp chin pointed upward, hands drifting at her sides as her long legs fluttered, propelling her toward the glittering ceiling of the water. Her dark eyes darted toward him, alarm melting into a smirk. She patted the bulging bag at her waist.

The little . . .

Nikolas somersaulted and kicked after her, irritation and amusement warring in his chest. To think, he'd been worried for her.

He popped up on the opposite side of the boat and hooked his arms on the edge, breathing hard. "I can't . . . believe you cheated."

She quirked a brow. "You started it."

He narrowed his gaze. "Me? You tricked me. I thought you were in trouble."

"I play to win." She grinned and flipped a gold coin toward him. It clattered into the bottom of the boat. "Speaking of winning, that doesn't sound like praise at all."

He stared at her. "You are an excellent cheater."

She tossed her head, droplets scattering from her drooping curls. "You clearly need practice. Try saying things like, *Demi, you're amazing. You're the best diver in Lycia*—or *the world.*" She smiled sweetly and blinked, resting her chin on one hand. "I'm fine with either title. Go ahead. I'm ready."

He studied her, a slow smile tugging at his lips, even as his heart started to thrum.

"Demitria, you're incredible." His voice emerged lower, huskier than he'd intended it to. Probably the salt water. But possibly, probably, *definitely* because he meant it.

Demitria knew it too because the moment he spoke, her face lost its playful smirk. The mirth left her eyes in a series of rapid blinks and was replaced with . . . shock? Fear? Panic? He wasn't sure what it was. Only that whatever she felt upon hearing those words was not what he'd felt speaking them.

She took a deep breath and disappeared.

The sinking stone of embarrassment and failure settled in his gut. Nikolas thumped his forehead against the side of the boat. What had he just done?

TWENTY-SIX

SHE'D OVERREACTED.

He was teasing. Of course he was. They'd *both* been teasing. Hadn't they? She might have sent a quip right back at him but for the honesty in his expression. She tried to tell herself it was only the way the sun hit the mottled green and brown of his eyes that made them seem so warm and sincere. That skipping lunch was the reason her stomach had flipped at his words. That diving all day was what made her limbs go weak. That her mouth had dried because of the brine, not because she was nervous . . . or thrilled.

Stupid. Stupid.

And now she was underwater waiting for . . . what exactly? A large fish to swallow her and carry her off to some other city? It wasn't a terrible prospect, but one glance around told her it wasn't going to happen. Just her luck. She'd have to come up in a few minutes and then what would she do? What if he tried to awkwardly explain that he'd only been teasing? A strange sense of disappointment clutched her stomach at the thought.

Act like nothing happened and maybe he will forget. Nydia's advice rang in her ears. Good advice, but was a quick duck underwater long enough to reasonably feign forgetfulness? And how unfair that he might forget, but she'd be left lying awake at night cringing over it for years. She turned toward the shadow of the boat in time to see Nikolas thrash his legs and haul himself inside. She ought to follow. Ought to—what, exactly? What was going on between them? They were simply partners. He'd lost his fortune and she'd been the only one able to recover it.

He was the pastor, and she . . . a coward.

He was everything she tried to avoid.

Reckless, dangerous—wonderful. Pure foolishness. Heartbreak waiting to happen.

It was a good thing they were all done recovering his money.

Air bubbled between her lips. She squeezed her eyes shut, letting the water carry her slowly upward, and then rolling to her back as the warm air washed over her face.

"There you are. I wondered where you'd gone."

Demi swiped water from her eyes. Nikolas stood in the boat, arms crossed, riding the rocking of the waves as if he'd been born in the boat same as her. The wind toyed with the waves of his hair, and she'd never noticed before, but Yia-yia Beatrix was right about his looks.

Pretend nothing happened.

"I . . . needed a moment to bask in my incredibleness."

His laugh clapped from his chest, erasing any of the awkwardness that might have lingered between them. There was no escaping the flicker of surprise. Nydia's advice had worked after all. She splashed to her stomach and stroked toward the boat. Nikolas flipped the rope ladder over the side and reached for her hand. He pulled her into the boat with an easy smile that sent warmth curling through her middle. Not unwelcome. Not exactly comfortable either.

"Thank you."

He turned his back as she stepped away to wring out her hair and pin her dry chiton over one shoulder.

"I wondered if . . ." He took a breath and held it a moment, jaw working as if in debate. When he looked at her his gaze was both hesitant and hopeful. "I spoke with Theseus about it earlier, but . . . what are you doing tonight?"

Demi shook her head as Nikolas pointed out a third-story balcony barely visible in the moonlight. Insects sang in the clumps of weeds edging the abandoned street, and the flagstones and whitewashed brick glowed a pale silvery-blue. The railing above their heads sagged, missing several upright supports that had either rotted or been used as firewood. Beyond the railing, the door leading into the apartment hung on crooked hinges, leaving a black gap near the top.

"There's no way you can reach that," she whispered, glancing over her shoulder to where Theseus had disappeared into a side street and had yet to emerge.

The apartment above belonged to an unchurched widow, wholly abandoned by her family. On the way, Nikolas told her and Theseus how he'd met the old woman on several occasions. She had no one and nothing. Rumor had it that this would be her last night in her apartment since she had no way of paying the rent.

Coins clinked as Nikolas tossed a small leather pouch into the air and caught it again. "I've failed at many things, but I've always had a good aim."

Demi squinted. The gap was tiny, barely visible in the dark. "That good?"

She could hardly believe Theseus had agreed to this, wandering the city at night, darting from street to street—armed with small bags of coins, no less. The perfect target for any street ruffians. Not that they'd seen any—yet. She glanced over her shoulder again. Why had Theseus ordered her to remain behind? And what was it about Nikolas that made her willing to break at least three rules just to slip out her door? And Theseus too. They were children of the day, as the Scripture said; how ironic that they must meet and work in the dark. Her heart began an anxious thrum.

"What are you going to do if you miss? Knock on her door and tell her to check her balcony? What if it lands on another balcony? Why not simply take it to the landlord for her."

"I told you. No one can know."

He had already told her what had happened in Patara. When word got out that he'd been giving money away to those in need, it wasn't long before he couldn't go anywhere without being accosted on all sides. Everyone had a sad tale, and it grew more and more difficult to discern who was truly in need and who only wanted a handout. He'd left Patara shortly after, disappearing into his uncle's monastery, only going out at night to help in secret.

She gave her head a little shake. "If you miss that crack in her door, no one will *ever* know. Including her."

Silvery light caught in his eyes as they met hers with a smile that stole her breath.

"Uncanny aim." He repeated, squinting upward, as if calculating.

"Where was this uncanny aim on the river when you nearly scraped every flake of paint from my boat?"

"You're not going to let me forget about that, are you?"

"It amuses me."

"I'm not certain you know what amusement is." He cocked his head, eyes shifting toward her. "If I make it, you'll sing my praises?"

"Far be it from me to withhold praise when it is due."

He chuckled, drew back his arm, and tossed the coin bag in a perfect arc toward the crack in the door.

Demi rolled to her tiptoes and held her breath.

The little bundle sailed through the air, a black spot against the starlit sky. She heard a muffled thump. Then a startled cry from within the apartment.

Nikolas grabbed her hand. "Quick."

He pulled her down the street, breaking into a run that was faster and smoother than he'd ever swum. Her pulse bolted after him, her shoulder slamming against his as she struggled to keep up. If she was at home in the water, this was his element, racing down darkened streets. It was not a comforting thought. No wonder he'd been mugged.

They swung around a corner and stopped, backs pressed against the side of a moon-washed shop, gasping for breath. She slumped beside him, the thunder of her pulse slowing only slightly when she realized no footsteps pursued them. Not yet. Was it just the chill in the air that made her knees shake? She tilted her chin toward the sky. Nikolas's thumb twitched against her knuckles, fingers still twined around hers like the cord around a diving stone, and she . . . she was going to drown.

She tugged her hand free of his, pressing it flat against the building behind her. A surge of embarrassment rolled over her like an incoming wave, cold reality dousing the feelings that had nearly taken root.

Twice, Nikolas inhaled as if to speak, and twice he said nothing. They stood like that for an eternity. Side-by-side and silent. Or maybe it had only been a few seconds.

Nikolas let out a breath, head turning toward her with a smile that was somehow sheepish and mischievous at once. "Well?" He raised a brow. "I'm waiting for you to sing my praises."

Awkwardness dissipated; she huffed a laugh and bit her lip. "Nikolas, you are—" What was she doing?

The breeze toyed with the hair at his brow, carrying with it a wisp of temple incense that soured her stomach. She couldn't deny that there was something attractive and free about Nikolas. But this thing she could easily feel for him—it had to stop. His position in the church netted him in a place he would not escape from alive. He was her pastor, and she would do well to remember that and keep her distance.

Soft footsteps around the corner drew their attention. "Nikolas? Demi? Where are you?"

Demi let out a breath of relief. Theseus never left his debts unpaid for long and he'd just rescued her. She moved past Nikolas into the street.

"Where have you been?" she whispered, hoping he'd not return the question.

"An errand of my own. Doesn't matter." Theseus looked toward Nikolas. "What now?"

TWENTY-SEVEN

Nikolas wasn't in the mood to argue. He wasn't in the mood for much of anything except for maybe curling up on his mat and sleeping for a day or four. Maybe he was coming down with the spring plague—in the middle of summer. It probably wasn't because the night with Demi and Theseus had ended awkwardly, nor the fact that she'd avoided him for nearly two weeks, nor that the trip upriver last night had been quiet with an odd tension between them. He could still recall with tortured clarity, the feel of her hand in his. That's when it all had gone wrong. Had he overstepped? Or was there something else? . . . Someone else?

"Timothy's a good man."

Nikolas blinked, the statement jolting him from his thoughts and back to the elders crammed around him inside the empty riverside tomb. Beyond the doorway, covered in a thick wool rug, the night cacophony of non-Latin-speaking frogs threatened to drown out the arguments within. The declaration wasn't wrong, exactly, but Timothy's "goodness" had nothing to do with the meeting Nikolas had called. He'd already spoken with Timothy privately. Several times, and with no result. Bringing his concerns before the elders was the next step before they all met with Timothy together.

The elders stared at him, shifting and muttering to one another in tones that said they didn't quite agree with his concern over Timothy's errant beliefs.

"I never said he wasn't a good man, only that—"

"He's been a leader among us for years."

And Nikolas had not. Though it wasn't argued in so many words, the sentiment was clear in the tone.

Nikolas glanced at Titus, who sat against the wall near the door. The older man met his gaze with a nod of encouragement, though he didn't offer to speak or ease the argument. This was a situation Nikolas had to handle on his own. He drew a breath.

"We cannot pick and choose the parts of God that suit us and disregard the others. In doing so, we create a god of our own making. It's heresy, a false religion, and has no place among us. We must stand for the truth or be swayed by every changing feeling." He might have begun pacing if the room wasn't so suffocatingly full. Why did they have to meet in such small spaces? "We aren't suffering, starving, and dying for a belief we've made up. If that were true, we should have picked something less dangerous. God is three in One, or He is not." The beliefs that had swayed Elder Timothy would separate God into three separate beings, each wrestling the other for supremacy.

"You can't mean to remove Timothy from eldership." Elder Matius spoke up from his perch on a salt cask. "He's been among us since childhood. Pastor Tomoso appointed him. You'll upset and shame him in front of everyone. That's not right."

Murmurs of assent answered.

"My goal isn't to shame him, but to lovingly correct his aberrant beliefs, draw him back to truth before he leads a whole group of believers astray. Marcion and his teachings have been denounced for over a hundred years by everyone of note. It is not a new misunderstanding of God, but it is a persistent one."

Lord, help them understand. I'm failing to explain.

It shouldn't have come as a surprise. He'd failed at nearly everything else he'd set his hand to.

The original objection surfaced again. "He's a good man."

"And good men can be wrong just as easily as anyone else. None of us are exempt." Not even him—*especially* not him. Nikolas grimaced and shifted. Was that what had gone wrong with Demi? Perhaps it had all been just a job to her. A task given by her pastor that she couldn't refuse. But his company? His friendship? Easily refused—because she'd been doing a job. That was all it was. There was no reason to feel such a sense of loss.

But he could think on that all night. Probably would. For now—"We've been entrusted with the care of God's people in Myra."

"And we've been doing that." This from Xeno, who crouched near the entrance, looking about as eager to dart through it and escape as Nikolas's students were at the end of Latin class.

Nikolas nodded, glancing again at Titus, who simply gave another encouraging nod. "And we've done well. Food distribution is running smoothly, arrests are down . . . We've done well with their physical well-being, but our greater responsibility is to care for their souls."

The cave fell silent. No more objections. And yet, the silence only made Nikolas's heart sink. *Forgive me for not speaking up sooner.*

"Let us pray." Nikolas lowered his eyes and turned his palms heavenward in his lap, silently begging for the right words, the right way to lead these people who chose him to lead, then didn't want him to. What a human thing. Wasn't he the same way? How often had he longed for his pater's attention, only to shove it away when it finally came?

Lord, forgive me.

As he prayed, heartfelt amens rose about the room. Others joined in prayer, voice echoing voice, the words spoken in low reverence forming invisible cords that tightened around them all, binding them together in unified worship. As it should be.

The meeting ended with the decision to spend a week in prayer and then meet with Elder Timothy. They dispersed in ones and twos, cutting back to the city in differing routes.

Nikolas walked back to the school with Titus, the evening air washing over them, thin and fresh.

"Do not interpret my silence tonight as disapproval." Titus said quietly. "The men needed to see you hold your own as their leader. And you did well."

The praise sent a sudden surge of heat to his eyes, and Nikolas was glad for the gathering darkness. When was the last time he'd heard *well done*? Had those words ever come from his uncle's mouth? His pater's? For Amadeo, certainly, but never once directed toward him or anything he'd done. It shouldn't matter so much. And yet, he felt the words binding up something broken and dragging inside of him.

The feeling lasted into the city, and several steps into the school halls where Titus bade him goodnight. For all the exhaustion he'd felt earlier, Nikolas knew neither his mind nor his body would allow him rest.

He might as well sit with a cup of warmed water and read at the worktable in the kuzina tonight. The firepot was still warm when he entered and poured water into the clay bowl on top.

Now, what to read? The fake wine amphorae were lined up in the back of one of the cupboards. Nikolas nudged aside the family shoes piled in front and tugged the door open. He selected one, not knowing what book lay inside, and pushed the door shut again, pausing to straighten the shoes once more. Nydia's blue slippers were last in line. His fingers paused on the worn toe, an idea lighting.

It wouldn't fix his mistakes. He was in too deep for that.

But it might make him feel better.

TWENTY-EIGHT

20 QUINTILIS, AD 310

Demi tucked a stray curl into the thin scarlet headband crisscrossing around the mass of curls pinned atop her head. She'd taken more care than usual on her appearance and told herself it was because they were celebrating the betrothal of Theseus and Nydia this night. Not because Nikolas would be in attendance. The thought sent an uncomfortable rush of anticipation and dread that swirled in her stomach like oil and water.

Theseus eyed her as they slipped into the alley, as if he suspected the traitorous reasons for her sudden interest in hairstyling. She could hardly understand it herself, only that something had changed in the days since Nydia had come to her gushing about the mysterious gift of coins tucked into her shoes. A pagan might have ascribed the gift to Poseidon, who was believed to come out of the sea in December and leave gifts in the shoes of sailors' families before he disappeared beneath the waves to wreak havoc on ships. But the dowry had been no guilt-gift of Poseidon, though Demi knew it had come from the sea.

"You look nice." Theseus faced forward as he spoke, though there seemed to be a question in his tone.

"It isn't every day my little brother celebrates his betrothal to my dearest friend."

The heat, oppressive even in the shadowy evening, stuck her chiton to her back as they pressed up the street toward the school, where Iris had invited them to dine with the family. She snuck a glance at her brother, standing taller since his appointment as deacon, eager to learn, glad to be put to work. Pater and Mitera would have been overjoyed to see him so.

"You're sure it has nothing to do with Pastor Nikolas?"

"What? No." She snapped the words too fast and feigned interest in a clump of weeds growing against the side of the alley.

"I talked to him."

Her mouth went dry, and she took several steps before she could respond. "Why?"

"I know what he did for us. Gifts like that don't just appear in shoes."

An odd rush of relief loosened the tension in her chest. Of course. What else would they have talked about? "What did he say?"

"He begged me not to speak a word of it."

"And yet . . ." She slanted him a look.

"It isn't as if it's a surprise to you either."

She shook her head and glanced at Theseus. "It was kind of him."

His throat worked. "What sort of person does that?"

"A good one."

The city had fallen quiet over the dinner hours; shops sat dark and closed for the evening. The falling sun cast one last shaft of bronze light toward the cliff at the city's back with the ferocity of a warrior throwing a spear. Light shattered across the rocky hillside, illuminating the carved temple-fronts of the tombs.

Theseus eyed her, a slow smile quirking the side of his mouth. "You look nice," he repeated.

She looked straight ahead. "And you're about to wear a bruised eye to your betrothal dinner, if you don't stop insinuating things."

He laughed fully then. "If you say so."

Her brother was a fool. Or maybe she was, for the way her traitorous mind wandered to Nikolas and the way he'd gripped her hand in the dark. Demi dropped her gaze. Someday she'd awaken to the news that Nikolas was dead. Men who took the risks he did always ended up dead. Imagining it sent a swell of emotion to her throat.

She'd spent days trying to ignore the allure and importance of Nikolas's mission. It tugged at her heart, even as all the rules he was breaking ran through her head in warning. Nikolas had somehow brought hope with him to Myra. Infused it into everything he did. Tomoso had made them all believe there was no future, that Jesus would return any moment and they best huddle in and wait for rescue. Nikolas shared the belief in Christ's imminent return, but instead of waiting in terror, he set to work, sharing food and spreading good news. As much as she struggled to convince herself otherwise, a determined hope had begun to push back at the gnawing dread. She wanted it, wanted to live like Nikolas.

And it terrified her.

After a knock at an alley door, Iris ushered Demi and Theseus into the warm glow of the school's kuzina.

"Come in, come in!" She kissed their cheeks as they stepped inside. "Go on in and sit with the men, Theseus. The food is nearly ready."

He hesitated. "Can I carry anything in for you?"

"So helpful!" Beatrix sighed from where she hunched over a bubbling pot of lentils. "Careful, Nydia, I might fight you for him."

Nydia laughed and whisked a tray off the worktable. "Here. Take the amphora and cups." She settled the tray in Theseus's hands and followed him through the doorway where they paused in the hallway and lowered their voices.

Demi turned to Iris and Beatrix. "How can I help?"

Iris set her to work mixing a salad of purslane and herbed yogurt. "You go upriver soon?"

Demi nodded. "At the next new moon."

"Theseus is looking so much better. Will he accompany you?"

Demi shot a glance toward her brother's back, still visible in the doorway. He balanced Nydia's tray on his good hand, still favoring his injured wrist. "No. He'll be joining the deacons to haul and deliver supplies once they're here. It's a little . . ." She lowered her voice though she doubted Theseus was paying any attention to her with Nydia three inches from his face. "I think simply being in the boat is difficult for him."

"I can understand." Iris gave a sympathetic nod, then brightened. "But Nikolas says Theseus has been a great help to the deacons and is doing wonders in the shantytown near the river. So many people need help."

Demi scraped the edges of the bowl with the spoon. "He's certainly been less miserable to be around, since he's started doing something."

Yia-yia spun around, wooden spoon dripping lentils. "Does this mean Pastor Nikolas will accompany you upriver, then?"

Demi tried to mask the flipping of her stomach with a casual lift of her shoulders. "Perhaps." She lowered her chin and stirred faster.

"How do you get along?"

"Fine."

"*Fine?*" Yia-yia spat the word like a bitter olive. "You'd think it was a sin to fall in love once in a while."

"Mater." Iris took the dripping spoon from Yia-yia's grasp and shot her an exasperated look. "Leave them be."

The old woman snorted. "Titus would have never spoken of his feelings for you had I not encouraged him."

"If you call 'encouragement' throwing a hornet's nest at him, then yes. I have you to thank for my marriage."

"Exactly. That is all I'm trying to say." Yia-yia gave a satisfied smile. "I've got one foot in the grave already, and I'd like to witness a bit of joy before I go. Is that too much to ask?"

Demi pressed a hand to her chest. "If I fall in love with someone, you'll be the first to know."

Yia-yia shook her head. "Everyone always says that, and I never am." She poked a finger toward Demi. "There's nothing wrong with Nikolas, you know."

Except for how he disregarded rules, took risks, and wouldn't be around long enough to marry anyway.

Demi bent and hugged Beatrix, whose wrinkled cheek was soft against her own. "Find me someone safe, Yia-yia, and I might be interested."

She pulled away, face lighting. "What are you looking for? I can help you find it."

Iris pulled the pot of lentils from the stove and caught Demi's eye, shaking her head with a *be careful what you wish for* look.

Demi squinted. "Blue eyes. Like the Mediterranean on a clear day."

Yia-yia nodded, waggling her wispy brows. "Exotic. I'll do my best." She took the bread basket and angled for the dining table.

Iris lifted a meager platter of fish and tipped her chin for Demi to carry the bowl of purslane. "You know how Mater gets. You shouldn't encourage her."

"She'll get her wish for a wedding in, what, ten days?" Demi scooped up the bowl and followed Iris into the dining room where the men reclined around a low table. It had taken some getting used to the Didius Liberare family's Roman custom of men and women eating together at the same table, but Demi rather liked it. She stepped through the doorway to a hum of male voices, punctuated by Rex's higher, tumbling words.

Demi's gaze was drawn to Nikolas first, almost of its own will. Dressed in a faded red tunic and reclining on a green dining cushion, Nikolas smiled at something Rex said, but his eyes were trained on her. Warm, flickering in the lamplight with an expression of . . . welcome? Regret? Hope? A rush went through her, heating her neck and sending her heart into a confusing stammer of thrill and anxiety.

The corner of his mouth twitched in a smile that looked unsure. How could one man be so courageous and timid all at once? The prospect of all he could be terrified her. And yet, he'd restored hope to the two people she loved most, and that wasn't something she could overlook.

Thank you.

His gaze dropped to her mouth as her lips formed the silent words.

Demi made the mistake of catching Theseus's eye as he looked from Nikolas to her. One dark brow slid toward his hairline. Wonderful. That would make for an exceedingly irritating conversation later. She lowered her gaze and the bowl of creamy purslane to the table, then settled between Yia-yia and Nydia. As Titus prayed over the meal and the upcoming marriage, Demi steeled her resolve. No matter what, she would not look in Nikolas's direction again.

TWENTY-NINE

A BAG OF COINS HEAVY AGAINST HIS THIGH, Nikolas kept his head down as he wove through the agora, trying to convince himself he wasn't being stupid. That it wasn't illegal to walk through a market without libelli—only to purchase something without it. Never mind that was why he was in the market to begin with. He flicked his gaze back and forth over the merchants crowded in the rectangular court. To his left, a man showed caned chairs to a squinting couple. Farther up, tables covered in a mountain range of colorful shoes teetered beneath an orange awning. Chickens squawked in wicker cages and the hum and haggle of the crowd droned in his ears, nearly as confusing as the roar of the sea when he dove with Demitria. Though he could hardly blame the sea for the confusion tumbling through him today.

He'd fallen in over his head.

And Demi had responded by avoiding him with the same fishlike deftness she employed while diving. Perhaps memories or lingering affection for Alexander held her back. Demi wanted safety, security, and she wouldn't find it with a man risking his life at every turn.

As long as he avoided arrest, he might win her with time and patience. He glanced over his shoulder now and saw nothing but the chaos of the agora. Already the port village and city were readying for the revelry and rest that marked the small, three-day festival of Artemis that reoccurred from the sixth to the ninth of each month. The August celebration would be upon them in six days and the market was crammed with last-minute shoppers. Definitely not the best day to go looking for a wedding gift, but fewer merchants bothered to ask for libelli in such a rush.

Women with market baskets hanging from their elbows and children in tow moved to and from various stalls, expressions varying from pleasant to frazzled depending on the level of protest from the children. Someone bumped into him, knocking him into the path of a basket seller laden with stacks of crackling wicker. He dodged again, jarred fully into the present. Into his mission. Find a gift. Find a frazzled merchant. Preferably at the same stall.

Under a drooping brown awning, pungent spices piled in colorful triangular pyramids fragranced the air with cinnamon, cumin, and turmeric. Nikolas paused and inhaled. Perhaps spices would make a good gift? He glanced at the woman planted behind the table with a dour expression, as if she dared anyone to attempt a purchase. No wonder the mountains of spices had yet to reduce to mere hills. He moved on.

Vegetable and herb sellers crowded the edges of the market, bunching beneath the shade of the covered colonnade where their wares would not wither so quickly. Butchers, cheesemongers, candlemakers, and cosmetic sellers also spread in the shade, fanning their goods to ward off swarms of black flies. Nikolas moved to the vast courtyard in the center where colorful awnings sagged over tables of imported cloth, woven rugs, casks of vinegar, and barrels of brined olives. Belts, bowls, shoes, chickens, jewelry, spoons . . . nothing was quite right.

A table filled with lamps caught his attention and he swerved beneath the red-and-yellow-striped awning. Lamps of every shape and size spread before him, some made of metal and others of clay. A lamp in the shape of a mermaid caught his eye, glazed in brilliant turquoise. He couldn't help but think of Demi, slipping through the water as if she too were part fish. She'd turned a smile on him the other night—his pulse thrummed anew at the memory of it—but just as a spark relit the hope that they might still be friends, she'd refused to look at him again. How could this woman wield such power over him, to be able to raise and lower his hopes as easily as she did the sail on her boat?

He picked up a bronze lamp engraved with vines of budding flowers. Light and new life entwined in one piece. The perfect symbol of marriage. He raised it, catching the seller's eye. "I'll take this one."

"Libelli?"

His pulse jolted.

The sun glinted on the silver chain around the merchant's neck where his libelli hung as a proud signal to all. Why hadn't he been paying attention?

Stupid, Niko.

Nikolas set the lamp back on the table and patted his chest as if his libelli hung from his neck like it did on so many others. If he searched long enough, perhaps the seller would simply grow impatient and take his money.

"Sorry, I . . ." Nikolas drew out his money pouch, combing his fingers through the coins.

The seller waited. Didn't offer to negotiate at a higher price for the absence of libelli.

Sweat dampened Nikolas's back. How to back out? He cleared his throat. "It . . . doesn't look like I have it."

The merchant blinked.

A man stepped up beside Nikolas with a laugh. He leaned toward the merchant. "Don't mind my brother. He's always forgetting something."

Nikolas's head jerked toward the man. Xeno flashed a wooden tile at the merchant and shook his head at Nikolas with a long-suffering grin. "All set now."

The merchant gave a satisfied nod, then turned to Nikolas and named his price.

Nikolas stood stunned. Where had Xeno gotten a libelli? He took a step back and Xeno's hand snapped to his wrist, clamping him in a vise and staying any stumbling retreat he might have made.

"This is the perfect gift for Mitera's birthday. She'll love it." Xeno met Nikolas's eyes and jerked his chin toward the merchant.

No way to back out now without making a scene. He'd never once purchased anything with a libelli. Stomach turning, Nikolas counted out the coins and took the lamp. Xeno had some explaining to do.

"Thank you." Nikolas forced himself to look the merchant in the eyes and wish him a fine day before turning away. *Do not look guilty.*

Xeno flung an arm around his shoulders in a brotherly gesture and tugged him away. "Come on. We don't have all day."

His steps faltered, but Nikolas allowed the ruse until the crowd cut off the lamp seller's view, then he pulled away.

"What was that?"

Xeno shook his head and lifted his hands. "I saved you. And you got your lamp. It seems like a thank-you is in order."

"Why do you have a libelli?"

"I made one. Gets me out of all kinds of scrapes like that. Amazing what a little wood chip can do, yes?"

They exited the agora, passing through a statue-lined forum, dotted with lawyers and philosophers in various huddles.

Nikolas shook his head and lowered his voice. "The words *Kyrios Caesar* are carved into those tiles. You declare that every time you use it." He set the lamp on the pedestal of a statue as they passed. The gift, tarnished by the means used to purchase it. "God forgive me."

"Don't waste it like that." Xeno snatched up the lamp. "And I do no such thing. I've never said those words in my life."

"You don't have to. Using that tile is statement enough that you trust those words and that tile to save you from trouble. Not God."

Xeno's face flushed. "Easy for you to say when you have a purse full of gold. How'd you get all that money, anyway?"

"Not with libelli."

"There's no need to be judgmental, Nikolas. Some of us didn't get the privilege of hiding away in a monastery. Some of us suffered greatly."

"And you think I haven't?" Nikolas tried and failed to blink back the images rushing his mind. "When the monastery was attacked, I saw my uncle sliced to ribbons before my eyes—and not quickly. Men dismembered, lit on fire, impaled and lined along the road." The street blurred. "I'm not asking you to seek out death, but to consider whether or not the God who did not spare His own Son for your sake, who rose from the dead to give you hope and life, is worthy of serving at any cost."

The only noise Xeno made was the scuffing of his sandals against the pavement.

Nikolas lowered his voice. "If He isn't, then we might as well burn the incense for real and live in peace."

Titus met Nikolas at the door of the school when he returned without Xeno, who'd stalked off.

"You have a visitor."

"Who?" Nikolas's mind ran in seconds. Timothy? Not likely after the elders had decided to remove him from leadership. Perhaps one of the deacons or elders. He wouldn't allow himself to hope it was Demi.

Titus didn't answer as he shut and barred the door. "He's in the office."

He? The image of the stone-faced lamp merchant leaped to mind. Also improbable. But not impossible. "Do you know him?"

"Never seen him in my life."

Nikolas started for Titus's office, then hesitated when Titus headed for the kuzina instead. "Aren't you coming?"

Titus gave a slight shake of his head. "He doesn't want to meet with me. Very adamant. But I'll be around in case he's trouble."

Trouble? Nikolas's hand tightened around the latch and he opened the door. Perhaps he ought to have let the boys teach him how to use the wooden swords that afternoon after all.

A balding man with nervous hands whirled toward him as he stepped inside.

"Nikolas? It *is* you." The man rushed forward, arms wide as if to wrap Nikolas in an embrace, but instead he stopped short, clapped his hands together, and dropped into a bow. "I've been looking everywhere for you, my lord. Thank goodness you're alive. I feared the worst."

Nikolas faltered, recovering from the shock. It *had* been Basil he'd seen while in the agora with Demi those weeks ago. "I know I left Patara without telling you, but I thought it would be for the best."

Basil heaved a sigh and studied him. "I thought for certain you were dead, my lord. You always were as nimble as a cat, and now I see you have as many lives too."

"I'm not your lord, Basil. Nor are you steward of anything. What you have is your own."

"Your pater risked his life to save mine when I was swept off his ship into stormy seas. I owe my life to him and swear to repay his courage."

"Which you have done, time and again, though I've released you from that oath at least a dozen times." Nikolas sighed, the argument old and valiantly fought on both sides.

Basil's jaw twitched. "Forgive me, my lord, but my vow was to your pater. And I will keep it. You may have given me control of your pater's fleet to keep it from being confiscated after the edicts, but believe me when I say everything I've done has been for you. I don't care if you take an interest in shipping or not; I'm here to help you. I've always been here to help, if you'll just let me. You can trust me."

Nikolas hesitated. Even though Basil had staunchly refused the Christian faith, he also refused to believe that killing Christians was the way to solve the problems in the empire. It wasn't that he didn't trust Basil, it was just . . . some things were easier done alone, weren't they?

"That wasn't the reason I gave you control of the fleet."

"I know." Basil shot him a good-natured smile. "You also hate business."

That he wouldn't argue. Nikolas sank down on the stool across the desk. "It's good to see you again."

Basil slumped into Titus's chair, resting his elbow on the curved armrest and dropping his chin into his hand. "What were you thinking?"

Nikolas waited. "When?" He'd done a lot of questionable things lately.

"You just . . . moved to a new city without telling me."

"I worried a message might be intercepted. After the monastery— I didn't want you to find yourself in trouble on my account."

"You have a curious way of avoiding trouble. Quite a stunt, taking a boat."

"You know about that?"

"Only with great sleuthing. Did you sink it? Hide it? There's no record of it in the harbor."

"Sank it."

Basil shook his head. "And here I thought you outgrew frivolous wastes of money."

Best not tell him he sank his inheritance too. "I'm glad to see you're well, Basil, but why have you come? How did you find me?"

Basil shifted. "The, erm . . . *investments*—have returned, and I received a curious message from one of my captains. It seems a tutor at the school for laborers' children in Myra saved his son's life and asked for a reward of grain to be sent to the city, under the care of a man named Nikolas. Sounded like something you would do. I told myself it was too good to be true, but I had to know for myself if it was really you."

His stomach dropped. Mind whirled. Investments, captains, grain . . . he'd never been very good at keeping track of all that.

"Well?" Basil hesitated. "I await your instructions."

"For . . ."

"Where to deliver it. I imagine you'd like it secreted away somewhere?"

"You have . . . grain?"

"*You* have grain, my lord. Half a shipload, after the contracts were filled. Where would you like me to deliver it?"

Nikolas faltered, words and meanings failing him. "I'll . . . have to ask."

Basil sat back and clasped his hands in his lap. "There. That wasn't so bad, was it? Making a decision, instead of running away?"

Nikolas fidgeted. "I didn't run."

"Forgive me. You took a boat and sailed away and almost drowned yourself."

"I—I know . . . I'm sorry."

"Did you sink your inheritance too? I noticed the vault was empty after you left."

"I recovered most of it."

Three times Basil took a breath to start a reprimand and three times he snapped his lips shut. Finally he sighed. "You can trust me, you know."

Nikolas shrugged. Nodded.

Basil steepled his fingers in his lap. "So, who's the woman?"

"Who?"

"Yes." Basil waved a hand impatiently. "That's what I asked. My captain mentioned a woman."

Nikolas shifted. "Not the subject of our conversation." He stood and moved toward the door. "I'll find out where to have you send the grain. Where can I reach you?"

Basil stood and smiled. "Fortunately for you, I'm expanding the business to Myra. I've got an office front near the harbor."

He raised an eyebrow. "Stalking me?"

"Someone's got to keep an eye on you."

Nikolas chuckled and swung the door open, gesturing Basil out first. He followed, tugging the office door shut behind him. When he looked up, Xeno stood from where he'd been sitting on one of the benches, shifting the bronze lamp from hand to hand. Titus was nowhere in sight. Xeno didn't speak until Basil had left, then he turned to Nikolas, fidgeting.

"I came to apologize. You're right, you know. I . . ." He tilted his face toward the door Basil had disappeared through. "Sometimes I get tired of it all. The starving, hiding, threats of prison and death—it's exhausting . . . Waiting for God to come through when it seems like He's left us." He sighed and held out the lamp. "I brought you this, and"—he held out the wooden tile in his other hand—"this. To . . . to burn. Get rid of it and start anew."

He didn't want the lamp, but Xeno pressed it at him, insistent.

"No. I know you think there's a stain on this lamp, but what happened today is a good thing. It's given me a new understanding in . . . so many ways." He smiled, but it didn't quite reach his eyes. "Take them, Niko. Please."

Nikolas took the lamp, warm from Xeno's hands, and held it as he balanced the wooden tile on top.

"Thank you, my friend." Xeno covered Nikolas's hands with his own, meeting his gaze with a steely look. "I leave here a changed man."

THIRTY

DEMI'S ARMS ACHED AS SHE WORKED olive oil through her curls, combing her fingers through the tangles and twisting the hair back into its usual coils—sans frizz. She sighed, letting tired limbs droop to her sides. Why couldn't she have sleek, silky hair like other women? Hers frizzed and grew in humidity like a tropical plant. She admired her best chiton instead, the fabric dyed in a mixture of green and blue, rendering it a somewhat mottled shade of turquoise. It matched her sea to perfection. If only her hair could behave.

"You look lovely, Demi." Theseus smiled at her from across the room, tying his best belt around his waist.

She gave up on her hair and wiped the excess oil on a cloth before jumping to her feet. "And you look very handsome. Nydia's going to swoon. But your neck's bleeding."

He rubbed his neck and winced. "My razor wasn't as sharp as I thought."

Demi dabbed at it with the oil-soaked cloth. "There. Better." She stepped back and looked up at him. "Are you nervous?"

"No. Yes. I don't know." He swallowed. "I'm eager to have her as my wife, but there's a measure of relief knowing she's not my responsibility yet. If anything happens to her in my care . . ." He shook his head. "That terrifies me. *Titus* terrifies me."

"Our days are in God's hands alone, Theseus. There isn't a thing we can do to add or subtract from them." Demi spoke the words, knowing they were true, and yet, the question lingered in her own mind. Why was she still here when the rest of their family wasn't? "Pater and Mitera would be so proud of you."

He smiled slightly, then bent to scoop something off his sleeping mat. "Here. I made this for you." He held out his hand, a necklace of polished sea stones draped across his fingers. "Actually, I made it for Nydia, but then I found prettier stones and made her a better one." He winked.

Demi swatted at him and took the necklace, running her fingers over the stones. Red, brown, yellow, orange, green. She looped it over her head and admired the contrast it made against her blue chiton. "It's beautiful. Thank you."

He shifted and gave a nod. "We'd better get going."

"Wait, I have something for you too." Demi darted for the corner and returned, cradling a large pot with a sapling sprouting from it.

"A . . . *tree?*"

"Not just any tree. An orange tree." Demi set the pot at his feet and straightened, her eyes suddenly hot. "I want you and Nydia to be happy. And Mitera always said, you can't be sad while eating an orange."

Theseus's throat worked. He bent to examine the tree. "I wish they were here." His words emerged husky with tears.

"Me too."

He ran a finger over one of the glossy leaves. "There won't be oranges for a few years yet."

Demi sniffed. "Well, I heard the first few years of marriage are hard no matter what."

Theseus barked a laugh and stood.

"Come on." Demi scooped up her mantle and started for the door. "Nydia hates being late, and you don't want to start the night with her upset."

He followed her out and coughed. "About tonight. Nikolas is still going with you?"

She hesitated. "Yes." He would have to. She'd hardly seen him since the betrothal dinner, but it was better that way. They needed the distance. *She* needed the distance.

Theseus gave her a side-eyed once-over and made a noise in his throat.

"What?"

"Nothing."

"Why are you looking at me like that?"

He shrugged. "No reason. The way you look tonight is starting to make sense, is all."

"It's your *wedding*, Theseus." So why was her face getting hot? *Do not turn red.*

They reached the cove as the sun set, spreading a rainbow across the sky and sea. Unlit torches lined the rocky backdrop of the cove, pale cliffs towering on either side. Driftwood planks, washed ashore from shipwrecks, spanned logs and rocks, creating a low feasting table stretching across the sand. Baskets of bread, dates, and figs nestled in the greenery and wild pink roses cascading down the center of the tables, tiny clay lamps flickering in between.

Titus and Iris must have saved their flour and oil rations for a month in preparation. Demi's contribution to the feast had been a huge kettle of mussels that two of the deacons' wives were preparing over a bonfire near the water's edge.

Her breath caught. How lovely, to be married at sunset with the Mediterranean crashing at your ankles. Demi unfolded her mantle, revealing the wedding wreath she'd woven earlier that day. Theseus dipped his head and allowed her to settle the laurels over his dark curls.

She smiled as he straightened. "You look like an Olympic champion."

"I feel like one." He offered a lopsided grin. "Sweaty. My heart's pounding."

Demi chuckled. "Nydia is the best of women. From this night forward, please know I'll take her side in everything."

He shook his head. "So, nothing's changing then?"

"A beautiful evening for a wedding, is it not?"

They turned as Nikolas approached in a sand-colored tunic that made his sunbrowned skin glow deeper. His smile flashed white against his bearded cheeks. He looked well . . . very well. Why was she noticing? She shouldn't be noticing.

Theseus nudged her.

"Hmm?"

"Pastor Nikolas asked you how you were."

Heat climbed her cheeks again. "Distracted by . . . everything." She gestured toward the enchanting scene on the beach. "Doesn't it look so lovely? Like a dream."

"Yes," Nikolas agreed, shifting to take in the sight behind him.

"Demitria! You fixed your hair!" Yia-yia Beatrix hobbled over, hands raised. "Praise the Lord!"

Theseus dared to laugh.

Demi rammed an elbow into his ribs and avoided Nikolas's eye as she embraced the old woman.

Yia-yia drew back, running both hands down the curls on either side of Demi's face, drawing it forward over her shoulders. "How lovely you look, my dear. Don't you agree, Pastor Nikolas?" She turned to him, smile freezing as her fingers tangled in Demi's hair and she tried to discreetly extricate them.

Nikolas shifted and murmured a noncommittal "Mm-hmm." He turned away. "Excuse me."

Demi tugged her hair from Yia-yia's grasp and glanced around the meager gathering of close friends. "Where's Nydia?"

Yia-yia's eyes glowed. "She's the most beautiful thing you've ever seen. Angelic."

"No, no, no. I don't want an angel." Theseus shook his head and held up a hand. "There's a reason the first thing they always say is 'don't be afraid.' Eyes. Everywhere. If Nydia looks angelic, you can take her right back home."

Yia-yia laughed and swatted at him, then drew him into a hug. "You dear boy." She reached up to cradle his face in her bony hands. "There's no better man in the world for our Nydia. We all know it. The Lord's hand be upon you both." She pulled his face down and kissed his cheeks before releasing him with a little push. "Now go on. Claim your bride. I assure you, she's only got two eyes tonight and they're both on you."

Theseus wiped his palms down his thighs as he crossed the beach to where Nydia had appeared between Iris and Titus, draped in a saffron-yellow veil.

Beatrix gripped Demi's hand and dragged her closer.

The crashing surf drowned out the words Titus spoke to Theseus and Nydia, but both of them nodded, and Iris swiped a tear from her cheek and leaned into Titus's side.

As joyous as she was to be gaining a sister—and Nydia, at that—a pang of loneliness struck. Her family was growing again, but also dividing. She'd been the remainder many times before. She should be used to it by now. And yet, heat swelled in her eyes and throat.

Yia-yia's fingers tightened around her own. "You are not forgotten."

The whisper came so faintly, Demi couldn't be sure it was Beatrix who had spoken, naming the tide of swelling emotion rising in her chest. The fear that everyone was moving forward, and she remained stuck fast and left behind. She ran her fingers over the heavy string of stone beads Theseus had given her. The weight a comfort and a reminder that she hadn't been completely forgotten—though just now, Nydia and Theseus might as well have been the only people on the beach.

The couple walked hand in hand toward Nikolas, Nydia's undyed chiton flapping around her ankles and the yellow veil dancing in the breeze. Demi, Beatrix, and the other friends and witnesses gathered close and laid hands on the couple as Nikolas prayed over them. They stayed clustered around them as Nydia and Theseus pledged themselves to each other, to honor, serve, and love each other as Christ loved His own with a sacrificial love.

Demi watched her brother's face, shining with delight, eyes for his bride only. And as Yia-yia had said, Nydia's gaze was fixed on Theseus alone, confirming her declaration that there was no one else for her. Guilt smote her heart, leaving a jagged gash. If marriage was a picture of Christ and His church, Demi had not been a faithful bride. How could God possibly look on her with such delight and love? Tears spilled over her cheeks, but they were not the tears of joy mirrored on the other faces.

Nikolas rested his hands on Theseus's and Nydia's heads. "May you live in God."

Cheers erupted, nearly drowned by the booming surf.

Demi hugged and kissed her brother and new sister, then edged out of the joyous cluster of wedding guests eager to offer congratulations and advice. She headed for the water, the cool breeze lifting curls off her neck.

"Lovely evening."

She turned. Nikolas labored toward her through the deep sand.

"It is." Demi let her gaze move toward the sunset, where purples and blazing orange streaked the sky and left rippling trails in the water.

They admired the horizon in silence, awkwardness blooming between them. Well-wishers began to trickle toward the low table and seat themselves on the sand.

"Thank you," she whispered.

He didn't answer, but his brow furrowed when she dared a glance his way.

"For what?"

"For leaving Nydia money for the dowry." She raised a brow. "A bag of coins in her shoe? You might as well have left a note."

His chin and voice lowered. "You're the only one who would know."

"She's been dreaming about this day since she was twelve. And look how happy she is." Demi glanced over her shoulder as Nydia's laugh pealed above the murmur of voices. When she turned back to Nikolas, he was watching her, a tiny smile flickering at the corner of his mouth.

"I'm glad." He was looking at her like he had in the boat that day. Hazel eyes warm and hopeful. An unwelcome warmth prickled in her stomach. She broke free of his gaze and drew in a breath. The sharpness of rosemary and cedar mingled with something crisp and comforting on the breeze.

"What is that smell?"

He tugged at the neck of his tunic, uncomfortable or amused. "Beatrix wanted me to try a new scent she'd made. She was quite insistent, and I hated to disappoint her. She assured me I'd smell wondrously mysterious and exotic."

Demi nearly choked. "She said *exotic*?"

A half smile. "And *wondrously mysterious*."

She would. Little sneak. Demi shook her head. She'd also told Beatrix to find her someone safe.

"What do you think?"

She squinted. "You don't have blue eyes."

He laughed. "Is that what it takes to be mysterious and exotic?"

"Everyone knows that. What are you even teaching your students?"

"Maybe I'll have to use extra to make up for my mundane eyes."

She gave a decided shake of her head. "I wouldn't do that."

He winced. "Is it that bad?"

Demi tucked an errant curl behind her ear and waited to speak until she spied Beatrix making her way to the table. "According to Nydia, Yia-yia made that scent at least forty years ago and it's taken her this long to pawn it off." She bit back a smile. "If not mysterious and exotic, I think wearing that perfume at least makes you the kindest man in Myra."

He inclined his chin. "I'd rather be kind than mysterious and exotic, wouldn't you?"

Demi sucked in a breath to answer, then snapped her lips shut. What was happening? Of course she was supposed to agree with him. But had Yia-yia told him *everything*? She scrabbled for a rule, a guide to get her out of this dangerous territory that felt alarmingly close to crossing the lines of flirting . . . or possibly blackmail.

Demi cleared her throat and turned toward the tables, her bare feet slipping in the powdery sand. "Well, hopefully the guards don't catch a whiff of you tonight and feel the need to investigate your mysterious . . . kindness."

Running away was always a good option.

He chuckled. "Are we leaving after the wedding?"

She nodded. "It should be late enough by then."

"I'll be waiting."

Something about the way his voice dropped and gentled when he spoke sent her stomach into a confusing tumble.

Nikolas moved toward an empty space on the men's side of the table.

Demi inhaled, forcing her mind to slip into the place where she readied herself to dive.

She wasn't falling for Nikolas. *Relax the body.*

Yia-yia's ancient musty tree scent wasn't remotely enticing. *Steady the heart.*

He didn't have blue eyes. *Clear the mind.*

She released her breath and moved to sit in the last remaining space at the table—in the middle of a passel of boisterous children who sent her sticky, date-filled grins and welcomed her into their debate of which was softer, sand or rocks. They all declared her answer wrong. She glanced down the length of the table and caught sight of Nikolas pounding his chest and laughing at something Yia-yia had said.

It wasn't right, to feel a twinge of envy over an aged woman when she wasn't interested in Nikolas.

THIRTY-ONE

HE'D DONE HIS BEST NOT TO STARE.

If he'd believed in such things, Demitria might have been a sea nymph this night, swathed in a fluttering chiton the color of the Mediterranean, her dark curls smooth, shining, and dancing in the breeze at her bare elbows. Though they were seated at opposite ends of the table, he could still see her out of the corner of his eye.

Her grin flashed at something Rex said.

Nikolas had never been so envious of an eight-year-old boy.

"Such a joyous night." Beatrix turned sparkling brown eyes on him. "Don't you just love weddings?"

He snagged a round of bread and dragged it through a bowl of herbed olive oil nestled in the lamplit greenery in the center of the table. "I've not attended many." His lips lifted in a crooked grin. "I spent a few years in a monastery."

Beatrix chuckled. "No cause for weddings there, I imagine."

"No."

She cocked her head, white curls frizzing around the edges of her Roman-style palla, dyed a shocking pink. "Have you taken a vow of celibacy?"

He nearly choked on the bread. Pounding the center of his chest, he swallowed, eyes watering. "No," he wheezed. "I was . . . more of a guest."

Beatrix smiled and nodded, as if he'd passed some sort of test, though the question had nearly killed him. "Marriage is one of God's greatest gifts—aside from salvation, of course. My nephew, Valentine, believed such. Lived and died for it actually. But that was many years ago." Her gaze grew pensive and she tilted her head as she studied him. "Something about you reminds me of him. Not your looks. You're much more handsome—something very Alexander the Great about you—but that's between you and me, you hear? When we get to glory, you're not to speak a word of this conversation to Valens."

Nikolas chuckled and put a finger to his lips. "Your secret is safe with me."

He accepted the wide platter of mussels moving from hand to hand down the table and held it, motioning for Beatrix to take what she wanted. She dragged a large clamshell scoop through the center and poured a small heap of butterflied black mussels onto the plank in front of her.

"Every time I start to miss Rome, I think of the food here, and I'm satisfied." She leaned forward and inhaled the steam. "Demi must have gathered these. She looks so lovely tonight."

The perfume, the marriage talk, now Demi . . . he doubted any of it was a coincidence. Nikolas scooped his own helping of mussels before passing on the plate and the invitation to talk about Demi with a scheming matchmaker.

"You've left your home, I've left mine, Myra isn't the home our friends remember . . ." He picked up a mussel and cracked one shell from the other, using it to scoop out the peach-tinted morsel stuck to the inside. "It's as if we're all being reminded over and again that this world is not our home. That our family is less of our own blood and instead our brothers and sisters in Christ. The world feels more and more temporary all the time."

Beatrix chewed thoughtfully, pausing to swipe a bit of shell out of her mouth. "And in this season, we find ourselves in an advent of hope. For the here and the not yet."

Nikolas nodded and popped the bite in his mouth.

"Now. You've taken no vow of celibacy, so are you going to marry?"

The mussel slipped down his throat and he choked again. Why did she ask these questions when he'd just taken bites?

Beatrix handed him a clay cup and he gulped warm wine. It burned on the way down. He set the cup on the table, stomach souring at the memories the flavor brought. He'd drawn the line long ago at only drinking wine for the Lord's Supper. He was no longer the man he'd been.

Beatrix folded her hands primly, waiting for an answer.

Nikolas cleared his throat. "That's a question and an answer that's in God's hands alone."

"Of course." Beatrix's smile was a tad condescending. As if she knew something he didn't.

THIRTY-TWO

NIKOLAS JOINED THE LAST of the guests as they disappeared over the rocky rise, taking the dismantled tables, garlands, and lights with them. He wished a few good night, and edged out of the crowd, slipping toward those without lights until he faded into the darkness at the edge of the path. He waited until the last few stragglers passed and turned back to the cove. He hadn't seen Demitria in the group. Perhaps she'd stayed behind.

As he descended back to the cove, he saw her pacing along the shore. All that remained of the celebration was scorched sand from the mussel kettle and black shells scattered over the sand like discarded beetle wings. Even those would all disappear when the tide came and went. All but the memories would be erased.

The stretch of sand was shrinking, crowded by rolling water. A single torch remained, burning low to the ground and casting more shadows than light on the rocky cliffs above. The night was not advanced enough to take the lateen without notice, but it would be in an hour or two. The thought of spending that time with Demitria wasn't without appeal.

He walked toward her, sinking ankle-deep into cool, damp sand. "Hard to believe this place was full of light, food, and laughter only minutes ago."

Demitria wadded the hem of her blue chiton up to her knees and stepped into the water. "It was lovely."

He tried to keep his gaze fixed on the shadowy sea and not let it slide toward her. "Very." His voice must have betrayed him because her eyes jerked to his and bore the same expression she had that day he'd praised her in the boat. Panic. Hope, maybe. But not revulsion. That was something.

Her expression smoothed. "Did you and Yia-yia have a nice conversation over the meal?" A wave buffeted the backs of her knees and she stumbled forward a step.

He squinted. Did she know what Beatrix had been hedging at? Did Demitria's feelings mirror his own? He lifted his shoulders in what he hoped looked like casual indifference. "We discussed marriage, celibacy—the normal things one talks about at weddings."

She blinked, as if taken aback by his answer. "I see."

"And you?"

"Not against marriage, but content as I am."

He coughed. "I was asking about your dinner conversation but . . . I'm glad to hear that."

Demi's cheeks went dark and she turned away. "Yes, well, that was a riveting discussion on which was softer, sand or rocks."

"Sand."

"Wrong. The answer is rocks."

"I don't understand."

She bent to scoop up a rock in one hand and sand in the other, then held them out. "They wouldn't admit it, but they were confused about the words *soft* and *smooth*."

He held out his hands and she transferred the rock and sand into them. "But they're the same substance. The true difference is their size. The more broken one is, the softer it becomes." He rolled the sand through his fingers, damp clumps falling. A wave rolled over his feet, and he crouched to rinse his hands.

"Not always." Demi's whisper cracked and broke in his ears, though he was not meant to hear it.

He straightened, catching her troubled expression before she shuttered it. "Demi—"

She darted away, chiton falling from her hands as she chased down something tumbling in the surf. Light caught on her bare arms as she bent and scooped up a dark object. She hunched toward the torchlight, turning it over in her hands.

He followed, and she turned a wobbly smile on him. "A tun snail," she said, raising her palm with the empty fist-sized shell balanced in the middle. "You don't see these every day."

The faint light cast a golden sheen across her sharp features, softening the freckles flung across her nose and cheekbones with abandon. Her eyes raised to his as he stepped closer, the darkest brown unable to mask the anguish hiding there.

"What's wrong?"

"Nothing." Her answer came too quick, eyes sliding away. "We should probably go." A wariness edged her tone. She took a step back and turned away, a wall going up between them yet again. Or maybe it had always been there. For her perhaps, but for him? Every time he experienced it, he staggered anew at the immensity of it.

"Not yet."

Wet chiton slapping against her legs, Demi paced back toward the sea, ever encroaching on their patch of beach. He followed her again, feeling more and more like a lost dog scrounging for crumbs and companionship. He'd thought they were friends, that they shared common interests, passions, and yet, she closed him off again and again. He'd never understood the monks who beat their bodies in an attempt at holiness. And yet, was he doing the same now? Demi had become agony to be around. Yet he couldn't bear the separation.

"What are these walls you're putting up between us?"

Demi dropped her chin and whispered, "Please, Nikolas. Let it be."

"Whatever burden you're carrying, you don't have to bear it alone, you know."

She hugged her elbows and angled away from him. "I do." Tears thickened her words, breaking something in him. How many years had he done the same? Hiding away his grief and questions from his father, his uncle?

"You don't." He reached for her, touching her arm. "I'd carry it with you if you'd let me."

Carry it with me?

If she told him the secret weighting her heart like so many diving stones, he wouldn't dare carry her. He'd let her tumble. Would he even listen to her whole story? Demi closed her eyes, painful heat searing through the center of her chest. His hand on her arm was warm, an invitation to accept him as a friend. As one who saw her pain and wanted to share it, rather than let her bear it alone. But could she trust him with it?

She made the mistake of looking up at him, of seeing the warmth in his eyes. The sincerity. It was all made worse by the idiotic thrill that accompanied the realization of how close he was. If he didn't let her fall after hearing her secret, she'd fall in another way, and that would be just as disastrous.

She slammed her eyes shut, tears squeezing through the lashes. Memories buffeted. Alexander's ready smile. Love blooming. Hope rising. All severed from her with a single swing of a sword. How could she willingly endure that again? If both men traveled the same path, Alexander had walked it, and Nikolas was racing toward the end waving both arms and shouting. It was only a matter of time before he was dead too.

And the other thing—her family, her cowardice and guilt . . . Nikolas was all black and white. He might understand her hesitation to love him, but would he still offer his friendship if he knew what she'd done? Never.

Demi pulled from his touch and bolted past him.

What made the waves rush headlong and heedless into the rocks? Their smooth rolls and curls broken and dashed. What made them return again and again to the same place with the same result? Mitera had always said Demi was born of the sun and sea. Maybe that was truer than she had realized.

A wave crashed over her legs, nearly sweeping her into the brine. She'd been under too long already. Floundering beneath the weight of fear and guilt, and there was nowhere to surface. Her lungs screamed for the breath she couldn't pull in.

Running away wasn't going to work this time. She dropped onto a boulder. The surf crashed against the rocks, misting her in spray. Waves and tides were predictable. Dependable. They rolled over the same sand, crashed against the same rocks. It was the rogue wave that upset everything, left destruction in its wake. She'd witnessed enough of them to know when to stay away. And maybe he wasn't her rogue wave. Maybe she was his.

Gravel popped beneath Nikolas's sandals as he approached.

"Demi." He appeared in front of her, his form slowly folding to sit on another stone—not too close, as if he was afraid to spook her again. The torchlight caught his face and turned his eyes dark as they settled on her. "Why do you keep running from me?" His tone, so gentle, threatened to send fresh tears down her cheeks.

A breath finally scraped through her lungs like a boat over boulders. "This . . . this thing between us, it cannot happen." She started to push up from her seated position but he caught her hand and tugged her back down.

"Why not?"

Alexander in a pool of blood flashed through her mind. She felt her sister's hand torn from her own, heard her mother's scream, smelled the sickening odor of incense. Pain shot up the center of her chest, tightening a fist around her throat.

Her voice cracked, the reasons stacking and tumbling. "If you knew who I really was, what I've done, you wouldn't ask that."

His fingers only tightened around hers. "I do know you."

She shook her head. "You don't."

"Then tell me."

She let out a long breath. "I told you about Alexander. He was like you. Handsome, caring . . . courageous. He seemed invincible. Part of me believed he was . . . And then he wasn't." The words began to tumble from her lips faster and louder. "And then Pater was arrested, and Mitera and my sister, Hediste—and I was too." She turned shimmering eyes on him, her voice dropping back to a whisper. "They took me too. And while my family stayed strong and true, I . . . I didn't. I'm a coward,

Nikolas." She smeared her palm across her cheek, then drew the backs of her knuckles beneath her jaw, catching drips.

"You're not a coward."

"I am lapsed." The last three words emerged in a strangled wail. She dropped her head to her knees, pressing her fist to her mouth.

A rush of air seemed to leave his lungs all at once. As if she'd rammed her diving knife into his chest and crushed the last beating bit of his heart. Maybe she had. Nikolas said nothing, but she could sense him pulling away before he'd moved an inch. He couldn't love her. Not after he knew. And she couldn't mar his own reputation and position with her mistakes. It was better this way.

But why did "better" feel so much like misery?

He would leave now, tell everyone what she'd done, and she'd be alone. Forever. Cast out and cut off as Pastor Tomoso had insisted be done to those who fell away. It was no less than what she deserved. And though the thought seemed to slit the breath from her own lungs, it also brought a strange relief. The ugly, festering truth was out, no longer smothered behind a bandage of good deeds that had covered the problem but couldn't cure it. Perhaps, like Theseus's wrist, her wounds needed air and light.

Nikolas's fingers slipped from hers and she gave a tiny nod, steeling herself for the words that must be said, and knowing they would be easier to hear coming from her own mouth rather than his.

"Right. You should go. I—I'll keep my distance from now on." She twisted her fingers into the fabric over her knees. "You won't have to worry about seeing me at the gatherings anymore. And once you tell everyone else, they'll understand."

"What are you talking about?" he breathed.

Fresh tears burned her eyes and the words tumbled out in a panicked tangle. "Don't blame Theseus. It's not his fault. He only knew I ran away; he didn't know . . . everything." Her voice broke. "I know I should have left earlier, but I couldn't bear it. I thought that if God could see how sorry I was . . ." She trailed off, hearing Pastor Tomoso's voice thundering in her ears.

Whoever denies Me before men, him I will also deny before My Father who is in heaven.

Stones scraped as Nikolas moved, and a cool sea breeze washed over her in his absence.

Despair spiraled. Her forehead sank to her knees. There was no hope for her.

His hand touched her head, warm fingers tunneling through hair until they found her chin and tugged. She slowly lifted her head, preparing herself for judgment, disappointment, chastisement, a lecture. Pastor Tomoso had always known exactly what to say at the slightest mishap. She had no doubt Nikolas did too. Instead, torchlight flickered in hazel eyes brimming with compassion and pain as he crouched in front of her.

"I understand, Demi," he whispered.

She started to shake her head. He couldn't. Not truly.

"I do."

Tears flowed anew. This was not the response she'd expected. How could he possibly understand? She'd revealed the worst, darkest part of her soul. Unredeemable blackness. She'd denied the Name of the only One who truly mattered. She knew that now. Why couldn't she have known it then, lived it? Died for it?

Nikolas stared into her eyes, the torchlight reflecting her broken guilt and pain in his own. His fingers fell away from her chin, sticky with tears, and found her hands instead. "I *do* understand."

Demi shook her head and pushed to her feet, pulling free from his grip. There was no way he could understand. She'd fallen too far. Perhaps it was only his feelings for her that were speaking. She had to put distance between them. Allow him to think clearly.

"Don't do that."

She froze at his words, or maybe it was the pleading tone that emerged with them.

"Don't walk away and put up your walls again. Talk to me."

"We should go." She hardly recognized the fragile hollowness of her own voice.

The torch flickered against the sand, guttering in the wind for a few violent seconds before snuffing them into darkness. Nikolas sighed and stood, following her toward the path lit by the faintest shred of moonlight.

They walked to Andriake in silence.

Gravel bit into the soles of her bare feet, cooling with familiar dampness as they neared the river's edge. As they approached the dock, she quickened her pace so the night guard would see her first and not sound the alarm. Kyros climbed out of the first boat moored to the dock and met them at the shore.

"How is it?" Demi whispered.

"Raucous evening, but it's quieter now," Kyros answered. "A new squadron of guards was sent down here from the city. They don't always settle in right away, but you should be all right going upriver."

They followed Kyros onto the dock. "I know you don't hoist the sail until you're past Myra, but make certain you don't tonight. I'll push you off. I moved your boat to the very end."

Demi nodded. "Thank you."

Planks creaked beneath her feet, the sound familiar and somehow far too loud for the night. She stepped aside and gestured for Nikolas to climb down into the boat first. She swept her gaze to the river, avoiding him as he passed, then climbed down after him. Shuffling toward her place in the stern, her movements were rote, perfected over years of practice, but the deep, cutting pain in her heart, sharper than ever—that was new.

The boat lurched as Kyros launched them without warning. Demi's arms flung out for balance and she found herself held in a solid grip. Her heart crowded her throat as she regained her footing.

Nikolas let her go.

It was what she'd asked him to do on the beach, and his compliance now sent tears to her eyes. She sat and took up the oar.

Focus, Demitria.

The boat angled for the opposite shore. Demi switched her oar to the other side, balancing the way Nikolas dug his oar into the river. Crickets rasped in the rustling grasses at the river's edge, and farther off, the boom and crash of waves echoed past the mouth of the river. The night sounds were achingly lonely.

She didn't have a rule to apply in this instance.

Act like nothing happened and maybe he will forget.

That one didn't work. If she acted like nothing had happened, she'd only look unrepentant. He wouldn't forget. And she shouldn't forget. Wasn't it the remembrance of sin that drew one to repentance? How many times did she have to repent? Was there a number?

The boat turned back to the shore where the city lights of Myra burned orange in the distance. The temple crowning the acropolis shone like a beacon. Gloating as if it had the final say over her life and those left in it. Her stomach churned, threatening to expel all she'd eaten at the wedding feast. Had that only been hours ago?

Demi shook her head to clear it and gripped the paddle tighter, forcing her mind to the present. Which wasn't much better. Wafts of Bea's "mysterious and exotic" scent floated on the edges of the breeze and just in front of her, Nikolas's wide shoulders shifted in the starlight as he rowed.

The boat angled back the other way, zigzagging back and forth up the river. At this rate, they'd row four times the distance, wearing themselves out long before they reached the cache.

"The wind is against us," Demi whispered. "We'll have to row together."

For a moment she wasn't sure if he'd heard. Then Nikolas glanced behind him and gentled his motion to allow them to synchronize.

Myra loomed large and towering to their left. Lamps burned in few windows at this hour and might have been mistaken for fireflies the way they winked with the movement of the boat. Demi and Nikolas hugged the shore, staying hidden by the willows and scrub clustered at the banks. Just as the river carried them past the steep cliff of the mountain at Myra's back, they drew the boat ashore and moored it.

Others had filled the cache cave throughout the month, and while it wasn't nearly as full as it had been in the past, there was still enough to fill the boat. Nikolas hefted a cask of sea salt to his shoulder and marched toward the river.

Feeling around in the darkness, Demi rolled three more casks of salt to the mouth of the cave, followed by bags of dried fish, rolls of wool cloth, and a crate of imported medicinal herbs and spices. Stones clattered on the narrow path outside. She paused, letting out a breath as Nikolas's shadow moved into the mouth of the cave, backlit by the sky. She only realized she'd hoped he'd speak when he tossed another cask of salt to his shoulder and turned away.

She tucked two rolls of cloth under her arms, hurt prickling in her chest. As it should. She'd made the mistakes. This distance between them was her fault. Much less than what she deserved.

Mist spat from the sky as they finished loading the boat and then fell harder as they navigated the rocky portion of the river. The only words passing between them were Nikolas's one-word directions as they wove between the river boulders. No talk of friendship or sharing burdens. This was a weight for her to bear alone.

THIRTY-THREE

OF ALL THE EXPLANATIONS NIKOLAS IMAGINED Demi would give, the one she'd offered hadn't even made the list. *Lapsed.* He'd stared at her, unable to reconcile the words she'd spoken with the brave, selfless woman he knew. The woman who sailed the Mediterranean, dove with sharks and eels, made dangerous and illegal trading trips at night. Demi, lapsed? It was possibly the worst thing she might have confessed, and yet, as he'd looked into those dark eyes, broken and shadowed by years of guilt and pain, he saw himself. And he couldn't leave her, couldn't—and wouldn't—walk away in revulsion the way she'd obviously expected him to.

And yet, he hadn't known what to say. Hours later, he still didn't.

Rain gushed from the sky, pouring over the entrance of the cache cave in a waterfall. He and Demi stood just inside, streaming water as if they'd had to dive for all the equally soaked goods that lay in muddy puddles behind them. Demi had said they couldn't leave until the rain let up and they could see to navigate.

He felt around for a seat on one of the salt casks they'd hauled in and shivered as the heat of exertion wore off. Water splattered across from him as Demi wrung out her hair or chiton. In the darkness, he couldn't tell which. If it wasn't as black as obsidian in here, he'd organize the goods, clear his mind. His knee began to bounce. Sitting idle with his thoughts had never been his strength—a trait the monks had declared sinful, and Nikolas's cross to bear. He'd been relegated to many of the manual labor tasks around the monastery. A punishment, Uncle called it. But couldn't God use a pair of hands willing to *do* something?

Not at the moment, apparently.

A thud followed by a soft hiss of pain.

"Are you all right?"

"Mm-hmm."

She'd probably never admit it if she wasn't. Demi would suffer in silence as long as she could before she'd burden anyone else.

"The salt casks are over here, if you need a place to sit."

A beat of silence. "I'm fine over here." Her voice was tight. A mooring line, set to break.

"Demi?"

No answer.

He repeated her name, louder.

A sharp inhale and a watery "Yes?" She was crying, and trying not to let him know.

Guilt smote him. He'd offered her friendship, urged her to share her burden with him, and when she had, he'd not said a word. *What do I say, Lord?*

"Will you . . . tell me what happened? I should have asked sooner but . . ." He sighed. "I'm sorry."

She didn't answer.

The silence between them stretched further until the gap seemed too far to bridge. A trickle of rainwater slid down his neck. He lowered his head into his hands, raking his fingers through his dripping hair. Too little. Too late. He'd failed again.

Then her voice broke through the storm. Wavering and heavy as she spoke of the day in the market, of how she'd been distracted when the merchant questioned her father. How they'd been dragged to the basilica and tortured one by one until they died or caved. Demi had been last. Had stood by her pater, forced to watch her mitera and sister horribly murdered. And when her pater's turn came—

"The more they hurt him, the more he screamed, the more it seemed like such a trifling thing to toss a bit of bark and dried flowers into a firepot. I wouldn't mean it, and perhaps if I did it, they would stop, and I could spare my pater." Her voice rose, erupting in wild sobs that seemed to tear her in pieces. "I couldn't bear it, Nikolas. I burned the incense. I spoke the words. And the way Pater looked at me . . ."

Nikolas pushed to his feet, feeling his way through the crates and bundles, following the sound of her broken cries. His fingers traveled over a crate of clammy cabbages and then tangled in damp curls. He knelt and found her shaking shoulders next, gently tugging her into his arms and holding her the way he should have done earlier.

"Why does He still let me breathe His air? I should be the dead one."

It should not have been Amadeo. His father's words still accused him. Perhaps Demi had made a coward's choice, but his own selfishness had left him with the same result. He too carried blood on his hands, guilt on his shoulders.

"We all should be," Nikolas whispered. The words came from his tongue but didn't feel like his own. "Not one of us deserves to breathe God's air, and yet, here we are. A second, third, fourth chance in every breath."

Demi shook her head. "How can that be true?" She pulled in a shuddering breath and drew back from his embrace. "Pastor Tomoso said God will not forgive those who deny the Name. It says so in Scripture."

"We are human and fail every attempt at perfection. Jesus's own disciples ran. Peter declared Jesus to be the Christ, the Son of God, but when he grew fearful, he denied he knew Jesus not once or even twice, but three times. Tell me God does not forgive and restore." When he'd prayed for words, he hadn't expected them to come out of his mouth like this. Aimed at his own heart as well as hers.

"But that was *Peter*," she argued, as if who it was made all the difference.

"Yes. Rash, angry, fearful Peter. Is he more worthy of forgiveness, of grace, than you or me?"

They both fell silent, Nikolas pondering the question as much as she seemed to be. The answer was no. Of course it was. And yet, why did he struggle against it so? As if even though he knew he could never be worthy of forgiveness, he ought to try anyway.

"How can you say you understand?" she whispered. "Why don't you cast me out? Others would have."

He drew a breath. Then another. She'd cracked open her heart, shown him the darkest corners; could he do the same with his?

"My brother, Amadeo, was supposed to inherit everything. Not me. Everyone who knew him loved him. He was the favorite of our tutors, excelled in every subject and I . . . I didn't. My pater favored Amadeo and encouraged him to learn and excel in every aspect of shipping—which he did. And most of the time I didn't mind because my mitera favored me. When the tutor would send me home early and in trouble, Mitera would hand me a basket and we'd spend the rest of the day delivering food and medicine to the poor. Pater would say she was the best of women." A burning rose in his throat, choking his words. "After she died, Pater poured himself into the shipping company, Amadeo did the same, and I floundered. I felt alone and abandoned. Tried to find happiness wherever I could. I was not a good son, a good brother."

He leaned forward, resting his elbows on his knees. "When Pater planned a two-year trading trip for the three of us, I wanted to go, was glad to be included for once, but . . . it made me so angry that it had taken them so long to do so. We argued bitterly when he told me of it, and I refused to help with the preparations. To my endless shame, I wanted him and Amadeo to feel the same rejection I felt . . . I can still hear my father's voice telling me I wasn't worthy of his name. That he'd cut me from his household, and gladly." The sharpness of those words lingered still. A shattered blade in his chest. "I wasn't supposed to inherit. I wasn't supposed to . . . be his son any longer. But later that day, a loading crane at the docks broke. The arm snapped and hit my brother. He died that day, and part of my father died with him."

It should not have been Amadeo who died.

"Amadeo's death shook me from all that I had been, but it was too late. Pater didn't disown me, but he never let me forget that I was not the son of his heart, and nothing I could ever do would change that."

"Nikolas . . ." Demi's whisper broke the stillness; her hand rested on his back.

"Could I have prevented Amadeo's death if I'd not tried to punish them by refusing to go to the docks and help? Is his blood on my hands?" He smeared a palm across the wetness on his cheek. "Pater thought so. He died on the return voyage and with his last words told me it should not have been my brother who died." His voice broke over the admission and he couldn't breathe.

"Where does that leave us, then?" Demi asked softly. "Peter wasn't worthy of forgiveness. None of us are." She let out a breath. "That is why Jesus came in the first place. That is the reason for the gospel. We aren't worthy of it."

"No." Nikolas tilted his face toward her and her damp curls brushed his cheek. "But it's offered to us anyway. And instead of condemnation, He calls us chosen, beloved." His voice dropped. They were tender names. Names he could easily ascribe to Demi, but he couldn't imagine God saying the same of him.

Her hand crept into his, and he gave her fingers a gentle squeeze. She responded with a tightened grip. Nikolas leaned back, tipping his head against the wall as the rest of the story flooded over him.

"After Jesus rose, He met Peter by the sea—in the same place He first called him to follow—and for each time Peter had denied Him, Jesus offered him a chance to make a different choice, then gave him a job to do."

"*Feed My lambs,*" Demi murmured.

"*Tend and feed My sheep,*" he finished. "Peter wasn't just forgiven and sent off to live out the rest of his days as a fisherman. He was restored, reestablished as a member and a leader. And he lived after that as a changed man."

Conviction smote. Was that how he was living? He was working, yes, doing good and helping, but to what end? And why? Out of love, because he was loved and forgiven, or because he felt he had to earn it?

She let out a breath. "I suppose that leaves us with a choice to make."

THIRTY-FOUR

BIRDSONG WOKE HER.

Demi shifted, warm, and somehow uncomfortably damp. She blinked. The opening of the cave glowed faintly gray against the darkness, silhouetting the mess of dark bundles. She jerked upright, warmth falling away with the length of wool spread over her like a blanket. She didn't remember doing that.

She pushed to her feet, heart leaping into a panicked rhythm. How long had she been asleep? When had the rain stopped? Where was—

Nikolas huddled against the opposite wall, draped in another length of wool. He must have covered her. She flung the cloth toward the pile of goods they were leaving behind and moved toward him.

"Nikolas."

He made a noise in his sleep, part moan, part grunt, and tucked his chin deeper into the folds of the fabric.

She gripped the edge of his blanket and pulled. "We fell asleep. We've got to go."

His eyes flew open and he scrambled to his feet. Demi dropped the cloth and reached for a crate of cabbages. "If I don't get this boat back to the docks . . ." She let the worry dangle and darted outside.

The morning air was cool, turning her skin to gooseflesh. A glance at the sky told her it was earlier than she'd originally thought, but they were still going to be hard-pressed to make it back to the docks before the other divers arrived. They loaded the boat in record time, Nikolas hauling the goods from the cave and Demi bailing water from the boat and loading as quickly as she could.

They made the return trip in the kind of urgent silence that implied internal prayer and extra rowing, even with the current and sail.

Demi left Nikolas and the goods at the drop-off point nearest Myra. Normally they might have spread out the goods in different spots, but there was no time this morning. As she neared the docks, her pulse thumped at the sight of the other divers already moving about the docks, readying their boats. Her breaths went ragged, and she forced herself to practice the breathing patterns Pater had taught her. Racing heart, racing mind. Neither was good for diving or solving problems. She blew out a whistling breath, slowing her pulse. Calming her mind.

They had a rule for this. A plan. She'd never been late enough to have to use it before, and she prayed it worked, that Kyros had waited for her, and remembered it too.

She freed the wooden pin holding the rudder fast and replaced it with a smaller one tied beneath her seat for just this occasion. The rudder wobbled and the boat veered. She strained to steer and waved at the docks as she coasted nearer, grateful to see the night guard still standing among the other divers.

"Kyros!" She waved at him and drew on a frustrated tone. "It didn't work. The rudder's still loose, and now I've got water coming in." *Thank You, Lord, for the rain.*

Kyros moved to the end of the pier and caught the front of her lateen as she docked. "Still loose, mmm?" He tied her off and climbed inside. The attention of the other divers, on her when she first called for Kyros, dissipated as they focused on getting their own boats ready. Kyros had made a reputation for himself by helping with their boats. Demi wasn't certain if he'd done so because he was actually good with boats or if it was in preparation for such an occasion as this. Either way, she was grateful.

She let out a shaky breath and stepped aside, gesturing to the rudder.

He crouched, moved it from side to side. "Everything all right?" His low voice reached her, though he never looked her way.

"Yes."

"The water's . . . from the rain?"

"Mm-hmm."

He cleared his throat and spoke louder. "Bail it out so I can find where it's coming in."

She set to work, glad to have something to occupy her hands.

"Demi!" Feet thumped up the dock. "Don't leave without me!" Rex barreled up the pier, dodging divers with ropes and baskets.

She straightened and aimed a tense smile at the boy. "I wouldn't do that. I can't dive without my spotter." She'd nearly forgotten Theseus wouldn't be diving today and Rex would be joining her instead. *Lord, guard the boy's tongue.* She brightened her voice. "Kyros and I are trying to fix a problem with the rudder."

"Is it fixed?" Rex leaped into the lateen, making it heave. Demi caught his arm before the boat threw him out.

"Easy, Rex," she chided.

"It's fixed now," Kyros announced. "I'm going to fetch some pitch for this crack. I think I've found your leak." He clambered back to the dock and strode toward Mersad's warehouse that squatted beside a tavern and greasy eatery.

Demi and Rex set to work bailing the rest of the rainwater from the bottom of the boat.

"Demitria." A familiar heavy tread thumped toward her.

She straightened as Mersad approached, the thick fringe on his upper lip drooping with disapproval.

"We need to speak."

Demi climbed to the dock, the ground seeming to rock beneath her for a moment before solidifying. She could not say the same for her stomach. Instinctively, her spine straightened. A fight was coming, if the lift to Mersad's shoulders was any indication.

"I'm a businessman, Demitria, not a decurion. You know I don't have the capital for philanthropy."

Lies. Mersad's tunic, striped with red, blue, and green and festooned with embroidery, had surely cost a year's wage. He was wealthy beyond belief, especially if he paid his other divers the same pittance he reserved for Theseus and Demi's precious hauls. She didn't risk calling him out but waited in silence. Her stomach turned with dread.

"Your hauls have been dropping since Theseus was injured."

"I know. We've spoken of this before, and I promise to do—"

"So you *do* remember our conversation."

She nodded, her heart starting to thrum with panic. "We've had to go farther out to find coral and—"

"I've examined your account and you're not even keeping up with your own half from before." He held up a meaty hand, silencing any protest or excuse she might give. "Because I'm a fair man, and you and Theseus have always been my best team, I'm warning you one last time. Ennio and Pelos have made a compelling argument to separate and give their sons control of this boat. You're welcome to dive with them, but—"

Her mouth dropped. "Mersad—"

"If you don't meet your quota, I'll have no choice but to accept Ennio and Pelos's request."

The hair on her arms and neck prickled. Mersad's threat was unmistakable. For all his pretending not to care about her beliefs or lack of libelli, her employer was shrewd. Everything he did was for his own benefit, and she was only safe as long as she remained an asset to him.

She lowered her chin, a creeping fear edging up the center of her chest, gripping her throat, drying her mouth. "I do admit that our numbers have fallen in recent days, but we will do better."

"See that you do." He squinted at her, studying her face too closely. "You look tired. Make sure you get some rest when the festival starts tomorrow."

She nodded, but the dread only built. Three days of pagan festivities meant three days confined to the safe room. She'd be able to rest some—when she wasn't worrying about her quota.

The dock shifted and trembled beneath her bare feet as Mersad sauntered toward the shore, passing Kyros hurrying toward her with a jar of pitch and a brush.

Her breath slowly leaked from her lungs, leaving her wobbly and deflated. Exhaustion rushed over her. Too many depended on her. She couldn't lose the boat.

THIRTY-FIVE

DEMI READJUSTED THE SAIL, directing the boat up the eastern coast. Rex hunched in the prow against the cool wind, eyes closed and probably asleep. Unlike Nikolas, who looked like he never slept, especially if there was work to be done—except for last night. She didn't remember falling asleep. But she couldn't forget their conversation.

Could it really be so easy as simply accepting that Christ had forgiven her, and then living like it? Easy, yes. And so difficult. Especially when suffering seemed the better option. It was what she deserved, after all. And yet, Jesus had not turned away Peter. He'd not let him live in shame and disgrace, though that was what he deserved. Instead, Peter had been reminded that he was chosen, called, beloved. What would it be like to live with those names over her head instead of trying to run from the names of *coward, disappointment,* and *disgrace* that dogged her every step?

Specks on the horizon jolted her from her thoughts.

Demi squinted. The waves reflected the slate gray of the sky, capped with frothing white and dotted with colorful boats far ahead. She couldn't tell if one of them was the red-and-blue devil boat. But it couldn't hurt to dive within sight of other boats. Ennio and Pelos wouldn't dare bother them in the presence of witnesses, would they?

Please, Lord. Bless our efforts today. We need this boat.

The treed mountains rippled along the coast, hazy, green, and punctuated with pale limestone cliffs. The boat curved around a rounded peninsula and into a bay playing host to a few other dive boats already anchored over darkened patches of water that signaled rocky reefs. Unwilling to get into a territorial feud, Demi steered further out off the coast, away from the others, but still within shouting distance. She dropped the sail.

"Time to wake up, sleepy." She nudged Rex's shoulder. "Help me toss the anchor."

Rex bolted upright, stretching his eyes wide. "I wasn't sleeping."

She laughed. "It's not a sin to sleep."

Rex scrambled to help heave the anchor over the side with a splash. Demi eyed the remaining anchor rope in the boat to determine their depth before diving. Deep, but not dangerously so.

"I'm just going down quick to see if this is a good spot."

He nodded.

She unpinned the shoulders of her chiton and stepped out of it as Rex leaned over the side squinting toward the other boats. Balling the fabric, she tossed it on the floor before hopping onto her seat and launching herself over the side of the boat. Cool water shocked her body. She moved her arms and legs until the tightness in her chest eased. She opened her eyes and scanned the murky shadows of the bottom, kicking lower until she could make out clumps of rocks. A waving wall of kelp rose to her left, hemming in the shallower waters of the bay to her right. She pressed lower, noting the spiny urchins dotting the bottom around the base of the kelp. The bottom was rough and rocky, studded with clumps of seagrass and ruffled yellow coral resembling cabbage leaves. It wasn't a bad spot. If only the light was better. She explored the bottom, air bubbles slipping from her lips.

The seafloor here might as well have been a garden. Short brown coral resembling a stand of mushrooms grew at the base of a bulbous yellow coral. Sea bream darted between the bright-orange branches rising above others sprouting like bouquets of flowers. She waved her arms and twisted in a circle, scanning for the familiar fan of red coral. She needed a good haul today.

Please.

Nothing. She spent a few more minutes circling out wider before surfacing. Spitting water, Demi wiped her eyes, empty coastline meeting her gaze.

"Well?"

She turned toward Rex's hopeful voice and swam for the boat.

"Nothing. We need to go deeper."

He flipped the rope ladder over the side. "You were down a long time."

"Was I?" She clambered into the boat.

"It always feels like a long time from this side."

She laughed. "I'll put you to work soon enough. Heaven forbid you sit still for five minutes." She shook out her chiton and wrapped it around her shoulders. "Let's pull up the anchor then, if you need something to do."

They moved the boat farther out. Then farther out again.

The third reef was new to her.

Fish darted in streaks of color among a cacophony of stunning coral. Demi kicked, the dread of Mersad's threat close, even as curiosity and wonder took hold. How both could exist in wrestling tandem was a wonder in itself. She twisted through a rocky arch and emerged on the other side of a coral-studded ridge shaded by an outcropping of rock overhead. A rush of bubbles escaped her lungs.

A fan of lacy red coral the size of a small shield spread inside a shadowy hollow. This spot might have been new to her, but surely not to others. How had anyone missed a branch of this size? She kicked to it, running her fingers over the white polyps beading strands that grew outward like frozen snakes. Smaller fans grew nearby, filling the shady underside of the outcropping in a swath of red.

Demi broke for the surface and stroked for the boat.

Rex stood. "Anything?"

She nodded. "We need to move the boat." She climbed inside and anchored the boat closer to the spot before diving again. Rex threw the coral basket out and it sank beside her, releasing silver bubbles that rose up along the rope securing it to the boat.

Everywhere she looked, coral sprouted from the ridge. She pulled out her hammer and set to work, loosing a precise blow to the base of the largest coral fan. It tumbled forward into her arms, rough against her skin. She nestled it into the basket, nearly filling the space. Oh, for the look on Mersad's face when she showed him this. She moved to harvest the next piece, choosing the best, most mature fans for the basket and leaving the smaller ones to grow. When the basket was full, she gave two sharp tugs on the rope and remained next to it as she ascended toward the glittering surface, ensuring it didn't tip or snag on the way up.

Stubborn hope rose again. This haul would solve everything, restoring her back into Mersad's graces—such as they were. And while the work seemed vain and destructive, it was all she had in order to keep the boat, and that was the only thing keeping food in the bellies of her friends. What else was she to do?

The ascent stopped. Rex must be getting tired. Demi tilted her head back and looked up to determine the distance left to go. Two shadows stained the surface. The familiar yellow hull of her dive boat, marred with gashes from the river trips, bobbed next to another boat that had appeared out of the depths of Hades. She abandoned the coral basket and kicked for the yellow boat, dread building with the pressure in her chest.

She spat in the direction of the red-and-blue boat when her head broke the surface.

"Good morning, beautiful." Ennio's smooth voice grated on her ears.

"What do you want?"

Ennio gave a lazy grin. "Come now. That's no way to greet your partners."

"We are not partners."

"Sure we are. Are we not partners, Pelos?" Ennio looked toward her boat and Demi followed his gaze, floundering when she saw Rex seated in the prow, Pelos holding a diving knife to his throat.

"Let him go."

Pelos didn't move.

"He's just a child. Let him go."

Pelos hesitated, then lowered the knife, keeping it in hand.

Ennio's son Tychon straddled both boats, naked but for a small loin-cloth. He yanked the rope out of Rex's hands and pulled her coral basket into the red boat.

"Magnificent." He lifted the large fan and held it up for the others to admire.

She gritted her teeth. "Put it back."

Ennio tsked and looked toward Pelos. "Demanding for a traitor, isn't she?"

"I'm not a traitor."

"Are you not?" Ennio's eyebrows drifted upward and his upper lip twitched. *"Our Father in heaven, hallowed be Your name . . ."*

Ice and regret sank her stomach. *Oh, Rex.* Why hadn't she told him to say something else? A harmless children's song, perhaps?

Rex's eyes flicked to her, apology and fear written on his face, but he didn't speak.

"It's too bad that we're obligated to turn them both in." Tychon tipped the basket of coral into the bottom of the red boat.

Ennio picked up the largest fan and nodded in mock sympathy. "It is."

Demi heaved herself up on the edge of her boat, flinging her legs over the side. "Give it back. You can't prove anything."

Ennio laughed. "No? Perhaps we ought to ask his parents at the school for laborers' children?"

Demi's heart sank, his threat to her friends and Rex's family unmis-takable. *Rex, what did you say?* Rex dropped his chin.

Her lips and voice went tight. "What do you want?"

"Your coral."

"Bad choice. Mersad is ready to requisition my boat and send me packing because of my poor hauls."

Ennio twirled the fan of coral. "This suggests otherwise. And we saw you sending a man ashore several days in a row with bulging bags. What will Mersad say when he finds out you've been keeping your coral, selling to someone else?"

She blinked, her skin prickling with gooseflesh. They'd seen her drop off Nikolas in the cove? Had they also seen where he'd hidden the gold?

Or did they only think he'd taken coral? *Only coral?* If they told Mersad, she'd not just lose her boat, her place as a diver. Mersad would have her beaten, thrown in prison. If he thought she and Nikolas had stolen from him, he'd stop at nothing to hunt Nikolas down.

Ennio and Pelos glanced at one another. "How much more coral is down there?"

"None."

"Think before you lie again." Pelos raised the knife toward Rex, the edge in his voice as razor-sharp as his blade. Rex whimpered.

She exhaled a long breath through her nose before admitting it through gritted teeth. "Enough to fill a boat."

Ennio's ocean-colored eyes rolled to Tychon and the three other boys before he gave a slight flick of his chin. They all disappeared over the side in booming splashes.

Why had she ever thought blue eyes exotic? They landed on her now, cold and calculating. The hair on her arms rose.

"Well? Go on, beautiful. Get me my coral."

She turned to the snake with the blade. "Put the knife away, Pelos. Does it make you a strong man to threaten a child?"

"I don't think you're in a position to barter with me."

"Do you want me to dive for you or not?"

Ennio hesitated, then glanced at Pelos and gave a nod. Pelos slipped the knife into the sheath strapped to his bare thigh and stepped away.

"Well, go on." Ennio flicked his hand toward the water.

Demi slid a sorry glance toward Rex and jumped.

Demi's limbs shook as she guided the boat back to Andriake, empty. Ennio and Pelos had decimated the coral on the ridge, taking every bit and heaping it on the prow of their red devil boat. She'd harvested her fair share, but every basket she'd filled, Rex had been forced to pull up and dump into the red boat.

Rex hunched next to her, head down. "I'm sorry, Demi." He sniffed, and his shoulders trembled.

Demi wrapped an arm around him and squeezed. "It isn't your fault, Rex, not a bit."

"But I said it out loud. They heard me."

She shut her eyes. "I told you to say the Lord's Prayer. And can you think of a better thing to do than pray when we're in trouble? When we're waiting? Or bored? Or afraid? I can't."

"But now we're really in trouble."

"Yes," she agreed, drawing in a steadying breath. "But I'd rather be in trouble for praying to the true God than anything else, wouldn't you?" Oh, that it would be so easy to say when she wasn't with people of the same mind.

Rex hesitated. Then nodded. "Will they come back tomorrow?"

"They said they would."

"And you have to dive for them?"

She shrugged. "Only until I can think of some way to get rid of them."

Rex moved to the prow, ready to catch the dock as Demi dropped the sail and coasted in.

Ennio and Pelos and their four sons stood in a circle of divers—everyone admiring the large fan of coral she'd found. Anger and injustice swelled.

Eels, all of them.

Rex caught the dock and steadied the boat as she climbed to the front.

"Go home while they're occupied, Rex. I'll be along soon. No need for them to follow you."

"I can wait for you."

She forced a smile, though it felt wobbly on her lips. "Go on. I'll be fine."

Rex hesitated a moment, then scurried off, keeping as much distance as possible between himself and the divers.

Demi tied off the boat and gathered her dive bag, ensuring the knife was handy. Not that it would do much good in an attack, but it made her feel better to know it was there.

She joined the others in the accounting line, a few sober and staring straight ahead and the rest congratulating Ennio and Pelos on their record haul. Ennio jostled his way through the group, angling for her. Demi lifted her chin and stepped up to the table where Mersad's accountant sat, record book open.

"Nothing today, Rasmus."

The accountant's thin eyebrows raised. "Nothing?"

Ennio bumped the table as he stepped beside Demi. "I never thought I'd see the day when Mersad's prize diver comes back with nothing."

Her jaw tightened and she kept her face forward. "It happens to everyone, Ennio. You of all people would know this."

Rasmus coughed.

Ennio's eyes flashed but his mouth stayed in the same smug smile. "I have a feeling the tides are changing. Mine are coming in; yours, going out."

"Perhaps." She shrugged. "Have a good evening, Rasmus. See you tomorrow."

Demi's chin stayed high, her spine straight as she left the line, but her legs wobbled once her feet hit the street, and when she'd turned the corner behind the dockside tavern, she stopped, bracing herself against the grime-covered wall with a shaking hand.

"What am I to do?" she whispered. If she dove for Ennio and Pelos, they'd take her coral and Mersad would take her boat. She'd not be able to trade for supplies and the church would suffer. If she refused to dive for them, they'd turn her in and cast suspicion on the school, on Nikolas. She'd lose the boat and endanger her friends.

She was as stuck as Theseus had been. Trapped between a reef and a moray, and fast running out of air.

THIRTY-SIX

ANDRIAKE RANG WITH THE CLAMOR OF TRADE. Overseers barked at laborers while carters loaded heaps of goods to be carried off to warehouses lining the streets behind the docks. Sailors of all nations staggered from shop to eatery to tavern, filling themselves with luxuries only afforded on land. Nikolas dodged a man whose shoulders were weighted with a pole hung with cages of squawking chickens.

Had Demi made it back on time? He'd raced to Andriake before going back to the school, but her boat was gone by the time he reached Mersad's docks. Rex hadn't joined classes today and there was a measure of relief that he hadn't returned early. All must be well. Was she as exhausted as he? His limbs had grown heavy on the walk. It was a wonder Demi had energy to dive at all.

He turned down a side street, past a stack of crates overflowing with peaches that perfumed the air in a scent thick and sweet. His mouth watered. The rushed anxiety of the morning had erased his appetite and pushed aside all thoughts of his conversation with Demi until now. What a weight she carried. How cumbersome his own had become. Why was it so hard to release them?

He massaged the bridge of his nose and sighed, too tired to delve further. After the long night on the river, and the morning spent teaching, his head pounded and he wanted nothing more than a meal and his bed. Maybe just his bed.

All of that would have to wait. Basil had sent a message during Latin class, asking Nikolas to meet at his new office in Andriake.

Nikolas paused before a freshly painted storefront. According to the directions on the missive, this was it. He raised a brow, taking in the scarlet paint covering the entire building, offset by a door the color of lime rind. The sign above the door depicted a poorly rendered image of a ship filled with gold, or grain, with the words *Shrieking Peach* scrawled below. He squinted. Or maybe it said *Shipping Office*. That would make more sense.

He entered without knocking. "Could you have picked uglier paint, Basil?"

Basil straightened from where he'd been slumped over his desk, scribbling in a ledger. "No. The painter was cheap."

"Yes. We can all see that."

"It's eye-catching and that's all I care about." Basil waved a hand. "Bar the door behind you and sit. Thank you for coming."

Nikolas obeyed, then lowered himself into the chair opposite the desk.

"Now"—Basil rubbed his hands together and leaned across the desk—"the grain arrived, and I've unloaded it into a warehouse I'm renting. It can stay there however long you wish, or you can move and distribute it as you see fit. Either way, it's safe."

"Thank you, Basil. I never expected you to—"

"I also inspected the insula you told me about—terrible investment. But I have a list of others that would be a far better value . . ." Basil slid a square of papyrus across the desk with a hopeful look.

Nikolas pushed it back. "I want the one I told you about."

"That's ridiculous. It's crumbling and sinking. You'll never get your money back on it."

"I don't want my money back. I have my reasons for wanting it. What did you find out—besides how terrible it is?"

Basil sighed and leaned back in his chair, crossing his arms. "It's owned by Kazan, 'purveyor of hearth and home.'"

Nikolas raised an eyebrow. "A nice epithet for a slumlord. What is his price?"

"Exorbitant. Criminal." Basil waved a hand. "That insula would be worth more if the river swept it away."

"So you got it?"

Basil's eyes fell shut and he released a long exhale. "Unfortunately." He turned to the pigeonholed shelf behind him and tugged a roll of paper from it. "Congratulations, Nikolas, you are now a slumlord. You take possession in two weeks."

Nikolas unrolled the scroll to inspect the hastily written terms. "That's far less than I was willing to offer."

"Like I said. Exorbitant. He should have paid you to take it." Basil stood and crossed the room to a small table set with an amphora and two cups. "Wine to celebrate—or console?"

Nikolas shook his head and raised the scroll instead. "Thank you, Basil."

The man shrugged and scratched his head. "I can't imagine a way that this turns into a good business deal, but you've always had an odd sense about you."

A thrill went through Nikolas at the prospect of all the place could be. "Can we meet later this week to discuss repairs? I want to walk through it again."

"Repairs? Niko, that building is half sunk into the silt. You're better off tearing it down and rebuilding."

"Ahh, I nearly forgot about the legendary optimism of Basil of Smyrna."

Basil shook a finger at him. "You mock me now, but I'm telling you. This project will drain every coin in your coffers."

Nikolas stood and rerolled the scroll. "Speaking of coin, I'm out."

"So soon?" Basil crossed to the tapestry hanging behind his desk that appeared to have been designed by the same person who chose the paint colors outside. "No matter. I have a new list of needs for you." He drew back the tapestry to reveal an ironclad door set in the wall which he proceeded to unlock with a series of keys.

"I don't know how you find these people."

Basil turned, waving his fingers around his sweaty face. "It is the curse of handsome men. People approach you, tell you their problems."

Nikolas chuckled. "Thank goodness I have you then."

The ironclad door swung open revealing a stack of iron chests. Basil selected one and opened it, pulling out a jingling pouch. "This should be sufficient."

"Thank you for storing the gold for me." Nikolas held out his hand and Basil dropped the pouch into it.

"Thank you for trusting me." Basil relocked the door before pulling a scrap of parchment from a stack on the desk and holding it out to Nikolas. "These ones are in especially dire need. Go as soon as you can."

THIRTY-SEVEN

11 AUGUST, AD 310

"Thank you for coming with me, Theseus." Nikolas spoke in a low tone, though the busyness of the streets in the rush of early evening covered his words. "Since you know more than most, I thought it best to show you first. I've made plans on my own, but another set of eyes is always a good thing."

Theseus gave a hum of acknowledgment, running a hand through the unruly mass of curls crowning his head. "I have to admit, your proposal is intriguing."

The shadows grew longer as they left the city and its buildings of pale stone that reflected the day's heat. Yet even as the men neared the river, warmth seemed to radiate from the ground like an oven, filling the air with the stench of decay. Children played and scavenged through the heaps of trash, their arms bony twigs as they tossed bits of pottery and shouted at each other. The line between the riverside shantytown and Myra's prosperity was unmistakable.

"I'm not sure this is the most secure place for a food cache."

"I admit, I am more concerned with proximity to need and ease of distribution than security."

Theseus glanced at him. "You mean to distribute grain to them?" He waved his hand in a vague gesture toward the shantytown.

Nikolas sighed. "I can't keep singing about light shining into darkness while hiding behind a light-blocking curtain. We have rules to keep ourselves safe and fed, but what about our neighbors?"

"None of them are being arrested for trying to buy bread. That is what all the elders say."

"And what do you say, Theseus? Look around us. I can't in good conscience keep a storehouse of grain under lock and key when these little ones scrounge for rotting bits of food among the trash. Our people are suffering, yes, but is our own suffering the greatest thing at stake? Or have we become lamps under baskets? Salt is useless left in its barrel. It needs to be poured out and put to use. Where has our compassion gone?"

"Safety has been our highest priority for a long time. I don't disagree with you. It's only . . . difficult to imagine a different course."

"There is no safety. Only the illusion of it. If I'm to be arrested, then let me be arrested while doing the Lord's work—feeding the hungry, spreading the hope of Christ—not while hiding in comfort."

Theseus sidestepped a pile of animal dung. "Some say you're a reckless man, Nikolas. But your heart is true, I'll give you that." He shook his head. "And I cannot dispute what you say. There's an allure to shaking off the confines of hiding, to facing off against the darkness and shouting *do your worst*. And yet, I fear for my family."

"I don't fault you for that." Nikolas shrugged and watched a mangy dog trot across the street before them, tail low. "It's different for me, I suppose. I have . . . no one."

"You have us."

The bridge of his nose burned as a sudden lump rose to his throat. Those three words carried a power he hadn't realized they could, both awakening and soothing a long-empty ache in him.

He was glad the insula rose before them and seemed to save him from replying.

The top two levels had crumbled already, leaving the remaining main and upper level a labyrinth of open-air halls, tunnels, and billowing moth-eaten curtains forming walls where there were none.

Inside the gaping doorless entry, a man leaned against the inside hall, clutching the neck of an amphora of cheap wine and breathing heavily in wine-induced slumber. Nikolas's heart pinched, knowing this wouldn't be the only person he saw in such a state. Rubble and cobwebs lined the dim hall—but it was only a few steps until he and Theseus emerged into the central courtyard that more resembled an edible jungle than anything else. The church widows living in the insula had taken it upon themselves to turn the place into a garden. Cucumber and melon vines cascaded down entire walls, fruits hidden by wide, prickly leaves. Basil, lemon balm, chamomile, and rosemary burst from between cracked floor tiles. All around, some form of life reclaimed the ruins of the broken building.

Theseus kept his gaze fixed ahead. "Speaking of my family, I feel it's my duty to ask what your intentions are toward my sister." He angled a sideways glance toward Nikolas. "I've noticed the way you are with each other . . . the way she is with you, and . . . if you intend to take further risks, I feel I need to ask you to leave her be. She's lost so much already."

A broken bit of pottery skittered and hopped across the uneven tiles, set into a burst of motion with the toe of his sandal, only to clatter into a wall and break.

"I know," he murmured. Any relationship with Demi would have a similar outcome once set in motion. Best he sidestep it now.

Theseus didn't press further. He peered down a hall. "I'm no carpenter, but we might be able to put up walls there, and there. If we added doors to the other rooms, no one would notice an extra here."

Nikolas blinked, trying to shake the prior conversation from himself as easily as Theseus had done. He followed the movement of Theseus's finger as he pointed. The idea was a good one.

They walked through the remainder of the building, avoiding the inhabited corners, pointing and planning in low voices. He'd tempered his enthusiasm before then, unsure if his plan could truly come to anything. Theseus seemed to catch the excitement though, to see more than Nikolas had thought possible. They edged past the man in the hall clutching his empty wine amphora and wove through the shantytown trash heaps back toward Myra.

"You've a gift of vision."

Theseus shrugged. "Just because I can dream it up doesn't mean it's possible to do. It'll take a fortune to fix that place."

"That might be the least of our difficulties."

"Ah, yes. I nearly forgot." Theseus glanced at him, then toward the deepening sky. "You're welcome to eat with us this evening. Unless you need to be with others."

"I do, but not until later. I'd be glad to join you."

"You look exhausted," Nydia greeted, as Demi crawled through the tunnel opening of the crumbling hut in the dumping grounds where Nydia and Theseus had stayed in the days since the wedding. Nydia had set Nikolas's gift to work and had made the place a home with green curtains hanging from the newly repaired section of roof. Warm smells of spiced lentils and flatbread perfumed the air, wafting from a new clay cylinder stove in the open center of the garden. Demi's stomach cramped.

"I am." Demi crossed the space and slumped against the wall next to the firepot. "Where's Theseus?" The three-day festival over, she'd dived for two days hoping Ennio and Pelos would forget about their forced agreement, and for two days she'd kept silent over their continued thievery. But she couldn't anymore. This was not a problem she could solve on her own, no matter how much she wanted to.

"He's at the shantytown with Nikolas, looking at that old insula." Nydia gave the lentils a stir.

"Why?"

"They're looking to see if they can repair some things. For the widows there." Nydia studied her. "I've missed you."

"I've been trying to give you two space."

A smile turned up Nydia's lips. "I don't need that much space. Now, what's going on? You look troubled."

A surge of emotion flooded her with the violence of the evening tide crashing toward the harbor. But unlike the stone jetties that broke the waves, Demi broke instead. Exhaustion, frustration, and fear spilled down her cheeks as she explained about Ennio and Pelos and the impending loss of the boat. She'd just finished when the coded whistle sounded at the tunnel. Nydia hopped to her feet as Theseus and Nikolas crawled inside.

Demi's pulse jolted. She scrubbed at her face, her first thought a hope that Nikolas wouldn't stay. Then a sinking feeling that he would leave.

"Are you hungry? Sit and eat with us, Pastor Nikolas." Nydia's tone left no room for protest.

Demi held her breath.

"Thank you." Nikolas stood and brushed off his tunic.

She let out a breath and stood as well, her limbs feeling oddly unsteady. But of course it was only the aftermath of strenuous diving. That was all.

Nydia darted for the food she'd left sitting on the tiny worktable that doubled as a storage shelf along one wall. Theseus followed her, probably to snag an olive or—something else. Nikolas surveyed the room, his gaze falling on Demi, and was it her imagination, or did it soften?

She plastered on what she hoped was a benign expression and unrolled Nydia's new dining mat. "Good evening, Pastor Nikolas."

He walked toward her, his eyebrows flickering in confusion at the formal title. "Good evening." He drew out the words as he studied her face. "Are you well?"

Now was not the time to explain it.

"Just tired. As you must be also. Please, sit."

Nikolas obeyed and sat at the edge of the mat while Demi sought out the crate that served as a table.

"How were your students today?"

His mouth twitched. "They managed to roll a tiny snake into my scroll of Latin verbs, which was actually quite helpful since I was able to illustrate several verbs, like *jump* and *shout*. They found it very amusing."

Demi chuckled and settled a low table in front of him. Another result of his gift. "Oh, to be a fly on the wall of your classroom."

He shook his head. "That would be a dangerous thing to be—on account of all the frogs they bring."

"Don't tell Rex, or I might lose my spotter." She sat across from him, grateful for the way his presence could ease the tension from her shoulders if not her mind.

"I think he might be the supplier. How is diving?"

And the tension was back. Nydia and Theseus bent between them, saving her from replying as they lowered a pot of lentils and a basket of flatbread to the table. They sat and Theseus blessed the meal.

Demi held back as all hands went for the flatbread, her appetite erased as quickly as the tension had revived in her shoulders. Nydia sent her a side-eyed look, then betrayed her.

"Demi said Ennio and Pelos are making a move for the boat, Theseus. I don't think she should be out there alone."

Demi's eyes slammed shut as the men turned toward her. She'd not wanted to speak of this in front of Nikolas.

"Did they threaten you?" Theseus's voice took on a dangerous edge.

Demi kept her chin down, knotting her hands in her lap. "I don't know what to do," she whispered. "They know everything. About the school, our faith . . ." She met her brother's hard gaze. "If I don't give them my hauls, they'll turn everyone in. But if I give them everything, I'll lose the boat and then there's no way to go upriver—" She clapped a hand over her mouth as her voice broke. She should have told him—all of them—earlier. Should have warned them to start taking precautions.

Theseus muttered under his breath and ran a hand through his hair.

Nikolas stilled at her words, gaze locked on her. "Have they hurt you?"

Demi shook her head. "The only way they'll ever convince Mersad to give them my boat is if I dive for them and increase their coral quota. They won't hurt me." At least, not until they got what they wanted.

"So, they're using you to get the boat." Nikolas dropped his bread. "You can't mean to continue."

She lifted her shoulders. "Their hauls are poor on their own. If I quit now, there's a chance Mersad won't give them the boat, but they might turn us in to get even."

Theseus nodded, chewing at his thumbnail in thought. "But if you continue to dive and Mersad gives them the boat, I think they're more likely to say nothing and let us live with the knowledge that they have our family boat."

"Why do they hate you?" Nydia's brow wrinkled.

"They don't hate us. Not exactly." Theseus shook his head. "Some men . . . they must tear others down to feel they can stand. They do it to everyone."

"You can't keep diving for them." Nikolas turned the weight of his attention to Demi.

She lifted both hands. "Whether I do or not, the boat is gone. How are we supposed to—"

"I'll buy you a boat." Nikolas silenced the room in five words, his earnest gaze locked on Demi.

Her mouth dropped.

"I'll buy you whatever boat you want. Name it and it's yours, just don't . . . go back there." He shifted as the last words came out of his mouth, eyes darting toward Theseus, who stared at Nikolas with a look Demi couldn't quite discern. It hung somewhere between admiration and a sudden desire to throttle him.

"You'll need a libelli to buy a boat." Theseus shook his head. "Or a fortune. Not to mention the matter of docking it and paying for a space at the pier. A boat small enough to hide won't be large enough to haul supplies."

"You're worried about *libelli*?" Nydia wrinkled her nose. "Where would he even find money to buy a boat? . . . What? Why are you looking at me like that?" She blinked and snapped her lips shut with a slight shake of her head as if she'd just remembered that not all information was shared. Her tone lacked any petulance at being left out and turned grave. "Would you like me to leave so you can discuss?"

"No need." Nikolas shook his head. "I have . . . funds. And a contact who may be able to help."

"And if he can't help and I stop diving? What then? We'll lose the only way to trade for supplies."

"I'll go with you until we know for certain," Theseus said without hesitation. He eyed Nikolas with a squint, as if he suspected Nikolas might volunteer if he did not. "My work with the deacons can be done at night. They'll understand."

Demi wasn't convinced that even Theseus's presence would have much effect on their rivals, but she nodded anyway. Silence dropped over them, punctuated only by the dull knocking of Nydia's spoon as she scooped watery lentils into small clay bowls. Demi accepted her portion, appetite reviving after a bite.

"There is another matter." Nikolas drew a breath. "I've received a message from upriver, claiming plagues of Egyptian proportions have wiped out the harvest. Disease, locusts, fire . . . They've asked for aid."

"How soon?" Demi asked.

Nikolas shrugged. "As soon as possible, I'd think. How soon can we get the grain moved from Andriake to the cache cave?"

Theseus stopped chewing and stared into the corner, calculating. "Two weeks? Perhaps as little as ten days. That's a lot of grain to move without causing a riot. Unless . . ." His gaze shifted to Nikolas. "What if we moved it in the open?"

"What do you mean?"

Theseus spoke slowly, mulling an idea even as the words came from his mouth. "You spoke of hiring the deacons to make repairs on the insula, yes? They'll need to cart in bricks, plaster, timber. Why not hide the grain beneath a layer of supplies? The cache cave isn't far from the insula. We could haul so much more in plain sight and be ready in a few days."

"That is good." Nikolas nodded. "I'll have Xeno start spreading the word tonight."

After the meal had been reduced to crumbs, Nikolas stood to leave. "Thank you for letting me share your meal. I need to get back. Xeno will be waiting. He seems to arrive earlier and earlier every evening."

Demi rose with the others.

"We bid you good night then. God go with you." Theseus gripped Nikolas's hand, then turned to help Nydia gather the dishes and remnants of the meal.

Demi followed Nikolas to the tunnel entrance.

"Thank you," she whispered. "A boat feels a selfish thing in light of everything else and yet, the supplies—"

"I loathe the thought of you diving for those men." Nikolas lowered his voice.

His concern warmed her. How could he be so kind after all she'd told him? She deserved to endure a little danger, did she not?

Demi chewed her lip and slowly met his gaze. "They threatened you too," she whispered, eyes darting toward Theseus and Nydia, then back to him. Nikolas watched her but didn't speak.

"They saw me put you ashore with the bags—and they assumed you were taking my coral and I was double-crossing Mersad." She gripped his arm. "No one double-crosses Mersad. If Ennio and Pelos tell Mersad what they saw, he'll stop at nothing to find you. And thanks to Rex, they already know about the school." Her voice dropped further. "If anything happens to any of you, it'll be all my fault."

"You heap blame upon your shoulders that isn't yours to carry." Nikolas shot a nervous glance toward Theseus. "You forget that I asked you to dive for me. That it was my stupid mistake that drew you away from filling your coral quota. If anyone's to blame for this, it's me."

She let out a breath. "Niko—"

"I'll get you a boat, I'll do whatever I can, but . . . please. Don't go back alone."

An ache crawled up the center of her chest. "Theseus will be with me."

"I still don't like it—and don't say 'everything we do is dangerous,' because that doesn't make it easier to accept."

"You prowl about the city at night with money. That isn't safe either."

He took a quick breath, as if to argue, and then let it out. "I don't think we're going to convince each other to stop, are we?" His words were more realization than question as his gaze caressed her face.

A thrill stirred through her, and her breath caught. "No," she whispered.

Theseus cleared his throat.

"Yes, well, I best be going." Nikolas ducked into the tunnel.

"You too." Demi watched him flee, her insides cringing as his words registered too late. *You too?* One more thing to keep her awake at night. She turned and froze.

Theseus and Nydia stood near the worktable, his expression as thunderous as hers was enraptured.

"Demi—"

"Yia-yia is going to be thrilled!"

Stupid heat rushed up Demi's neck. "Why?" she muttered, plowing toward her sleeping mat, rolled and propped against the wall.

Nydia beamed. "You and Nikolas—"

"Shouldn't even consider—" Theseus broke in.

"Falling for each other!" they finished in unison.

Nydia's grin fell and she spun at Theseus. "What?"

Demi unrolled her mat with a snap.

"You heard me." Theseus crossed his arms. "He's a good man, Demi, but he takes too many risks. You'll only end up hurt again. I've already talked to him and—"

"You *talked* to him?" Demi spun toward Theseus, who raised both hands. Was it possible to be more mortified?

"He knows he's not in a safe position for a wife and family—"

"Who is?" Nydia argued.

Demi flopped onto the mat, rolling her back to them and squeezing her eyes shut. "No one's falling for anyone. And I'm sleeping, good night." The words barely made it out around the lump in her throat. Had Nikolas said he wasn't interested in a wife? A family? It was a wise decision. One she shared. But that didn't keep the ache from burning in her chest long after Nydia and Theseus's sharp whispers had been exchanged for the deep, even breathing of sleep.

THIRTY-EIGHT

5 SEPTEMBER, AD 310

Nikolas crossed the courtyard garden and went deeper into the labyrinth of walls newly shorn up with bright patches of fresh plaster. Solid wooden doors lined the halls and he ticked them off one by one until he spied the open doorway ahead. They'd expanded that apartment and then cut it back to its normal size with a new wall of plastered timber. The new safe room could be accessed through a cupboard inside the apartment or a small metal door locked and hidden in the overgrown brush tangling around the outside of the insula between it and the river.

Light spilled out of the apartment door, flung wide and splashing the stained walls of the hallway in golden welcome.

He hesitated, then hurried forward at the sound of arguing voices that didn't belong there. His pulse kicked up as he ducked through the opening and into the humid warmth of a single room, crammed with more people and bodily odors than there should be in an apartment shared by three poor widows. He lowered the bundle of wood to the floor, searching faces for the three elderly women he'd come to see. Alarm shot through him. Where was Amata? Phoebe? Kore? Who were all these other people?

"Phoebe? Kore?"

A handful of ragged people milled about the room, chattering, eating. None of them seemed to mind or notice his sudden appearance.

"Amata?"

"Niko." The familiar voice spoke his name with drawn-out delight.

He smiled with relief as the elderly woman emerged between two tattered men arguing over philosophy—of all things. Back slightly humped, gray hair frizzing in all directions, Amata cupped his face in her bent hands and kissed both of his cheeks. "Glad to see you, my boy."

He lowered his voice. "What's going on here? Are you all right? Are these people taking your food?"

"Not at all!" She beamed and surveyed the room. "We are doing as you suggested."

"What do you mean?"

She leaned closer, hazel eyes sparkling. "You're not as subtle as you might think."

Nikolas cocked his head, one eyebrow flicking up. "Oh?"

"It isn't a great secret to anyone what you've been up to since you arrived." She lowered her voice. "You and good deeds in the night came to Myra hand in hand."

His stomach twisted and he shook his head. How did she know these things?

Amata studied him. "Your courage, your kindness, is not without effect. Courage never is. It's a spark to a fire that can't help but draw others to the blaze."

He raised his eyes to the others in the room. Ragged outcasts, half-starved misfits gathered in a room too small to house them, too few chairs to seat them, but full to the brim with welcome. His throat burned.

"I do not mean to offend your position as pastor, Nikolas. But the greatest work of the church does not happen at the morning river meetings, but in the markets, at the wells, in the shops and kitchens—in our lives, and how we live and give the gospel."

"I am not offended, Amata." His voice went husky, and he gripped both of her hands. "I have long believed such, and I am deeply relieved to have another coconspirator."

She giggled and squeezed his fingers. "Come, meet my friends. We all bring what we are able and together it is enough for everyone to share a meal." She glanced at the bundles of wood at his feet. "And we were wondering how to cook the fish Leo brought. The Lord provides. I hated to burn the door so soon."

She introduced him to the others, but he declined the tempting offer to stay and eat. "I've got a meeting tonight, but I wanted to see that you all are well."

Amata gripped both of his hands with a knowing look. "God go with you, Niko."

The trip upriver went smoother than any other had, and it left Demi on edge. The whole month had been too smooth. Though the damage to Theseus's lungs had kept him from diving, simply having him in the boat with her during the day had proven enough of a deterrent for Ennio and Pelos that all month they'd lurked about their boat but never bothered them. Perhaps they'd noticed that with the water beginning to cool, and the currents signaling the fast-approaching end of the diving season, Demi's coral finds remained poor.

She'd tried not to panic at all that meant.

After dark, Theseus had accompanied her to the docks and upriver as far as the cache cave where Nikolas and Xeno met them to load the boat with grain. When Nikolas climbed into the boat with her, she could sense Theseus chafing at being left behind as he shoved them off. "I'll meet you at the fountain with four faces, when you get back. We'll stay at the sponge shop tonight."

Kyros was waiting at the pier when they returned and docked without a word. He simply tipped his head and turned his back as they moored the boat and tiptoed from the creaking dock.

The sweet, dusky scent of ripening citrus enveloped them as they angled for the orange groves between Andriake and where Theseus would be waiting to walk Demi to the sponge shop.

The night was still, quieted by the admonition of crickets singing *hush-hush-hush*.

Nikolas swallowed, the sound loud against the shushing of crickets. "I've missed this," he admitted in a whisper.

She smiled. "Aren't you running about the streets most nights?"

"Not with you."

A jittery warmth spread through her. How could he miss something that had only happened once? Instead, she asked, "How do you know who to help?"

His shoulder bumped hers as he shrugged. "I have an old friend with a unique . . . gift. People reveal their troubles to him, tell him things, and he—if he cannot repeat their stories—at least tells me what they need."

"It must be nice. To see a need and be able to fill it."

He kicked at a stone, sending it skittering up the path. "Sometimes it seems worthless. The world is full of needs that cannot be filled with gold. Needs that can be filled by anyone with a bit of patience and a listening ear. I'm not the best with those."

"You prefer actions and results."

"To a fault."

"Were your parents like you too? So . . . giving?" She realized that while he'd spoken of their deaths, of the inheritance they'd left, he hadn't spoken much about who they were.

"My mitera loved our Lord," he began softly. "Pater claimed the faith as well, but never acted on it the way she did. She was always bringing a meal or medicine to someone. While my brother worked with my pater, I used to accompany her, carry things, fix what I could while she visited. Pater used to laugh about it and say that he worked so she could give it all away."

Nikolas spoke with a fondness in his voice that faded when he stooped to retie the loose straps of his sandal, shifting the other foot forward and doing the same. "He changed after she died. Blamed the people she helped for making her ill. Blamed me for . . . taking her to them. Not long after, Pater dragged me and Amadeo on a trading trip to distract us. Amadeo took to it like a fitted garment, but I hated it. Instead of finding myself distracted from my grief, I only felt more lost, more alone. Aimless. I . . ."

"What?"

He stood. "It's silly, but we stopped in Andriake just before going home and the beach looked so much like the one my family used to picnic on in Patara. It made me weep like I'd never done before." He swallowed. "Then this little girl appeared out of nowhere, ragged and wild and toothless. And she gave me the only fruit she had, and told me I couldn't be sad while eating an orange."

Her heart made a strange leap at his words.

Nikolas heaved a dry laugh and pushed to his feet. "I was envious of her. Wildly envious. I had everything, and none of her joy. She had nothing and yet possessed the only thing I wanted." He dared a glance in Demi's direction.

She squinted at him, mentally subtracting his height, his beard, most of his muscle. "That was you?" She breathed the question more than spoke it.

"Me?"

"The boy . . . crying on the rocks."

THIRTY-NINE

NIKOLAS STARED AT HER, mentally subtracting half her height, half her teeth, half her hair. "You . . . you're the girl with no teeth."

She blinked. "After everything else you said, that's what you remember about me?" Her fingers went to her mouth. "I was six. They grew back."

"You remember me as the boy crying on the rocks."

"*Sobbing*, actually. I was trying to be nice."

They fell silent. The city of Myra sprang up between the trees ahead, the fountain with four faces only a few streets away.

Demi drew a quick breath. "I didn't mean to—"

"I never forgot you. What you did. I . . . I've made mistakes, but you have to know, you changed something in me back then."

She shook her head. "It was just an orange."

"To you, yes. But not to me."

The path they'd followed through the grove changed from gravel to stone as they entered the streets of Myra. Ahead, the street widened into a small plateia, the center crowned with an ornately carved fountain pool. A huge block of limestone dominated the middle, carved into a single head with four grotesque faces that melted from a smirk to a grin to a grimace to a frown dribbling water from its sagging jowls.

Nothing moved in the square and Nikolas shifted into the shadows of a carpentry shop called Woodhouse. One word. Letters so large and shoved together it appeared to have been made by the same painter who'd done Basil's shipping office. Demi stepped beside him just as the clouds broke, splattering moonlight onto the streets.

Muffled voices and laughter suddenly burst onto the street in full volume as a door opened farther up the road. Orange lamplight illuminated a staggering group of men as they exited and attempted to retell differing versions of the same tale. Nikolas froze. Why didn't they move on? Why leave the tavern and yet linger?

Demi's hand crept into his, fingers tightening. Keeping his eyes on the men, he edged closer to the alcove of the carpentry shop's inset doorway, kicking himself for not stepping into it sooner. Demi crowded against him, her breath brushing his neck. He tried to focus on the men, slowly dissipating up the street, but her nearness left him in a heady rush. He was running out of time. Theseus would arrive soon, and the ache in his chest wouldn't ease unless he spoke the words that grew more and more difficult to suppress.

"Demitria . . ." Her name left his lips like a caress and he paused, waiting for her to interrupt, to tell him not to speak, not to say the words he needed to say and she probably didn't want to hear.

But Demi said nothing, her chin tilting upward and her expression so still in the moonlight that he could see her pulse flickering in her neck.

His mouth dried, heart pounding in time with hers. "I've never met anyone with a heart like yours. Tender and courageous—yes, courageous. Don't shake your head like that."

The moonlight lit a silver streak on her cheek. He reached up and smeared it away with his thumb, letting his fingers linger along her jaw, brush against the pulse in her neck. Again—*always*—waiting for her to pull away, give him some sign that his affection was unwanted, that this endeavor would meet the same failure as every other.

"I cannot stay silent any longer. You have to know how I care for you. How much I . . . I love you."

He felt the sharpness of her inhale against his fingertips, and still, she didn't pull away. But then, he did have her backed against a door. *Stupid Niko.* He swayed backward but before he could take a full step, Demi touched his arm, that one tiny movement effectively freezing his feet and breath.

She released a ragged breath. "You hold my heart, Nikolas. But I'm afraid to let it go. What if I lose you too?"

The soft words loosed a flood of relief within him and buoyed a resilient hope. "I know you're afraid, Demi—and not without reason. You've loved and lost, and that is a deep wound only God can heal." He ran his thumb over the swell of her cheek. "Love is never without risk—I took that plunge the moment I laid eyes on you, and I know you may never return my feelings. But I can't leave them unspoken any longer." He swallowed. "I can't promise to love you until I'm old and white-bearded. But however long God grants me life, whether it's a century, a year, or only a day, I will love you until my last breath."

Her dark lashes lowered, and she turned her face into his hand, lips pressing to his fingers in a way that made his heart sink. The rejection was coming. He could sense it in the turmoil of her expression. How foolish of him to think he could profess his love and she would respond in kind.

Her lips parted and she took a quick breath as if to speak, but she didn't. Instead, she reached up, fingers threading into his hair as she tugged his head down.

He resisted. "I don't want to say goodbye like that."

She rolled to her tiptoes. "It isn't goodbye."

Her lips brushed his, tentative and sweet, and the last of his hesitation crumbled. He lowered his head, mouth finding hers in a kiss full of risk and promise and hope. Demi felt right in his arms, as if she'd always been meant to fit there, a piece of him he didn't know was missing until that moment. If he'd been called to lead this church, he could think of no one else he wanted by his side than this woman. Kind, generous, brave.

Nikolas broke the kiss and drew in a shaky breath, and Demi dropped flat-footed once more. She ran her fingertips over his stubbled cheeks, her lips quirking.

"What?" he whispered.

"I'm imagining you with a white beard. You're rather striking."

He laughed and tugged her against him, pressing another kiss to her hair, which smelled of sun and sea. Soft footsteps scraped into the plateia, and Nikolas's gaze darted toward the figure who stopped in the shadows at the edge of the square, facing them.

Demi shifted and a rush of cool air separated them. "Theseus is here," she whispered.

FORTY

As they angled back through the city toward the school, Theseus managed to stay between Demi and Nikolas in a way that might have been comical if it hadn't been so terribly annoying. When had he grown up and become the mature, responsible adult looking out for her? And why at this exact moment? Beneath her bare feet, the paving stones were cool, the temperature the only thing ensuring she wasn't actually floating. The thrill of Nikolas's kiss washed over her again in a warmth she felt clear to her toes. He loved her. And she loved him.

Her heel connected with something sticky on the street. Definitely not floating. And yet, that bit of reality made the moment in her mind all the more real.

Demi glanced at the sky. Any moment, dawn would break like a wave over the harbor seawall, spraying a burst of light into the heavens. She should be exhausted. Should be longing for her bed. Dreading a new day of diving with Theseus, who'd obviously seen or at least suspected what had gone on between her and Nikolas, and who wouldn't be as quiet about it once they were alone. Instead, a rush of energy filled her. How was she supposed to sleep after that? She'd head to the dive boat now if she could see.

Ahead, the columned portico of the school shone a pale gray in the starlight. Almost back. Instead of Nikolas walking her home and turning back to the school alone, they'd leave Nikolas at the school and then—

Theseus turned into her, stepping on her foot, his shoulder ramming into her chest.

"Hey—"

Her protest was cut off as he gripped her arm and spun her around. "Run, Demi." The words ground between his teeth as Theseus yanked her into motion.

Male voices, raised in shouts, echoed behind them.

Panic laced her limbs and her heart rammed into her throat. Demi cast a glance over her shoulder in time to see shadows peel from dark walls, puddling in the street with a glint of starlight on swords. In a breath they were running back the way they'd come, Demi in the middle hemmed in by Theseus and Nikolas.

"Who are they?" she gasped.

Whether or not they knew, neither man answered, the pounding of booted feet behind them a clear enough explanation that someone had known where they'd be and had alerted the guards. Who would have done such a thing? Ennio and Pelos? But how could they have known they'd be here now?

Theseus bumped her shoulder and Demi careened into Nikolas, who caught her by a miracle and gripped her hand. Ahead, the road brightened with a cross street.

"Split up," Theseus wheezed. "Niko, take Demi."

There wasn't time or breath to argue, but Demi tried anyway. "We're not splitting—"

"Can't run anymore, Demi." Theseus faltered, coughed. "Niko, take her." He twisted down one arm of the cross street, visibly slowing as his injured lungs betrayed him. Betrayed them all.

Demi bolted after him, but Nikolas pulled her in the opposite direction, spinning her in a circle.

"No!" She wrenched against his grip, straining toward Theseus. "We can't leave him."

"I don't want to leave him either, but he's trying to protect you, Demi." Nikolas's words came fast. There was no time to argue. "If they catch us, it's one thing, but if they get you . . ."

The clank of armor and boots emphasized his words. She hated that he was right. Tears slammed in her eyes. Perhaps Theseus would have a better chance hiding alone than if all three of them stayed together. *Lord, protect him.*

Nikolas dragged her feet into motion. Demi threw one last glance toward her brother. The horde of shadows divided behind them. Nikolas's hand tightened around hers, his breath coming in sharp gasps. He started to pull her down a dark side street, but Demi yanked back, recognizing the shop front.

"Dead end." She careened into a different street, dragging Nikolas after her.

He glanced over his shoulder. "They're gaining."

"Keep going." They couldn't give up. She'd witnessed the horrors inflicted on her family, and the memories sent new energy lacing through her limbs. Nikolas's breaths came in bursts and a dagger rammed her ribs with each step. They wouldn't outrun the guards. Her throat and eyes burned but it wasn't the exertion. *Lord, help us.* Why was every man she'd loved cut down in the street? Her fingers tightened around Nikolas's.

At every turn, the booted feet followed, gained. She could hear the grunts, the ragged breaths. Panic seized her chest. There was no way out. *Please, please help us.*

Ahead, the moonlight fell on a torn-up section of road cluttered with stacks of bricks, paving stones, and an unmistakable stench.

"Demi," Nikolas gasped. "There is a way . . ."

She was already shaking her head. "No."

"It's the only way."

Tears choked her throat. "Don't. Please don't. Niko—"

"I love you." His words slashed her heart like a goodbye as his fingers tightened around hers. He jerked her in front of him, propelling her toward the opposite side of the road where a pile of paving stones and bricks nearly obscured the gaping hole in the street, even if they couldn't disguise the smell. He shoved, hand tearing free from hers as her feet lifted from the ground. As she fell, a dark shape lunged from behind, engulfing Nikolas and taking him to the street.

FORTY-ONE

DEMI WAS FALLING INTO BLACKNESS.

Her arms and legs thrashed in midair, the world dropping away beneath her. And then it was back, crashing into her knees, stinging her palms. The impact jarred her shoulders into her ears. Stars streaked through the blackness around her before reality snuffed them out.

The ground struck first, but the smell of sewage and rot landed a double blow that nearly sent her senseless. Why couldn't her breath have been knocked out? She shoved to her feet, stumbling until the curved wall of the sewer tunnel met her outstretched palms. Her throat and chest burned.

Nikolas.

Curses rang out somewhere above her. She looked up and caught sight of the circle of midnight floating in the blackness above. Darker shapes moved in the opening. Bodies and glinting blades. A thud and grunt of pain followed by the sickening sounds of angry fists connecting with flesh.

Nikolas, what have you done? It should have been her. A panicked sob burst between her lips and she clawed at the impossibly curved sides of the tunnel, nails catching on rough stones as she searched for a way out, a way to put up one last valiant fight by his side. It wasn't fair, for him to take that from her. *Coward. Coward.* The word circled her mind as if, instead of being shoved—saved—she'd once again taken the easy path.

No way out.

At least, not the way she'd come.

On the street above, the beating concluded. Muttering voices and laughter replacing thudding fists. A louder thud and a grunt of pain made her look up. Niko's face slammed into the circle of faint moonlight above, a foot on his neck.

"*Demi.*" He groaned her name, his shoulders jerking as if his arms had been yanked behind his back. The men trussing him up before dragging him away forever.

"Niko—" Her mouth moved but no sound emerged.

"Feed the sheep."

The men jerked him upright, his face disappearing as quickly as it had appeared. She reached toward him, her fingers finding nothing but empty air over her head.

"Wasn't there another one?" The strange voice was loud and rough.

"Jumped into the sewer like a rat," another answered. "Doesn't matter. We got the one we wanted."

Her body shook. Demi slumped against the wall, pressing a fist against her teeth, choking on sobs and the stench—and why couldn't she scream? *I'm here! Take me too!*

The voices and coarse laughter faded, replaced by a faint trickle of water and scuttling from further up the sewer tunnel.

Feed the sheep.

The task was daunting. Overwhelming. Impossible. She squeezed her eyes shut, the charge weighting her ankles like too many diving stones. It was too great a task to bear. And who was she to undertake such a thing? Hadn't she proven herself a coward so many times before? How could this be any different?

Stone bit into her spine through her thin chiton, reminding her of where she stood, ankle deep in sludge and filth. Nikolas had saved her. Given himself up for her to live, to go on. He'd offered her a second chance—Theseus had too. How could she stay here and make their sacrifice meaningless?

Feed My sheep.

The three words echoed in her mind, both firm and gentle. A command and an invitation. A realization that what Nikolas had done for her was only a shadow compared to what Jesus had done. The second chance He offered. She'd failed Him, yes. But He stood ready to forgive and restore.

The choice was hers.

Wallow in guilt, wearing the filth of what her shame told her she was. Or walk out with purpose.

"But how, Lord?" Her whisper broke against the stone walls. "How am I to care for Your people? Without Nikolas? Without—"

My grace is sufficient for you. My power is made perfect in weakness.

The words came to her mind bidden by the Spirit alone. The whirling questions stopped for a moment. Pressure built in her chest.

Weak was exactly what she felt. Powerless. Everything she'd done had guilt at its beginning, worry in the middle, and unworthiness at the finish. Her service had been motivated by guilt and fear, not power and love. She leaned her head back, pressing into the tunnel walls, tears scalding her raw cheeks. What if she failed?

Come back, Lord. Won't You come back? You promised You would. Don't You see the evil? When will it end? When will You make all things new? I'm tired and afraid.

The silence was answer enough. The instructions had been issued. The choice to obey was hers.

The trembling in her limbs slowly firmed with a courage beyond herself. Those men, and whoever sent them, wouldn't win. For the moment, yes. But not really. The end was written, and God be her help, she wouldn't stop resisting the darkness creeping over the world. No matter how strong it seemed, the darkness was doomed. And she would remind it of that until her last breath.

FORTY-TWO

BLOOD AND STARS.

Pain radiated through his ribs, throbbed between his eyes. Nikolas stumbled when the men—guards—shoved him through a screeching door. The ones who'd captured him on the street had dragged him to the basilica and turned him over to the city guards, claiming they'd caught a thief. Nikolas had refuted the charges—what was he to have stolen? He demanded messages be sent to Master Evander and Basil. The guards had barely said a word to him, only muttered something about the magistrate settling it after the festival as they escorted him to the tiny carcer. There'd be a three-day wait before his trial, and a shorter period between the trial and his release, or execution.

Nikolas collapsed on the slick floor with something of relief. He suspected ribs were broken, knew his nose was. Each breath cut like a knife. His mouth tasted of copper. The door slammed shut, locking him in darkness.

He touched his lip, tender and swollen. The night watch hadn't been gentle. Nor had they considered he might not actually be guilty of theft. What theft? The city guards had been kinder. If one called locking an innocent in the carcer kind. At least they hadn't found Demitria.

Lord, protect her.

"Nikolas?"

His chin jerked up at the familiar voice, heart beating a double rhythm of dread. *Lord, no. Please not*—"Theseus?"

A rustling in the darkness to his right answered. Then a hand bumped against his knee, gripped his arm. "Where's Demi?"

Nikolas shook his head. "Not with me." Theseus's fingers tightened, and Nikolas lowered his voice to a whisper. "There was an open sewer grate in the street. It was the only way . . ."

Theseus let out a breath and loosed his grip on Nikolas's arm. "She's free?"

"Yes." As far as he knew. *Lord, let it be so.*

"Thank you."

"Are you hurt?"

Theseus coughed. "I've been in worse fights."

They lapsed into silence. Nikolas slumped to the rancid floor, curling against the daggers in his side. His head swam. Perhaps the fact that he was a tutor at an esteemed school would help exonerate him. And yet—what about Theseus? Perhaps he'd only been arrested on Nikolas's account and would be freed.

Even as he smoothed the situation in his mind, he knew the question they'd ask, the sign they'd demand.

Are you loyal to the empire? Prove it.

Would Master Evander and Lady Isidora place themselves, the school, and the church at risk to try to exonerate him? He was no thief. And yet, his stomach sank with the realization that the risk would be too great. That they'd cut him free to protect themselves. Wasn't that part of the code? What he'd agreed to? A good shepherd gives his life to save his sheep. He'd give it up a hundred times to know for certain Demitria was safe.

Guilt nagged at the edges of his mind. She'd not be in danger if he hadn't invited her into it. Theseus would be home with his new wife. All would be well.

"I'm sorry, Theseus," he whispered. "I fear I've led you down a dangerous path and there is no turning back now."

Theseus shifted and let out a grunt of pain. "The path we walked was already dangerous. How much better to walk it with a friend. A brother."

Nikolas was glad for the darkness. For the way it hid the sudden tremble in his chin when the word *brother* sent a flash of memory to his mind. Amadeo, crumpled in a sticky pool on the docks. Blood draining from his crushed skull. Would he always bring death to those closest to him?

He couldn't breathe. When would it end?

God, forgive me. Grant us strength.

FORTY-THREE

ONE HAND BRACED ON THE CURVED WALL, Demi slid her bare feet over the precarious ledge built into the side of the tunnel for the sewer inspectors to use. When Rome had taken the Lycian region under its control, the first things they'd introduced to the major cities were public latrines and sewer systems, followed closely by the circus. Though she'd never set foot in the latter, she'd never been more thankful for the sewer system until now. Although she couldn't be certain of her direction. Would she end up at the mouth where the sewer drained into the Myros River? Or wander forever in the dark maze beneath the city?

"Lord, help me." Her whisper seemed to echo back to her, reminding her that she was not relying on her strength alone. The knowledge wrapped her in warmth.

Squeaks and splashes preceded her slow shuffle, and she was grateful the rats were moving away from her instead of toward. She'd been chased enough for one night.

Tears stung her eyes and her chest tightened with quick breaths. Had Theseus escaped? Where had they taken Nikolas—and why? Had they only beaten him, or left him dead in an alley? A sob bumped past her lips, and she struggled to swallow it back, drowning the others that followed. It wouldn't do to cry in an echoing sewer. She pressed forward, drawing slow breaths that threatened to gag her as much as calm the anxious tumble of her thoughts.

The tunnel curved ahead, and around the bend, a trickle of gray light filtered in through a grate in the street. Dawn had arrived. Demi hurried and paused beneath the grate, hoping to catch a glimpse of a building and piece together where she was. Nothing but sky in the grate—and yet, the air stirred around her. Was it just the holes in the grate allowing it in or . . .

She pressed on, the stir in the air growing stronger as she went and then, far ahead, a pinprick of light, a glint in the sludge. The ledge seemed to widen as the light grew brighter, larger. Her feet moved faster, each step growing firm with purpose. No stopping now, no turning back. She was running when she left the foul mouth of the sewer, bursting into the clean air and vibrant green of the reeds spread along the riverbank. Demi flung herself into the current, allowing the water to flood over her in a welcome rush, cleansing the filth from her.

A declaration.

A baptism of body and soul.

Her head broke the surface as her feet struck rock, knees straightening, propelling her upward. Droplets streamed from her body as she slogged to the bank, the cold water setting fire in her veins, or perhaps it wasn't the water after all.

Titus opened the door in hesitant response to her pounding fists. "Demi." His eyes went wide, and he tucked his dagger into his belt as he stepped back to let her in. "Are you well? What happened?" His gaze flicked over her dripping form.

Demi's chin trembled, tears burning the backs of her eyes. "Nikolas is gone." Exhaustion, hunger, and relief shook her limbs and choked her words. The back of her hand went to her mouth, then jerked away as the faint smell of sewer struck her nose. "Mugged or arrested—I don't know."

"Come." Titus barred the door behind her and gestured toward the kuzina.

Demi's knees wobbled and Titus took her arm as they entered the kitchen, already warm with a fire and pot of boiling water.

Iris turned as they entered. "Demi?" She skirted the worktable, bolting toward her as Titus gently pushed Demi down on a stool. "What are you doing here? What's wrong?" Worry creased her brow.

Demi's eyes squeezed shut. She bit her lip. "Nikolas and I went upriver last night. Theseus met us to walk me home, and we were attacked."

Iris's hands went to her mouth.

Titus looked grim. "Where are they?"

Demi shook her head. "We split up. I don't know where Theseus is. And I . . . Nikolas sacrificed himself for me." Her voice wavered and broke. "He pushed me through an open sewer grate. I heard them beat him and drag him away." The reality of it struck the air from her lungs. She dropped her head into her hands, emotions rising to a tidal wave that could not be suppressed any longer.

"Are you hurt?" Iris touched her shoulder.

Demi shook her head, scrapes and bruises nothing compared to what Nikolas had endured. She looked up at Titus. "I don't know what they did with him—or where Theseus is. If they're hurt somewhere or—"

"I'll go look. Where were you?"

She shrugged, mind scrambling. "The sewer grate was open because someone was working on it. There were bricks piled nearby."

Titus gave a quick nod and ducked out the door, one hand on his knife.

Iris tucked an arm around Demi's shoulder. "Come. Let's find you a dry chiton."

They'd only stepped through the doorway when Nydia darted up the hall, Rex in tow.

"Mater—*Demi*? Where have you been? I've been so worried. Where is Theseus?"

Demi's stomach sank and new tears burned her throat. "I don't know," she choked.

Nydia paled, taking in Demi's drenched clothes and the smell of sewer clinging to her. "What do you mean?"

Demi explained again and Nydia's knees wobbled as her hand shot out to steady herself against the wall.

"But you don't know that he was caught?" Nydia's voice sounded strangely breathless. Her shoulders twitched and she pressed the back of her hand to her mouth.

Demi shook her head. "I didn't see him after we split up."

Nydia's shoulders jerked again and she bolted for the kuzina. The sounds of retching followed.

Iris pushed Demi down the hall, twisting to call to Rex over her shoulder. "Get your sister some water. We'll join you shortly."

Titus didn't return for hours. Demi helped Nydia in the kuzina until exhaustion collapsed her on the dining cushions. She awoke to the scrape of an opening door and voices just above a whisper.

Demi lurched upright, pushing matted curls from her face. Titus slouched against the door, his posture bearing witness to the news he carried. Dread curdled her gut. She couldn't make her body move.

"What is it, Titus?" Her whisper lifted his head, and light glinted in his pale eyes as they rested on her, then shifted back to Nydia.

"I spoke with Lady Isidora." His voice rumbled low and sent a flood of quivering anxiety rushing through her veins. He let out a long breath. "Nikolas has been arrested."

Demi blinked, the words slipping over her like a wave that struck and retreated, but didn't stay long enough to stick.

Nikolas.

Arrested.

The wave came again, this time dragging her under and stealing her breath. *Nikolas, arrested.* Old images flashed through her mind. Unwanted, unbidden, undimmed by years. The glint of blades and the thick shine of blood on the pavement. *Not him too, Lord. Not him too.*

A strangled whimper cut through the room's silence. Demi clapped both hands over her mouth and only then realized the sound was not her own. Titus put a hand on Nydia's shoulder and she crumpled into his hug. Truth settled in Demi's gut like an anchor. She shook her head. "Not Theseus, too, don't say it."

"We're not certain of Theseus yet," he murmured. "Only that no one's seen him." Titus sighed, shoulders drooping in a way that made him look even older and careworn. "My contact at the prison informed me that there were several arrests last night, though he couldn't tell me for certain who they were."

Demi's hand shook as she braced herself against the wall and pushed to her feet. "Then he could be fine. He's just . . . being cautious." Her voice came high, desperate. It would all be fine. A misunderstanding. People were always late, or showing up at the wrong location. Communication failed, messages were missed—and Theseus was fine. He had to be.

FORTY-FOUR

THE WORLD HAD GROWN SINCE HE'D LAST SEEN IT, or perhaps it had always been too large to see clearly through the slit of one swollen eye. Quick stabs of pain sliced between his ribs with each step. Nikolas hunched, cradling the pain with folded arms. Theseus stumbled beside him as they were transferred from the carcer cell to the basilica where the trial would surely be a sham.

He might have admired the architecture had he been able to see more than a few stones at a time. Instead, he concentrated on not falling as they climbed uneven marble stairs to the government hall. A humid dampness embraced them, somehow less welcoming than the clammy warmth of the carcer cell. Footsteps clacked on polished marble, pages and scribes bustling down hallways, arms laden with codices and scrolls. A rumble of low voices, both in argument and agreement, vibrated through the air, broken by the clink of chains shackling him and Theseus to the guards escorting them.

The trial had already begun before they'd arrived. Or at least Basil had begun arguing.

"Are you trying to tell me that Nikolas of Patara—*the* Nikolas of Patara, son of Euodias—is a petty thief?"

"Who but thieves creep about the city at night?"

"Where are his accusers?"

"It is early yet—ah, Nikolas of Patara." A chair screeched across the floor as the magistrate stood. "Honored to meet you, sir."

The guards escorted Nikolas to the desk and tugged him to a stop as the magistrate rounded the desk, his white tunic nearly blinding—even through the slit of Nikolas's eye.

A slight smile left Nikolas's lip bleeding again. "It would have been preferable under different circumstances."

"What have they done to him?" Basil thundered. "Beat him to a pulp before his trial? Are you well, my lord? I would like to press charges."

The magistrate clapped his hands. "Why don't you unchain him? Not that one—*Nikolas*."

Nikolas pulled away as the guard reached for the shackle on his wrist. "Leave me chained if you won't release my friend as well. Neither of us have done anything wrong."

If the magistrate looked surprised at this, Nikolas couldn't tell. Chair legs squeaked as the man sat behind a desk littered with papers. He cleared his throat. "You've been accused of theft."

"What am I to have stolen?"

"Your accuser has yet to arrive."

"Who is he?"

"I . . ." Paper crackled. "I don't have his name written down."

Beside him, Theseus muttered something under his breath. The emperor's third edict, which revoked the right of Christians to defend themselves in a court of law, allowed suits brought against Christians to be awarded in favor of the accuser. The charges, however obvious the fabrication, no longer mattered.

"There's no evidence against them," Basil argued. "You cannot hold him."

Another set of footsteps slapped into the hall, growing louder and more determined. The owner of the determined feet cursed.

The chair scraped again as the magistrate stood and bowed. "Master Evander."

Nikolas turned his head and tilted his chin in various angles until he could fit Master Evander's frame into the slit of vision.

"What is going on, Cosmo?" Master Evander's voice wielded a hard edge. "Why is my Latin tutor here? Do you think I would hire a thief to teach the children of our fair city?"

"That is what we are gathered to discover."

"Where are his accusers?"

"Not here yet."

"Then if there is no one here to bring a suit against him, I suggest you let him return to his students."

"*I* have a suit against him."

The voice sent stones plummeting in Nikolas's stomach. Theseus let out a sharp breath, as if the air had been knocked from his lungs. They both turned toward the voice, Nikolas angling his head to find the accuser, to confirm the betrayal cutting through him like shards of pottery.

Theseus gave a violent jerk of his chains as he swung around. "What are you *doing*?"

"And you are?" The magistrate let the question hang.

"Xeno of Myra." The voice continued, smooth and cold as the Mediterranean in winter. "As you've already confirmed, this is Nikolas of Patara, heir of Euodias and owner of the largest shipping company on the Mediterranean."

"Shut *up*, Xeno!" Theseus growled, and then grunted and doubled over as the guard brought order to the courtroom with the hilt of his sword.

"Leave him be." Nikolas reached toward Theseus, the movement shooting blades of pain through his chest.

"Order," the magistrate barked, his voice echoing. "Speak."

"I am Xeno of Myra and I bring a suit against these men."

"And what is it?" Evander snapped.

"These men are Christians. Ask them. They'll not deny it."

"As are you," Theseus spat.

A flicker of hesitation betrayed Xeno's resolve—just for a moment. His shoulders straightened. *"Kyrios Caesar,"* he said. "Go on, Theseus. Say it."

FORTY-FIVE

NO AIR MOVED IN THE TINY CHAMBER ASIDE from the huffing breaths leaving Yia-yia Beatrix's lungs.

Body exhausted, eyes swollen, mind wide awake, Demi lay on the sleeping mat beside Nydia and stared at the cracked plaster ceiling she knew was above her head though she couldn't see it in the dark.

Are You there too, God? Because it's hard to see You in all of this. I'm ready to obey, but I don't know what to do.

No answer save the creaking of crickets both inside and out.

Had it only been five days since Nikolas was arrested and Theseus disappeared? It felt like moments, and a lifetime. Word of the arrest had spread throughout the church, along with other stories. Deacons ambushed as they made their rounds with bread and medicine, whole families taken. So many dead. Missing. Her brother and Xeno among them. How had their carefully laid network been so quickly overcome? There was a crack in the boat. There had to be. And Nikolas had been taken first. Anger and fear had revived old rumors. Nikolas of Patara. The degenerate heir. Lazy, selfish—they were lies, all of them. She knew it, and yet, he had been taken first.

Please God, do not let it have been Nikolas who gave us up.

Titus had returned with word that the prisoners were being transported to the capital city of Nicomedia. No news of an execution had brought mingled feelings. Relief that Theseus, Nikolas, and the rest might still be alive—and dread over the tortures they would face in the emperor's city. Rumors swirled that Emperor Diocletian and his

son-in-law and successor, Emperor Galerius, had killed twenty thousand
Christians in that city alone. Hope and despair rode opposing waves. If
they were not executed immediately, might it mean they could escape
on the journey? That they might be spared?

Nydia shifted beside her. Demi wasn't certain she was asleep either,
but she wouldn't risk waking her to find out. What would she say anyway? *Are you wondering where Theseus is? I understand how you feel*—No.
She couldn't say that because she didn't. Couldn't. Theseus and Nydia
had been married. Man and wife. A bond Demi would never know.
Had she even told Nikolas she loved him? The pain of love lost couldn't
possibly be greater than this suffocating regret. Why hadn't she spoken
the words?

A burning sensation spread in her chest, rolling up her throat. How
could regret cause physical pain like this? No use trying to sleep now. She
sat up and gathered her mantle around her shoulders before she stood
and crept into the hall. Trailing her fingers along the wall, she headed
toward the kuzina. Her breaths shortened and she pressed the corner of
her mantle against her mouth, muffling the sharp inhales and the sobs
threatening to tear her open.

Her fingers went from plaster to wood and she stopped, not at the
door to the kuzina but the room Nikolas had slept in. Dare she?

She pushed the door open and found herself blinking into indiscern-
ible darkness that smelled of something mysterious and exotic. Demi
stepped inside, sliding her feet across the bare floor until they brushed
the softness of a blanket. She knelt and gathered the weight of it into
her arms, crushing the familiar scent against her face as the tears came.

She didn't hear Nydia enter until a hand touched her shoulder, and
Demi's head jerked up.

Nydia set a bronze lamp on a table Demi hadn't seen and knelt beside
her, wrapping her in a hug.

"You loved him, didn't you? Pastor Nikolas."

No use denying it. Not to Nydia.

"Yes." The word came on a mewling cry, the fissure that broke the
dam.

"Oh, Demi."

There was nothing more to say, not then. Nydia held her and stroked her hair until Demi's cries weakened to ragged breaths.

"I knew when Theseus became a deacon that this outcome was possible. That one night he wouldn't come home," Nydia whispered, words breaking on shuddery breaths. "But I thought I'd have a warning somehow. I didn't think the last time I'd tell him goodbye was with a casual kiss."

Demi had left Nikolas with a kiss too—only it had tasted of hope, of future promise. How wrong she'd been. How naive.

"What do we do now?" Nydia whispered.

FORTY-SIX

13 SEPTEMBER, AD 310

Iron shackles burned against his raw skin. The butt of a spear jabbed his lower back and Nikolas stumbled forward, barely keeping his feet under him. The sun broke free of the sea as they left the city of Myra, turning the Mediterranean a glittering blue by the time they reached the harbor. His eyes went to the waves of their own accord, searching for a yellow boat trimmed in white, a slender figure at the helm, wild curls flying free behind her.

Foolishness.

He didn't even know if Demi was alive. If she'd made it out of the sewer, or if the guards had found her too. She certainly wasn't at sea. He knew this, but the knowledge failed to convince his eyes to stop searching. If Xeno had betrayed the entire church, Nikolas didn't know. He and Theseus were the only two prisoners bound for the harbor of Andriake. Thinking of it all again brought an agony that made it hard to breathe. He couldn't even warn anyone of Xeno's treachery and the danger the rest were in.

Rough planks met his bare feet as he was shoved up a gangplank toward a ship, crawling with guards and sailors. He twisted his neck, the sunlight catching on the city of Myra, illuminating the walls and towers and transforming the ordinary stone to copper and gold in a marvelous magician's act.

The sun shone on a balding pate on the pier, drawing his attention. Basil's expression, set in solemn grief, matched his. They'd been able to speak for only the briefest of moments, words rushing between them so quickly he could barely recall what was said.

"Help them." He mouthed the words now, pleading with his eyes.

Basil blinked, lowered his chin in a nod of farewell—all he could offer.

The chains on Nikolas's wrists jerked.

Hope and light faded to black as he climbed down a slick ladder into a dank hold devoid of illumination aside from what leaked through the cracks above his head.

Lord, protect them all.

A guard clamped Nikolas's ankles into manacles secured to the ship and removed his wrist chains. A few of the other prisoners cursed. Most were as silent as he was. As the guards left, Nikolas sat back, inspecting the rawness of his wrists, hopeful they would soon scab.

Theseus sank back against the planks, forearms draped over his drawn-up knees. "Nicomedia," he murmured, staring at the square of sky above their heads. "Never once did I imagine I'd see the emperor's city. Never once have I wanted to."

Nikolas fought a burning in his throat. "I'm sorry your marriage was so quickly interrupted. I feel I'm to blame."

Theseus lifted a shoulder in a gesture that was neither agreeing nor disagreeing. "You are the reason I had a marriage at all."

Nikolas felt the breath squeeze from his lungs. He should have been more careful. Not let Theseus or Demi join him. It was too dangerous. He should have known . . .

"Theseus . . . I . . ."

"Thank you, Nikolas. No matter how short, it was a gift I will never regret." The light caught a glimmer in Theseus's eyes before the sailors shut the hatch above them and locked them in darkness. His tone carried a hint of desperation, as if he needed Nikolas's joy because he couldn't bear the pity.

He sighed. "I wish things could be different."

Rope thudded against the deck above them and the ship creaked.

"Me too." Theseus's voice was muffled by the shouts of sailors. "But while we have life and breath, we have purpose. Isn't that what you say?"

Nikolas nodded. The words had tumbled so easily from his lips before, when he'd been free to move and work. But what purpose could he have now, chained in a dark hold, unable to do a thing?

He sank back, rough wood supporting his bruised back. Sailors shouted. Chains clanked. Wind snapped in the sails. Nikolas closed his eyes, letting the rocking of the ship lull him into prayer and memory. Of waves splashing against a white-and-yellow prow. Of sun and sea. Of Demitria's laughter.

FORTY-SEVEN

Demi spat and sluiced cool brine from her eyes as she emerged near the boat. Rex strained at the rope where the coral basket hung below the rippling surface.

"Hang on, don't let go. I'm coming to help." She struck for the ladder and scrambled inside where together, they hauled the basket over the side, spilling the blood-red coral into the bottom of the boat. They both flopped back, breathing hard.

Demi had thrown herself back into work. What else was there for her to do? She'd lost everything. She wouldn't lose the boat too. Mere weeks remained in the diving season, as the cooler currents moved in and diving to the coral depths grew more difficult. For several days, Ennio and Pelos had kept their distance. Could she hope they'd remain that way until the end of the season?

"Is it time for the noon meal yet?" Rex panted, squinting at the sun only beginning its arch overhead.

She followed Rex's gaze and couldn't suppress a smile. "We've got at least two hours before we head back."

Rex groaned, throwing both arms over his eyes. "I'm going to starve to death."

"Hardly." Demi poked his belly, and he curled forward, giggling.

"I'm still hungry," he insisted.

"I'm sure. A growing boy like you." She squinted toward the shore,

268

then pointed. "I think there's a few wild fig trees somewhere over there. Shall we go look?"

Rex's response was enthusiastic. He might have drawn up the anchor single-handedly. A short time later, they'd anchored the boat a safe distance from the rocky shore and both splashed into the glittering turquoise.

"You're getting faster, Rex!" Demi called over her shoulder.

She slowed to let Rex plow ahead of her to the shore, where he clambered onto a boulder, raising both fists above his head like an Olympic athlete. Demi laughed and scrambled up after him, hopping from boulder to boulder over a rise to where several fig trees sprawled in a verdant bowl in the rock. Rex swung up the limbs with a whoop. Demi hesitated, the place full of bittersweet memories. Pater napping off the afternoon heat in the shade while Mitera built a fire and cooked shellfish. They'd rest their quivering muscles, fill their lungs with air, and then they'd all leave together, bellies filled, ready to work once more.

The hidden grove was quieter now, save Rex's enthusiasm, and Demi felt the cut of loneliness. One by one, everyone she loved was being chiseled away. And she could do nothing but bear it and go on.

How long must I bear it, Lord? When will this end? How could it possibly end without a miracle?

Demi dropped into the grove and gathered a handful of figs before settling into a familiar crook of the tree with the figs on her lap. Her limbs quivered with her need for food, but she felt as though her stomach might refuse it all. She was in a constant struggle, wrestling against the continuous barrage of accusations in her mind and casting them out with the truth that she was forgiven. It seemed that once her choice was made, the real struggle in her mind had begun.

Pinching the rounded base of the fruit, she peeled it open, baring the pink flesh before popping it into her mouth. Nutty sweetness rolled over her tongue. The others were devoured in moments. She was hungrier than she'd thought. Tilting her head back, she surveyed the fruit-laden tree, wishing she could fill the boat, and knowing she'd only get a berating for wasting Mersad's time on "worthless" figs.

"Why don't we come here every day?" Rex shouted from above her head.

"Because we'd never get any work done." Demi plucked another fig and pulled it apart. Rotten inside. She tossed it aside and picked another. "Eat your fill and then we need to head back."

Rex clung to the branches, stuffing his mouth even as a short while later, Demi turned back to the sea and crested the rise to look down the steep drop to where the boat bobbed. Deceptively warm and cheerful, the intense glare of the sun set the cooling sea shimmering in a crust of white pearls. She braced a hand over her eyes, her blood chilling far colder than the winter tides at the sight of the red-and-blue boat edging around the rocky peninsula.

"Rex! Come now!" She plunged down the hillside, stones scraping her heels, shins jarred at every rocky drop until the water gave way beneath her. Ennio and Pelos had left her alone while Theseus had been with her. How quickly the vultures circled at the first hint of ill news.

The red-and-blue lateen reached her boat before she did and Ennio and Pelos stood back like a pair of scrawny roasted chickens while their sons leaped aboard her boat, tossing her coral onto their own meager pile. Her haul hadn't been a good one, but it was hers.

Her blood lit. She gripped the rope ladder and hauled herself up. "Get out and go away." Weak.

"Why are you here?" Ennio sneered. "Your brother's dead. Give it up and go back home or to the nearest brothel, where you belong."

"This is my father's boat, my grandfather's boat. I was born just there." Streaming water, she pointed toward the prow where Ennio's son took a quick step back. "Where do I belong if not here? Am I not a diver, same as you?"

"No," Ennio shot back. "We're men, trying to provide for our families. You don't even have one."

The words cut deeper than they'd been intended to. Her mouth gaped like a fish's, drawn out of the water. No words, no breath. He wasn't wrong; she had no family other than the memories of the one she'd lost, and yet—

"Demi!" Rex's voice bounced off the rocks behind her. "Don't leave without me!" His final shout was punctuated by a splash as he flopped into the sea.

She did have a family, not born of blood, but bound by it all the same. And she'd been given a responsibility to help them. "I have every right to be here, same as you."

The boats erupted in laughter. "Rights?" Ennio repeated. "You have no rights . . . A woman . . . and a *Christian*."

Her lips pinched. "Get out."

"I heard about your brother. How he refused to honor the emperor. News like that does not stay hidden."

Pelos spat into her boat. "Traitor."

Demi bit the side of her cheek. *Stay calm. They want to rile you. Do not give in.*

Ennio shook his head. "What happens when Mersad finds out? What shame and disgrace he will find himself in for hiring a Christian. He'll do anything, *anything* to avoid disgrace—bad for business, you know."

She couldn't breathe. What could she say? Everything he said was true, his threat unmistakable. She could think of no way to refute it.

Rex sloshed to the edge of the boat and reached for the ladder. Ennio's son Tychon swung a foot over the side, pressing it against Rex's forehead and pushing him under.

"Don't—" Demi lunged at him.

Tychon caught her arms, wrestling her back against his oily chest as Rex popped up, sputtering.

"Leave him alone. He's not part of this."

"Isn't he?" Tychon's hands slid over her body as his brother or cousin heaved the ladder into the boat and shoved Rex down again.

The rule. Pater had a rule for this. What was it? She flung her head back, connecting with Tychon's nose. He cursed and swung her around, slamming the side of her face against the mast. Shock numbed the impact and for a moment, the glittering of the sea danced in the blackness that flashed across her vision. A roaring pain cleared it, and throbbing heat flooded her cheekbone. She stumbled toward the edge of the boat.

Rex surfaced, coughing.

"Stay calm, Rex. Swim back to shore!"

His round blue eyes met hers, scared and panicked. "I can't," he gasped, reaching up for the edge of the boat. She bent to meet his hand only to be hauled back by two of the cousins.

"He's a little boy—leave him alone!" She thrashed and kicked, holding Rex's gaze as if that connection alone could keep him afloat. His movements grew quick and jerky as he flailed an arm, gripping the edge of the boat with his fingertips.

"You will not return to Mersad's employ. Agree to stay away." Ennio's voice slithered in her ear. "Refuse, and the boy drowns."

Tychon moved toward Rex and lifted a heel above his small fingers, holding the boat in a white grip.

Her mind was made up in an instant. There was no hesitation, no lingering doubts. The boat was the last tie she had to her family; diving, her means to provide and protect. She'd attached herself to it, bound to her boat and occupation as tightly as a diving stone cinched to her ankle. And now? She was about to drown.

She locked Rex's desperate gaze with her own. The words came more easily than she'd expected, cutting the bonds like her stone knife cut through the twine on the diving stones.

"The boat is yours."

FORTY-EIGHT

THE SCHOOL WAS IN A FLURRY WHEN Demi and Rex returned, sunburned and breathless.

"We have to leave," Iris's tone was urgent as she and Nydia layered things into baskets in the kuzina. "Lady Isidora was here. With Nikolas's arrest, investigations are being made at the school. She's warned us to leave while we can."

"I have news of my own." Demi helped gather cooking items as she told what happened at the docks.

"We can go to the insula at the shantytown for now," Titus surveyed the kuzina as he entered.

Iris removed a cellar of salt from Nydia's basket and set it back on the shelf. "Take only what belongs to us. Though Lady Isidora would not mind if we took everything, I don't want Master Evander to think we've pilfered a thing from him."

"Nothing goes if we can't take the books." Yia-yia opened the cupboard and began pulling out the amphorae containing the books of Scripture they'd hidden. "One's missing. Demi, check Nikolas's room."

Demi headed for the door off the main hall, the one she hadn't entered since the night after Nikolas's arrest. She pushed the door open, the same low table greeting her, stacked with codices and waxed tablets covered in scrawled writing. She bent and sorted through the papers, none of which she could read. Which was the Scripture? Not the waxed wooden tablets nor loose sheets of parchment. She picked up one codex, then the other and turned, eyes traveling over the sparseness of the room until they snagged on a chest next to the sleeping mat.

She rushed to it and knelt, setting aside the books and lifting the lid. Several tunics lay folded on top, a rolled belt beneath. She shifted those aside, chest constricting at the familiar scent of cedar and rosemary wafting from them. As she removed the clothing, three things remained beneath. A leather-wrapped scroll, which must have been the missing Scripture, a scrap of parchment scrawled with careful lines of text, and a heavy leather pouch that gave an unmistakable *clink* when she lifted it. Her heart began to thrum.

"Demi?"

She jerked the bag to the floor, pushing the fabric of her chiton over it as Rex entered the room.

"Did you find it?"

She handed him the codices. "Is it these or—" She reached for the scroll.

"Not those." Rex shuddered at the sight of the codices. "That's our Latin lessons."

She held up the scroll and he brightened.

"That's it. Nikolas used to teach me to read it before the evening meal when I missed lessons." He took the scroll.

Demi held up the scrap of parchment next. "What's this?"

Rex scanned it, squinted. "Names and . . . I don't know." He pointed, "This says, *Needs ten sesterces. Third window.*" He scrunched his face. "What does that mean?"

"Demi, have you found it?" Iris's voice echoed up the hall.

"Yes," she called back. "Take it." She waved Rex out the door and looked down at the parchment clutched in her hand.

Names and instructions. A bag of coins. There was no mistaking what Nikolas had been doing with it. She'd gone with him. The thrill she'd felt that night coursed through her again. The list crackled in her hand. It meant only one thing. That these people were in desperate need of help. That they were *still* in desperate need.

Footsteps clapped down the hall. No time to decide, only time to act.

She bundled the coins and the parchment into her mantle and rushed out of Nikolas's sleeping chamber and into the one she shared with Nydia and Yia-yia, where she piled her swimming tunic and an extra chiton and mantle on top of the coins and tied it all into a neat bundle. She'd decide what to do about it all later.

By the time Titus led everyone to the edges of the shantytown, light was fading fast, the sky streaked with a joyous pink and gray. How could a sky look happy at such a time? Demi trudged at the rear, her feet feeling weighted with diving stones and her eyelids not much lighter.

Titus held out an arm to slow the others. "Step carefully so you don't slice your feet. There's broken pottery everywhere."

Demi had been to the insula several times, but how odd it felt to be visiting while the sun still shone. To be entering unladen with secret grain, and with the intent of staying. And without Nikolas. Where was he now? Dead? In prison? Was Theseus with him still?

The coins weighed heavier with each step, Nikolas's footprints seeming too large and purposeful for her to possibly fill. And yet, she was here, and he was not. His work had found its way into her hands, and she could not ignore it.

Titus led the way down a hall Demi barely recognized, each doorway covered by newly installed doors. They crowded around Titus as he paused at a door in the middle of the hall. Instead of knocking, he pulled out a key hanging from a string around his neck and pushed it into the lock.

"We can stay here." Titus swung open the door to reveal a tiny, windowless room, two of the walls newly plastered, as if they had not always been there. He stepped back and waved them in ahead of him.

Everyone moved into the room, Iris carrying necessaries in a market basket to avoid suspicion on the street. Beatrix carried her own market basket of "necessary" items she couldn't bear to leave behind.

"Light that lamp before I close the door." Titus pointed to a niche in the wall that held a small clay lamp. Iris dug a covered pot of coals from her basket and used one to light the lamp. Titus pulled the door shut, dropping a large bar across the entrance.

"How did you know about this place?" Demi picked up the lamp and placed it in the niche, its tiny flame casting a dim circle of light and leaving the rest of the small room in darkness.

"Theseus showed me after the new owner installed doors for everyone. He said it was a new safe room and to come here if we ever needed to leave the school."

"We best settle in and rest while we can." Iris spread a thin blanket on the floor and gripped Yia-yia Beatrix's hand, easing her down. The old woman looked winded and worn as she leaned against the wall and closed her eyes. Exhaustion rolled over Demi as she followed suit. Rest had never sounded so good.

Demi had just closed her eyes when someone shook her shoulder.

"Come. It's time to go to the river." Fabric rustled as Iris moved through the darkness as if she could see.

Demi rolled to her feet, trying to avoid the obvious, painful question: Who would lead them at the river?

She followed the others out of the airless room and into the insula hall, still empty and quiet in the predawn hour. Yia-yia shuffled beside her through the courtyard, clutching an amphora to her chest. Their number grew as they picked up stragglers along the way, and when they reached the river, the clouds parted and moonlight shone cold enough to illuminate huffs of breath. It looked like everyone had come.

Yia-yia turned and held a cup and an amphora of wine toward Titus. He balked. "What is this for?"

"The cup of Thanksgiving."

He pushed it back toward her. "I can't do it."

"Yes, you can."

Titus shook his head. "You were teaching the catechumens long before I ever believed. Why don't you do it?"

Yia-yia squinted up into his face. "Because He hasn't called me to lead, Titus. He's called you."

A breath left his lungs. "How do you know?"

She smiled and pressed a hand to her heart. "I just know."

"I'm content as I am."

"Contentment is good. Godly. But don't let contentment turn into fear of stepping into the next thing God is leading you to do."

The conversation was not meant for her, but Demi's breath caught at it all the same, her hesitations about Nikolas's gold mirrored in Titus's responses.

"How could He lead me to this? *Me?* Of all people." He shook his head, expression pained.

Demi didn't know much of Titus's past, only the bits he'd revealed over the years. That he'd once been a Praetorian investigator, that he'd hunted down Beatrix's nephew, a church leader in Rome. That though Titus had run in shame, God had found him anyway.

"There are better men, more equipped—"

"God does not call those already equipped, Titus. Who better to preach to the Jewish leaders of Jerusalem than Paul, who was trained up in their religious ways from his childhood? And yet God called Paul to preach to the Gentiles and sent uneducated Peter to preach to the Jews. His ways do not always make earthly sense, but they are never without result. The church here in Myra came from Paul's obedience. What can God do with yours?"

Titus blinked. Swallowed. Took the cup and wine. "You've been nothing but trouble since I first laid eyes on you."

Yia-yia chuckled and waved a hand for him to go toward the front where Nikolas had always stood.

The collection of believers waiting at the river consisted of women of all ages, and children, but few men. There were few men left.

Breeze tugging at her curls, Demi knelt in the gravel near the river-bank, the burbling of the water calling and calming her. She bowed her head, begging God to protect Titus, strengthen Theseus and Nikolas. To free them somehow as He'd freed Paul.

Send an earthquake. A shipwreck. An angel. Something. Anything. Were they not doing Your work here? Why do You allow the men doing Your work to be taken? Don't we need them to lead us? As soon as her heart voiced the words, she knew her mistake. She'd been looking to Theseus for security instead of the Lord. Looking to Nikolas for direction. Oh, that she'd seen it earlier. They were good men. Godly men. But they were not the ones to follow with her whole heart.

"Forgive me, Father," she whispered. "Forgive me for following men instead of You. I will follow You, if You will show me what to do."

The Lord is my shepherd. I shall not want.

Demi pressed into the group, emotion welling in her throat. What a wonder that even with her family gone, she had a family still. What a wonder that God could bring life from death, joy from sorrow. Beauty from her ashes.

He restores my soul.

She joined the line of believers moving slowly forward, Titus's voice rising above the rustling of fabric and the clatter of stones.

"Remember, O Lord, Your Church, and deliver her from all evil. Perfect her in Your love, and from the four winds assemble her, the sanctified, in Your kingdom, which You have prepared for her. For Yours is the power and the glory forevermore. May You come and this world pass away."

"Hosanna to the Son of David." Demi lifted her voice and joined the others in the refrain.

Titus shifted in the light of the lamp set in the empty tomb alcove behind him, shielding the light from searching eyes but casting enough for the readers to see the scrolls. He cleared his throat. "You all know by now that Pastor Nikolas has been arrested with many others."

Murmurs of assent moved through the assembly.

"We've not heard what has become of him, but we know many will be sent to the emperor's prison in Nicomedia." Titus swallowed. "We are faced with a choice, brothers and sisters. To fall back to our old ways of cowering and hiding or to endure and press on. Christ counted us worthy of His own suffering. Are we willing to do the same? Not to die for the glory of our own names, but to serve at any cost for the glory and worthiness of His."

He paused, letting the challenge hang over them. Demi felt it settle over her own shoulders, the weight both heavy and well balanced. Energizing rather than exhausting. She thought of Theseus and Nydia's wedding. The way Theseus had gazed at his bride with a love nothing could break. And Nydia, holding that gaze in the strength of her own love for Theseus. No one else would do.

Demi lowered to her knees, raising her chin.

No one else would do. No one else was worthy.

Sniffles and murmured prayers told her that many of them felt the same conviction. They'd carried the weight of trouble and care for too long. Had grown weary from looking only at the mounting trouble. They'd neglected the Source of strength. *She'd* neglected Him.

Pebbles clattered underfoot as penitent believers shuffled toward Titus and Elder Lysias, who read softly from a scroll.

"For as often as you eat this bread and drink the cup, you proclaim the Lord's death until he comes."

The wind shifted, carrying with it the faint odor from the sewer downstream. But it was enough to remind her of that night. Of the sacrifice Nikolas had made for her, which mirrored only in part what Christ had done for her. For all of them. She rose to her feet and joined the line, tears of joy and gratefulness streaking her face as she tore a bit of bread and placed it between her lips.

"His body broken for you," Titus murmured.

She took the clay cup from his outstretched hand and tipped it to her lips. The wine was warm and dry on her tongue.

"His blood poured out for the remission of sins."

Hers. All of them. Forever. Not because of what she'd done, but because of what He had. It was finished. It was done.

How could a simple *thank-you* ever be enough? A new fire lit within her, an eagerness for action—not bound of obligation or guilt, but *love.* How could she have done anything without it?

She returned to her place near the water's edge, resolution strengthening her limbs as she thought of the gold and the list left behind, tucked even now in the bundle of her belongings. *Where there is life, there is purpose.* Around her, the sniffles of conviction and confession soon poured out in songs of praise that strengthened in volume and shot through the predawn darkness with all the defiance of a battle cry.

PART THREE

*"We are not of those who shrink back
and are destroyed, but of those who
have faith and preserve their souls."*

HEBREWS 10:39

FORTY-NINE

Light shot through the darkness with a gust of cold wind and swirling dust. Nikolas lifted his head, blinking and marveling that something as ordinary as opening a hatch could infuse such life and hope into a hold of stinking prisoners.

Gulls wheeled and screeched in the square of light, and beyond the edges he couldn't see, men shouted. Mingling with the baser stench of the hold, the breeze carried the scent of sea and shore, of rotting wood and fresh bread. Feet and legs appeared on the ladder, followed by a rusty tunic and the sun-bronzed arms and head of the guard.

"We've arrived in the emperor's city" was all he said as he unlocked the chain running through all their shackles and released them one by one. "Try to escape, and you'll be killed slowly."

Nikolas's limbs were stiff and aching as he climbed into the fresh air and cool sunlight. He tilted his chin to the sky. How long had it been since he'd seen the sun and sky in its fullness? One month? Two? A trip this far in spring or summer would take only a few days. Now December, the journey north had been fraught with winter storms and lengthy layovers in various harbors. They'd picked up illness and supplies in one port, buried crew members and picked up new ones in another. Somehow, he and Theseus had survived the storms and sickness. A miracle they would most likely rue.

"Blessed are You, O Lord," he murmured.

Behind him, Theseus added, "Amen."

Nikolas held out his chafed wrists, clamped in irons, and allowed the guard on the deck to thread a new chain through the shackles. They were prodded off the gangplank; their stench, once invisible in the hold, now permeated the crispness of the breeze.

Fishermen and carters cursed them as they marched down the docks and swayed and stumbled on the stillness of the street. The sudden instability of the earth made Nikolas's stomach heave, though there was nothing in it to lose. Their guards marched them on through the vastness of the port city, rivaling Andriake by ten.

Beyond the port, the empire's capital gleamed. Sun shimmered on colorful marble and gold-capped domes, light glinting in every window. Tall, pointed cedars speared the cloudless sky as flat-topped stone pines spread shade over wide, paved streets of pale stone. Every window and doorway dripped with colorful flags and garlands of greenery and late winter blooms. Nicomedia was gilded and stunning. A true capital of the empire.

Peddlers clotted the streets, pushing carts laden with candles, wax fruit, and statues.

"Io Saturnalia!" echoed on a breeze flavored with festivities and music.

Saturnalia. The festival of Saturn and light. Of music and gifts.

"Get a move on."

A spear butt jamming into his lower back brought Nikolas's gaze to the ground.

The emperor's city was gilded with blood as well as gold. When Emperor Diocletian passed the edicts to hunt down Christians in the whole of the empire, he'd begun in his own city. The stories hadn't taken long to reach the outer borders of the empire. The beheadings, torture, the burning of hundreds within their own meeting places. Even though Emperor Diocletian had since abdicated the throne to grow cabbages, his successor, Emperor Galerius, had upheld the edicts. For all its shine, compassion ran cold in this place.

The path they took through the city was circuitous and passed temple after opulent temple, each bearing signs of recent beautification. Nikolas couldn't help but wonder how many of the improvements had been funded with the pilfered coffers of murdered Christians.

The palace dungeons bore no such improvements.

The prison yard was square and plain, worn gray paving stones making way for whipping posts bearing rust-colored stains. Four guards lolled around an upturned barrel rolling dice and sharing the contents of a chipped amphora. As the prisoners entered the courtyard, the guards paused their game and sauntered forward, wiping wrists across their mouths. More guards spilled out of doors set beneath the pillared colonnade surrounding the courtyard.

A man who was clearly the commander strode before them all. "We'll take them from here. This is all of them?"

"The ones that survived the voyage."

The commander tilted his head and looked them over. "They'll live to regret it." He stepped out of the huddle and snapped his fingers.

Guards surrounded the cluster of church leaders, swords drawn and stances ready as if they anticipated a fight from half-starved men and women. Metal clanked and rang as the chain threading through all of their bonds slid free.

Nikolas and four others were hauled forward and kicked down to kneel and embrace the whipping posts. His cheek rubbed against the wood as his wrist shackles were chained to the post.

"Io Saturnalia." The commander gave a mock salute and raised his voice. "We welcome you to the emperor's city. And today we show you his mercy."

The guard chaining Nikolas's wrists to the post stepped back, his hobnailed boots clacking to a point behind him where they fell silent. Nikolas's skin prickled and twitched, anticipating and dreading the first lash. One of the other men screamed. Another grunted.

Fire raced across Nikolas's shoulders. He sucked in a breath and released a groan, digging his fingers into the post as the whips cracked and cries rang out.

"You will each experience the mercy of our great Emperor Galerius, and you will think on this day during the many that will come and wish for the mercy of this moment. For this is the least of what you will experience within these walls. Hades and Ares reign here."

The lash bit his skin again, tearing the flesh of his lower back, his arms, his legs, the soles of his feet.

"Your god is weak. Why would a god subject his devotees to such pain?"

He did not spare His own Son.

Another lash tore at his neck, catching his ear, his cheek. Fire and numbness wrestled back and forth across his skin.

"Curse him and live."

Nikolas pressed his face into the post.

He was half-conscious when they released him and rolled him aside, grit stinging into his wounds. He heard the grunts and clinking chains of another prisoner taking his place at the post. Hobnailed boots clacked and screeched to a stop near his feet. The ring of a blade from its scabbard. A burning and pop at the back of his left ankle. A rippling in the back of his calf as the severed tendon retracted.

"Take these ones below."

A hook snagged the shackles on his wrist and jerked his body to slide across the paving stones. The slit in one eye caught the brilliance of a puddle reflecting the blue of the sky. And for a moment the heat in his skin was the summer sun beating down on a turquoise sea that echoed with Demi's voice. His heart had not been reached by the guard's whip and yet it burned and ached all the same.

FIFTY

The skies had grown cloudy with the onset of winter. Rain polished the marble facades of homes and temples and washed the summer dust from the streets, sending streams of muck through the shantytown slumped on the mudflat along the Myros River. Everywhere Demi looked, the world was bathed in gray. The river and sea reflected the gloom of the sky, and even the golden tones bled from the cliffs as trees shed their summer leaves in favor of skeletal sleep.

Feet coated in grime, Demi trudged through the tumble of shantytown huts and makeshift shops, Rex ambling alongside her, kicking stones.

"What does this one say?" She angled the tattered parchment toward him. It had taken weeks for her to go through the list, to find the courage to sneak back in the night to the places she and Rex had scouted during the day. The bulging bag of coins had slowly reduced to a meager pinch. But there had been enough. She wondered where Nikolas had hidden the rest of the gold. How he'd made the list.

Rex heaved a long-suffering sigh and peered at the parchment again. *"Erastus. Four children. Food only, no coins."* He looked up at Demi. "Why do you read this so much? It's not even a good story."

She shrugged. "It makes Nikolas feel . . . closer."

"He's better at reading than writing," Rex said decidedly. "This is boring."

Demi felt her lips twitch as she pointed to the next line that usually listed the directions. "And this?"

Rex took the parchment. "I know where that is." He led the way, consulting the scrawled writing and doubling back several times before he pointed out a shack made of driftwood and reeds leaning against a collection of other huts as if for moral support. "There."

Demi studied it, memorizing its lines and the roundabout way they'd come upon it. "You're certain?"

As if in answer, four children tumbled out the doorway, scattered by a ragged woman shooing them out.

"Don't come back empty-handed." The woman dragged the door shut behind her and speared Demi with a glare as she propped an empty basket on one thin hip. "What are you looking at?" She spun away before Demi could respond.

"She seems nice," Rex muttered.

Demi had seen enough. She returned Rex to the insula, swapping out the scrap of parchment for her diving tunic and mesh bag before slipping out alone. With the winter solstice upon them, the diving season had long ended, water growing too cold for diving to the depths where the coral hid. But shellfish were plentiful if one could stand the chill of the water long enough to reach them.

Damp wind blew ragged curls into her eyes. She pulled her mantle over her head, shivering and longing for the sunny heat of summer. She followed the river only as far as the citrus groves that grew up between Myra and Andriake. The orange and yellow fruits hung in the evergreen trees like jewels and scattered the ground beneath the branches. The tangy-sweet smell of broken oranges filled the air alongside the rumble of harvest carts. Festive singing and shouts of "Io Saturnalia!" seemed to come from the trees themselves as harvesters climbed the branches to pick the fruit.

Demi turned into the grove, eyes suddenly stinging as her mitera's voice filled her head. *You can't be sad while eating an orange.* A silly sentiment, but one that brought to mind a time of peace and security, if not plenty. A world where hope wasn't so hard to keep hold of.

"Will we ever live in such a world again, Lord?" she whispered. "Or only when You return?"

She ducked drooping branches, her questions remaining unanswered and weighing as heavily as the fruited trees. Her feet quickened, chin lifted, as she feigned the purposeful stride of a worker on task. No one stopped her or even called out a greeting. She wouldn't linger overlong, not in the grove, nor on the questions. Neither would benefit, nor would they change what she must do. What she would do. Theseus and Nikolas were not coming back, and she wouldn't turn back either.

Had they reached Nicomedia? Were they even now in the dungeons of the emperor, or in the courts of heaven?

How much longer must we endure before You return?

Tension eased from her shoulders as she left the grove behind, slipping into the soggy dumping grounds in the salt marsh in the mouth of Andriake's harbor. The roofless safe house came into view, tilting and covered in leafless thorns. They'd long ago stripped the inside garden of all vegetables and herbs, leaving an empty shell to bleach in the winter sun.

The hidden cove, too, seemed abandoned and forlorn in the winter chill, filled with finger-numbing wind and heaps of brown seaweed rolling in the foam on the sand. She picked through it, gathering the edible strands before stripping to her swimming tunic. Cool wind caressed her skin, raising gooseflesh as she waded into the brine. A wave crashed into her stomach, stealing her breath and shoving her backward into a boulder. It would have been better to leap headfirst before the temperature changed her mind. She pressed both hands against the rock at her back, recalling the way Nikolas had slogged out of the sea, ready to both collapse and help at the same time.

Surely she could do the same. They'd both had a great Teacher to emulate. To show what true love, true service looked like. She drew a breath and plunged beneath the water, fighting the shock of cold that sent her heart racing, limbs moving faster than they ought.

Calm.

She broke for the surface, gasping for air. Was she truly so out of practice? Or was it simply the cold? Initial shock wearing off, she took another breath and ducked under, forcing her eyes open. The water was rough today, murky with grit and roaring in her ears. She kicked toward the rocky bottom, hunting for mussels and other shellfish hugging the crevices. She gathered until she shook too hard to swim, then sloshed to shore.

She stripped off her swimming tunic and redressed in her dry chiton, wrapping her mantle snuggly around her wet head and shoulders. Leaving the gray sea and sky behind, she rushed back through the citrus groves, near abandoned in the gathering dusk, and hurried along the river path until it broke into the meandering streets and abrupt stops of the shantytown.

Instead of houses and shops, huts and sagging tents lined the debris-covered path, some marked in hopeful advertisements scrawled on shards of pottery. Laundress, weaver, carver—and an unsigned gray-bearded man with one eye who simply watched her pass. She lifted a hand in a greeting he didn't return, then angled down an alley leading to the next street, the bag of shellfish clattering against her leg.

She made her way back toward the sagging driftwood hut Rex had pointed out earlier, arriving as the woman barged around the corner, crashing into Demi. Demi stumbled backward while the woman's basket slipped sideways, spilling two half-rotten oranges and a string of curses into the dust.

"Touch those and I'll cut your thieving fingers clean off!"

Demi jerked her hand back. "I was only going to help you."

"Help yourself, you mean," the woman snapped, turning a pock-marked scowl toward her. "Stick to your own street. You can't just go barging through anywhere you please." Dark eyes flicked to the bag of mussels at Demi's calves and seemed to harden against the longing flickering behind the anger. "Well? Go on then!"

"Have you eaten today?"

The woman drew herself straight. "Don't you dare be insulting my man. Erastus works hard."

Demi shook her head. "No, no. I meant no insult. Only that there's a meal at the insula tonight. We're preparing food for whoever will come, and there will be plenty left over. It would be a shame to have any go to waste. Will you come?"

The woman spat. "So you can kick me out of those fancy walls and laugh at the stupid woman who followed you home like a stray dog? I'd starve here first."

"We can't have that." Demi opened the mouth of her dripping bag, gesturing for the woman to hold out her basket. "I've got fresh shellfish to share."

The woman's longing gaze lingered on the bag, but she hugged her basket to her chest. "I can't pay you."

"I'm not asking you to. I'm sharing as a friend."

"I don't have friends."

"Now you do." Demi drew out a handful of tightly closed shells and held them out. "What are you called?"

The woman moved back, hugging the basket tighter. "Doesn't matter."

Demi stooped and dumped a pile of shellfish onto the ground. "I'm Demitria, daughter of Anatolios. We've begun gathering three times a week for shared meals at the insula. When you come next time, tell them I invited you. You will be welcome."

The woman glanced into the hut behind her and scowled, shaking her head. "You're a fool. Get out of here before my man comes out."

Demi straightened and turned away from the scowling woman. At the cross street, she glanced back over her shoulder, but the woman—and shellfish—were gone.

Ragged women clustered in the insula courtyard when Demi arrived. Three widows of the church huddled around bubbling pots balanced over coals on the ground, and Beatrix and Iris squatted nearby, flipping flatbread on hot stones.

Demi lowered the bag of remaining shellfish to the ground beside her bare feet. "Is there an empty pot?"

"You can use this one soon." Nydia banged her spoon against the dented rim of her pot and smiled up at Demi. "My lentils are almost done."

Beatrix gripped Iris's shoulder and pushed to her feet with a wince. "I have a pan for you over here." She waved Demi to follow. "Isn't it wonderful? All of us, together like this instead of segregated into little safe rooms?" She sighed. "I can't help but wonder if this was what the First Church was like."

Demi nodded. "I like it."

Bea brushed dirt out of a shallow pan and held it out. "For your shellfish."

Demi dropped the seeping bag of mussels onto a plank of wood across from a teenaged girl smashing chickpeas and herbs into a paste. "Hello, Chloe."

The girl gave a shy smile. "Demi."

As more women appeared with their mantles wrapped around meager offerings of food, Beatrix stepped in to order women and ingredients together with a practiced confidence. Demi hoped the food would turn out better than her "mysterious and exotic" scent for men.

"Virana, if you chop your bowl of purslane, we can mix it with Lydia's yogurt and make a fine, large salad. Eunike, what have you brought?" Bea leaned forward to peer into the jar a small, tattered woman hugged to her chest.

"Grape leaves in brine is all I have," the woman murmured, dipping her chin as red seared her cheeks. "I know it's silly—"

"Nonsense. That's absolutely perfect." Beatrix gripped Eunike's arm. "Xenia and Diana are over there mixing delicious bits of all sorts of things into a filling we weren't sure what to do with. We can fill these marvelously. Thank you for offering what you had." Beatrix's grin spread to Eunike, who offered a timid smile in return.

Nydia joined Demi with a pair of rusty shears. "Here. I'll take over the mussels if you'll open the urchins. The crunching turns my stomach."

"How are you feeling?"

"Fine." Nydia glanced at Chloe. "I think the sickness has passed."

Demi picked up one of the spiny urchins and cracked it open, glancing at Nydia's stomach that had only just begun to swell with her brother's child. Theseus might have been taken from them, but his name and memory could live on in a new life. Her family, ever diminishing, was finally growing.

FIFTY-ONE

The ragged hem of his tunic was rough with dirt, but Nikolas tore strips from it anyway. There was nothing else to use as bandages, and he was glad to give up his tunic if it meant he wouldn't have to sit against the wall and roll his thumbs. Groans and murmurs resounded through the cell, echoing in a way that might have reminded him of prayers in the monastery had it not been for the smell. He knelt beside the man most recently returned from the torturers, who lay crumpled on the floor.

The smell of burned flesh turned his stomach, and Nikolas was glad the cell was too dark to see clearly what had been done. Knowing that they'd burned the man's eyes was enough.

"Can you hear me, Menas?"

A grunt. "I'm blind, Niko. Not deaf."

His dry lips cracked as a smile tugged at them. "They have not broken your spirit, I see."

"Never."

"I have a bandage for you."

"God bless you."

Nikolas tucked a hand behind Menas's head and lifted enough to wrap the cloth around it. *Lord, how long? How long must we suffer? How long will You let evil men relish the tortures they inflict upon Your people?*

Menas reached up, stilling Nikolas's hands. "You are troubled, angry."

Nikolas shrugged. "I lament the suffering. Why doesn't God stop this? He could come back at any moment, end the suffering, bring justice . . ."

Menas's fingers tightened around his hand. "Look around you, Niko. This cell contains only a few of the vast number of sons and daughters of God. We may suffer here, but there are so many others doing work beyond these walls. Spreading hope and life. We are a distraction, allowing them to work undetected. But more than that, if we are not here, then who would sing praises that our guards will hear? How will our guards know the truth if we do not proclaim it to them, around them? Our mission is not over because we've been thrown in prison. It has only begun in a new place."

The words burrowed deep, sure and strong, building up the weakening places where doubt might ram a dagger. Nikolas secured the end of the bandage with a tuck, emotion swelling in his throat.

"They do not understand, Niko"—Menas spoke through pain-gritted teeth—"that no matter what they do, they cannot break us. They cannot kill us. We are a new people rising. Mortals and yet immortal. We cannot fear death if we have already died with Christ. We cannot die because we have life everlasting."

"Thank you, Menas."

"Thank our Lord Jesus. What other king does what He does? Our emperors take and take, fearing a loss of fleeting power, but our God gives, and gives abundantly and full, because His power is unshakable."

"Be careful or they may take your tongue next."

"It would be an honor to make such a holy noise that the enemies of God wish to have me silenced. So long as they don't take my ears. If we are silenced, the rocks will cry out. Wouldn't that be a wonder? To hear the stones of this prison shout praise to their Maker?" Menas laughed, then grimaced and drew an arm over his ribs. His next words came labored. "You will have to describe to me the look on the emperor's face when the marble halls of his palace break forth in hallelujahs."

Nikolas covered Menas's hand with his own. "I will. For now, you rest."

More strips from his tunic draped over his arm, Nikolas crawled to the next man. His left foot dragged behind him, flopping and loose from the severed tendon, unable to support his weight. His knees ached, tunic stuck to the scabbed lacerations on his back. He wished he had

Menas's gift of speaking as he moved from one prisoner to the next, tending wounds that grew ever more elaborate and painful as the guards' boredom and creativity increased. His tunic was gone before all the wounds were bound. He continued to make rounds, praying over the rest. Wondering, dreading, when it would be his turn.

FIFTY-TWO

Demi stirred a pan of mussels simmering in seawater and thyme. On her way back to the insula that evening, she'd invited the gray-bearded man with one eye to join them for the meal, but he'd only stared at her, then pushed to his feet and stalked away. It seemed rejection was the only response she'd get from her invitations.

And still the church had begun to live as it never had. Throbbing with a defiant life that wouldn't be quenched. The tethers of safety and security had snapped with Nikolas's arrest, and the unspoken drive of self-preservation had been cast aside for something reckless and free. For the open study of Scripture, the care of not just those within the church but of the poor and needy around them. No longer hiding their hope behind the safety of shuttered windows and barred doors but shining it bright. A lamp on a stand. A city on a hill. A shantytown on a river.

Demi had never felt more alive.

When the mussel shells butterflied, she pulled the pan from the coals, inhaling the fragrance.

"Demi?"

She looked up as Nydia approached. Wiping her hands on her chiton, Demi stood and stepped away from the fire. "What is it? Have your mitera and Yia-yia returned?"

Nydia shook her head. "No. But they should have been back already. That sick woman was not far away." Her brow creased. "There's someone here asking for you."

Demi frowned. "Me?"

"A woman. Ragged, pockmarked—rather angry."

A vague recognition struck. It had been nearly a week since she'd first invited the woman. "She came?"

"You did invite her then. I thought you must have if she knew your name."

"I did. I am glad she showed up, but I confess, after all the spittle, I am surprised."

Nydia chuckled. "She's standing outside. Refused to come in."

"Now that sounds like her."

Outside the shelter of the courtyard walls, the woman stood beneath the scraggly branches of a cedar, tattered mantle draped over her head and shoulders and pinched firmly beneath her chin with one fist. Her face was dirty, and her dark eyes skittered across the yard, no longer hard and defiant, but uncertain.

Demi pulled her own mantle over her head as she came nearer, shivering against the wind and mist beginning to spit from the sky. Around the insula, the sounds of Saturnalia celebrations continued as they had for several weeks. Bonfires smoldered in the mist, while music and singing filled the spaces between laughter and the clink of wine amphorae.

The woman squinted. "You are Demitria?"

"Yes." Demi offered a smile. "I'm so glad you've come to join us."

"A diver?" the woman pressed, ignoring the invitation.

Unease prickled up Demi's spine. "No . . . not anymore."

The woman studied her a moment. "I don't know about diving. Seems unseemly for a woman, but I've kept my eye on you and you seem a decent sort."

Demi waited, jellyfish beginning to flip in her stomach. She'd been watching her? To what end? "Won't you come inside?"

"No. I'm here to warn you. My man's a diver and said there's a reward out for a woman diver—Demitria. After you left those shellfish . . . I . . . thought you should know."

"Th-thank you," Demi stammered, mouth suddenly dry.

"Best be—"

"Demi!"

Her head whipped toward the panicked voice. The woman scurried away as Demi's gaze landed on Iris, staggering toward the insula and dragging a brightly colored bundle stained with dirt and blood. Demi's heart slammed into her throat as her body jerked into motion.

"Help me." Iris's knees buckled as she scrabbled for a better grip on Yia-yia, who slumped to the ground.

Not Yia-yia. Please.

Dirt bit into her knees as Demi dropped beside Iris, who cradled Yia-yia's still form. "What happened?"

Iris's lip was swollen, a bruise darkening one cheek. "We've got to get her inside. Where's Titus?"

Demi shrugged. "Not here." Titus was forever in and out, making rounds of Myra and meeting with the deacons and small gatherings the way Nikolas had done.

Iris's voice shook with barely checked emotion. "If we work together, we can lift her. She's not heavy."

They locked arms around Yia-yia's back and beneath her knees, lifting her between them like a child. Demi didn't ask any more questions. Iris's whole face trembled as if she might have strength for this task only and she'd fall apart if asked to speak as well. Nydia's cry of alarm greeted them as they crossed the courtyard and shuffled into the windowless safe room they'd occupied for months now. Nydia unrolled a reed mat and they laid Yia-yia upon it.

Nydia threw her arms around her mother as Iris sank back. "Mater, what happened? I thought you were just going up the street?"

"We did." Iris smeared the back of her hand beneath her nose, her shoulders beginning to shake. "We prayed with Eunike before we left. I think a group of . . . boys overheard . . . They were drunk, caught up in the Saturnalia celebration . . ."

"So they beat two women?" Nydia spat. "Wait til Pater hears this, he'll—"

"Hears what?" Titus stepped into the room, holding the door for Rex before shutting it behind them. Rain dripped from their cloaks.

Iris shoved to her feet and rushed to him with a sob. Titus caught her, wrapping his arms around her as his gaze fell on Beatrix. "What happened?" His voice was flat and sharp as a dagger.

Demi's hands shook and tears burned the back of her throat as she peeled back Yia-yia's pink mantle to reveal swollen and bruising flesh. How could anyone be so cruel to a sweet elderly woman? *Strike them down, Lord.*

Titus shared her sentiments—only he volunteered to do the striking. He cradled his wife in one arm, cupping her cheek to inspect the cut there. "I'll kill them," he muttered.

"You can't kill anyone, Titus," Iris protested with a wince. "You're the church leader now."

He shook his head. "That is why I didn't want to lead the church in the first place." He gave a growl of frustration. "I had more options before."

"No, you didn't." Iris tried to pull away. "Let me help with Mater."

"The girls are looking after her. Let me look after you."

Nydia knelt beside Demi and poured water onto a clean cloth.

"She's still breathing," Demi whispered and accepted the cloth. A lump rose in her throat as she gently swept it along Yia-yia's forehead, wiping blood-matted hair away from her face. Her eyelids twitched and remained closed. Short lashes resting on the bulbous swelling of her cheek.

Nydia pressed the back of her hand to her mouth, sucking in a jagged breath. "I don't understand . . ."

Demi shook her head. "I don't either." *How long, Lord? And why?*

Yia-yia moaned, her breathing labored and rattling.

Nydia looked up and caught sight of Rex still pressed against the door, lamplight gleaming on his wide eyes. "Oh, Rex." Nydia opened her arms to her little brother. "Come here. It's all right."

He stumbled forward, gaze glued to Yia-yia's battered face. Choking back a sob as he reached Nydia, Rex suddenly pitched forward, flinging his arms around his sister and burying his face in her shoulder.

While Nydia consoled Rex, Demi swallowed back her own tears as she cleaned Yia-yia's wounds with water and olive oil and redressed her in a clean chiton the color of a sunset. It was all she could do. It was nothing at all. This dear woman had already endured much pain and loss in her life. She'd lost two husbands, lived through and escaped persecution in Rome that had claimed the life of her nephew. She'd been faithful and courageous during the last six years of fear and persecution. Why must her end be like this? One of suffering and pain, and not peace. It wasn't fair.

Titus cared for his wife and then left to find Phineas, anger in the sound of each step. Iris murmured prayers after he'd gone, anxiety in the creases of her face as she stared at the door, as if she wasn't quite convinced he'd gone to seek the physician and not revenge.

They gathered close around Yia-yia, Iris gathering her bony hand and lifting it to her own bruised cheek.

"We're here, Mater," she whispered, her lips shaking. A stream of tears slid over their mingled hands.

Yia-yia's fingers trembled and twitched as they tightened around Iris's. The eye that wasn't swollen slowly opened and shut.

"Don't . . . weep," she whispered, her voice a mere breath that grew in strength as she spoke. "How exciting . . . to be . . . such"—a labored breath—"a threat to the darkness . . . that it must . . . come after me. At my age . . ." She smiled and let her eyes fall closed, face sagging with the toll those words had taken.

How like Beatrix to see the darkness of the world in such a way.

"There is still so much to do, Yia-yia," Nydia sniffed. "How can we do it without you?"

"The joy . . . of the Lord is . . . your strength," Beatrix wheezed. "Not . . . whoever is . . . with you." She seemed to fall asleep then, chest rising and falling in quick, shallow motions.

Titus arrived with Phineas later that evening, after he'd tracked him through several rounds of patients. There was nothing Phineas could do for either woman that hadn't already been done. When Phineas left, the room dropped into the weighted silence that bespoke silent prayer and pleading. As the night stretched on, they organized into shifts, Nydia taking the first as the others settled on mats to sleep.

Demi lay down, the air thick and close with the smell of blood and the herb-infused water Phineas had left for them to wash wounds. The smell of death clogged the room. Demi tried to position her face to catch the draft of evening air creeping in beneath the door, her eyes swollen and burning.

She must have slept because the next she knew, Nydia was shaking her shoulder.

Demi sat up. "How is she?"

"Sleeping still." Exhaustion carved dark moons beneath Nydia's eyes.

"Why didn't you wake me sooner?" She scrambled off her sleeping mat, gesturing for Nydia to take both it and the mantle she'd used as a blanket. "Here, rest."

"Wake me if there's trouble." Nydia lay down and pulled the mantle to her chin.

Demi moved toward Yia-yia's too-still form, wanting to be near her and wanting to run to the sea until the horrible waiting was over. She tucked the blanket higher, smoothed the thin curls still stubbornly springing every which way, and wrapped her fingers around the wrinkled hand that had so often held others.

"It isn't fair, Yia-yia . . ." she whispered, her lips tight with the grimace of grief. "That you should suffer." Demi squeezed her eyes shut and pressed the back of her hand against her teeth, failing to stifle the gasp of tears.

The next three days became weary stretches of sitting at Beatrix's side, ladling scant spoonfuls of water and fish broth between her lips. Praying, inexplicably, that she would both recover and pass in peace. Iris had endured the same abuse but in a younger body, less fragile, though Titus was still determined to keep her abed.

On the third night, Demi sat slumped against the wall, back aching, eyes burning. Iris and Titus slept against the wall opposite, with Rex sprawled across the floor at their feet. Nydia curled on her side along the back wall.

How long since Demi had been outside, seen the sun glitter across the winter blue of the Mediterranean? Were Nikolas and Theseus trapped in stale darkness also? *God, give them strength.*

Yia-yia stirred and shifted with a grunt of pain. "There's my girl."

Demi started and opened her eyes as Yia-yia's wispy voice broke over the deep breathing of the others. Beatrix's eyes were open, blinking slowly through the dark swelling around them.

"Yia-yia?" Demi bent closer. "Don't try to move. Are you thirsty?" She grabbed the cup of tepid water and ladled a spoonful.

Beatrix accepted several sips, water dribbling down the lines carved on either side of her mouth. "That is . . . good." She lay back with a sigh as if the simple action of swallowing had sapped her strength. Her hand moved, fingers twitching toward Demi until Demi took her hand in both of her own.

"I'm glad to see you awake." Demi's lips trembled.

"I'm glad to see your face." Yia-yia's lips twitched in a smile that turned to a grimace. "Does mine look as bad as it feels?"

"The bruising will go away with time."

"Iris?"

"She's sleeping. Recovering. As you are."

A weak shake of her head. "Tell me, what have you been doing?"

Demi tried to tip another spoonful of water to her lips, but Yia-yia shook her head again, seeming to settle back, though she was already laying flat.

"I've been . . . here with you."

"But there is so much to be done."

"We'll get to it in time, Yia-yia."

Demi jumped at the sound of Nydia's voice and moved over to make room for her friend. As she did, Titus rolled over.

"Is she awake?"

Demi nodded. "And talking."

He sat up and touched Iris's shoulder, murmuring something in her ear before she stirred. He helped her move toward Yia-yia's mat.

"Mater?" Iris murmured. "You're awake?"

Beatrix dragged in a breath. "Not for long."

Rex shuffled into the circle, rubbing sleepy eyes. "Hello, Yia-yia."

Beatrix's smile was tender and weak. "I've missed you."

"Are you getting better?" Rex asked.

"She just needs to rest and she will get well." Titus reached toward Beatrix and tenderly brushed several limp curls off her forehead. It wasn't right that even her curls had lost their energetic spring.

"Listen to me." Yia-yia shook her head, lips tight against the pain visible in her swollen eyes. "Our time is short. Do not grow weary. We are hated . . . but He was hated first." Her breathing grew labored and shallow, the dim lamplight flickering across her bruised face.

Demi's stomach sank, Yia-yia's words taking on the tenor of someone saying goodbye. Her throat felt raw with unshed tears. It was too soon— too many goodbyes already said. How could God make her say another?

"He gave up His life for ours . . . and we find life in Him that doesn't end with these bodies. Who else can offer hope like that?" Yia-yia seemed to settle again. To sink, though there was nothing to sink into. "Don't forget." She closed her eyes, chest rising and dropping in breaths that seemed too heavy for her frail body to carry any longer.

Nydia sniffed, pressed the back of her hand against her mouth.

Yia-yia's hands twitched outward toward Demi and Titus who sat on either side of her. Both tried to pass her hands to Iris and Nydia, but Beatrix's fingers tightened around theirs with a fierce strength.

"God makes no mistake in His mercy."

FIFTY-THREE

Muscles quivering, Nikolas did his best to keep up with the guards as they dragged him down the poorly lit corridor, passing door after door, barred and secured with rusted locks. His head spun, pain shooting through his limbs, the scorched skin on his back burning as if the red-hot brands pressed there still.

Where was the light?

His eyes searched in vain for the faintest crack of sunlight, anything that spoke of a world beyond these weeping stone walls. Even the guards were pale.

"Think he's going to die?" one asked.

The guard on Nikolas's left grunted. "They usually do."

"Not *him*. Emperor Galerius. I heard he's rotting from the inside out, and that he had his physicians executed because they retched at the smell of him when they walked into the room."

"Who says?"

"Justus."

"*Justus.*" The left guard spat the name. "You can't believe a word he says."

"He says Empress Valeria prays at the emperor's bedside." He lowered his voice. "To the Christos."

"How would Justus know that? Galerius has gone to Serdica. Do you really think he would allow his own wife to go against the edicts? Lies, all of it."

They paused near the end of the corridor before a wall of small doors stacked one upon the other like a row of cupboards. They were too small. Too short to be the entrances to cells. Why so small?

As if in answer, one of the guards unlocked a little door on the bottom row, the hobnailed iron square scraping across the uneven floor. A tiny black mouth in the stone.

"Head or feet?"

"Feet. I hate it when they kick the door."

"Feet it is."

A foot crashed into the back of Nikolas's knees, buckling him. Pain sent white streaks through his vision, and before he could protest, the guards had shoved him to the floor and pushed him feetfirst into the hole, little more than a shoulder-width tunnel drilled into the stone. His heart swelled and rose to his throat, blood and panic racing through his limbs.

"Please!" The word burst from his lips on a gasp.

They fought his arms to his sides and shoved, the pain nearly sending him senseless as his blistered back grated against the stone. Fire and ice raced over his body in turns. It was pointless to fight, to thrash and yell, but he did it anyway, even as the tiny door slammed over his head, killing the last flicker of torchlight. His breaths came quick and shallow, panic closing in with the walls. Keys rattled in the lock, as if it weren't impossible for Nikolas to wrestle his arms over his head and pry open the door from the inside. The walls held him tight on all sides.

No light. No movement. A tomb in the depths of the dungeon.

He couldn't breathe.

His limbs went limp.

How many times had he jerked awake, limbs flailing, only to find a barrier before they'd moved an inch? Breaths coming too fast, using up too much air, and not enough, before his body went limp and it started over again . . .

Panic slowly surrendered to resignation. Tears burned the backs of his eyes, and he let them come. There was no one here to see him break. No reason to be strong anymore. No one to help or encourage. Nothing to do.

The last thought sent a race of panic through him that had little to do with the tightness of the walls. He was going to die; that much was certain. The tortures would end, the pain soon cease . . . so why was he so afraid?

You are selfish, Niko, and stupid to think you will find joy in it.

Amadeo's angry words rang through his mind in such clarity, his brother might have been in the cell beside him. It was the first time Amadeo had been wrong.

They had been friends once. As close as any brothers could be. Amadeo always the encourager, the uplifter. Always the leader, the honest one, the one Pater had counted on. The difference grew more pronounced as they grew older. When Pater wanted something done, something done well, he always asked Amadeo. Never him. As Nikolas seemed to struggle through friendships, school, and learning the business, Amadeo floated on the praise of his tutors and everyone who knew him.

Nikolas had never minded being set free from the confines of ledgers and desks, free to accompany his mitera as she made daily rounds to the ill and elderly. He fit there. Better than anywhere else. He could carry bundles of firewood, baskets of food, tinker with broken doors and leaky roofs. Mitera had looked on him with pride. Pater had only seen a boy and then a young man unskilled in shipping and trade and assumed it was because he would not apply himself in order to succeed.

Kindness, then, was not success.

It was Nikolas and Mitera, Amadeo and Pater. Together, yet always separate.

It remained that way after Mitera died—Pater and Amadeo, sometimes inviting Nikolas along but mostly leaving him be. As if after all that time, they didn't know what to do with him.

Perhaps he ought to have tried harder. Pretended to love shipping the way Amadeo did, while dreaming of other things. But he didn't, and grew angry as they poured themselves into the same things they'd done before Mitera had died, as if her death hadn't left a gaping hole in their hearts and in their days. And so he'd given in to the words his pater had muttered about him.

Lazy, aimless. Selfish. Drunkard.

It wasn't right.

But neither was Amadeo.

He hadn't been trying to find joy. He'd been trying to find his father. To have his father see him. And it had taken so long. So long in misery before Pater had finally invited him on a trading trip. To this day, Nikolas didn't know why, when his heart had leaped, his mouth had spilled venomous insults.

Why hadn't he gone after them? To help or . . . apologize? Might he have kept his brother from standing where he had? Might he have been struck instead?

His brother's face flashed through his mind, still and smashed against the docks. His father's voice echoed in his ears, weighted with grief. *It should not have been Amadeo.*

Pain sliced up the center of Nikolas's chest, sharper than any of the torturer's blades. Regret as well as rejection.

I should have done more.

"It should have been me." The words nearly choked him. Nothing he could ever do would make up for how he'd turned his back on his brother, his father. He'd chosen to turn his back, to repay neglect for neglect, and now they were both dead. And soon, very soon, he'd stand face to face with God and how would he explain? His good deeds, his acts of helpfulness would never wash his brother's blood from his hands. All he could do was throw himself upon the grace and mercy of God.

His conscience smote.

He'd grown up in a world of transactions and trades, barters and exchange rates . . . How easily those ideas had slipped into his view of God. God was not swayed by his goodness, his generosity, his work. The only thing that mattered was that the blood of Jesus Christ covered him. There was nothing less, nothing more he could do to affect the love and grace God bestowed on him. On all those who believed.

And throwing himself on that grace? Wasn't that all anyone could do? He'd believed these things from childhood—how could they have grown so twisted and backward in his heart? He let out a ragged breath. Since the accident he'd not allowed himself to be still, to rest. He'd already lived his fair share of idleness, and then action, no matter how exhausting, had seemed a satisfactory punishment to inflict on himself. And yet, God had never asked him to punish himself. He'd taken the punishment already. God was not his earthly father who'd heaped shame on his shoulders over his mistakes. On the contrary, He'd taken on Nikolas's mistakes, his sins—all of them—and paid for them with His own blood. What a slap in His face for Nikolas to live as though that were not enough.

Tears rolled from the corners of his eyes, tickling into his ears.

Lord, forgive me.

FIFTY-FOUR

RAIN STUNG DEMI'S CHEEKS AND FOREHEAD, her face the only thing exposed beneath the edges of the mantle gripped beneath her chin in one fist. With the other hand, she clutched the bundle of bread against her chest, praying the rain would not render it a bag of mush by the time they reached the little cave tucked into the oceanside cliffs opposite the harbor from Andriake. But making the mile-long trek in the rain was the easy thing. Doing it while carrying a body for burial in the dark was another matter altogether.

Demi's heart felt as raw as the skin beneath her eyes. She could hardly fathom that Yia-yia Beatrix was gone. Her smile, her energy, her relentlessly awkward quest to see everyone around her married . . . How could it all disappear so quickly? How many more times would Demi have to say goodbye to someone she loved?

Titus led the way, twisting past the citrus branches that clawed at his shoulders, cradling the wrapped body that seemed too small to have been Bea's. And yet the way he stumbled betrayed how great a weight he bore. Iris steadied him, her own form hunched and limping still. The two of them led the way to a place Demi had rarely been in recent years. Ironic that the last six years spelling death for so many Christians had led to the fewest burials in their cemetery.

When Christos returns, we will rise to be with Him.

It was that very belief that drove the emperors to such brutal executions so as not to leave a body to be raised, declaring it illegal for anyone to bury the body of a condemned Christian, and instead ordering them exposed to the birds, dumped into the sewers to be swept out to sea. In so doing, they thwarted any attempt to create a martyr's memorial. But stories were more powerful than graves.

Stones and pottery clattered underfoot as they skirted the fishermen's village and crossed the upper end of the dumping grounds. Ahead, rising even blacker against the stormy flickering of the sky, the sea cliffs heralded the end of their journey. The end of Bea's. Waves boomed and hushed along the coastline in thunderous applause, as if the sea itself rejoiced that Beatrix had run the race and finished well.

The entrance to the cemetery was hidden, the mouth normally covered with stones. Tonight, the stones had been cast aside and the opening hung with a thick curtain to hide the flickers of lamplight within. Titus ducked through the low opening followed by Iris, Nydia, and Rex. Demi drew one last fresh breath of briny air before shifting aside the curtain and hunching through the entrance.

The cave was a natural tunnel, walls cut with niches to hold the remains of the faithful. Lamplight flickered over the rippled walls, illuminating triptych paintings of Jonah centered inside a great fish, Jonah bursting forth on land, and Jonah reclined beneath a leafy plant rendered in such stunning green that it looked like a true living thing. Others bore a simple fish or the Greek word for it, *ichthus,* whose letters formed the code for their creed: *Jesus Christ, the Son of God, the Savior.*

They wound deeper into the tunnel and Demi was finally forced to take a breath of stale air tinged with must and earth and other odors she refused to think more on. She nearly bumped into Nydia, who'd slowed in front of her. The hall ahead was lit with the warm glow of lamps and lined with silent friends who'd come to lay Bea to sleep. Demi let her mantle fall to her shoulders and drew out the bread as Titus tucked his burden into an empty niche. Iris laid an evergreen sprig plucked from an orange tree over Bea's body. Life, even here. Especially here.

Nydia held out the amphora of wine to Titus and Demi offered the bread. Titus took both, his throat working as he struggled to find and form the words. When he did, they emerged rough with emotion.

"Brothers and sisters, we do not want you to be uninformed about those who sleep in death . . . For we believe that Jesus died and rose again, and so we believe that God will bring with Jesus those who have fallen asleep in him." He swallowed and uncorked the amphora, pouring a measure into a clay cup. "Tonight we lay a dear sister to rest, and tonight we celebrate that our Lord defeated death and the grave. We remember and celebrate His death and resurrection, knowing one day we will partake of the same."

Titus passed the cup down the line and opened the bundle of bread. "His body, broken for us. His blood poured out for the forgiveness of our sin."

Somewhere in the line, a voice lifted in song, passing it down the line of mourners after the bread. The words whispered, wavered, and swelled into something majestic. Defiant.

Now sunset comes, but light shines forth,
The lamps are lit to pierce the night.
Praise the Father, Son, and Holy Spirit,
God who dwells in eternal light.

Worthy are You of endless praise,
O Son of God, Life-giving Lord;
Wherefore You are through all the earth
And in the highest heaven adored.

Tears pricked the backs of Demi's eyes, and she squeezed them shut. How fitting to be gathered in a tomb, a place of death and decay, worshipping the One who destroyed death forever and made it but a slumber until the dead would rise with Christ. They might bury a body this night, but they celebrated a victory. They were a new people rising. They would not fear death, because they had died already, crucified with their Christ, and living a life that could not truly be taken.

The taste of the bread and wine lingered on her tongue as Demi opened her eyes. They had gained courage in reaching out to their neighbors, offering food and hope. And now the question remained: In the face of all that seemed dark and hopeless, would they continue?

When the sun had risen and the rain ceased, they walked back to the insula in scattered groups, the sky still shrouded in gray, though it no longer wept. The elderly widows who could not make the trek to the cemetery in the dark and rain had kindled a fire in the courtyard and brewed herbed ptisana to serve if they did not have enough food. The winter months had eaten away their rations, already meager since Demi had not been able to make the final trips upriver for supplies.

Demi stood in the crowded courtyard, warming her fingers around a steaming clay cup that smelled faintly of mint. She brought it to her lips as a stranger stepping through the doorway caught her eye. Balding head, robes that did not befit a beggar or resident of this insula.

Unease sent a twinge to her stomach. Her gaze darted around the courtyard and back. Where was Titus?

Their eyes caught. The man gave a nod and moved toward her. She had no choice but to let him approach.

"I believe we have a mutual friend," he said, by way of greeting.

"Oh?" Demi crossed her arms, gaze darting toward the group. Was he a spy for Mersad, sent to search for her, bring her to justice?

"Are you Demitria, daughter of Anatolios?"

Warnings thumped in her chest. "I don't think I know you."

He extended a hand. "Basil of Smyrna. I am the loyal steward of Nikolas of Patara."

The name sent a strange thrill through her, followed by the familiar choking crush of grief. Nikolas of Patara, *her* Nikolas, was no more.

Basil turned to survey the insula. "I thought buying this place was a terrible decision on his part. I see now I was right. He'll never get his money back."

She didn't dare confirm or deny his words in case he told the truth— or a lie.

"He asked me to find you, and I'm sorry it's taken me so long to come. There's been several . . . hang-ups with my work."

She said nothing and he continued.

"I don't know if you heard of his trial?"

She shook her head, throat feeling tight. "Only that he's been sent to Nicomedia."

"He was accused of sedition. Of leading illegal gatherings. Of being a Christian. He denied none of the charges against him."

Her nose burned, tears welling in her eyes. "Who . . ." She swallowed. "Who accused him?"

"Xeno of Myra."

Her knees jerked. "Xeno . . ." They'd assumed he had been captured when he'd disappeared. Her stomach soured.

"You know him?"

"I . . ." Had she known him? Had any of them truly known him? Demi turned away, the courtyard seeming to spin around her. All the arrests, the way the guards had seemed to know their every move, their every hiding place . . . Xeno. Not Nikolas. Anger came hard on the heels of relief. How could Xeno have done such a thing?

Basil took another step toward her. "He was awarded all of Nikolas's possessions . . . including the shipping company and warehouses. I've spent the last months trying to convince Xeno he still needed me to run things. Got him to trust me."

How could she be hearing this? Shipping company, warehouses, Nikolas—and Xeno. *Xeno.* They'd added his name to their list of captured brothers and sisters, praying for the strength and witness of each one. And to think, all this time he'd been the betrayer. The Judas. Feasting off the spoils of his treachery. She was going to be sick.

"What are you doing here?" The words emerged in a breathless whisper. Why had he waited so long to find them? Why now?

"I know Nikolas worked closely with you." He glanced around and lowered his voice with a slight shake of his head. "And while that . . . *usurper* has possession of . . . what you dove for, I have access to the grain again. The rest we didn't move out of the warehouse when Nikolas was working on this place. I can get it to you."

Her breath caught, the promise of grain warring against the knowledge that Xeno was now this man's master. Xeno, who had betrayed Nikolas. Betrayed them all. Could they trust this Basil of Smyrna? She'd rather starve than endanger her friends.

"I was able to meet with Nikolas after the trial. He told me to find you." His lips pulled in an uneasy smile. "He said you would not believe me, but to say that . . . that . . . you were the girl with no teeth. Which doesn't make sense, but—"

She pressed her palm to her mouth. *The girl with no teeth?* Who but Nikolas would know that?

"Demi? Who is this?" Titus's voice sent a rush of relief that cleared her whirling head.

She turned. "This is Basil of Smyrna, Nikolas's steward. He has grain for us."

FIFTY-FIVE

THE GRATING OF STONE AND IRON OVER HIS HEAD. Or was it behind him? A murmur of voices. Curses. Laughter.

His? No.

Nikolas tried to pry his tongue from the roof of his mouth. No. Definitely not his. He hadn't spoken in hours. Not had food ladled into his mouth in days. How long had he been confined here? Weeks? A month?

Teeth bit into his shoulders and tore at his skin—no, not teeth— fingers. Hands. He felt his body sliding, the skin of his back tearing where it had stuck to the stone. The pain pulled the breath from his lungs and he was unable to even cry out.

"Ugh. Another dead one?"

"No doubt Clovis forgot to water these ones down on the bottom."

Nikolas tried to shake his head, to open his eyes. "Water," he croaked.

His body slid free of the tomb. From darkness to light. Death to life. Hades to—well. So, he wasn't dead after all. What a shame.

Water crashed against his face, and for a fraction of the moment between shock and his next sputtering breath, he was in the sea. Body floating free. Demitria, near him, wild curls waving in the water like tendrils of seaweed. Her smile, aimed at him, bright and playful.

Lord, I miss her.

The ache in his chest turned to a cough, and he was no longer in the sun-drenched Mediterranean, but curled on his side in the musty damp of the emperor's dungeon.

315

"This one's alive still."

"Put him with the others then."

Hands wrapped around his upper arms and pulled. His heels dragged, catching on the uneven stones and shooting spasms of pain into his hamstrung calf. He moaned.

Golden light flickered over his eyelids and dropped into darkness as they passed between torches along the corridor.

"What are we saving them for?" one of the guards muttered. "If the rumors are true, and Galerius dies, Maximinus Daia is going to seize this region and execute them all anyway."

"Orders is orders. We do as we're told."

All? How many of them remained? Was Theseus among them still? *God, grant us strength. To glorify You in all circumstances. In every . . . means of execution.*

Fire rolled through his body. How could he still feel? He shouldn't be able to feel. He'd long stopped feeling the pain of hunger. Barely felt his own hands clasped together over his belly. But the fire nearly stole his breath. Would this pain be his undoing? It racketed through his limbs, his back, his head.

Why didn't they kill him now? Why wait? Why prolong the suffering? His uncle's words, spoken to him so long ago, spun through his mind. Chastening.

To die in times like these is easy. To live, that is the difficult thing.

It was true. How easy it would be to welcome death—paradise at this moment. To put an end to the pain. To leave the struggle far behind. How much more difficult to persevere through it. To endure. To live. To love. To praise.

Stars crashed through the backs of his eyelids, more pain rushing hot and sharp through the base of his skull. He hissed through his teeth, riding the waves of pain until they became mere ripples. He was no longer moving. They'd dropped him and his head had hit the floor.

Keys clanked. Iron hinges protested.

The guards hauled him into a cell and dropped him again, but he barely noticed them leave over the crushing pain in his head. He moaned.

Rustling in the dark nearby.

"Who are you?"

That voice. Familiar, but too weak to be right.

"Niko . . ." His own voice was wrong. Creaking and snapping like an old merchant ship.

A hand clasped his. "After all this time? We thought you were dead."

Another voice. "Who is it?"

"Pastor Nikolas of Myra."

His name, and yet so much more. A lump rose to his throat. How could three words hold so much? *Nikolas of Myra.* No longer a stranger from a distant city, but a fellow citizen. A brother.

Murmurs filled the cell. Voices. More rustling. A hand went beneath his head. A cup found his lips. Water trickled into his mouth.

"Not so fast." The cup disappeared. "Here, try this."

A paste of ground grain and water filled his mouth next and went down with another sip. Hunger struck then. Nikolas lurched forward, eager.

Hands pushed him back, gentle, unlike the guards. "No more for now. Let it settle."

That voice.

"Theseus?"

"I'm here. We are glad to see you alive and with us still."

"How many?" Nikolas worked his tongue over the words. He tried to open his eyes, gritty and sticky with lack of moisture. They burned with each blink, as if he'd been diving with Demi. A lantern hung in the center of the cell, falling on the men beneath who might have been living skeletons. He shut his eyes, unwilling to look at Theseus, to see how he'd fared. How he'd changed.

"Who else is with us?"

Theseus listed names, some Nikolas remembered and most he did not.

"We've been telling our stories. Encouraging each other with how God called each one of us from death to life." Theseus raised his voice. "The guards have been listening, and one has even joined us in here."

"Menas?"

"He is with our Lord. Though no one has been taken out of here for days."

Nikolas opened his eyes, finally turning them toward Theseus. His skin was pale and lacerated with cuts and scabbed burns, his beard torn and scorched, but his eyes remained compassionate.

"Your back is bleeding. Let me help you."

Nikolas rolled to his side, all he seemed capable of, and gritted his teeth as Theseus set to work. The breathtaking pain made it difficult to discern whether Theseus was washing his wounds or tearing the very flesh from his back.

Theseus spoke, as if to take Nikolas's mind from the pain.

"The guards seem confused. There are wars and rumors of wars. Some say that Constantine, the emperor of the west, is determined to have sole rule, and that Emperor Galerius is dead. Others say he is not."

"What does it mean?" Nikolas moaned.

"I don't know. But something has changed and we can all feel it."

"Good?"

"Time will tell."

Theseus tugged at the shredded bits of Nikolas's tunic, stuck to the wounds on his back. White-hot light raced through him, and he lost what little he'd eaten. His eyes fell shut as if weighted with stones, mind teetering on the edge of nothingness, sounds fading in and out. How long he stayed there, he couldn't say.

Somewhere near him, someone started to sing, the sound low and haunting and full of worship. Was he dead? Or was it possible for such heavenly sounds to rise from a tomb? He wavered in the place between nothingness and sound, searing heat and mind-numbing cold. Water and grain paste pushed between his lips, the exertion of swallowing sending him to sleep once more. Voices murmuring, singing, praying. Then nothing and silence.

Nikolas shifted, body stiff and cold, but not wracked with the same brain-searing pain. He raised his cheek from the stone floor, then his whole head, shoulder, and side. The cell was quiet. Water dripped from somewhere in the passage and a fiery thirst swept over him. He sat all the way up, head spinning and slowly calming.

"Nikolas?" A rustle beside him as Theseus sat up. "I'm glad to see you awake, brother. I wasn't sure you would come back to us."

Brother.

This time the word brought comfort instead of guilt.

"Where are the others?"

"Sleeping. Are you hungry?" Theseus reached out and gripped his hand, dumping a crumbling cake of dried grain paste into his palm. "It needs salt."

Nikolas took a bite, the grit scraping between his teeth. "Salt . . . among other things."

Theseus chuckled. "Reminds me of Demi's attempts at bread."

Nikolas's throat went dry, from the bread or the mention of Demi's name, he could not be certain, though there was one thing that was. "I miss her," he dared to admit aloud.

Theseus was silent for a breath. "I know," he whispered. "I'm sorry I dissuaded you. I didn't want to see Demi hurt again . . . though perhaps I only denied you both a chance at happiness."

The sentiment comforted, even if it could not change what had happened. "If anything, she would probably thank you. You were right, I was not a safe choice."

"But you are a good man." Theseus reached through the dark and gripped his shoulder. "I'm glad they brought you back to us."

Nikolas gave a nod Theseus could not see. "Me too."

FIFTY-SIX

Over the course of several months, Basil had kept up a steady delivery of grain to the insula. It was abundance unlike anything they'd seen in years. Nydia and Demi joined the dwindling ranks of deacons and deaconesses, carrying market baskets filled with bread and grain, medicine and messages to various drop-off points throughout the city. Yia-yia's death had lit something in all of them. If she could risk her life to love their neighbors, surely they could too. After all, wasn't extravagant, costly love the very reason they'd been saved? How could they go on hoarding such a gift?

They served a meal several times a week in the courtyard of the insula, word spreading like the green of spring blanketing the Taurus Mountains. The grain ran out, but the food did not. Strangers began bringing what little they had to share, combined into a common meal that was eaten until no crumbs remained. Each day, more food was brought. Each night, more people crowded into the insula courtyard, hungry for more than just physical food as Titus and others took turns reading small portions of Scripture. Each day was a miracle—handfuls turned into bowls of leftovers. Only possible because they served a God of the impossible. Of the miraculous. The God who sees. Satisfies.

Demi settled against the wall at the back of the courtyard next to Nydia, taking in the room, full to bursting. People clustered on the crumbling stairs and lined the balcony of the second story. The gray-bearded man with the eye patch had eventually heeded Demi's invitation, and since the first time, he'd not missed a meal, nor the readings that came after. Tonight, he'd brought a bag of pine nuts. Demi had served food into hands and on shards of pottery that clinked against the floor as they were set aside, empty. The cleanup would carry them far into the evening.

At least the work would take her mind from the tension gripping the city. The festival of Thargelia began in a few short weeks, heralding the birthdays of Artemis and her twin brother, Apollo. The celebration was one of purification and eradication of filth followed by welcoming with sacrifices of that which was good and beautiful. A nice sentiment. Unless you were considered the "filth."

Lord, hold us fast.

Titus emerged through a curtained doorway, a codex cradled in his palms like the most precious of treasures. The voices in the room dropped away to expectant rustling as Titus lay the codex on a table beside a lighted lamp, and paused, resting both hands on the book.

He prayed and began to read. His Greek was accented and his voice oddly halting and lacking confidence. But the delivery didn't matter, because the words he spoke were the words of God.

"Present your bodies as a living sacrifice, holy and acceptable to God, which is your spiritual worship."

Living sacrifice.

What did it mean to be a living sacrifice, a continual offering? Surrendered over and over to a will greater than her own?

"Rejoice in hope, be patient in tribulation, be constant in prayer. Contribute to the needs of the saints and seek to show hospitality."

Was that it? An active love, one that kept its focus on heaven?

Her eyes opened and settled on the table laden with leftover bits from the meal. The room blurred and swam. All those pieces were wholly inadequate on their own. Each ingredient offered wasn't enough. But offered willingly, in sacrifice and trust, they served the needs of everyone in the room. It was worship.

A warmth filled her. The knowledge that the offering of her gifts, given not to earn approval or erase her wrongs but as an act of worship, was accepted. Welcomed.

Tears rolled down her cheeks.

The sounds of the room fell away; even the sound of Titus's voice seemed to quiet, though he read on. The moment was holy. As if the only ones in existence were her and God.

And then it broke.

The door.

The silence.

The peace.

Hobnailed footsteps, shouts, screams. The sickening meeting between fists and flesh.

Demi leaped to her feet, only to be shoved back against the wall by panicked bodies rushing past. Stars flashed in her eyes.

"I'm not one of them! I'm not one of them! Kyrios Caesar. Hail the Sol Invictus!"

No. Not again.

She clapped a hand over her mouth, but the shouts remained. Not hers. Friends and neighbors shoved past, angling for doorways and disappearing out windows. Babies and children screeched and wailed. A hand gripped hers, and Demi turned to meet Nydia's wide eyes as her gaze shifted over Demi's shoulder. Demi squeezed her hand and turned toward the doorway, blocked by city guards, swords drawn. One raised both hands to his mouth, shouting.

"We've received word of seditious meetings taking place here. All those who declare allegiance to the emperor and Sol Invictus are free to leave. No harm will come to you."

His gaze traveled over the remaining crowd, too old, young, or unwilling to run. "Those of you who will not will be taken to the prison to purify our fair city."

Demi's throat dried. Heart thundered in her chest.

Rejoice in hope, be patient in tribulation, be constant in prayer.

"No matter what comes, He is worthy." Nydia breathed the words and Demi nodded once.

"He is."

FIFTY-SEVEN

22 APRILIS, AD 311

Mersad's face paled when Demi stumbled into the courtroom, her wrists shackled in front of her, chiton slipping off one bruised shoulder. The corner of the basilica at the city center held only a few men wearing pristine tunics and irritation. Only Mersad looked concerned.

"Has she been maimed? She's no good to me maimed."

"She's fine," the guard grunted.

Mersad stared at her until she allowed the tiniest nod in confirmation. No, she'd not been maimed, not sliced down like so many of her friends. She'd been spared—if one could call it that. Upon news of the raid, Mersad had rushed to the prison to single her out, order that she be brought before the magistrates. So many of her friends lay wounded, dead, and all Mersad cared about was getting his prized diver back in his grip.

"Let's get this over with." The magistrate, seated behind a wooden desk clotted with papers, glanced up at her. "You are Demitria, daughter of Anatolios?"

She nodded.

"Yes or no."

She tried to keep her bruised lips from moving. "Yes."

"Mersad of Andriake has offered—"

"Mersad of Andriake, *jeweler of the seas*," Mersad corrected. "Coral, pearls of all colors—excellent pricing on everything."

The magistrate blinked.

"Do go on, sir." Mersad bowed.

The magistrate's eyes slid back to Demi. "Mersad of Andriake, *jeweler of the seas,* has petitioned to offer you life, on the condition that you become his bondslave and renounce your seditious cult. Do be aware that if you refuse this pardon, you submit yourself to execution in two weeks during the festival of Thargelia."

A shiver laced up her spine.

They were willing to wait two weeks to execute her, but not a second for her answer. A scribe at a desk beside the magistrate beckoned her over, unrolling a sheet of papyrus.

"Make your mark here." He pointed.

"I don't want a slave collar put on her," Mersad broke in, hovering at her shoulder. "It's not good for diving. Piercing her ears will be enough."

The scribe handed her a pen and tapped the papyrus again. "Right here."

Could her heart beat so hard it would burst? She backed away, bumping against the bulk of Mersad. "I can't."

"If you can't write your name, just make a mark." Mersad's arm came around her, grasping her wrist and herding her back toward the table where he pushed the pen between her fingers. "You'll be safe, under my protection. No harm will come to you, I promise. Ennio and Pelos won't bother you again."

She believed him. He would take good care of her. Mersad cared for his possessions very well. Boats in good repair brought higher yields. So, too, would divers. But he didn't understand.

"I can't, Mersad." Demi let the pen drop to the table beside the contract. "I will not renounce my God."

"Don't be foolish, Demitria." Mersad's mouth froze in a smile as his eyes darted from her to the magistrate and back. "That is foolishness. Death. And not a quick one. Do you know what they plan for you all during Thargelia?"

Demi shook her head. It was best she didn't know.

"Sign the document, girl." The magistrate inclined his head, boredom and irritation flickering in the tightness of his lips. "You're wasting our time."

A bead of sweat edged her hairline, burning in the cuts and scratches, a tiny precursor of what would come.

"I will not. A diver I am, but more than that, I am a Christian. And I cannot be anything else. How can I turn my back on a God who has never once turned His back on me?"

"No?" The magistrate barked a laugh. "And what do you call this then? Hmm?" he gestured to the courtroom. "Do you think your god will save you?"

She lifted a shoulder, peace flooding through her aching body. "He's saved me already. You may kill me, but you can't touch my soul."

"That is your choice?"

"Yes." She'd never been more sure.

"Demitria, no." Mersad's hand fell heavy on her shoulder. "Give her time to consider. Obviously the stress of the prison has affected her mind."

Demi shook his hand off. "I am perfectly able to make a decision, and I've made it."

The magistrate flicked a hand. "Get her out of here."

The guard stepped forward and took her arm, turning her away.

Mersad trotted after them. "Change your mind, Demi. There's still time."

She twisted to look at him over her shoulder, her lips cracking as she tried to smile. "Thank you for trying to help me, Mersad. I pray you find the truth."

FIFTY-EIGHT

The clack of hobnailed boots echoed up and down the prison halls for two days. Always rushing. Never stopping to offer the prisoners water or food. More and more battered men and women were returned to the cell until they sat shoulder to shoulder, knees drawn up to make space for others.

Nikolas sat against the wall, stomach cramping. He folded his hands across his knees, the stingy light from the barred grate high on the wall illuminating the thin bones, knobby joints, ragged nails.

> *"Let the luminous stars not shine,*
> *Let the winds and all the noisy rivers die down;*
> *And as we praise the Father, the Son and the Holy Spirit,*
> *Let all the powers add 'Amen, Amen.'*
> *Empire, praise always and give glory to God,*
> *The sole giver of good things, amen, amen."*

His voice echoed. Resounded, as his brothers and sisters joined the song. For once the guards didn't shout for silence. The boots went clacking past. Not stopping. No hesitation.

Something was happening beyond the walls of this prison, but it would not be long before they were affected. His body itched to move. To pace. To press his ear against the door, his face against the crack. To learn what was going on. To prepare.

Be still.

He forced himself to stay where he was. Whatever was happening was out of his hands and there was nothing he could do about any of it. What would be would be. The only thing he could control was his response to it. He leaned his head against the stones and closed his eyes.

Footsteps stopped at the door.

Nikolas's eyes snapped open, his stomach spiking at the noise. Would the arrival bring food or torture? Not knowing was often worse than the torture. Hope could be devastating.

Keys clanked in the lock.

His legs tensed.

The door opened with a groan, a broad-shouldered guard silhouetted in the doorway, golden torchlight at his back.

His heart sank. No bucket or bowl in hand. Torture it was.

The guard put a hand to the sword at his waist. "Everyone out."

Nikolas caught Theseus's gaze. They pushed to their feet, aching and sore, scabs pulling and tearing as they stretched limbs that had lain still too long. Nikolas's legs burned and shook with the effort of obedience.

The prisoners formed a line. Nikolas braced himself on the back of the man in front of him and the man behind him did the same. Left feet dragging, maimed, some blind, the line of men and women moved slowly and steadily out of the cell. The soldiers' words from weeks ago ran again through his mind. *If the rumors are true, and Galerius dies, Maximinus Daia is going to seize this region and execute them all anyway.*

So this was it then.

Nikolas left the cell behind and entered the lantern-lit corridor, dull pain shooting up the back of his leg from his maimed ankle. Even after all these months his foot still hung limp and dragged. At least the infection hadn't set in like it had with so many others. Or maybe death by infection was a mercy shown to his other brothers. What horrors awaited him above? Shadows licked the walls, bending and dancing as if hell rejoiced at their coming fate.

As the hall tilted upward and the line of prisoners stretched up the stairs, Nikolas saw the line of hands connecting the first man to the man in the back. Each one drawing strength and courage from the one who'd gone before, even if it was only a single step before. A chain of brothers and sisters, united as one.

Maybe it was his imagination. Maybe it was a final gift of grace. But the pain in his legs seemed to subside as they climbed the stairs, the red lantern light bleeding out into a cold, gray dawn. More armed guards joined the procession at the top of the stairs, winding out of the prison and into a colonnaded yard of scarred gray stone bearing rusty stains and yellow lichen. The sky arched overhead like the gray dome of the sarcophagi lining the road from Andriake to Myra.

The line of prisoners broke into two, and Nikolas found himself facing Theseus. A cool breeze ruffled the rags of Nikolas's borrowed tunic and carried with it the scents of roasted meat and fresh bread. One final torture.

Guards lined up behind them, hands on their sword hilts. The commander barked an order for the prisoners to kneel.

This was it. Nikolas locked eyes with Theseus, his lips moving in a murmured prayer. "Lord Jesus, we lived our lives in Your service, and we give our last breaths to You now."

Gravel on the paving stones bit into his knees as Nikolas knelt.

The double doors at the far end of the courtyard opened with a bang, clattering against the stone walls as an ebony litter entered the courtyard, borne on the backs of four muscular slaves. Resplendent green-silk curtains billowed from the litter and fluttered to hang still as the slaves halted. The guards pivoted and slammed their fists to their chests in salute as the curtains were drawn back and a man emerged, dressed in rich robes betraying him as, if not a member of the royal family, then a high-ranking government official. He surveyed the prisoners with a disinterested lift of his shaved chin.

"I am Felix Junta, servant of the great Emperor Galerius. I am here to ensure his will be done."

Nikolas's pulse stuttered. What would make an emperor send a messenger like this? Was their impending execution a sacrifice to his health?

Felix Junta peered out at the double line of prisoners, his lips tightening. He raised a pouch of herbs to his nose, covering the smell. "Are these all that remain?"

"Yes, sir."

"Hmm." The set of his mouth said he'd hoped for more. He looked at the commander and gave a single nod. "Well. Get on with it then."

Nikolas caught Theseus's gaze and let his hands fall to his sides. He raised his chin.

Here I am. I'm ready.

FIFTY-NINE

6 MAIUS, AD 311

Footsteps sounded in the passage, the clicks of a guard's metal-studded cingulum belt betraying the approach of morning. Nydia's fingers tightened around Demi's. The night before, she'd been dragged from the cell by several guards only to be returned bruised, tear-streaked, and whispering that she'd not be executed with everyone else. That she could not be punished while pregnant, and she would remain in the prison until the child was born.

"How will I endure it, Demi?" Her whisper shook. "Over a month . . . alone with . . . *them.*" She shuddered. "What if I break? What if—"

"You won't." Demi gripped her hand, resisting the urge to tell Nydia that she shared her fears, that in a time of testing, she'd fallen. But it would not bring Nydia comfort. Instead, she repeated the words Titus had spoken the night before when one of the guards he knew had brought them wine and a loaf of hard bread.

"We cannot allow ourselves to dwell on what is coming and what we must endure. But instead set our eyes on our living hope. God will be our strength." She repeated the words to remind herself as much as encourage her friend. She would no doubt feel the same.

The footsteps paused outside the cell, orange light flickering around the black rectangle of the door. Keys clanked in the lock, and the hinges screamed in protest as the door gaped open in a square of flickering light, as if a doorway to hell itself had opened.

The guard stepped inside, lantern in one hand and sword in the other. "Out, you dogs."

Demi's knees shook as she pressed to her feet.

Nydia's abandoned sobs echoed after her as she joined the shuffle of prisoners moving down the passage and up a set of uneven steps.

Demi blinked as she stepped from darkness to light. From damp dungeon to warm sun. Paving stones turned to sand as they left the prison and made the short trek to the amphitheatre. Statues of Artemis, Apollo, Poseidon, and Leto lined the back of the semicircular stage, the images set into open arches that framed a backdrop of the turquoise sea and clear blue sky beyond. Demi inhaled the clean air, tinged with salt, and perfumed with the scent of citrus blossoms and smoke.

Smoke?

Her footsteps faltered as she caught sight of the raised dais taking the center of the stage and bearing the gold relief of the Sol Invictus. An altar smoldered beneath the image and a basket of pungent incense rested on the bottom step.

Her stomach lurched as the old memories and images surged.

God be my strength.

The stands roared with spectators. When the line of prisoners shuffled onto the stage, the chatter and laughter turned to jeers. Gnawed bones and trash rained from the tiered seating, along with the growing chant, "Great is Artemis of the Lycians."

The huddle of prisoners jostled with murmured prayers and snippets of song. A few sobbed. Demi turned to find Iris and Titus close. No one had seen Rex since the raid. Demi hoped he'd survived it and was even now with friends. Iris gripped her hand, her face calm, even if her palm was clammy. Titus's expression wavered between one that dared anyone to lay a hand on his wife and resignation as he looked at the crowd, as if he'd known all along that this was what his last day would look like.

The sun was high overhead. The sand spread over the stone floor already clumped and stained red beneath her feet. Demi squeezed her eyes shut against the sight. Against what it meant. The mornings and afternoons were reserved for exciting shows—the gladiator matches and beast fights. The midday show—when the sun was high and hot, and some left the stands to nap—that was the time reserved for executions.

"Oh, Lord, hold us fast—hold *me* fast."

The sun warmed her head, heavy, as if a palm rested against it.

Peace, child. Soon.

A sharp pain shot through her side. Iris cried out as Demi stumbled and fell to her knees, her hand wrenched from Iris's and going to the spot, expecting blood. Only throbbing and fabric met her probing fingers.

"Get up, wretch."

Searing pain in her scalp. She jerked to her feet, pedaling the slipping sand as the guard yanked her toward the dais by her hair.

The altar smoked, swirling before the gilded image of Helios, personification of the unconquered sun, who seemed to smirk as if to say, *Here you are again. A wave crashing headlong and heedless. A woman who repeats her mistakes. There is no glory in rebellion. Only suffering.*

Another sharp kick to the back of her knees sent her sprawling before the image, her hair tearing in the guard's grip. Gravel and blood bit into her palms and knees.

"Declare your allegiance to your emperor and your country." The guard's fist slammed to his chest. "Kyrios Caesar."

Her breaths came quick.

The bowl of incense rested by her right hand, the pungent, sickly sweet smell of it turning her stomach as her fingers slipped inside. Her knees shook as she pushed herself to her feet and stared at the steps of the dais. At the top, the image of Helios waited for her to crumble into cowardice as she had before.

Whoever strives to save his life will lose it, and whoever loses his life will keep it. The words came unbidden, and with them, peace. Her feet moved, up one step.

You are the daughter of the King most high.

Her spine straightened, shoulders rolling back as she climbed the second step.

You are chosen.

Her chin slowly lifted. She stepped to the platform.

You are dearly loved.

Was it the smoke or her imagination, or did Helios's carved smirk tremble?

"Kneel and declare your allegiance to your emperor and your country."

Demi pivoted, turning her back to the image. She flung the incense to the dirt.

The guard started up the steps, fury twisting his features.

"I have but one country, and one King. *Kyrios Iesous.*"

The guard's fist flew. Demi's head snapped back, and her feet left the dais. For a moment there was nothing, then pain exploded through her whole body as she hit the ground.

The stands erupted with shouts that seemed to swell and fade with the darkness wavering across her vision. Hands gripped her arms, dragging her across the stage as someone else was forced up the steps of the dais behind her.

"This isn't what I thought it would be." The guard on her left sounded young, unsure.

The other only grunted in response.

The amphitheatre roared into clarity once more as the haze in her head cleared. The guards shoved her back against a post, the older of the two yanking her hands behind and tying her wrists together while the young one held her in place, trembling hands pressed to her shoulders. She raised her eyes, meeting his gray and uncertain gaze, only inches from hers. His breath was shaky and smelled of wine that had clearly done little to steel his nerves. Was hers the first life he would take? He didn't want to, that much was clear. If given the choice she was sure he'd run from the amphitheatre faster than she would.

"No matter what you've done, what you do, God's mercy is for you," she whispered. "He loves you."

His chin trembled. Lips pressed into a sharp line as he turned his head.

"Thrax. Back here," the other guard ordered.

His hands dropped from her shoulders as he moved to obey. The tiered seating of the stands expanded before her, a cacophony of voices and colors. Hands shoved her hair forward, baring her neck.

"I don't want to do it."

"You're going to do it. Make a fool of yourself, and Drusus will have you flogged. Just swing hard. There's nothing worse than having to do it twice."

The hairs on her arms raised as the voices behind her went quiet.

Lord Jesus, receive Your servant. I am unworthy, but I fall on Your mercy and grace.

The volume in the stands rose. Voices shouting, calling for blood, calling for her head, calling for . . . silence?

A trumpet blared, repeated and unmelodic against the cacophony—not a trumpet of heaven.

"Silence! Silence in the name of Emperor Galerius!"

The crowd hushed to a restless stillness as Imperial guards in shining silver breastplates swarmed the amphitheatre stage, forming a barrier between the prisoners and the spectators. A man in a crimson cloak swept into the semicircle, a piece of parchment gripped in one hand. He raised his voice.

"One day before the Kalends of Maius, Emperor Galerius issued an edict of toleration."

The words fell on senseless ears. *Toleration?* What did that mean?

"These Christian prisoners are under the emperor's toleration and must be released. These proceedings are hereby illegal in the Roman Empire."

Demi blinked. A shudder went through her. She'd never heard the word *illegal* applied in such a way that it meant salvation rather than condemnation.

Heat seared through her chest, pressing out of her eyes. The strength she'd felt only moments ago on the dais seemed to leak from her limbs. The bonds on her wrists were cut so suddenly, she fell forward, dropping to her knees. Sobs rose in her throat as the words sank in. The meaning.

They could not be killed. Not this day. Not for being Christians.

Thank You.

Someone knelt in front of her, the brightness of a breastplate nearly blinding her through the tears.

"You are free to go." The relief in Thrax's voice sent more tears down her cheeks. He gripped her arms and pulled her to her feet, escorting her back into a huddle of welcoming arms.

Iris clasped Demi's trembling hand in her own, her voice weak with disbelief and awe. "How can this be possible? I've never heard of such an edict, and yet . . ." She shook her head. "God's stories never end in ash and blood."

How surreal to walk free and alive from a theatre that only moments before promised torture and death as crowds watched and cheered. How odd to strip off the rags of a prisoner and put on the clothing of the living. To see Nydia's face, tear-streaked and dazed, as she joined them on the street. To pass the downcast eyes of neighbors ashamed of their actions, the glares of the pagan devout, thwarted by a greater hand. How sobering that an edict passed a week ago had spread through the Eastern Empire to reach them now. In this moment.

How merciful that God, as He'd done with Peter, had offered her forgiveness and a second chance. Not because He needed it, but because she had.

SIXTY

THERE WAS NOWHERE ELSE TO GO but back to the only place they
knew. Neighbors and old acquaintances watched in solemnity as Titus
and Iris led the shuffling group of wounded prisoners back to the crumbling insula near the river. No one stopped them as they slipped through
the now doorless entry and moved into the courtyard.

Rex knelt with a codex open in his lap, a scraggly gathering of children and adults around him. He stopped reading as the group entered,
his face going still and white.

"Mater? Pater?" His voice trembled. He slid the codex to a little girl
next to him and leaped to his feet, barreling across the courtyard. "We
prayed you'd come back." He slammed into Iris and Titus, sobbing.

Demi and the others spread into the courtyard. She stared at the
place, speechless. No longer were the walls gouged and cracking, but
covered in new plaster. Holes had been patched, portions of the roof
replaced and repaired. She turned in a slow circle. Had the time spent
in the prison altered her memory of the place? Did it now seem like a
palace?

Her gaze caught on a balding man who'd stood from where he'd
gathered around Rex. She moved toward him.

"Basil."

He bowed. "At your service."

"Did—did you do all this?" She lifted a hand.

"I thought he would want me to."

"He? Nikolas?"

Basil shrugged. "I thought so, at first. But . . ." He glanced toward Rex. "I realized it wasn't the memory of Nikolas prompting me after all. He's a good preacher, that little boy."

The place they'd used to bring hope to their neighbors brought hope to them all that night and many nights after. The people they'd risked their lives to help this time brought their offerings and cared for them, binding their wounds, filling their bellies. News of Emperor Galerius's death reached them only days later. The man who'd sought their destruction had become their means of rescue.

SIXTY-ONE

DEMI'S FEET MOVED FASTER AND FASTER as the pounding of the surf on the shore grew louder. Tears pricked her eyes. How she'd longed for the sound. For the sun on her skin, water burbling over her head. She'd spent the last week at the insula, sleeping, eating, healing, and praising with the new church that had exploded under Rex's simple care. A handful of city guards had begun showing up for evening readings, Thrax among them.

But she couldn't stay any longer. She was fairly running through Andriake when a familiar voice shouted her name.

"Demitria!"

Her heart slammed into her throat as her feet skidded to a stop. She turned toward Mersad as he trotted toward her. No small feat for a man of his size. He looked her over, gaze catching on the bruise still marring her cheek in a mottle of blue and green. An expression of mingled pity and relief crossed his face.

"I heard the news. I'm glad to see you are alive." He swiped a hand over the sweat beading his brow. "You are well?"

She shrugged. Nodded. "Overall. Yes." Her glance darted toward the waves. Turquoise. Glittering. Calling her name with a greater urgency than Mersad had done. She could nearly feel the welcome embrace.

"Come. Come. I want to give you something." He waved a meaty arm for her to follow.

Demi didn't move.

"It is only right that you have your boat back. I took it after your pater's arrest in hopes I could one day return it to you, and I will not sit another day with it tied to my dock. You must take it as a token of our friendship."

She hesitated. What friendship? His attempt to spare her life had been an offer of slavery.

"What of Ennio and Pelos?"

"*Pfft.*" Mersad waved off the question like a pesky fly. "They mean nothing to me. They tried to steal coral from Balik. Can you believe it?"

She could.

"They are hard-pressed to find buyers here after that. There are rumors that they will move to another city. Good riddance, I say. So"— he paused, clapping his hands and rubbing them together—"do we have an agreement?"

Demi nodded. "I will accept the boat."

Mersad's face relaxed into a smile that bore an eerie similarity to a predatory moray whose prey had just appeared.

"I will accept, because it belongs to my family, and it is rightfully mine." Her chin lifted. "And since you value honesty so deeply, I must tell you that I will dive again, but not for you—unless your coral prices rival those of your competitors."

His smile seemed to freeze, to lose a bit of the triumph.

A smile tugged at the corner of her mouth. She dipped her head. "I thank you, *friend.*"

Freedom swelled in her chest only minutes later as waves slapped the hull of the little yellow lateen. Demi loosed the sail and caught the wind, passing through the mouth of the Myros River and into the glittering Mediterranean. The wind tugged at the curls around her face like the tender brush of a father's fingertips. She shut her eyes and raised her face to the sun, tears streaking out the corners of her eyes, blowing back into her hair, her ears. Why had the news reached Myra when it did? What if the messengers had been delayed a day? An hour? Why had her life been spared?

There was purpose yet for her. While breath filled her lungs and life flooded her limbs, God would use her yet.

I am willing. Here I am.

She drank in the coastline, peace filling her soul as her eyes feasted on the pale almond limestone tumbling into the azure sea. She steered nearer the shore, the hidden cove opening only from the perfect angle and distance. She stopped just shy of it, lowering the sail and letting the boat drift and settle before heaving the stone anchor over the side.

The diving season had barely begun, the water still clutching the spring chill, but Demi couldn't resist. She shimmied out of her outer robe and kicked it aside before hopping to the bench and curving head-first over the side. Water met her ears with a crash and a roar, the chill clenching her chest.

The pounding in her heart slowed, the muscles in her limbs relaxing as her skills revived. The rush of bubbles faded to a burbling hum, like the comforting sound of an old friend's voice. She kicked and rolled, reaching up to thread her fingers through her hair, scrubbing it clean of the prison's filth. Her head broke through into the humid heat above, and she filled her lungs with briny air that felt like a gift. She loved it so well, had missed it so much.

Her strength was not what it had been last summer, or even a few weeks before. Demi had only gathered a handful of mussels and a single branch of coral before her body shook with exhaustion. She climbed back into the boat, laying in the sunshine to rest and dry. The rock of the boat and crackle of waves on shore soothed like a lullaby, but she couldn't allow herself to sleep. She'd need to return soon, or the others would worry.

Limbs no longer shaking, Demi repinned her chiton over one shoulder before gripping the anchor rope and hauling it in. It knocked against the boat and tumbled into the bottom with a hollow, empty thud that rang in her ears and stole her breath with a sharp catch. She turned in a slow circle, taking in the emptiness of the boat. The thing she'd wanted most now held loneliness and loss.

Do you love Me more than these?

The question drifted to her mind and her gaze fell on the meager harvest clumped in the bottom of the boat. She shut her eyes.

"What would You have me do?"

No answer came, but might that be because it hadn't changed? *Feed My sheep.*

A splash opened her eyes, gaze drawn toward the sound that was decidedly not a wave crashing on the shore. She squinted. *What in the sea?*—Was that a person?

Hoisting the sail, she angled the boat toward shore and braced a hand to her brow, pulse kicking up. It wasn't another diver, not without a boat bobbing nearby. But the movements were definitely human. They were too far from shore to be out for a leisure swim. Had they been caught in an undertow?

The swimmer's arms appeared to flail rather than stroke. In need of aid.

"I'm coming!" she called. "Hang on."

Coasting closer, she dropped the sail and rushed to flip the rope ladder over the side. She wrestled her chiton over her head and curved over the edge of the boat, water crashing in her ears.

She bobbed up next to the floundering swimmer, snaking an arm around his chest. "I've got you now, don't fight me."

The back of his head pressed against her cheek as Demi angled for the ladder and grabbed hold. She kicked, twisting him around. "Grab the ladder, that's it."

One of his hands gripped the rope and Demi loosed her hold on him.

"I'll climb up and help you in, just hang on."

"Wait—"

She ignored him, scrambling up the ladder and turning to grip a handful of the man's tunic, her father's words running through her mind with eerie familiarity. *In the event of an accident, secure, leverage, and pull.*

He sputtered and coughed, head drooping.

She shifted her grip to his upper arm and pulled. "Come on, get your foot up there. That's it."

The boat tilted up behind her, threatening to capsize over them as the man gripped the ladder and she pulled at his arm. He scrambled over the side, both of them collapsing into the bottom of the boat.

Demi flopped back, panting as the boat rolled from side to side and the waterlogged swimmer struggled to sit up across from her.

Bony fingers reached up and slicked dripping brown hair from hazel eyes that locked onto hers with a tenderness that cut the air from her lungs.

"Demi."

Had her heart stopped beating? Her hands shook as they pressed over her mouth. It couldn't be. He was dead. Long dead.

"Nikolas." She breathed his name, the last bit catching on a sob.

Nikolas didn't move. Just let his eyes drink her in as her mind rearranged what she thought she knew.

Demi shook her head, trying to make sense of him. Here. Her eyes flooded. "I thought you were dead."

"I thought *you* were dead."

"Theseus?"

Nikolas nodded. "He came home with me. He's with Nydia and the others. When Titus told me you were gone, I . . . well, I might have broken something when I threw the chair."

Demi didn't respond. Her heart began beating again. Coming alive in her chest like it had been replaced by a thrashing fish.

Nikolas shrugged. "*Then* he finished telling me you'd gone to the shore. I owe him a chair."

She lurched forward with a sob. He caught her, arms coming around her, pulling her against him. His face buried into her neck. Neither spoke, the moment between them one of extravagant grace.

Demi finally drew back in his embrace, cradling his bearded face in her hands, her thumbs tracing scars on his cheeks. His nose had been broken. She drew a finger down the crooked line. "Where have you been?"

"In the emperor's prison in Nicomedia."

"All this time?"

He nodded. Swallowed. "I thought—we all thought—the time had come. They brought us to the courtyard and ordered us to kneel. But the man we thought was to order our destruction, brought a message from

Emperor Galerius and set us free instead." One of his hands cupped her cheek, thumb brushing the fading bruise.

It twinged beneath his gentle touch, but it wasn't the pain that brought tears to her eyes. It was the pride in his.

"I heard of your courage," he whispered. "The way you stood strong and confessed your faith before a mob that called for your blood. The way you offered God's mercy to the man about to . . ." His fingers caressed her neck, as if marveling that it remained unmarred. Unlike his.

She let out a shaky breath. She'd been marveling over the same thing. The way she could be a daughter of God, chosen and beloved—not a disappointment. The way even her earthly label had shifted from lapsed to confessor. A feat not of her own doing, but of God's. Such mercy. Such grace. And now Nikolas. A tear slipped from her eye, and he brushed it away.

"How did you get here?"

His mouth twitched. "Would you believe me if I said I had boat trouble?"

A laugh huffed from her chest, and she swatted at him. "You might have drowned."

"You looked closer from shore."

"For a man with uncanny aim, you have terrible perception."

He smiled, tugging at a curl coiled near her eyebrow. "I made it, didn't I?"

Demi trembled, eyes welling with grateful emotion. "You did." She leaned closer. Hesitated. The last time she'd kissed him, he'd been taken from her.

Nikolas rested his forehead against hers, their noses touching, his lips brushing the corner of her mouth.

"I don't want any more goodbye kisses," she whispered, threading her arms around his neck.

"No more of those." His mouth found hers as if in agreement. "Not if I can help it."

EPILOGUE

"I can't believe it's true."

"Can you not?" Nikolas threaded his fingers through Demi's and tugged her close. The sun beat down on the top of his head as he smiled down at his wife, whose belly mounded with new life. "God restored the inheritance of His people, Israel; how hard can it be to believe He'd restore ours as well?"

She shrugged.

After all that had happened, the order from the joint emperors Constantine and Licinius to return all confiscated goods and property back to the Christians seemed the stuff of stories. The stuff of God's stories. The edicts allowing for the confiscation of Christian goods in a court of law had also created records of the accused and the accuser and the goods transferred between. For those who survived to claim them, all that had been taken would be restored. What had once seemed a curse had become a blessing.

"And you get your shipping company, and the villa Xeno purchased? Where will he go?"

Nikolas shifted the crutch beneath his arm, the severed tendon in his left foot preventing him from ever walking without it. "He claims to have repented. I wish he'd done so before the emperor's edict instead of after. It is difficult to discern how true his repentance is."

"But you believed I had repented."

344

He looked at her. "Your actions proved your repentance was real. God can and does forgive all. I hope Xeno's repentance is true, but that doesn't mean I'll trust him to—" Nikolas stopped and stared, his breath catching in his throat.

Demi followed his gaze. "Is that it? The white one?" The words squeaked past her lips, fingers tightening in his.

He nodded. "The one on the hill." Just outside of the city proper, a white-walled villa crowned a green hilltop covered in a grove of orange trees. Pointed cedars stood sentry along a winding road to a pair of welcoming red doors.

The place truly was the stuff of dreams and stories. They'd been living at the riverside insula the past two years, though the spring floods had repeatedly filled the lower level with inches of silt. But what was he to do with all of this? Sell it?

He didn't realize he'd asked the question aloud until Demi's laughter drew his gaze down toward her.

"We're not going to sell it." She lifted her face to him, eyes sparking with the same light that shone in her smile. "We're going to build a church."

Step back in time with another powerful historical novel from Jamie Ogle

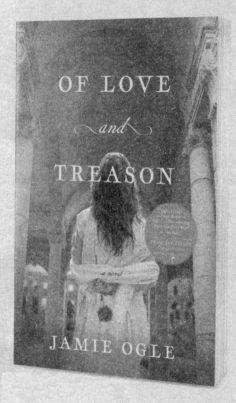

"A beautifully wrought tale.... Jamie Ogle is a brilliant storyteller."
Joanna Davidson Politano, author of *The Lost Melody*

AND WATCH FOR HER NEXT NOVEL COMING IN 2026

JOIN THE CONVERSATION AT

CP2013

A Note from the Author

MY ONLY CHILDHOOD MEMORY OF CELEBRATING "Saint Nicholas Day" was terrifying. Apparently, my parents paid my uncle to come over and run around the outside of our house pounding on the walls and roof before leaving a bag of candy on the steps. It was supposed to be a fun, "better be good before Santa comes later" situation, but I just remember hiding under the bed crying. We all laugh about this now, but to my knowledge, we never mixed Santa into our Christmas or celebrated Saint Nicholas Day again.

Despite the childhood fear of a strange man trying to break into our house, my favorite holiday has always been Christmas. There's something overwhelmingly beautiful about the dark, cold winter (at least in Minnesota) being transformed by this hope-drenched celebration of light, joy, and divine rescue. My favorite Christmas carol says it best:

Long lay the world in sin and error pining,
Til He appeared and the soul felt its worth.
A thrill of hope, the weary world rejoices,
For yonder breaks a new and glorious morn.
Fall on your knees!

It makes me cry every time. That God would step into our world. That He would deign to call me chosen and dearly loved, rather than depraved wretch.

So how, from this act of great love and divine intervention, did we end up with stories of a jolly man in fur-trimmed scarlet, dropping gifts down chimneys while transported in a sleigh pulled by flying reindeer? I'm not sure. But what I do know begins in the year 303.

Emperor Diocletian ruled the Roman Empire, and it was so vast, he divided it between himself and three other rulers, forming the tetrarchy. The empire was in shambles, and Diocletian worked hard to stabilize it and bring it back to its former glory. When a seer claimed that Christian prayers were hindering his ability to divine the emperor's future, Emperor Diocletian passed a series of edicts that would further divide his empire. The first edict prohibited Christians from gathering for worship and ordered the imprisonment of church leaders and the destruction of church buildings and Scripture. The second edict expelled Christians from the military and government positions and revoked their civil right to defend themselves in a court of law. Anyone who brought a suit against a Christian who refused to swear allegiance to the gods of the empire would be awarded all of the goods and property of the accused. The third edict allowed the church leaders in prison to leave—if they offered pagan sacrifices. If they refused, they were to be tortured until they did so or died in the process. The fourth edict was a general decree commanding all people in every region to offer sacrifices to the gods.

This final edict was enforced in different ways. In some regions it was mostly ignored. In other regions, citizens who offered sacrifices were given libelli to prove they'd done so. In the region ruled by Maximinius II Daia, there are accounts of towns rounding up all of their citizens and offering a choice between an altar and a chopping block. The number of martyrs varies widely based on city and region, but in Diocletian's city of Nicomedia alone, there were an estimated 20,000 martyrs.

This is the world the stories of Nikolas emerge from.

And this is where things get tricky.

You may have recognized some of the traditional "Saint Nicholas" stories included in this book while noticing the absence of others. This is because there were two Saint Nikolases from roughly the same region, though they lived centuries in time apart. Though they have the same name, the word used for "saint" is different for each of them. Nicholas of Sion is called oisos—the Greek word for an ascetic, monastic saint. Our Nikolas of Myra is called hagios—the Greek word for a saint who was a martyr, a confessor (one who withstood torture but wasn't killed), or a church leader.

Nikolas of Myra was born between 270 and 290 to wealthy Christian parents. He was orphaned as a young man, and a few versions of the stories say he spent a short time with an uncle in a monastery near Patara. During that time, he began using his wealth to help others in need. One of the most famous stories of Nikolas involves a man who found himself so deeply in debt, he had no other options but to sell his three daughters as prostitutes. When Nikolas heard of this, he dropped bags of money through the windows at night, enabling each of the girls to have a dowry and be able to marry instead of being forced into prostitution. (You may have recognized Lady Isidora as one of the daughters from this story.) Other stories involve Nikolas saving three men wrongfully accused and facing execution, and others tell of him reuniting lost children with their parents. I tried to include versions of all these stories as well as his surprise election to church leader in Myra.

It really happened that the leader in Myra died and the elders decided that whoever walked into the house first for the funeral would be the next leader. (Note: none of them volunteered.) According to the story, Nikolas didn't know of the funeral or this decision when he walked inside. But he didn't refuse the dangerous position. Nor did he weaken when he was captured, imprisoned, and tortured. And he stood strong against heresy even as an elderly man, when he traveled to the Council of Nicaea and allegedly slapped—or punched—another man in the face for spouting a blasphemous heresy. Apparently, Nikolas decided that fists were not out of the question when blasphemy was involved . . .

In the late 900s, Symeon Metaphrastes compiled a history of confessors and martyrs in which he combined the lives of oisos Nicholas of Sion and hagios Nikolas of Myra into one larger-than-life character. Perhaps he wanted to write one grand story, or maybe he didn't realize they were two different people whose lives were separated by over 200 years. Either way, the stories of the man who used his vast wealth to meet the needs of those around him were mingled with the more mystical stories of Nicholas of Sion.

As I struggled to find a way to tell the story of the church leader Nikolas of Myra, I stumbled across information about the coral industry in the Mediterranean and how skilled divers were used to harvest red coral. It was disturbing—especially considering what we know about the fragility of coral reefs today—and utterly fascinating at the same time. The character of a diver named Demitria instantly came to mind, fully fleshed out with her wild curls and hidden pain. Though Demi's involvement in Nikolas's gift-giving escapades is entirely a work of fiction, it's not too far of a stretch to believe he might have had a wife, especially since Nikolas of Myra wasn't an ascetic monk like Nicholas of Sion. Though various councils discussed and enforced clerical marriage bans at a local scale throughout the early centuries, the Catholic Church didn't universally ban priests from marrying and having children until the twelfth century.

Tradition states that Nikolas of Myra died on December 6 at the age of seventy-three.

Nikolas did his good deeds in secret, so this story is not intended to shine a spotlight on him or raise him to a pedestal he'd cringe to be on, but instead to use the story of his life and legacy to point to the One he lived his life for. This is a story of deep love and sacrifice. A story of darkness and light, of peril and rescue. It's a story we still find ourselves in centuries later. And our call remains the same.

To go and tell.

To feed the sheep.

To do it all in love, because He loved us first.

Jamie

Acknowledgments

FOR A LOT OF REASONS, this story was the hardest thing I've ever written, and while I wrote most of it alone at my desk, I'm so grateful for all the other writers and friends who came alongside and strengthened my arms with prayers and encouraging words. We did it.

I have to begin with a special thanks to my in-laws, Pean and Nell, who thought they were coming for a "quick visit" and ended up living with us for a month and doing all the things while I frantically finished the first draft. You two are the real MVPs here. Thank you.

To everyone who had to read that first draft: I'm sorry.

There's a Shannon Hale quote about writing first drafts and remembering they're like shoveling sand into a bucket so later I can build sandcastles. I am deeply grateful to my editors, Elizabeth Jackson and Sarah Rische, for taking my bucket of sand, digging through it to find all the best things, and encouraging me to keep building on them. Thank you.

To the entire, incredibly wonderful team at Tyndale: I still cannot believe I get to work with you all. Thank you for everything you do.

To Phil, Ellery, Maebel, and Henry: Thank you for being my biggest cheerleaders and fans. For believing in my writing and telling me I can do this, even when it feels overwhelming. For your love and prayers, jokes and pictures, and all the hugs—I don't take your support for granted. I love you.

To my entire family for your relentless excitement, encouragement, long-distance road trips, and for all the cookies, flowers, and chocolate . . . I couldn't ask for better people in my life. You are the best and I love you all!

To my church family and small group who prayed this book into existence: Thank you.

To my agent, Kristy Cambron: Thank you for your guidance and excitement over my writing. For your willingness to read early drafts and help me sort out my wild ideas. I'm so grateful I get to work with you.

To Smokey Row Coffee Co. for letting me hang out for hours and write, and for the delicious London Fogs that fueled this story.

Thank you to Captain Leonardo Fusco for writing about his experiences as a coral diver, and for his work to study and protect red coral. His book, *Red Gold: Extreme Diving and the Plunder of Red Coral in the Mediterranean* is a fascinating read for anyone interested in this subject.

To Kristine Delano for answering my diving questions, for all the brainstorming calls, feedback, and for joining me in early morning writing sprints and texting me at 5 a.m. to make sure I was awake—I'm so grateful for your friendship.

My fellow Christian Mommy Writers and our den mother Kimberley Woodhouse: you ladies are an endless support system of laughter, solid encouragement, and prayer. Thank you.

To my heavenly Father, for guiding me on this difficult journey and letting me find Your strength in my weakness, Your grace and love in every breath. This is for You, and because of You.

Discussion Questions

1. The presence of a single orange makes Nikolas feel seen and cared for even as he loses his boat and the precious gold inside. Can you think of a similar moment or detail in your own life that illustrated God's love for you?

2. Demi remembers that "[Pastor] Tomoso had made them all believe there was no future, that Jesus would return any moment and they best huddle in and wait for rescue. Nikolas shared the belief in Christ's imminent return, but instead of waiting in terror, he set to work, making the best use of his time and resources." Which perspective do you gravitate toward? Which do you think is most represented in the church today?

3. How are Nikolas and Demi each motivated by memories of their families? What parts of this motivation are healthy, and which do they need to overcome or let go?

4. Xeno doesn't want to eat the food offered by church widows, whereas Nikolas believes that to refuse it dishonors their sacrifice in sharing the food. Who do you think is right? Do you agree with Nikolas that "being able to receive a gift is just as important as giving one"?

5. Nikolas is forced to confront errant beliefs in the church, like the separation of God the Father from Jesus, saying, "We cannot pick and choose the parts of God that suit us and disregard the others. In doing so, we create a god of our own making . . . We must stand for the truth or be swayed by every changing feeling." Have you found yourself tempted to pick and choose what to believe about God? Where do you think this temptation shows up in the modern church?

6. While Demi loves Christ and continues to live in her Christian community, deep down she believes she can't be forgiven for her past failure. How do you reconcile Scriptures like those quoted by Pastor Tomoso—*Whoever denies Me before men, him I will also deny before My Father*—with other passages like the restoration of Peter (see John 21)? What would you have said to Demi if she'd come to you with her confession?

7. Nikolas has "grown up in a world of transactions and trades, barters and exchange rates . . . How easily those ideas had slipped into his view of God. God was not swayed by his goodness, his generosity, his work." In what ways do you see Nikolas trying to earn God's favor? Have you ever found yourself trying to work for God's approval in a similar way?

8. Amata, one of the church widows, tells Nikolas, "The greatest work of the church does not happen at the morning river meetings, but in the markets, at the wells, in the shops and kitchens—in our lives, and how well we live and give the gospel." How do characters in this story live the gospel through their actions? Where have you seen the most compelling examples of the gospel in your own life?

9. Nikolas reminds Demi that God calls them chosen and beloved— "Names he could easily ascribe to Demi, but he couldn't imagine God saying the same of him." Why do you think it's easier to believe in God's love for others than for ourselves?

10. Demi thinks of the sea as "the very place that felt the safest, most unchanged despite the chaos on shore." What is an image or place that represents safety and constancy for you? How does Demi come to find her ultimate certainty in God?

About the Author

JAMIE OGLE is a predawn writer, homeschool mom by day, and a reader by night. Inspired by her fascination with the storied history of faith, she writes historical fiction infused with hope, adventure, and courageous rebels. A Minnesota native, she now lives in Iowa with her husband and their three children, and she can usually be found gardening, beekeeping, and tromping through the woods. Learn more about Jamie at jamieogle.com.

CONNECT WITH JAMIE ONLINE AT

jamieogle.com

OR FOLLOW HER ON:

f authorjamieogle

⊙ jamie_m_ogle

g jamie-ogle

CP1929

TYNDALE HOUSE PUBLISHERS
IS CRAZY4FICTION!

Become part of the Crazy4Fiction community
and find fiction that entertains and inspires. Get
exclusive content, free resources, and more!

JOIN IN ON THE FUN!

 crazy4fiction.com

 Crazy4Fiction

 crazy4fiction

 tyndale_crazy4fiction

 Sign up for our newsletter

FOR GREAT DEALS ON TYNDALE PRODUCTS,
GO TO TYNDALE.COM/FICTION

CP0021